Difficult Lies

Christopher T. Werkman

ISBN: 978-1-62420-169-1

Credits
Cover design by Designs by Ms G
Editor: Kitty Carlisle

Dedication

I dedicate this novel to partner-lover-friend, Karen Wolf, who believed in this story and in me when no one else did. She listened, read, and offered suggestions and solace as needed. She put up with and gave up a lot, all the while. I love you so.

I also must thank Kathie Giorgio, my dear friend, writing coach, and muse. She was instrumental in helping me get it right. I also must thank my "family" of fellow writers at Kathie's AllWriters' Workplace & Workshop. They, too, offered their opinions and expertise that helped me shape my thoughts into words.

Lastly, I must thank Christine and Arlo for offering me the opportunity to get my novel published. The "team" they organized for me (Genene Valleau, cover artist; and Kitty Carlisle, final edit) was wonderful to work with and their skill was over the top.

I only hope I have enriched all of your lives as much as you have enriched mine.

Chapter One

Allan "Vic" Vickery pulled onto River Road from Bittersweet Drive and booted the gas. Something thumped the right front fender of his RX7, and a small object skidded over the hood and across the windshield. In seeming slow-motion, it pirouetted above the sunroof, shedding dark gray and orange feathers like sparks. In his rearview mirror, Vic saw a robin land upside-down, beating its wings against the blacktop. "Damn," he muttered, stabbing the brakes. He was close to being late, and punctuality was an obsession with him. Still, no way would he leave a living creature helpless on the road, especially since he put it there.

After his car skidded to a stop, Vic looked to confirm there was no oncoming traffic, leaped from the driver's seat and broke into a jog. The robin's wings jack-hammered against the pavement, its beak open to the sky. "No. No, little guy," Vic said, stooping to grasp the struggling creature. At his first touch, the bird seemed to relax and Vic slipped his hands around it. He folded the bird's wings against its body and started for the curb. A man in a passing pickup swerved and honked. "Yeah, fuck you!" Vic shouted. Vic's Old Man used to fall back on rage to deal with guilt or sorrow and, like him, remorse frequently put Vic a mere pitch-shot from a flash of anger.

"You're going to be okay, little guy," Vic whispered to the bird. He believed it. The bird's wings were functioning, and Vic could feel its heart whirring like a little motor. The bird closed its beak and tried to peck at Vic's thumb. Vic believed that to be a good sign. "I think you're just stunned, buddy. I'm gonna put you down and let you get your bearings." As he bent to place the bird on the grass, its head slumped. Its heart stilled.

"Son of a bitch!" He stroked the bird's chest several times. "I'm so goddamned sorry. Why the hell weren't you twenty feet up in the air?" He looked for someplace to put the small corpse. He decided on the mulch surrounding a planting of evergreens, not far from the road. Tucking it up under the foliage, he gave the bird one last caress before he stood to leave. Vic glanced at his watch. "Shit, already after 9:30." He was supposed to meet the guys at the golf course in fewer than fifteen minutes. He started for his car. "I'm sorry," he said, over his shoulder. It sounded so paltry. "If I'd only been on time."

He jogged back toward his idling car. He'd been on schedule, but then he tried to arrange some after-the-round romance with Angie. Early in their marriage, Vic joked he could get sunburned if he stood too close to her. A mere decade later, it felt like a chilly overcast settled in.

Back in the driver's seat, he waited for a car to pass, let out the clutch, banged through the first two gears and settled in at fifty. As upset and harried as he was, Vic couldn't help but glance admiringly at the stately river houses he passed. A Toledo native, he spent his 1950's boyhood wishing he could live in a house overlooking the Maumee River, with steps leading down to a fast boat tied off at a dock. His grandparents lived on the river back then. Vic spent hours scampering over the rock gardens they maintained on the sloping bank. That, and tossing baited hooks into the muddy Maumee. Such a house wasn't in the cards for him thus far, but living just off River Road on Bittersweet was a close miss.

The dashboard clock said he had six minutes to get to the course. "God, after sacrificing the life of a robin, I hope at least I hit 'em decent," he grumbled.

To a large extent, Vic was late because Angie couldn't understand why, on a beautiful late September day with an eighty-degree forecast, Vic wasn't excited about playing golf. Sitting at her Ping-Pong table-turned-workbench, she was fashioning parts for the miniature house she was constructing. She saw an article about miniatures in a magazine several years previous and the build began as a lark, but grew to be a passion, the way brushing paint on canvas was for Vic. Angie bristled at the term dollhouse, so Vic always correctly referred to it as "the miniature." She was a skilled builder, and the inch-to-foot scale replica of a Georgian-style country house wasn't close to being a child's toy.

"So what's the deal?" Angie asked, when Vic stepped into her workroom to say goodbye. She gathered parts for a double hung window. "You're usually grinning ear to ear when you're headed out to play golf."

"Yeah, when I'm playing for fun." He stood next to her, watching her eyes as she positioned pieces of the window's frame. Angie's eyes were very close in color to cerulean, Vic's usual choice for the sky in summer landscapes. "But the Chili Open is the last big scramble of the season, and the winning team splits five hundred bucks. The guys are all hot to take it home."

"Look, nobody else would pony up the twenty-five bucks and fill in for Jay, right? You're doing them a favor "

"I'm not sure they see it that way," Vic said. He had only been playing golf for a few years. Some of his teacher friends started a league and talked him into joining, promising it was only for fun and beer. Vic dragged out the set of clubs The Old Man gave him, the last thing his father did before he skipped to California. At first, it was fun to whack the ball around, but Vic hated being mediocre at anything. He started reading golf magazines and watching instructional videos. He even took lessons. Regardless, it became obvious he had no natural ability and was destined to be a hacker. He fought to keep his score under one hundred, and was overjoyed when he managed to break ninety. He accepted his fate, and golf evolved into more of a state of mind than a competitive sport. On the course, he found respite from his troubles, fellowship with his friends, and the beauty of nature. Deep down, however, he harbored hopes somehow he would develop the kind of game he could be proud of. The kind of game Jay Carlin had.

Angie put down her razor knife, used the backs of her hands to push her humidity-frizzed blonde curls from her forehead, and looked up at him. "You all take a shot and the team plays the best one?"

He nodded. "That's a scramble."

"So statistically, you only have to contribute one shot in four."

"Statistically. But Jay was their secret weapon. The guys were counting on him to come through with a hell of a lot more than one shot in four. I feel like I'm on the hot-seat."

"Hey, if their 'secret weapon' was drunk enough to break a leg falling down the stairs in some bar last night, how many of his shots could they use?" Angie picked up her knife. "You need to lighten up and enjoy playing golf."

Though Angie had a point, Vic knew he couldn't make the shots Jay would have, even if hangover demons were firing cannons in the man's head.

Trying to fill Jay's shoes was scary, but Vic's inability to get Angie to understand how he felt bothered him more. It once was so easy to share feelings, fears and dreams with her. He missed that at least as much as he missed physical intimacy. Both seemed to have evaporated from their marriage. Angie hardly ever offered suggestions or insights regarding his paintings anymore, and she'd stopped asking his opinion on her miniature house. She no longer inquired about his classes or his students, and when he asked her about a legal case or the office politics at Jonathan Fairchild and Associates, "not much" was her likely answer. He wondered which they'd lost first, their mental closeness, or the sex.

After some super-legal speeds and a few NASCAR-like cuts and ducks through traffic, Vic slowed and turned into the parking lot at Heather Hills Golf Club. He found a parking spot, shut the engine down and glanced at the clock as the display changed to 9:45. On the dot.

Vic got out of his car. The pressure he felt to help the team win overrode his pleasure at being on schedule and made his stomach roil. The image of the dead robin was still fresh. He burped and wondered if he could get some Tums in the clubhouse. When he noticed a tuft of the robin's down still stuck on the wiper arm, he pulled it free, let it fall, and watched its final flight. A few seconds either way would have made all the difference.

Vic was nerved up, but he reminded himself every round of golf offered a fresh beginning. The way he played the last time, or any time before that, didn't count. Each round offered a fresh start. A clean scorecard. Teaching was like that; one reason Vic loved it so much. Start the kids on a painting or a drawing and in a week or two, that project was complete and it was time to begin another. Four or five projects later, it was the start of a new semester, with new students. Before long, another school year ended. He could make adjustments and changes in his curriculum with no carryover to influence each new beginning. If only marriage was like that, he thought. And if only he could play golf as well as he taught art. He pulled his clubs out of the Mazda and closed the rear hatch.

Phil Bartlett drove up on a golf cart, ending Vic's time alone with his thoughts.

"Throw your clubs on," Phil said, grinning like a carnival barker. "You and I are riding together."

Vic hoped he would be riding with either Sal Batik or Ron Stevens, the other members of the scrambles team. Phil was overbearing, always pontificating about things Vic already knew. *Yeah, like I'm a dumb-ass,* he often thought. Others had the same complaint. Phil never got off his teacher pedestal, even on the golf course with fellow-teacher friends.

"You ready to kick ass and take names?" Phil asked as Vic dutifully strapped his bag to the cart.

"Damned straight," Vic replied, with all the enthusiasm he could muster.

"Great. Five hundred big ones to the winners today. You gotta help us win it."

Vic sat on the cart and gazed off at the late September foliage that was showing tinges of fall color. It's going to be one fucking long round, he thought.

~ * ~

Phil Bartlett may have been the fifty-year old head of Alexis High School's social studies department, but forty-five minutes after they teed off, he bounced on his toes like a kid at a carnival. "Four under par after three damned holes," he enthused. "And a sweet two on a par four! That eagle should win us some money, for sure." The thought Phil was excited enough he might piss himself helped Vic mount a convincing smile. "We have to stay focused now," Phil said, the way he might to his American government class. "Gotta birdie this par three."

Vic was glad the team was scoring well, but felt detached. They hadn't used one of his shots, although admittedly, he hadn't made a shot worth using. While they waited for another group to putt out on the par three they were about to play, his attention strayed to a flock of robins who were prospecting for worms. He thought about the one he killed on the way to the course.

"Whatcha looking at?" Sal asked. A phys. ed. teacher, he was half a foot taller than Vic and could slam a golf ball three hundred yards with above average accuracy. Not only that, he was a good guy.

"Those birds," Vic said, pointing in their direction. "A robin flew into my car when I was driving over here today." The memory of the soft limp bird in his hands played in his head and he turned his palms toward the sky. "Nothing I could do."

Sal nodded, then began taking practice swings, so Vic pulled his seven iron and began swinging it, too. Regardless, his mind was on the final exchange he had with Angie before leaving the house.

"I'm leaving now, sweetie," he said.

"K," she replied, not looking up. "Remember, just relax. You'll play better."

"I'll try," he said, bending to kiss her on the cheek. "I know I'll be a heck of a lot more relaxed when this round is over." A thought crossed his mind. "Hey, maybe I'll pick up a couple steaks and some wine on my way

6

home. We could grill 'em up. Who knows what could happen?" He finished with a wink she missed when she didn't look up.

"We'll see," she replied, in a distracted sing-song. Over the years, Vic learned that was Angie-speak for, "don't get your hopes up."

He couldn't let that go. "Are you pissed at me?" he asked, trying to hide a flicker of exasperation.

"Pissed?" She looked up at him, squinting wrinkles into the skin on the bridge of her nose.

"Yeah. I just suggested some dinner and a little romance. Because I love you. Because we're married. Also, because you never make offers like this to me anymore. And you're not interested. So, what did I do wrong?"

Angie gave him her "I don't have a clue" look. The wrinkles moved to her forehead and deepened as she raised her eyebrows. "I'm not mad at you." She shrugged. "It's so early in the morning."

"I know. But I thought, well, tonight. We could have some steaks and wine and—"

"Vic, you're talking eight or nine hours from now. I don't know how I'll feel then."

He could feel his frustration and self-doubt peaking. Annoyance souped it up. Why was the template always the same? When Vic made an advance, she was too tired, or didn't feel good. But she had to feel good sometime, and she never made advances anytime.

"But it's not only today, babe. I understand you may be too tired today. But you hardly ever feel like making love, and it makes me feel like you don't you love me anymore."

Her eyelids began to flutter and redden. "It's nothing like that. I told you before, I just don't have much sex drive right now." She spoke in the softest of whispers. Her watery eyes extinguished his kindling anger, the way they always did. Vic wondered if she counted on that.

"But you haven't had much sex drive for a long time. And you're only thirty-two years old. You were going to ask if it was the birth control pills you're using. What did your doctor say yesterday?"

Tears overran her long lower lashes and she shook her head. "It didn't come up."

"Didn't come up?" he said, fighting to keep his volume from increasing. "You mean you didn't bring it up, like you said you would. Why not?"

"I take care of you," she offered, wiping at her eyes.

He looked for something she could use for a hanky. "You didn't answer my question. Besides, I'm not talking about a hand-job. I'm talking about lovemaking, where I make you come, too." He found a scrap of cloth that looked clean and offered it to her. "Where we both participate. It doesn't even have to be intercourse, as long as we're both into it." He knelt as she dabbed at her eyes, now looking more July-sky blue against their teary-pink surroundings. "It used to be so good, Ange. We used to make love two or three times a week. Are those days over?"

Angie snuffled. "Tonight," she whispered.

He stood, but he couldn't coax himself to smile.

"What? I said we'd do it tonight. What more do you want?"

Vic touched her shoulder. "And that will take care of today. But we need to get to the cause of the problem or it will keep coming back, like it has before. You're the woman I love, but you never come on to me anymore. Since I'm always the one who brings it up, it makes me feel like you're giving in to get me off your back."

Angie stood and touched his cheek. "Tonight," she said. "It'll be good—honest." She glanced at the clock on her workbench. "You better go. You're going to be late."

"Oh shit, you're right. I *am* late." He kissed her.

"Good luck," she offered, as he hurried out of the room. "Maybe you'll sink the winning putt."

"Green's open," Phil said, catapulting Vic back onto the fourth tee. "Vic, you're hitting."

In a scrambles, the weakest player usually hits first. Vic teed a ball and put his best swing on it. The shot started for the green, but side-spin made it veer to the right, where it plopped into the grass near a green-side sand bunker. "Sorry, guys," he said, sliding the club into his bag.

"An art teacher's shot *should* be creative," Ron Stevens, a math teacher, said as he teed his ball. "Shake it off."

"I guess," Vic allowed. He gazed down the sunny fairway and discovered if he squinted just the right way, his eyelashes refracted the light and made the course look like an Expressionist landscape. He wondered how Van Gogh would have hit it.

The others were unable to improve on their situation. Ron's ball fizzled like a dud bottle rocket. Phil's and Sal's shots both landed in the same greenside bunker Vic's ball narrowly missed. They decided to use Vic's shot for the first time that day, but apprehension settled in like a bad neighbor when none of them pitched a ball close to the pin. Phil's was nearest, a good fifteen feet away.

"Okay, we gotta make this putt!" Phil said, pumping his fist like a coach hammering out a half-time pep talk. He looked at Vic. "You putt first and show us the line."

Crouching, Vic studied the stretch of green between the ball and the cup. The putting surface sloped to the right, but because the putt was uphill, he knew the ball would tend to roll straighter. Putts almost always came down to speed. A player could visualize the line he wanted the ball to follow, but to keep it on that path required the correct pace. He was never sure about speed until after he struck a putt, unlike good players who have a sixth sense about how hard to hit it.

Phil stood behind Vic, hunched like an umpire at home plate. "Sal...Ron...make sure you watch and get a good read."

Vic noticed a dark spot in the turf and pictured the ball tracking over it to the cup. He stood and made several practice strokes, trying to synthesize a feeling for the speed that would keep the ball on line.

"Whatever you do, don't leave it short," Phil said.

"Fore!" a far-off voice called.

Vic felt a surge of confidence. "Don't worry. I'm sinking it."

"Fore!" The single voice became a chorus.

"Who are they yelling at?" Sal asked. "Is it coming this way?"

Vic stroked his putt.

"FORE! *Fore on the green!*" came another choir of shouts.

Vic's ball rolled over the spot he picked out and held the line, but he heard a hissing sound. Faint at first, it intensified into a piercing buzz. Then the ball vanished. Was it in the cup? He couldn't tell because he couldn't see the cup. The buzzing stopped, but he couldn't hear anything else, either. What the hell was going on? Something hit him hard on the right cheek. Whatever it was felt firm, but soft. It stuck to his face. He tested it, pressed and rubbed against it. It seemed like it was ... grass?

He heard voices, like the cross-talk bobbing on the surface of AM radio at night—indecipherable background speech. At times, he could make out a word, but the rest was unintelligible gibberish in the rhythm of speech. He strained to make sense of it. Suddenly, it was as though a circuit slammed closed.

"— the goddamned ambulance," he heard Sal shout. Vic caught parts of phrases, as though the radio had a bad cord. "I'll stay with him. They'll need to know – hell he is. You go – them – here!"

"Sal?" Vic asked. The sound of his own voice surprised him.

Sal's reply came in pieces. "— awake! Hey, Vic! You —"

"What?" Vic asked.

"Are you okay?" A complete sentence. Then Vic could see Sal's image, but it flickered as though someone switched the lights on and off.

"Yeah. What happened?" he managed.

"You got hit by some guy's tee shot."

"Where?"

"On the head. Lay still, buddy. You'll be okay."

"Am I bleeding? Who hit me?"

"Somebody from that tee over there. Here they are! They just rode up." Sal turned and shouted. "He's okay! He's talking!"

"No! Tell him I'm hurt bad. Maybe they'll buy me a beer."

Sal looked at him and grinned before disappearing into darkness again.

"Did the putt go in, Sal? Sal! Did it drop?"

It all went dead. Someone shut off the radio and turned out the lights.

Vic's next awareness was he levitated. He couldn't feel the pressure of the ground against his body anymore. Oh, shit, he thought. This is not good. He rode the edge of panic. No ground. No gravity. Neutral. Everything was static. He didn't feel like he was moving up or down. Hanging. Suspended. Physically and figuratively. A golf ball stopped his life. Forever?

He wondered if his eyes were open. It felt like they were, but he couldn't see anything. He wanted to check, but he couldn't find his arms. They weren't there. No legs either. He was aware of his existence. He was Allan Vickery, and he could remember everything about himself and his life, but where the hell was his body? He wanted to shout or cry out, but he couldn't find the route to his vocal chords.

He became aware of leaves. He first saw irregular blue shapes, and suddenly realized that was the sky. He shifted his attention to the leaves. He sensed he was rising through them, like in an elevator. He looked down now and saw he hovered above the tree, quite a distance from the grass below. That scared him. He'd fallen off a ladder once, and being more than four or five feet in the air made him nervous. Not panicky, but cautious and edgy. Strangely, now he was more alarmed by the thought he might float into the heavens than he was by the possibility of falling back onto Earth. He still couldn't feel his arms or legs, but he could alter his field of vision.

He looked around and realized this was his yard, on Bittersweet. The tree he hovered above was the big maple standing in the center of the lawn he'd mowed the evening before. Friday. The day before the Chili Open. At Heather Hills, where he was clocked on the head.

Vic saw his house. He peered down on the second floor where the two dormer windows rose in precision from the slope of the roof facing the street, looking like angular frog's eyes. He could see the balsawood glider the kid next door lost that morning, caught in the gutter. Little Freddy, crying at the front door. "Can you get it down for me, Mr. Vickery?"

11

"I have to leave for golf now, but I'll get it this afternoon, Freddy," he promised. He riffled the little guy's brown hair. "If the wind doesn't blow it down, I'll get it for you when I get home." It rested in the eave's trough, right below the dormer window of Angie's workroom. As Vic drifted closer to the house, the little plane was within reach, if only he could use his arms. He couldn't, or he would have picked it up and launched it into Freddy's yard.

He looked inside, through the dormer window, and there was Angie. She was still at her huge work table, the various parts of her doll house scattered like remnants from the aftermath of a tornado. Perched on the old bar stool, she wore one of his castoff dress shirts as a smock. With her blonde curls pulled back into a banana-shaped red barrette, she looked every bit the college coed he married eleven years earlier.

He began to drift away from the window. He didn't want to. Like Fred's little glider, he was lousy at controlling his direction. He felt like he was in a hot-air balloon. He wanted to stay. He wanted to look in on Angie and remember when she used to sleep in the nude with him, snuggled in his arms. He wanted to remember the happy times before he worried he was losing her, that she was drifting away. Now he was drifting away from her, and he couldn't do a damned thing about it.

~ * ~

Grass pressed against Vic's cheek again. He savored the sweet soothing aroma of the turf for a moment, and when he opened his eyes, he could see perfectly. Not only that, he had control of his whole body, and it was pain-free. *Oh, man, this is great,* he thought. *I blacked out for a minute. It was all a stupid dream. I'll let the guys know I'm okay.*

He pulled himself into a sitting position. He was fine. He rose to his feet and ran his hands over his head. He couldn't find any lumps, bumps, or sore spots from the shot Sal told him he'd taken, and he did a quick once-around to make sure no one witnessed his self-examination. It felt like a line of chilly dominoes ran the length of his spine. None of his playing partners were there. No one was. Then, another reality struck. He wasn't at Heather Hills. This wasn't even a golf course.

He struggled to understand. He'd struck a putt on the fourth green, and awakened into the weird floating dream. Now he stood in an open meadow near a large tree. To his left was a curtain of heavy brush and trees, which almost reminded him of the narrow area of woods that formed a barrier between Bittersweet Drive and the thirteenth fairway at Toledo Country Club. He ventured several steps in that direction, but it was obvious they weren't the trees at the end of his street. Besides, he reminded himself, I'm no country-clubber. We were playing Heather Hills.

A lacy veil of clouds diffused the sunlight, disguising east from west and offering no clue as to the time of day. He looked at his watch and saw the second hand wasn't moving. He tapped the crystal. "Goddamned thing," he said. "I got hit on the head, not on the damned watch."

That's when he noticed something was wrong with the timbre of his voice. It didn't sound like he was outside. Instead of melding into the surroundings, his words reverberated in an unusual way, almost as though he was indoors. He wanted to shout to test for an echo, but he had no idea where he was, or who or what might be within earshot. It was easy to talk himself into maintaining silence.

Across from the brush and trees was an asphalt road; smooth, and black as licorice. The nearby stretch was straight, but it curved and disappeared into a cluster of distant trees. He walked over to it and looked both ways. Where the hell does it go, he wondered. He wanted to see if there was a house or town nearby, but was unsure about wandering off.

"I don't know what to do," he whispered, wondering how long it would be until a car or a truck would come along. He walked back to the big tree and spotted an inviting space where its roots disappeared into the ground. He sat down there and leaned against the trunk to assess his situation. Arguments for staying where he was paraded through his mind. Your plane crashes, stay with the wreckage. Your boat capsizes, cling to the

13

hull. *This is where I'm supposed to be,* he decided. *I'll wait here until someone comes to tell me where I'm supposed go next.*

With a soft shuffle of wing feathers, a robin fluttered from an overhead branch and settled on the grass no more than ten feet from where Vic sat. The bird hopped around, cocking its head the way robins do when they're on the hunt for worms. He made a few soft clicking sounds with his tongue, and the bird turned in his direction. It looked at him with some curiosity, and little apparent fear.

"You're the one, aren't you?" he whispered, replaying the image of the robin that flew into his car. He reached out and the robin hopped toward him, coming close enough he could actually stroke its waxy feathers several times before it skittered off, to renew its search for dinner. Tears clotted at his eyelashes as a new possibility hit him like a hammer.

"I'm fucking dead."

~ * ~

Vic slumped against the tree trunk and blubbered like a lost child. Sobs as violent as dry heaves wracked his body. He was engulfed by a sense of loneliness. Is being alone the worst part of being dead? He used his fingers to squeegee the tears from his cheeks, and swallowed down the urge to continue crying. Does Angie know? Did one of the guys call her? He hoped she heard the news from someone closer than an impersonal policeman or paramedic. He wondered what her reaction was. Maybe it's a good thing our relationship's so shitty. My checking out might be easier for her to live with. That thought had him teetering on the brink of tears again.

But maybe I'm not dead, he countered, trying to apply some logic to his situation. The friendly robin didn't prove anything. Still, the fact was he'd been playing golf with friends, was hit by a golf ball, and now he was alone in an unfamiliar place. Another strange thought came to mind. *What if I'm not even Allan Vickery?* A fast inventory reassured him. He wore his favorite green pullover, cargo shorts, and the old running shoes he liked when he played golf. He yanked out his wallet. There were his credit cards.

Sears. Sunoco. His name, Allan T. Vickery, was recorded in plastic relief. He studied his driver's license picture. Brown eyes, dark brown hair, a square jaw and a stupid grin. *Yeah, that's me,* he thought, tears re-blurring his vision. As he slid the wallet back into his pocket, a powerful drowsiness overrode his emotions. He curled up at the base of the tree, pillowed his head on his forearms and slipped easily into slumber.

When he awakened, he experienced one of those groggy moments of peace, before reality backhanded him into full awareness. Nothing changed. The light was the same, there was no wind, and no sound disturbed the palpable layer of quiet blanketing him. Out of habit, he checked his watch. The hands were still motionless. He could recall vague memories of bewildering dreams; high-pitched beeps and unfamiliar sounds reminded him of the voice-like noises he'd heard when he first got hit, along with recollections of pencil-thin white lights swooping back and forth. Again, he was tempted to explore, but caution kept him where he was. He wasn't hungry or thirsty. He wasn't in any immediate danger. He decided to stay put until any of that changed. Remain at the scene. Wait for the authorities.

His sense of security shattered when Vic spotted a man on the road, walking in his direction. Vic was lonely and lost, and he wanted someone to tell him where he was and how to get back to Toledo, but the sight of another human made his heart rattle in his chest. The voice in his head screamed ... *Run! Hide*! But, like in one of those weird nightmares, he couldn't seem to make himself budge.

A second look reassured him. Walkingman didn't appear to be much of a threat. He wore a pair of tan Bermuda shorts, a collared white pullover shirt, and a pair of deck shoes with no socks. The wide brim on his straw hat cast enough shadow to obscure his face, and any hint of his age, but his relaxed athletic gait told Vic the man was at ease with himself and his surroundings. Rather than call out, Vic decided to wait and see if the man noticed him. If I'm dead, he might not be able to see me anyway, he figured. When Walkingman was no more than a hundred feet away, he happened to glance in Vic's direction. Startled, the man sidestepped and stopped, peering at Vic for several seconds before seeming to regain himself.

"Hello. Are you all right?" Walkingman called out, in a husky resonant voice, the kind that would make a radio speaker throb.

The sound of another human voice made Vic blink back tears again. He stood, but leaned against the tree for balance, maybe even for comfort. "Yes," he replied, his voice quavering despite his best efforts.

"Are you sure?" Walkingman held out his hands, fingers splayed like a piano player trying for full octaves. "Sit back down if you need to."

"I'm okay."

Walkingman came closer and pulled off his hat. He looked to be about Vic's age; in his mid-thirties, anyway. He was quite muscular from the waist up, but he was one of those men whose legs, though not spindly, didn't appear to match the heft of his upper torso.

"You just get here?" Walkingman asked.

"No, it's been a couple hours," Vic replied.

"Hours." Walkingman's face creased into a smile. "Do you know where you are?"

He studied Walkingman's clear green eyes, but they offered nothing regarding how he was expected to answer. For the first time in his adult life, Vic had no clue where he was. That was unsettling enough, but admitting it to someone else was terrifying. A moron wouldn't know, but he wasn't anxious to be included in that group. "I know I'm not in Toledo."

Walkingman's smile widened. "Toledo, Ohio?"

"Yeah." He felt a surge of excitement. "Are you from Toledo, too?"

"No, not by a long shot. Syracuse ... Syracuse, New York. But I've been through Toledo a time or two. On the turnpike."

"The turnpike?" Vic almost shouted, smiling for the first time since he'd awakened. "I live about a half a mile from where it crosses the Maumee River. I jog over a bridge that crosses the turnpike almost every morning." Even as he spoke the words, his happiness faded. He wondered if he would ever see the river or the turnpike again.

16

"Hmm, I can't say I remember that particular river, but I'm sure I've crossed it," Walkingman said, shaking Vic's hand. "My name's Bascolm and I'm on my way to drink a beer at a little place up the road. Join me?"

"Nice to meet you, Mr. Bascolm. I'm Allan Vickery and, oh Jesus, a beer sounds better than you'd believe."

"No. Bascolm's my first name," he said, as they started down the road. "Bascolm Traskett."

"Is it very far ... to this place where we get the beer?"

"Nah, not even a mile."

They soon rounded a curve in the road where a small cottage surrounded by trees came into view. The paint on the white walls and on the royal blue trim appeared to be fresh. A silvery metal roof topped the small building, and leafy shrubs flanked each corner. "Does somebody live there?" Vic asked.

"Not that I know of," Bascolm replied. "I think it's available."

They didn't cover another hundred yards before Vic decided knowing the worst was better than wondering what the hell was going on, even if asking the question *did* make him come off like some kind of whacko. He stopped. Bascolm stopped, too, and raised his eyebrows in that universal expression welcoming a question. "Bascolm, you asked if I know where I am. I'm gonna level with you. I don't have the faintest damned idea. Do you?"

"That might be something best discussed over a beer, or maybe even something stronger."

"Can I get a glass of Southern Comfort at this place where we're going?"

Bascolm clapped him on the shoulder. "That might be a good choice."

Chapter Two

Vic and Bascolm crested another hill, and a cluster of buildings interspersed with towering trees came into view. The little village had an inviting feel to it, almost Mayberry-like. Vic half-expected to see Andy Taylor or Barney Fife drive by in their squad car, although they would have constituted the only traffic. The silence that cloaked the town was eerie, but not at all threatening. A collection of stores, grocery, hardware, five and dime, a couple bars, and a gas station fronted the road where Vic and Bascolm walked. A scattering of small homes clustered in rows on several cross-streets. The little outcropping of buildings had a warm, friendly look to it, even in the flat gray light the batting of clouds overhead allowed. Without sun to cast strong shadows, the buildings didn't show their dimension, giving it the look of Grandma Moses' primitive paintings. It also had a vaguely familiar appearance, as though he might have seen it somewhere before, although he was certain he hadn't. An English Tudor structure had a sign hanging from a pole on its facade which read, "Gaylord's Pub." Bascolm gestured in its direction, and they walked to the front door. The clack of a cue ball breaking a tight rack greeted them as Vic followed Bascolm inside.

"God, does this place ever bring back memories," Vic said. "I used to hang out at a college bar like this back in Bowling Green."

"Identical to it?" Bascolm asked.

Vic thought that was a strange question and gave Bascolm a look, but he was hanging his hat on a hook and didn't notice. "Not exactly like it. Reminds me of it. Same decor. Why?"

"Just wondering," was Bascolm's offhand reply. He exchanged greetings with several of the other patrons, some of whom were playing cards or throwing darts. The lighting was low-wattage at Gaylord's, and peanut shells crunched beneath their feet. Stale beer was the odor of the day. *Probably every day,* Vic thought, remembering similar watering holes as he followed Bascolm to the bar. They chose some stools and sat down.

Vic's stomach began to roil like a sack of snakes. The vague familiarity of Gaylord's was soothing, but now he would learn the truth of where he, Bascolm and this village actually were. Did Bascolm know for certain? Would the news be as bad as he feared? Like someone standing knee-deep in a chilly pond on a hot summer day, he wanted to take the plunge and find out, but wasn't certain he was ready for the shock of cold truth. He figured if he kept talking, he could postpone the explanation he at once wanted and feared.

"The Canterbury Inn was the name of the place I was talking about, the one I remember from college," Vic continued. "Haven't thought about it in years. The owner had another bar just like it, up north in Toledo, called The Tabard. My sophomore year, the guy had the bright idea of staging a pilgrimage from the Tabard to the Canterbury. A bunch of us idiots dressed up like Chaucer's characters and found rides up there so we could walk back to Bowling Green. Must have been twenty-five, maybe thirty miles. It sounded like fun, but it took us all day to make the trip. Like a dope, I wore some stupid bedroom slippers because I thought they looked like medieval shoes. The next morning, my feet were so sore, I could barely walk." He and Bascolm finished laughing as an attractive young woman stepped up and wiped the bar top with a damp towel.

"Bass," she said, "how are you?" Her accent sounded Scandinavian. She was tall, solid and Nordic-looking. A Viking beauty, Vic decided.

"Same as ever, kid. How's yourself?"

"Never sure," she replied, rolling her impressive brown eyes.

"Cristianne, this is Allan Vickery. He just arrived."

"Very glad to meet you, Allan." She had a firm handshake and she was one of those people whose eyes seemed to project more light than they absorbed. "I'm pretty sure what Bascolm would like, but for you?"

"Bascolm says you might have some Southern Comfort?"

"Oh, yes. I think."

"Make it tall," Bascolm said. "Allan and I are going to be a while."

She stepped back, looking at the sizable stock of bottles lining the altar-like shelving behind the bar. When she spotted a fifth of the honey-gold liquor, she hoisted it onto the gleaming bar top. "Should I leave the bottle and you can serve yourself, sir? How would that be? I'll get you a glass. With ice?"

"Yes, please." Vic remembered he only had a twenty in his pocket. "How much is a shot?"

"If you've any money, Allan, keep it in your pocket," Cristianne said with a smile. "We don't use it here." She winked, and was back in seconds with a draft for Bascolm and the glass of ice.

Vic was about to ask her to explain, but Bascolm spoke first. "Still having your episodes?" he asked her.

"Yes. I tell you, Bass, I've been flashing very much, lately. Think I slept again and had very strong dreams." She rested her elbows on the bar and whispered, "Something is happening." Her eyes flashed in high contrast even when she appeared wistful. "Donald is getting crazy. I'm not doing so well, myself."

"Yeah, I know how you feel. It all gets so complicated," Bass said, patting her forearm. "You miss the ones you left behind, but you love the ones you meet here. And if you go back, on a selfish level, the friends you make here hate to see you go. I would. And Donald, of course." Bascolm turned to Vic. "Donald MacDougal, we're talking about. He's Cristianne's gentleman friend. Terrific young guy. He should be coming around, eh?"

"Yes, I think. I leave you to your talk. Call if you need anything."

20

Vic was really confused now. Not only did they not use money, but if Cristianne could leave Donald and this place behind, she couldn't be dead. He spilled some liquor into the glass, instigating a chorus of crackles and pops as the warm alcohol cascaded over the ice. If she isn't dead, then Bascolm and I must not be, either, he reasoned. He wanted to know for certain, but still wasn't ready to ask. He wanted a sip of the eighty-proof liquor before Bascolm started to explain what he and Cristianne were talking about.

"God help me, I love this stuff," Vic said. "Had some last night, although it seems like it's been longer."

"It may well have been," Bascolm replied. Then he inhaled audibly, almost as though he was girding himself for bad news. "What's the last date you remember before you woke up here?"

"Date?" Vic tried to mask his surprise at the question.

"Yeah. The day and date."

"Saturday. September 26th. Why?"

"What year?"

"Nineteen eighty-one." He waited for a punch line. It didn't come.

Bascolm shook his head. "And what were you doing on Saturday, September 26, 1981?"

He shifted on his stool. He'd seen clips of F. Lee Bailey doing a cross-examination, and Bascolm did a fair approximation, which made Vic more nervous than he already was. "Playing golf with some friends."

"Golf? You play golf, man?"

"Yeah. Not very well, but I play." Vic started telling Bascolm about the Chili Open and he seemed interested, so Vic gave him the unabridged version. Like most avid players, he could recount every shot in great detail—the kind of specifics that could often bore even a fellow golfer. Regardless, Bascolm listened intently.

"And you don't know if you sunk the putt?" Bascolm asked when Vic's story ended.

"No. It sure looked like it was dead center, but after I got hit, I don't know."

"And you say the last person you talked to was this friend of yours, this Sal?"

"Yeah. At first, I couldn't see or hear him, but then he started to cut in and out, kind of like a TV with bad reception. I missed a lot of what he said, but he told me I got hit in the head and the ambulance was on its way."

"Flashing," Bascolm said. "That's what Cristianne and I were talking about. It happens when you're right at the edge."

Vic sucked a big swallow of his drink. This was the moment he'd been awaiting and fearing. "The edge of what?"

Bascolm turned on his stool and rested the mug on his knee. "You haven't figured it out?"

Vic felt defensive. Am I supposed to have all this figured out, he wondered, especially when the most plausible answer I can come up with scares the hell out of me? He decided to go with the worst case scenario. "The edge of ... death? Am I, are we dead?"

Bascolm gave Vic a tight-lipped smile. "You ... we, are unconscious. Comatose. Actually, *you're* comatose. At this point, I'm in what they refer to as a vegetative state. Comas are relatively short-lived. Anything over a few weeks is vegetative."

"And you've been here, how long?"

"You say it was 1981 when you checked out?" Bascolm asked, holding up his empty mug so Cristianne would know he needed a refill. "That makes it coming up on sixteen years. November 22, 1965. That's the day I had my accident."

Cristianne hurried by to swap a frosty full mug for Bascolm's empty one.

"Nineteen sixty-five," Vic said. "Shit, I was in high school back then. So, what happened to you?"

"I'm a New York State Trooper, Allan," Bascolm began. "I had ten years in by '65. Joined the army as soon as I graduated high school and served four years as an M.P. Two of 'em in Korea. Mustered out, took the civil service test, and went straight to trooper school." He gave Vic a nudge on the arm with his cold beer mug. "I goddamn loved it. School was a breeze after the training I got in the military. I had to book it on the motor vehicle codes and civil law, but the rest was easy. Plus, they sent us to high performance driving school. We tossed cars around. Road course, high-speed control, pursuit. It was a ball. I got lucky and didn't even have to relocate when I graduated. I was stationed in Syracuse, and patrolled the New York Thruway fifty miles east and west of there."

"I've driven the Thruway," Vic said, warmed by this link he shared with Bascolm. "Angie—that's my wife—she has friends who have a cabin on Racquet Lake, up in the Adirondacks." The memory of happy times with her washed him with sadness. "We used the Thruway to get up there three or four summers in a row. It's a great piece of road."

Bascolm nodded and went on. "The night it happened, it was about, I'd say, three-thirty in the morning. I was headed eastbound. Turned out some yahoo shot up a bar outside Syracuse. Killed his wife and the man she was with. He was leading a west-bound high-speed at over a hundred miles an hour." Bascolm sipped his drink, but his voice still rumbled like a bad wheel bearing. "I came to a cross-over, pulled onto the median, and waited. Hardly any traffic at that hour, so I knew I'd be able to see the other cruisers' lights from a long way off. Sure enough, a couple minutes later, here they come."

Vic conceptualized what Bascolm said with painting-like images, but in action, not still images. The tape in his mind played with speeding headlights and flashing red overheads slashing through the cold darkness. They blurred like a time-lapse photo in his imagination.

"I had a brand-new car," Bascolm said. "A '66 Galaxie with a four twenty-seven cubic inch cop motor. Guar-un-damn-teed by the factory to do a hundred-thirty. I pull out and nail the pedal to the floorboards, run her up to a hundred, and hold it there. I'm biding my time. When they're about a half-mile behind me, I'm watching in the rearview, I flip on my overheads and straddle the lanes. He might try to get around me, but I'm ready to block him."

Vic's imagination placed him inside the powerful sedan now, as though he viewed the scene from the floor of the passenger side. The lights in the rearview mirror put a mail slot of flashing crimson illumination across Bascolm's face. Bascolm's eyes flicked back and forth from the road ahead to the reflected image in the mirror.

Bascolm slugged down some beer and went on. "Everything was textbook, at first. Whichever way he went, I got there first. He tried the left lane, I blocked. He swung it over into the right lane, or the breakdown lane, I blocked. All the while, I'm slowing down, see? We were down to about eighty. I figured it was a matter of time until he gave up. He swung left, I blocked, and Dex, a trooper buddy of mine, he pulled over on the perp's right side. First step in getting him boxed. Get him boxed, we have him." Bascolm shrugged. "Then the son of a bitch headed onto the median. Grass was wet. You ever try to control a car on wet grass, Allan?"

Vic wagged his head. "Slippery?"

"Slippery?" Bascolm repeated, the word riding on a chuckle. "Wet grass is like ice, especially at eighty miles an hour. A median's low in the middle, designed to move a car down and catch it. Keep it from coming back up into the traffic lanes." He paused for another sip of beer. "He was either good or lucky. Either way, he gathered that goddamned Buick up and drove it back on the road. Caught my cruiser on the right rear corner, broke me loose and I pitched left. Next thing I knew, my car spun like a damned roulette wheel. I saw a flash of something big and gray in my headlights. Probably a bridge abutment, I don't know. I woke up not far from where I ran into you."

They sat in silence, and Vic sipped his drink while the enormity of what he'd been told began to sink in. Unconscious. A whole world of people who are in comas, or vegetative? He thought of his student assistant the previous year, Elliot Patrick. Eli was riding his bicycle home from a night shift at McDonalds when someone in a pickup truck hit him from behind and high-tailed it. Eli was still in a coma, in Lake Park Nursing Home. Vic wanted to ask Bascolm if he'd come across the boy, but he looked spent. His normally drill sergeant-straight spine bowed. "I'm sorry. I didn't mean for you to have to relive it all," Vic said.

Bascolm regained his posture and even managed a thin smile. "Ah, not a problem, Allan. I think about it all the time, anyway. It's, when I talk about it ... " His voice trailed off, then he swiveled on his stool to face Vic full on. "I mean, don't get me wrong. It's great here. You'll want for nothing. But I miss the life I had. I'm married to an angel ... the most wonderful, most beautiful lady in the world, Sondra." His eyes began to blink rapidly. "But after sixteen years, well, I hope to God she's gotten on with her life. I mean, if I was coming back, I would have by now. And even if I did, my body ... " He dabbed at his eyes with a cocktail napkin, turning away for what Vic assumed was a desire for some privacy.

"Can I ask a question?" Vic shifted on his bar stool.

"I figured you'd have a few." Bascolm turned back toward the bar and rested his elbows on it. His eyes were still red. "Shoot."

"You don't look like you're old enough to have been in Korea. My Old Man was, but he died when he was almost fifty." He raised his eyebrows. "So, what's the deal?"

"I was born in 1931," Bascolm said. "Joined the Army the day I turned eighteen, in 1949." His mouth pulled into a grin. "I'm fifty, now, if it's 1981," he continued, brushing his hand across his dark brown hair, "but, no grey yet." He choked out a laugh. "I guess I'll look like I did the day I had the crash until I die." He shifted on his stool, and hunched against the bar. "See, we're unconscious. We don't know what our bodies look like anymore. It's a safe bet you look the same, but I don't have a clue. I look in the mirror, I only see what I know. I guess you see what I do."

"So how do you know we're unconscious, in comas or whatever? You're assuming that, right? We *could* be dead. How can you be so sure?"

Bascolm gestured toward a muscular young man with streaked blonde hair who looked as if he came off a beach. He wore shorts, sandals, and a sweatshirt with cut-off sleeves. Beachman was shooting pool with several others. "See that blonde guy over there?" Bascolm asked, pointing now. "That's Jason Reno. He went back. And he's not the only one."

25

"Went back?"

"Yeah. A couple of times, in fact. His body is in a sanitarium or some damned place. He couldn't move or talk. He says no one ever even knew he was conscious, but he could see and hear. And *feel*. He's plenty glad to be veggie again. You're in a coma for any length of time, your body shrivels up, curls into a ball. Jase told me the pain was unbelievable. Muscles all locked up in cramps."

Vic shuddered.

"Yeah. You gonna go back, you want to get right to it," Bascolm said.

"But do we have any control?"

"Nope. None I know of. If we did, I'd be in Syracuse right now instead of passing the time of day with you." He winked. "No offense meant."

Vic ignored Bascolm's joke. "So this is like a dream. One we may or may not wake up from?"

"I've wrestled with that one for a while, but I don't much, anymore. I mean, if this is a dream I'm having, then I guess I made you up. You don't really exist. But, I just bet you think you do, right?" Vic nodded. "So, I'd bet my left lung you're not dreaming me up, either. Nah, you and I, we had lives. Now, through circumstances we can't understand or control, we meet up here." He paused for another swallow. "I believe this is a real place. Not at first, but I'm comfortable with the idea, now."

"I don't know, Bascolm. It's all pretty wild."

"Try it this way. Where do you go when you die?"

Vic shrugged. "Heaven, I guess, if you're a believer. Or Hell."

"Are you a believer?"

The personal question caught Vic by surprise. They hadn't known each other very long. At the same time, Bascolm shared a very personal story, and Vic was beginning to feel a bond of camaraderie with him. He shrugged. "I used to, up until a few years ago, I guess. I think maybe I outgrew my superstitions."

"Yep," Bascolm said, "right where I was. I mean, I sat down to read the Bible, and about half-way through, God started to sound so man-made to me." He sniffed. "I won't belabor you with my thoughts, but I'm definitely out of the organized religion thing. Same time, though, I have to tell you, this place has more or less convinced me there's more."

"More?"

Bascolm looked as uncomfortable as a kid in the dean's office. "Seems like if there's a place like this for the comatose, then it's not too big a leap for me to think there might be a place for the dead." He rubbed at his jaw as though checking for stubble. "I don't know, maybe I'm only hoping. A life, an afterlife, and a place for the ones who are somewhere in between."

Vic refilled his glass while he mined for new logic. "Hey, but wait a minute," he argued. "People have come out of comas and never said anything about this place, or any place, for that matter."

"True enough. And people have been clinically dead, zero heartbeat or respiration. They get revived, but I've never heard any of them give accounts of what the afterlife is like, either. Floating toward a bright light, maybe. That's about all."

"Yeah, but they're only 'dead' for a minute or so."

Bascolm used his chin to point at Vic's wrist. "How's your watch working?"

Vic looked at the second hand, still motionless beneath the crystal.

"There is no time here," Bascolm went on. "That's one of the first things you learn. I had a real pretty Rolex Commander. Dead weight. Don't know where I left it. You could still be lying on that green. Your buddy Sal might be standing around, wondering where the damned ambulance is." He paused. "Or maybe months have gone by. I've been here a while, but it sure doesn't seem like it's been sixteen years."

Vic let his head drop, his forehead resting on the bar top.

"You all right, kid?" Bascolm asked, patting Vic's shoulder.

"Yeah, a lot to absorb all at once. Feels like my mind is swimming." He looked up. "Have I heard the worst?"

"Ab-so-damn-lutely. I told you, you'll like it here. Once you let go of your other life, this place is great. Never too dark, never too light. Never too cold or hot. Never windy, or even breezy. More like a constant draft. My theory is we're all hooked up to life support in air-conditioned rooms." He laughed. "I don't know all the answers, for sure, but I know my way around this neighborhood. I'll show you the ropes. You can bunk at my place until we're sure you're not going back. If that's going to happen, it's usually pretty quick. After a while, you can pick out a house for yourself. There are plenty around."

"Any rivers around here?" Vic asked. "I always wanted a place overlooking a river."

Bascolm grinned. "Big one. The Damascus. I think we can get you set up with a house down that way."

Vic decided to ask about his former student. "Have you ever run into a guy named Elliot Patrick? He'd be young, mid-teens. Goes by Eli."

Bascolm shook his head.

"He's the only person I know who's in a coma ... other than us," Vic said, raising his arms to include the others in Gaylord's. "A former student of mine, a hit-and-run. Happened about a year ago. Thought he might have wound up here, too."

"I know most everybody in this immediate area, but I've never run across him. He could be somewhere else. There aren't a lot of us around, not right around here, anyhow. Most are Americans. I figure it's probably because of the emergency medicine in our country. Cristianne, she's Belgian. Donald's from Scotland. I've only met a few other people from places outside America, but I've never traveled any, either. Never felt the urge to wander. Talked to some who have. From what I hear, it's pretty much the same everywhere. I like the people in this area. There's a great golf course that's an easy walk from my place. What more could you want?"

Vic grinned. "You sound like a real estate salesman. But, how about animals? I don't see any around."

"You're right. I don't know for certain, but I don't think many animals go veggie. They're injured, they die. The ones you do see are friendly, though."

Vic told him about the robin he'd hit on the way to the Chili Open, and how the one he saw by the tree, when he first awakened, allowed him to pet it. "I thought it might have been the same one. That's when I was figured I was dead." There was something else Vic couldn't let pass. "You said it's an 'easy walk' to the golf course. You don't drive anymore?"

"Don't miss much, do you?" Bascolm asked, smiling. "The fact is, I used to love cars. Tinkered with a hot rod I built up all the time. Loved patrolling out on the thruway. But, yeah, guess the accident sort of changed me. I'm not *afraid* to drive, now. I think I sort of lost interest. I've driven cars here, once in a while." He shrugged. "Maybe I associate cars with my previous life. I took up golf, which I used to think was the dumbest thing a man could waste his time on. Fell in love with it. Hey, we'll round up Jason and Donald, they're great players. Have a hell of a time. You won't be afraid to get back out on a course?"

Vic laughed hard. "Are you kidding? What's the worst that could happen? Get whacked on the head and wind up back in Toledo?"

~ * ~

Before they left Gaylord's, Bascolm introduced Vic to Jason Reno. They set up a round of golf, agreeing to meet Jason and Donald at the course after Vic rested up. Rest sounded wonderful. The Southern Comfort he'd downed made the pub feel like a sloop in a gale, not to mention he still reeled from what Bascolm told him. Vic felt a little better once they were outside, but wondered how he could feel drunk if what he experienced was only mental, not physical, as Bascolm explained. If Vic was on an I.V. drip in some hospital, he doubted Southern Comfort was part of the prescription. He was about to ask, when Bascolm began talking.

"From time to time, we take a break," Bascolm said, as they started for his house. "Rest is the equivalent of sleep to us. You close your eyes and you might get close to sleep, maybe daydream a little. But fall asleep, you're no longer 'veggie.'"

"But how's come I feel drunk if I only drank in my mind, so to speak?" Vic asked.

"I haven't a clue," Bascolm replied. "Seems like, no matter how much I figure out, there are still a bunch of things I can't put any sense to." He grinned. "I've had a few too many now and again, though, and one thing I can tell you for sure." He paused. "You don't have to worry about a hangover. At least, I never got one."

Bascolm's house wasn't far from the main street and Gaylord's, although as unsteady as Vic was, it seemed like quite a distance. Finally, Bascolm tipped his head toward a sprawling brick ranch with white trim, which was nothing like the little shack Vic spotted on their way into town. Bascolm led him through the door. It was neat and tidy inside, much the way Vic expected a state trooper would keep his home. Vic followed Bascolm through the living room to the kitchen.

"There's plenty to eat here. Don't be bashful," Bascolm said. "The pantry, over there, is full, and so's the fridge. Milk, pop, and of course, beer," he added, smiling.

"Oh shit, that's the last thing I need now. Where can I lie down?"

"Come on." Bascolm motioned for Vic to follow him down the hallway. "Bathroom's there," he said, gesturing with a tip of his head to a darkened room they passed. "You'll bunk in here." He opened a door at the end of the hall.

Vic stepped inside and froze.

"What's wrong?" Alarm rose in Bascolm's voice. "You okay?"

Vic didn't answer, but began to walk slowly around the room, his arms drawn up tight against his torso, like a man in a carnival fun house. He looked side to side.

"What? What's the matter?" Bascolm asked again.

Vic locked his eyes on Bascolm's. "Is this some kind of joke?" It came out more like an accusation instead of a question. Bascolm turned his palms up, and stared into Vic's face. "This is my room. The one I had when I was a kid." He waved his arm toward the wall with windows. "That's my goddamn wallpaper, Bascolm. It was cool when I was little, but my high school buddies razzed me about the cowboys and Indians." He pointed in the other direction. "And three walls papered, one painted. My mother saw that in *Better Homes and Gardens*—big decorating fad back in the '50s." Vic pointed at the floor by the foot of the bed. "This is where I used to play with my Fort Apache. I kept it set up on a piece of green plywood so I could slide it under the bed. Kept Mom off my back when she wanted to clean." Vic dropped to his knees and bent to look. The fort wasn't there, but he grasped the bedspread, working it in his fingers. "This is the one I had, brown corduroy." He jumped to his feet, all evidence of being tipsy gone. "My desk. My dresser." He pulled open one of the dresser drawers. It was empty. He hurried over and yanked the closet door open. There was nothing hanging on the clothes bar, but when he looked at the shelf above, an old adding machine sat against the wall. "Where'd you get that?"

Bascolm stepped forward and followed Vic's gaze. "Hell if I know. It must have been here when I moved in. Truth be told, I don't think I knew it was there. I don't come in here much. Cowboys and Indians aren't my style, either. I never had anyone stay with me before."

Vic lifted the heavy machine down and placed it on the desk. The outer shell was brown plastic, and the yellowed typewriter-like keys clicked when Vic pressed them. He pulled the lever on the side and it made the sound he remembered—dry gears meshing, followed by the trill of a small bell as the lever snapped back into its original position. The tape popped up like a thin white tongue, and Vic tore it off. Two plus two equals four, printed in pale gray against the white paper. "Still needs a new ribbon." Vic turned to Bascolm, who looked away, his eyes blinking quickly, fluttering irregularly. "What?" Vic asked.

Bascolm walked over and looked out the window. "This is your bedroom?" He didn't wait for Vic to reply. "That garage out there," he used a tilt of his head to point out back, "that's my garage, the one out back of the house Sony and I had in Syracuse."

"No way!" Vic said, walking to look out the window. "With your stuff in it?"

"Some of it. It's strange. Things are missing, like the car I drove to work. But the old hot rod is there. Most of my tools. Sony's bicycle." Bascolm turned to look Vic in the eye. "There's no logic to it. Some of my stuff isn't there ... whole drawers of tools empty, and some the way I left them."

"What the fuck is going on?" Vic nearly shouted. "I mean, you say this is no dream, but how the hell does your garage from Syracuse and my bedroom from Toledo wind up at the same damned house? Then the topper, you happen to stumble across me, and we wind up here together. Huh? Explain that one."

"Sorry, partner. No can do. I don't have a handle on it. I'm as confused as you are." He paused. "Get this. The gas station across from the pub? Jason worked in that one in Long Beach, California." Vic could only stare at Bascolm. "The scary part is, Jase poked around in the desk in the office, found the paycheck he'd have picked up if he hadn't had his accident, laying there in the drawer." Vic sat back down on the bed, but didn't say anything. "Crazy thing is, doesn't happen to everybody. Donald's never found anything from his other life. Not yet, anyway. But about everybody else I know has. Cristianne found a tree where she and some boy carved their initials, but nothing else. And she says he was no one really significant. She barely remembers the guy."

"So how do you explain it?" Vic asked again.

"Told you already, I don't." Bascolm barely whispered. "Not my job to explain, or to understand." He pulled out the desk chair and sat facing Vic, who remembered his father doing much the same thing more than once. "When I first got here, I wanted to know the answers to all the questions, like you. I finally came up with the theory we're all here sharing this experience, but we each bring a portion of ourselves and our other life along. That's the best I've ever been able to do."

"So, if I go back, will this room, my bedroom, disappear?" Vic asked.

Bascolm scratched his ear. "Nah, I don't think so. The room was here before you showed up. I accepted it as a room, like you accepted the kitchen as a room. This room holds meaning for you, but it'll still be here if you aren't. It's been here all along. Unless I miss my guess, you'll probably work yourself into a lather trying to get your thumb on all the answers. Now, after a bunch of mental wrangling and headaches, I chalk it all up to what I call the un-knowables, things you'll never be able to figure out. Things there aren't answers to. Like the ones in your other life." Bascolm stood and walked over to the window again, then continued. "Like, is there a God? Did God make man in his image, or did man create God? Where is this God if there is one? Did man evolve, or was it the way the Bible tells it?" Bascolm smiled, barely showing his teeth. "And, how the hell do you hit a tee shot smack into a tree branch a hundred-fifty yards away?"

Vic grinned. "Every player knows it's easier to hit a two-inch branch than it is a hit a two-acre fairway."

Bascolm laughed. "I've never heard that one, but ain't it the truth?" A serious look crossed his face. "To me, it's one of the many un-knowables. Maybe I'll find out someday, and maybe I won't." He shrugged. "Whether or not I will is un-damn-knowable."

Vic reached up and rubbed the back of his neck.

Bascolm patted Vic on the shoulder and started for the door. "Try and get some rest. Give me a yell if you need anything."

Vic nodded and watched the door close. He shucked off his shoes and lay on the bed. It was as comfortable as he remembered from when he was young, but this was his first time alone with his thoughts since the talk with Bascolm at Gaylord's. Thoughts of his other life surged into his mind, as uncontrollable and incessant as ocean waves.

Angie's face emerged from the darkness beneath Vic's closed eyelids. The image was from early in their marriage, perhaps even from college. She was laughing, and Vic could see her crooked front tooth. He called it her "snaggle-tooth," and he always considered it a perfect counterpoint to her beauty. He was certain she was beside herself now, but he would have been slow to bet money on the actual reason. He was certain she loved him, but on her own terms. He doubted marriage to a near-cadaver was one of them. She would be there, maintaining a bedside vigil with Vic's mother, Barbara, when she arrived from Charleston. His mother loved Angie and always said Vic gave her the daughter she never had. The two of them genuinely enjoyed each other's company. The last few years, Vic wished his relationship with Angie was as strong as his mother's was. His eyes fluttered open and he looked at the adding machine. His mother let him keep it in his room after her divorce from The Old Man.

Barbara Vickery was an attractive woman in her early fifties. She had sharp blue eyes, a bit of gray stealing into her mane of brown hair, and a serious commitment to exercise and running that kept her graceful body trim. As a boy, Vic thought of her as his very own beautiful princess, who was doting and attentive. She hung the drawings he did for her on the refrigerator. "Someday you'll be a great artist," she told him. He saw that as a huge compliment because she made all kinds of clothes with her sewing machine, painted and wallpapered every room in the house, and made beautiful centerpieces for all the holiday dinner tables. Not only that, she kept up on all the fifties and sixties music and dance crazes. His friends told Vic she was the prettiest and coolest mother they knew.

The image of his mother faded as one of Vic's father loomed. Tom Vickery wasn't quite six feet tall, but he was thick, and tough as gristle. He lifted weights and punched the heavy bag that hung from the rafters in the attic, when he wasn't cutting the grass or working on some other project around the house. Vic wanted to feel as close to his father as he did with his mother, but during the week, his dad left the house early and came home late. He owned Thomas Vickery Trucking, and what he lacked in creative nomenclature, he more than made up for in tenacity. And balls. When the Teamsters tried to organize his drivers, a concept lost on Vic back then, his father did all he could to prevent it. Once, according to what Vic overheard his dad telling his mother, a man named Jimmy Hoffa came down from Detroit, in person, to have a "little talk." Of course, Vic had no idea who that Hoffa guy was at the time, but, "The talk was little, all right," his father boasted. "I tossed his ass right out into the parking lot!"

To Vic's surprise, he and his father were together all the time after the Hoffa thing. Vic was confused because he no longer was allowed to walk to school with the other kids. Dad dropped Vic off at school on his way to the truck garage each morning, and picked him up again after school to take him back to the garage in the afternoon. Dad was always busy with the papers on his desk in the office, so Vic was able to hang out with the mechanics and drivers. They told Vic jokes and funny stories about each other. Vic learned how men talk and get along. He also learned he loved the trucks, and he decided he wanted to work for his father when he grew up. The mechanics sent "Al the go-fer" on errands, and gave him little jobs to do, sorting nuts and bolts and cleaning parts. And they about went crazy when Vic finally screwed up the courage to ask why he reminded them of a gopher.

One evening, Vic and his father were on their way home from work in his '57 Chevy. As they rounded a corner, an elderly woman teetered on the curb, as though she might step in front of the car. His dad nailed the brakes and a big silver revolver slid from under the seat. Vic reached for it and his father yelled. When he quieted down, he told Vic about union goons, something that Hoffa guy threatened him with when he showed up at the truck garage. "No union goons hanging around during recess at school or anything?" his father asked. At age ten, Vic had no idea what union goons were, but his dad was getting to where he didn't like "stupid questions." Vic thought hard. The only goon he could think of was Alice the Goon in the Popeye cartoons. He told his father the coast was clear.

Soon after that, the union trouble was settled—the drivers and mechanics voted to join. Vic's dad was angry for days, but from Vic's standpoint, it didn't make any difference the men were Teamsters. As usual, Dad sat at the dining room table on Sunday mornings and ran the adding machine. He drank special orange juice he called "screwdriver." When he finished, he'd call Vic into the room and show him how much money he'd made that week. The numbers always looked big, but the difference between two hundred dollars and two thousand was beyond a ten-year-old. His father would gesture toward the table and say, "Someday, all this will be yours." Vic didn't care much about the papers with the big numbers, but he thought the adding machine was cool. Vic loved to crank the lever on the side and listen to the neat "ting" sound the little bell inside made when he let it snap back. Vic couldn't wait to get his hands on that, and on the trucks, of course.

But Vic's life spun in another unexpected direction.

"Nah, you can walk to school with your buddies from now on," his father told him one morning when Vic opened the passenger-side door of the car. "The union bullshit is over."

"But can I still come to the garage after school and help the mechanics, Daddy?" he asked.

"No," his father barked. A slap on the face wouldn't have stung as much. "You need to get back to being a kid, and those mechanics need to get their union asses in gear and get some work done."

Vic held back tears until his father was safely out of sight because, as he told Vic time and again, men don't cry. But Vic cried a lot, as time passed. His father changed, and Vic couldn't figure out why. Was it the union thing? Did Vic do something to make him mad? On one day, Dad might come home happy and offer to throw a baseball around, or help Vic fly one of his model airplanes, after dinner. The next, or even a few hours later, Vic might catch one in the chops and never really understand why. Vic never knew what to expect, which scared him.

Doubly scary was the fact his mother became moody and sullen. Anytime Vic asked, she always assured him with hugs and kisses, but several times heard her crying while she talked on the phone. Vic's recourse was to stay as close to his mother, and as far from his father, as he could. His father was usually in good spirits while he tallied the week's business and drank his screwdriver, so Sunday mornings became one of the few times Vic lowered his guard. Finally, Vic began to refer to his father with a term that once made his skin crawl when the older tough guys used it. They tossed the term around from the sides of their wise-acre mouths to sound aloof and cool. When Vic began using it, he meant it in its most derogatory sense. His father was now The Old Man.

Vic recalled the afternoon his mother ushered him into her bedroom. "How would it be if it was the two of us, just you and me? Yes, your father will be living somewhere else, but you can still see him on weekends. No," she said, laughing despite the tears that overran her lower eyelids, "you don't have to. You can decide from week to week." Vic didn't have one friend with divorced parents, and felt strange mixtures of fright and happiness swirling through him. Regardless, he threw his arms around her neck and gave her a big hug.

When The Old Man finally rolled in that night, Vic's stomach roared like a blast furnace. He hid under his bed, hoping The Old Man wouldn't come after him. "What the hell is this?" he bellowed from the downstairs hallway. "Divorce? You crazy bitch! What the hell you gonna do without me? What the hell you gonna do for money?" As Vic began to wonder how much he'd squirreled away in his piggy-bank, he heard The Old Man's heavy steps on the stairs. "I'm calling the police," Mom shouted. "The phone's in my hand." More footsteps, but the front door slammed and Vic heard the screech of tires as The Old Man sped away.

The divorce seemed to take forever to happen. Sometimes, when he was supposed to be asleep, Vic sneaked to the top of the stairs and eavesdropped while his mother talked on the phone to her friends. She had a detective, like on *77 Sunset Strip*, and Vic heard his mother talking about The Old Man having girlfriends. Vic didn't understand all of it, and he didn't really care. The Old Man didn't come around anymore, and that was all that mattered to him.

In the meantime, Vic became Mom's "Little Man." That's what she called him. He'd gone from a kid with few responsibilities to one who cut the grass, raked the leaves and put up the storm windows—things The Old Man used to do. He couldn't disguise his pride when his mother praised him to her friends and the relatives, saying she couldn't get along without him.

The day of the divorce hearing arrived, and Vic remembered his mother coming home from court. "We won! We won!" she shrieked as she burst through the door.

"Won what, Mommy?"

"The house! The car! The trucking company! We got it all!"

"Even the adding machine?" Vic asked.

Vic eventually found out his father was given the choice of paying alimony, child support, and buying his wife's half-share of the trucking company, or giving up his half-share in return for the cottage the family owned on Devil's Lake, a sleepy little waterway thirty miles north, in Michigan. The Old Man chose the latter. Vic saw his father only sporadically after that. Sometimes the two of them went to the cottage. They definitely got along better after the divorce. His father seemed to try to go out of his way to be nice, but Vic still saw glimpses of The Old Man, from time to time. Once, they came out of a carryout, and a guy was leaning on the fender of The Old Man's car. "Get your sorry ass off my car," The Old Man snarled. The man and his friend thought they could take The Old Man on, but he ended it quickly. Two punches, and both men were down for the count. Vic remembered getting into the car, feeling a weird mix of pride in his tough-guy father, embarrassment, and unwavering fear of him.

Vic's mother changed the name of the company to High Hopes Trucking, and devoted all her time and attention to running the business. His father told her she couldn't do it, she explained. "You're not smart enough," he said. "You'll run it right into the ground." She made a vow to Vic she would prove his father wrong. Vic did all he could to help. He worked hard for good grades at school, kept up his duties around the house, and even learned to cook. On Saturdays, his mother dropped Vic off at the terminal and he washed the trucks. The mechanics were supposed to move the trucks to the wash bay for him, but they quickly tired of that and taught him how to drive the huge semi tractors. He loved the feeling in the pit of his stomach when he let out the clutch on one of the monsters, forcing the great mass of metal and horsepower to lurch into motion. On Sundays, he and his mother sat at the kitchen table and totaled the week's business together. She and Vic drank Diet-Rite Cola, and he ran the adding machine while she called out the numbers. He liked helping out, and besides, he knew it was good practice for when he someday ran the business.

One evening, in mid-October of 1965, the phone rang as Vic finished his homework.

"Is this Allan Vickery, Tom and Barbara Vickery's son?" the voice coming through the receiver asked.

It was a voice Vic couldn't place. When he confirmed who he was, the voice continued.

"This is your Uncle Bill, Allan. Your dad's brother. You remember?"

Vic was speechless, uselessly nodding with the receiver pressed to his ear.

"I have some terrible news," his uncle said into the silence on the line. "Your dad was killed last night in San Bernardino, California." There was a long pause. "I'm sorry to have to tell you this way, but I don't know what else to say."

Vic pumped his uncle for information, but it was apparent he didn't know much. There was a fight of some kind. The Old Man was outnumbered. To his surprise, Vic found himself overwhelmed with grief. Much as he'd carefully cultivated a bumper crop of hatred for who his father became, the loving father he once knew was dead, too. Vic began to understand a really strong case of hatred often fed off residual love, or at least, the memory of love. Part of him wanted to go into Mannix-mode: head for the coast, track down the men who killed The Old Man and bring them to justice. Or even mete out a little of his own. That thought made him grimace. Vic was indeed, he thought, The Old Man's son.

When Vic told his mother the news, and that Bill was having the body shipped back to Toledo for burial, she held him tightly and wept softly.

"I can't go, Allan," she whispered in his ear.

Vic would have been surprised if she did, but driving himself to the funeral was one of the hardest things he'd done in his seventeen years. His rib cage felt like it was full of panicked mice, but the reality of spending time with relatives he hadn't seen in years turned out to be pleasant. Seeing his father was a shock. Although a skilled mortician smoothed over all vestiges of the beating, it was obvious The Old Man had been on a path to self-destruction; a mere shadow of the man Vic remembered from only a handful of years before. After an hour or so of reminiscence, and even some laughter, the small group made its way to the cemetery. Cold wind-driven rain forced the planned graveside service into a small chapel. Vic cried all the way home, eventually giving up on hiding his tears from people in the surrounding cars, or from his mother when she met him at the door.

Vic's goal became finishing school so he could take over the business and buy it from his mother. That all changed one April night in 1966, toward the end of Vic's senior year of high school. He was studying in his room after dinner, and the minute his mother entered, Vic knew something was up. He had a feeling of unease he couldn't explain. Mom had a look on her face that reminded Vic of the afternoon she told him she was going to divorce The Old Man, and before she said a word, Vic sensed his life was about to change. He was afraid to find out how.

She inhaled deeply, and began to unload feelings Vic was certain she'd kept hidden for a long time. "Tired of it, Allan," she began. "Tired of the grind, of the hours. Tired of it all. I've taken the company your father started and quintupled its size. I've bettered everything your father ever did, except for tossing Jimmy Hoffa on his butt, and I'd like independent verification on *that* one." She looked into Vic's eyes. "I got a fat offer today. Enough to keep me for the rest of my life, and plenty to leave you when I die. You've always said you want to buy me out when you get out of college. If that's still your plan, I'll keep it until you graduate." She patted his knee. "Take some time to think it over, and let me know what you decide."

Vic's stomach felt like it was twisting around his spine that night. Of course he wanted the company. He always assumed his mother would retire on the nice monthly income he would send her when she moved to a warmer climate. He lay awake most of the night, ruminating over the choice he had to make. By breakfast the next morning, he decided he loved his mother more than anything, even High Hopes Trucking. If she wanted to get out from under the pressure and the hours required to run it, he didn't want to stand in her way. The Old Man was dead, and Vic imagined The Old Ghost laughing when Vic smiled at her across the breakfast table and told the biggest lie of his life. "Sell it, Ma," Vic said over his bowl of shredded wheat. "I'd rather be an artist, anyway." Vic left for college that fall, and never looked back at the door he closed on his dreams.

Shortly after his freshman year began, his mother moved to Charleston, West Virginia to be closer to her sister. She dated a number of men in the intervening years, but she never let it get serious. "Lousy at picking men," she told Vic. "I'm never going to put myself in the situation I was in with your father, again." Her current "friend," Hobart Early, a mountain boy who came out of an uncharted holler to build a successful tool rental business, would undoubtedly accompany her up from Charleston. Hobart's image, that of a man who seemed too homely and "back-woodsy" to date Barbara Vickery, joined the parade of faces in Vic's mind.

Angie's parents would surely be at the hospital, too. Angie's mother was the consummate socialite wife and hostess. In the last eleven years, Vic never once saw her in jeans, or even in slacks. Vic pictured her in one of her tailored Armani dresses, posturing as the bereaved and concerned mother-in-law, while privately seething over the fact Vic was injured while wasting his time playing golf. It seemed to Vic that Angie began to exhibit the same cold and distant mannerisms her mother had down pat, which angered and saddened him. Angie's father, a tall silver-haired man, wasn't comfortable with Vic calling him Dad, but he always treated Vic like a good friend. Her father was a mover and shaker in the Chicago commodities markets, and his way of dealing with problems was to throw money at them. Vic grinned when he thought of his comatose body lying in the finest private room in Toledo Hospital.

The grin vanished when Vic's musings were interrupted by a knock on the door. "Yeah?" he called. He realized he was bathed in sweat.

Bascolm cracked open the door. "You okay?"

"Yeah. Yeah, Bass, I'm all right," Vic croaked, swinging his legs over the side of the bed and clearing his throat. "Do we need to leave?"

"Not unless you're up to it."

"Yeah. I've had more than enough of this rest," Vic muttered.

"You sleep any? Flash at all?"

"Nope. Just a bumpy ride down memory lane." He forced a laugh. "Almost felt like I was dying—you know, the way they say your life passes before your eyes. A little recreational stress on a golf course will be a treat," he joked, pulling the door open. "Hey, how do we know Jason and Donald will be there when we roll in? There's no time here, right? How's all this work?"

Bascolm rubbed his chin. "Rhythms, I guess. That's the best explanation I can come up with." He leaned against the door jamb. "It's easier to know when we'll all meet up than it is to explain how I know. I've played a lot of golf with those two. We sort of sense when we'll all get there. And if any of us are wrong, no big deal. We find things to do. Practice our putting or chip shots."

"Do I have time to take a quick shower before we go?" Vic asked. "Resting was hard work, I guess. I sweated like a pig."

"No problem, long as you don't make it a career." He turned to start down the hall, then stopped. "I'd like to get there before they do," he said over his shoulder. "I want to watch you hit some balls before we start our round."

"That was my next question," Vic said. "What the hell am I going to do for clubs?" He raised his arms in exaggerated dismay. "I thoughtlessly left mine sitting next to a green back in Toledo."

"Plenty of sets down at the clubhouse," Bascolm said. "We'll get you fitted up good. Don't plan on using equipment as an excuse for a bad shot." He chuckled as he started down the hallway again. "You're gonna like playing golf here, Allan. I guar-an-damn-tee it."

~ * ~

The golf course was a short walk away, down a pleasant lane with big trees that formed a virtual tunnel of foliage overhead. It reminded Vic of River Road, where he wanted to someday own a river house. "Fat chance now," he whispered under his breath.

When they reached the golf club, Vic was struck by the beauty of the course and the buildings. The clubhouse looked a little like the Georgian mansion Angie was building, and it was surrounded by verdant hills and sleepy, meandering streams that cut across the fairways as they wandered from pond to pond. When Bass and Vic entered the pro shop, they were surrounded by racks of clubs. There were dozens of sets, ranging from wooden-shafted antiques to modern steel shafted clubs. The shop had a high ceiling and was surrounded by large windows that lined the wood-paneled walls to let in the flat gray light. Vic and Bascolm were the only two people in the building, and when neither of them talked, it was as quiet as a tomb.

"How does this one feel?" Bascolm asked, pulling a five iron out of a bag and handing it to Vic.

Vic took a full speed rip and the club head left a telltale mark on the pile when it brushed over the thick green carpet. "Good, Bass, real good. About like my clubs at home."

"I bet you fight the slice a lot," Bascolm said.

Vic gave Bascolm a look like he'd guessed his weight. "Yeah, how'd you know?"

"Look at the mark you left on the carpet." Bascolm pointed with the grip of the club he held. He used it to scribe a line in the lush green pile. "This is the direction your feet were set up in, but the club head came across that line from the outside—outside-in. Puts a clockwise spin on the ball." He twirled an upright finger in golf ball-sized circles. "Makes him want to start out straight, but turn right." He raised an eyebrow. "Sound like the flight your shots tend to take?"

43

Vic choked out a laugh. "A lot of them."

"Know why the club comes through that way?"

"No. It's supposed to go straight down the line, but I can't make it do that. Not consistently, anyway."

"Straight down the line or, better yet, from the inside-out. Puts a counterclockwise spin on the ball. Makes the ball want to go right to left," Bascolm said, his finger twirling in the opposite direction.

"A draw?"

"Ab-so-damned-lutely. A ball hit with a draw goes farther because it's already spinning in its direction of travel when it hits the ground. You don't drive it as far as your buddies, do you?"

Vic shook his head.

"Do what I show you and you'll not only lose the slice, you'll gain distance in the bargain. The swing shouldn't start with the arms," Bascolm said, gripping the club and taking his stance. "Watch." He coiled into a back swing, cocking his wrists so the club was parallel to the floor, pointing straight toward Bascolm's intended target line. He paused, then unwound like a tightly coiled spring. His hips and torso began to rotate, while his arms dropped straight down and through to where the ball would be waiting. When his wrists straightened before reaching the bottom of their arc, the club and Bascolm's arms became one long pendulum; a hammer with a six-foot long handle. He finished, his arms over his left shoulder and his stomach facing the target. He repeated the swing several times.

"Do you see what's happening? It's like cracking a whip. I pull with my left side, then my hips begin to turn—that's called clearing. The hips clear as my upper torso follows through, but watch my right elbow." Bascolm executed several partial swings, stopping as his elbow came into contact with his hip. "The right elbow drops straight down against my side. I've heard it referred to as 'pulling the rope,' like when you ring a big bell. It drops down to ride the right hip as it turns, and BOOM!" he exclaimed, completing the swing. The club head whistled through the hitting area like a scythe. He grinned. "Now you."

Vic swung, trying to do as Bascolm instructed. It was difficult to touch all those bases during a swing that lasted only a bit more than a second, but Vic felt like he'd come close. "How was that?" he asked.

"Not bad. Not bad. But you slid your hips more than you rotated them. You're a right-hander, and that's something that will work against a good swing. A righty, he'll tend to push the club with his right side on the follow-through. Makes the club do what we don't want, cross the target line from the outside in." Bascolm stepped into his stance and completed his backswing. "When you get the club to this point, you want to pull with the left side of your body and let your arms swing free. Hard for a righty to do, but it'll give you more of this," Bascolm said, swiveling his hips several times.

"Looks like you're doing the hula."

"You go ahead and make fun, kid. I'll hula right by you out on the course."

Vic executed several more swings, making sure he used his left side to pull the club down to where the ball would be waiting. His hips felt like they were rotating instead of sliding, and his elbow seemed to be hitting its mark at his hip.

"How's that feel?" Bascolm asked.

"Different. Different, but good."

"Yeah, and look at the marks you're leaving on the carpet now. Inside-out instead of outside-in." Bascolm glanced around. "I don't see Jase or Donald yet. We need to get you out on the range and hit some live balls before we tee it up with them. You think those irons will be all right?"

"Sure," Vic answered.

"What do you usually play with?"

"Clubs The Old Man gave me. Hogan Precisions."

"I have you covered on the woods, but I haven't seen any Precision irons around ... no complete sets, anyway. They're rare since AMF bought Hogan out, even here. You go back, make sure you don't give yours away. Might be worth some money."

45

"Yeah? If The Old Man knew that, he never would have given me his."

"Not exactly father of the year?"

"You got that right." Vic said, taking one more look around. "This is amazing. How did all these clubs get here?"

"Hell, kid, I don't know how *we* wound up here. You have to learn to take this place at face value. It doesn't pay to intellectualize."

"It's all so crazy."

"Maybe that's why the name of this club is Loon's Lair."

When they made it out to the range, Vic's first few shots were nothing spectacular. Bascolm patiently coached him, and his tenth or twelfth shot dropped out of the sky, bounced, and rolled past the 250-yard sign Bascolm told Vic to use as a target. "Damn! I've never hit a ball like that before." Bascolm put another on a tee. Careful to do as he was shown, Vic swung and the ball shot off like a mortar round. It started out to the right of the row of yardage signs, but drew left and landed in what would have been the middle of the fairway. Vic loosened his fingers, allowing the driver to fall over his shoulder to the ground. "Yee-ha! I feel like I did the day I learned to ride a two-wheel bike. Christ, you are one hell of a good teacher, Bass. I thought I was good, but you put me on the trailer."

"Helps to have a good student."

"I guess ... I don't know. All I know is I never hit a ball like that before." Vic picked up his club. "Man, I owe you big time. I mean, you can say we're in comas, and I guess we probably are, but as far as I'm concerned, this is heaven!"

"Then heaven comes at a higher price than I'd ever offer to pay," Bascolm said, slinging his arm over Vic's shoulders as they walked to where their golf bags leaned against a fence. "I'd trade a thousand under-par rounds here for the chance to go back to Syracuse." He sounded wistful. Probably thinking of Sondra, Vic figured. He was a long way from knowing all he wanted to about the comatose state, and he wanted to keep pumping Bascolm for all the information he could get. To do that, he wanted to keep the conversation focused on their comas, not their wives.

"But if you did regain consciousness, once you got back in shape, you'd be hitting it as well as you are here, right? I mean, you wouldn't forget everything you've learned by coming out of your coma, would you?"

"I don't know. We've kicked that one around a time or two, over beers. There're more than a couple ways of looking at it." They shouldered their bags and began walking across a meadow toward the first tee. "I don't think forgetting would be the main problem. Look, you dialed in a beautiful swing, and you did it hitting maybe twenty or thirty balls. Right?"

"Uh, yeah, with your help."

"Ah, but you've had instruction before, and read books and articles in magazines, I imagine. You've watched the greats on TV. You know how you're supposed to swing a club. So, what's the difference today?"

"There's a big difference between reading a book or watching TV, and personal instruction."

"Granted. But ... I guess I'm not asking the right way. Where are you right now?"

"Here with you, wherever this is."

"But what part of you is here? Your unconscious mind, yeah? Or your awareness, if you prefer. What part of you isn't really here?"

"My body?"

"Bingo! You left your body back in Toledo. Mine's in upstate New York someplace. We're free of them. I don't know about you, Allan, but I was never a great athlete. Most times, I knew what I wanted my body to do, but getting it to follow my brain's instructions was the problem. The great golfers, their minds work in a state of harmony with their bodies that make the likes of us look palsied."

They leaned their bags against the bench at the first tee. Bascolm started taking practice swings with his driver while Vic sat down and rubbed the sides of his head. "So you're saying the reason I'm hitting the ball so well is I'm doing it without my body?" Vic asked.

"Essentially," Bascolm said. "Back in your life, your mind sent good signals, your body couldn't follow them. That's my read on it, anyway. You go back, your mind, even if you remember any of this, will have your body to contend with." He punched Vic on the shoulder. "You'll be a hacker all over again." Vic still rubbed his head. Bascolm leaned on his driver. "What's the matter, you getting a headache?"

"No, but close. Every time we talk, it all gets crazier and more complicated."

"I told you, don't try to understand it all. Did you have a handle on every aspect of life back in Toledo?"

Vic immediately thought of his marriage, and shook his head. Being married to Angie wasn't the only aspect of life he hadn't figured out, but it was the most obvious.

"So, treat this place the same way. Ease up and enjoy it here. The less you try to figure things out, the more you'll understand. I know that sounds like double-talk, Allan, but it's the way it's worked out for me."

Jason and Donald walked up and put their clubs down. Donald, a tall, freckled man in his mid-twenties, with reddish-blonde hair and an impish grin, looked like a man dying to say something funny. Vic could sense the man's mischievous streak. Jason, on the other hand, had an open-faced, expectant quality that said he was ready to enjoy someone else's humor at a moment's notice. Donald stepped forward and grasped Vic's hand. "Donald MacDougal," he said in an engaging Scottish brogue. "Pleased."

"Allan Vickery, Donald," Vic replied, shaking both men's hands. Vic came close to using his nickname, but he decided against it. Bascolm was calling him Allan, and already introduced him around that way. It seemed foolish to change things up. Besides, Vic was his name back home. This was a new place. Another new start, like a new golf game. His nickname felt like unwanted baggage, so he let it go. Allan felt right for his new life, Vic decided.

"How many strokes are you youngsters spotting us?" Bascolm asked, leaning on his driver. "Allan, here, might not be at the top of his

48

game today. Might be a little spooky. The last time he was on a golf course, he took a tee shot to the head."

"No kidding?" Jason said. "That's how you got here?"

"It's a fact. Struck a putt and *wham*. You?"

"Water skiing. We were jumping and the ski ramp dried off, I guess. All I know is when I hit the damned thing, my ski stopped, but I didn't," he said, shrugging his muscular shoulders. Vic winced as his mind played the scene in Technicolor. "Never felt a thing," Jason added, with a shrug.

Vic looked expectantly at Donald. "A victim of me own stupidity, I'm afraid," Donald said, his grey eyes twinkling. "I was on holiday in Belgium, checking out the disco scene in Brussels. I met a lass and fell in love." His face went vacant of any humor. "She wanted me to stay. Cassandra owned a pub, and offered to let me live upstairs with her and work the bar. Anyway, I decided to go back to Scotland to mull it over, and clear up some business I had there. She came to see me off at the pier. I was waving goodbye from the upper deck of the ferry when I suddenly decided not to leave. As the boat pushed off from the pier, I tossed my bag over the rail and jumped. I don't know what happened after that, exactly, but I guess it wasn't good." Donald winked, his mirthful smirk returning. "But don't you be worried about gettin' hit out here," he added, swinging his club in slow wide arcs. "Us veggies are already hurt about as badly as can be. And no, Bass. You'll be gettin' no strokes from us. We're playing the game straight up."

"But Allan has never played at the Lair," Bascolm said, as he teed his ball and looked down the fairway, apparently picking a target. "You two are plainly out to take advantage of a couple of old men." He turned to wink at Vic. "You see what I've had to put up with? The two of them together don't have half a conscience."

"And we usually don't have half a chance of winning, either," Jason said, to Vic. "Bass takes the both of us on, lets us play our best ball, and we rarely win a hole."

"Hey, wait a minute," Vic said. "Bass, you told me we're all playing without our bodies, only our minds, right?" Bass nodded. "Then why can't Jason and Donald play as well as you?"

Bascolm looked like he was about to answer, but Jason cut in.

"Because we all don't have the same level of understanding," he said. "You gotta allow for individual differences. Bass understands the swing better than we do. He knows more than we've learned yet. I may get to where he is someday, but not so far." Jason turned and mugged at Bascolm. "All the same, I kick Bass's ass on the pool table. And Donald's game is poker," he said, clapping the Scotsman on the shoulder.

"So, you understand, Allan?" Bascolm interrupted. "If Albert Einstein was here, he couldn't teach all of us to understand relativity, not to the degree he did. We're all wired a little different. And, here's another thing I play with sometimes: our minds only operate within the confines of the body we had back in our life. It's like, if we're here with only our minds, then why aren't we all supermen?" Bascolm went on. "Why don't we all look like Paul Newman, or whoever? It's because our minds can only work within the confines of the bodies we had. That's all each of us can conceptualize." He pointed toward Jason's muscular upper torso. "You think my mind could operate that kind of machinery? Christ, I'd fall on my keister if I tried to swing a club with all that. Back when I used to drag race, we called it 'runnin' whatcha brung.'" He chuckled. "That's what we do here. We work with the body our mind knows and understands. So, even though we can make our body do what we want it to more easily, what we can do is also limited by the body our mind remembers. The one it's always been plugged into. Probably why we never look any older. Make any sense?"

"I'm going to think that over," Vic said.

"Remember," Bascolm concluded, "don't take any of this as gospel. I don't know any of this for sure; it's what I believe right now. I mean, we're here. There have to be explanations, and we don't have any. But that doesn't keep us from trying to figure it all out, even though I keep telling you not to try." He bent to adjust the height of the ball on his tee. "It's only human to want to figure it out, to put some kind of order to what I see as mainly chaos."

"It's a pretty good theory, though," Jason said. "I'd bet on it."

"Hey, speaking of bets, do you guys play for money?" Vic asked, reaching for his wallet, remembering he only had twenty dollars on him.

"No, lad," Donald replied. "If you've any money, throw it away. It's of no value in this realm. We're playing for the only thing worth anything—"

"Bragging rights," Jason cut in. "Donald and I win, you and Bass have to sit through a steak dinner at Mancy's while we rake you over the coals."

"No better steak than at Mancy's," Donald continued. "But you'll be lucky to enjoy even a bite if we take the match."

Bascolm hit his tee ball, punctuating Donald's threat with a strike that cracked like a rifle shot. Vic, Jason, and Donald turned to watch the ball sweep up and draw, following the fairway as it meandered to the left around a line of trees.

"Nice shot, Bass," Jason said. "You're up, Allan."

Vic swung several times, reviewing what Bascolm taught him.

"Aim for the willow out there and hit your draw," Bascolm instructed. "You'll be in the fairway and sitting pretty."

Vic's tee shot was as good as any he hit on the range. It proved to be the perfect start to a memorable round. Loon's Lair bullied its way over and between rolling hillsides. Vast colonnades of trees formed canyon-like walls stretching toward the lace-work canopy of clouds. The clouds made the light mimic the fluorescents Vic remembered in his classroom back at Alexis High. It had the same cold, clinical tonality, and seemed to worm its way under every object, diminishing any shadows. Vic could only imagine how beautiful Loon's Lair would be in the saffron rays of direct sunlight. That, and Vic couldn't lose the sensation of being somehow enclosed in a huge structure. There was a tinny, dead tone to the sounds of their voices, and even to the sounds of the clubs rattling in the bag as he walked. There was no breeze. It was bizarre. Nothing in this new world ever seemed to change, as far as Vic could tell.

"Nice of them to build this course for the four of us," Vic said, sweeping his arm toward the empty surrounding fairways.

Bascolm side-glanced. "Just don't go asking me who 'them' is. I don't have a clue. The course was here when I landed. That's all I can tell you."

"Okay, I won't ask," Vic said. "But I still can't believe there aren't more players out here. Gotta say it, some parts of this place are so logical, and other parts don't make any sense at all."

Bascolm chuckled. "Kinda like Toledo, huh? Or Syracuse?"

Vic blew a puff of air through his nose in grudging agreement. "I did see a foursome, though, teeing off on number one, earlier."

"You will, from time to time. It isn't private, that's for sure. Or else they wouldn't let the likes of us on it." He gave Vic a playful shove as they arrived at his tee ball. "Now, there're golf holes you can't milk for a stroke, Allan," Bascolm said, his voice changing slightly toward an instructive tone. "Those have to be played for par. On others, you can try for birdie because they invite aggressive shots. That's the tricky part of the game, reading a hole and playing it accordingly. Any idea which this is?"

Vic surveyed the landscape between where they stood and the par five's green. "It's still a long poke from here, over two hundred yards," he said.

"Yeah, and if you aim for the green and don't make it, there's lots of crap in your way; that heavy brush and the long grass," Bascolm said, pulling Vic's five iron out of the bag. "You probably ought to stay in the fairway and plan to come in at the green from the right side. The green's wider than it is deep. You'll have a better chance to get on and make par. With a really good third shot, you might even have a legitimate putt for birdie. Right?"

Throughout the rest of the round, each of Vic's new friends explained the merits and dangers of playing their shots in various ways, and helped Vic with his strategy. "Course management," they called it. Back in

Toledo, their pace of play would have been considered downright slow; but in the absence of time or any other golfers, their progress was comfortable. His new friends' advice about where to hit it, coupled with his new swing, made for an astounding difference in Vic's game. After missing his first putt on the eighteenth hole, he tapped in.

"When was the last time you shot a seventy-eight?" Bascolm asked.

"Never!" Vic said. "This is unbelievable. And I owe it all to you guys."

"We'll have to work on your chipping and putting," Jason said. "Hell, without any three-putts, you'd have been at par or under."

Donald looked up from the scorecard. "That's right. Two-putts on every hole would have given you seventy-one. I shot sixty-eight with the 'elp of me putter. Jason, sixty-three, me lad. And Bass, a smooth fifty-nine."

Bascolm, Donald, and Jason offered a number of tips and demonstrated how to play pitch shots and putts, then the four of them continued to practice on the eighteenth green.

"What it all boils down to, Allan," Bascolm concluded as they walked to their bags, "is that the short game, the last hundred yards to the hole, is the key to a low score. Practice getting it up and down. That is the most important thing you can do."

Vic slid his putter into his bag. He was riding a huge high, like he'd been handed the keys to a powerful car or a fast motorcycle. He never before played a round like the one he'd just finished, and he was sure the short game practice would allow him to shoot even better. He didn't want to wait to try it out. "You've made me a disciple. But hey, this round turned out to be more of a class for me than a match for the four of us. Are you guys tired?"

Jason fired off a toothy grin. "You're gonna fit in here fine."

"Yes," Donald added, "steak will taste that much better after eighteen more holes."

"Now that Allan knows his way around, you two might end up eating some humble pie for dessert," Bascolm said as they picked up their bags and set off for the first tee.

Vic immersed himself in concentration on the second loop. He allowed himself several practice swings before each shot, and never hit the ball until he identified a clear objective. If there was a hazard, he ignored it and focused on his target. He birdied a total of four holes on the front nine, and never three-putted. Donald handed him the score card as they walked to the number ten tee. Vic added numbers and realized he'd taken only thirty-four strokes, tying Jason. Donald resurrected his long game and carded a thirty-two. Bascolm, of course, lead with an unbelievable twenty-nine. They were even on the match. Each team won four holes and tied one. "Pressure's on, men," Donald said, as they walked onto the tenth tee. "The back nine will prove what we're made of."

Donald was right, the second nine was tough for Vic. Every swing felt effortless, but the prolonged cerebral gymnastics were wasting him mentally, and his swing began to erode. He was eager to finish so he could let his overloaded circuits rest. He sagged to the ground when they walked off the final green, pillowing his head on his bag.

"You okay?" Bascolm asked.

"Oh yeah, but whupped." He rose to a sitting position, wagging his head. "I can't remember the last time I focused so hard for that long."

"So that was it! We thought you didn't like us anymore," Jason joked. "You hardly spoke a word."

"Guess I was caught up in my game. How did we do, Bass?"

"Think it's fair to say we got our asses kicked," he said, grabbing Vic's wrist to pull him to his feet. "Fair assessment, Donald?"

Donald slid the pencil behind his ear. "I'm afraid so, Bass. We split on eleven and fourteen. You and Allan took sixteen and seventeen. Jason and I won the rest. We won, five up."

"You boys shot our eyes out today, but there'll be other rounds," Bascolm said. "Hey, what did 'Mr. Mental' shoot, anyway?"

"Blew up to a thirty-six on the back for a two under par seventy," Donald said. "Not bad golf for a hacker."

The idea he was lying in a hospital bed somewhere surfaced in Vic's mind. *Of course, I'm playing without my body.* Regardless, Vic couldn't remember when he'd been happier after a round of golf. He'd never finished under par before. Even if all this was only happening in his head, it felt real enough to leave him with a tremendous sense of satisfaction. He couldn't stop grinning.

Bascolm slapped Vic on the back. "My friend, you played one hell of a round. Damn, I'm proud of you. A few more rounds, you'll be deadly! Now, let's go eat steak."

"And a big helping of humble pie for the two of you."

Chapter Three

The soft yellow lighting in Mancy's dining room made everything look rich and warm, unlike the continual overcast outdoors that seemed to leach the color out of even the brightest of hues. Mrs. Mancy kept the heavy drapes pulled, and the artificial darkness enhanced the buttery light from the chandelier, making the meal a warm, visual treat, in addition to its succulent taste.

Donald put his fork down. "Can I ask you a question, Allan?"

Vic chuffed out a dry laugh. "Seems only right. I've done nothing but ask you guys questions since we all met up. Fire away."

"The Pope, did he survive that shooting?"

Vic's mind spun like a Rolodex. Donald surprised him with a question about life back in the world they were no longer part of. Vic couldn't make the jump immediately. "Uh, yeah. He did. They worried for a while, but he's fully recovered, far as I know."

"Thank you, Allan," Donald said, apparent relief softening the wrinkles on his forehead. "Someone who arrived right after it happened told me he'd been shot, but I never heard if he lived."

"I'm no fountain of information," Vic said, "but I'll tell you guys anything I know. You probably know President Reagan was shot a month or two before the Pope. He's doing fine now too. And man, did that turn out to be a squirrelly deal." He paused to finish his Southern Comfort. "The kid who shot him ... did you hear any of this?"

56

"All we know is someone tried to assassinate him," Bass said, leaning forward and putting his elbow on the table. He grinned. "Reagan was an actor when I checked out."

"That's right," Vic said, shaking his head. "Anyway, the kid who did it, he had this thing for Jodie Foster. You know, the actress." The absurdity of the whole incident he was relating made him chuckle. "Somehow, the kid, Hinckley was his name, thought killing the President would turn her on to him." Vic shook his head. "Sick puppy." He thought for a second. "So yeah, this is how you guys get your history, right? People tell you what's going on in the world when they get here?"

"Actually, we don't consider it 'history,'" he said. "It's really news to us ... kind of history in reverse." He chuckled. "Fact is, I don't even know who Jodie Foster is. She must be young."

Vic rolled his eyes. "Oh, that's right. Christ, she wasn't even around in the early sixties. Maybe not even born yet," he added.

"It's past history for you," Bascolm said, "but we weren't there for it, so it's news to us."

"Yeah," Jason said, lighting up with mirth. "Things that happened after we bonked out are history. Now we're all history, unless we go back." They shared some laughter, but Vic's was forced.

"To be honest," Bascolm said, "I don't really much care what happens back there. Not that I've become hard or calloused. It's not part of my world. I used to be huge on baseball, but I don't really care who won the last World Series."

"Good," Vic said, "'cause I don't follow the game, so I couldn't tell you, anyhow. Tom Watson won The Masters, though."

"Watson," Bascolm said, like he was trying the word out for the first time. "Don't think he was on the tour back when I was around, but he might have been. I didn't follow golf back then."

Donald cut in, "I'd love to stay a bit of a while to chat and raise another glass, but I know where there's a sweet young lass who'd love to serve me a tankard of ale." He raised and lowered his hands like the pans on a balance scale. "Cristianne? You guys? Cristianne wins, hands down," he said, grinning big and letting one of the "pans" drop to the table. "No offense meant, gentlemen, but it's no contest."

"Yeah, and I oughta get a move on, too. Enjoy your humble pie," Jason said. He folded his linen napkin and slapped it down on the table with a flourish. "I'd love to stay and watch you eat a big helping, but I think I know where there's a pool table." Jason gave Donald a wink. "Doesn't sound near as good as beer and a good woman, but, what the hell," he said, as he and Donald rose in unison to leave.

"Where the heck is that pretty gal you were seeing?" Donald asked, as they ambled toward the nearby door together.

"I'm afraid she went back," Jason said as he closed the door, sealing Vic and Bascolm off from any more of the conversation.

Donald's and Jason's talk of women made Vic think about Angie, and the dinner the two of them shared at a restaurant the night before the Chili Open. How long ago was that? How much time passed in the conscious world? Is it still the day I got hit, or has a week gone by? He wondered, and he knew beyond a shadow of a doubt that he *did* still care what happened back in Toledo. He cared very much. And he hoped to get back.

Bascolm's voice rumbled. "You look like a man who's in deep thought."

"Yeah, my mind's been floating. Started out by thinking how great this steak is," Vic said, resisting the urge to mention Angie or the world he left behind. "It's strange. I wasn't really hungry when we sat down, and I don't feel any different now that I've eaten."

Bascolm tossed his napkin on the table. "Your mind told you it was time to eat, not your body. Your body's being fed, probably by I.V. drip or a feeding tube. That's my take, anyway. I eat because I love the taste of steak, and June Mancy knows how to cook 'em." He drained his beer. "You good for one more?"

"What the hell, we're not driving."

Bascolm caught Mrs. Mancy's attention and signaled for another round.

"Does she own this place?" Vic asked.

"Still determined to figure it all out, huh?"

Vic shrugged.

"No, she doesn't own it," Bascolm said. "Nobody owns anything here that I know of. I don't own the clubs I played with today. They're mine while I'm here. When I'm gone, they'll be someone else's. Mrs. Mancy always wanted to run a restaurant. This place was available and she took it over."

"Are you still a cop?"

Bascolm smiled. "Not much call for cop-work in these parts, I'm glad to say. I guess that means I have what I've always wanted, a world that had no need for the likes of me. Of course, the world I had in mind included Sondra and Syracuse. What do they say? Be careful what you wish for?" He sipped his beer. "As far as this place is concerned, I guess it's a matter of no money, no possessions, no crime."

Bascolm's mention of his wife and hometown put Angie and Toledo squarely back in Vic's mind. He scrambled for another question to keep himself in the present. "Doesn't anybody ever get pissed off at anybody else? I mean, come on, people are still people, with normal human frailties. There have to be some assholes around, right?"

"You'd think," Bascolm said with a shrug, "but I haven't really run across any. Maybe a person I don't like, but no real criminals. Since nobody owns anything, and there seems to be plenty of everything around, so what's to get ticked off or possessive about?"

Vic couldn't let this alone. His mind churned out questions, and Bascolm never seemed to mind wading in with his opinion. At least, he hadn't so far. "Yeah, but what if somebody came in here and told Mrs. Mancy they wanted to take over the restaurant, told her to buzz off?" Vic asked.

"Hasn't happened, so I can't say," Bascolm said. "I think what it all really boils down to is all of us here have already lost our most important possession, the life we used to have." He held his fork loosely by its handle, moving it in small circles, the tines sliding noiselessly across the tablecloth.

"Now we're here, a second chance at another life before we die. So I guess we all want to make it as pleasant as we can. Why cause trouble when you're lucky to be anywhere at all? We were lucky to have the life we used to have, but losing that life makes us all acutely aware of how precious this one is. That's the way I see it, anyway. So no, I'm not a cop anymore. But, I *am* kind of the unofficial greens keeper at Loon's Lair."

"No kidding?"

"It doesn't take a lot. Grass doesn't grow much in the light we have. When the greens start to get slow, I mow 'em. There's an old Ford tractor I use to pull a set of mowers when the fairways need it. I could probably count on both hands the times I've mowed. Jase helps out, too. Everybody kind of does what they want to do based on what needs to be done," he said, smiling at their matronly hostess as she arrived with their drinks. "Isn't that right, Mrs. Mancy?"

"I didn't catch all of what you boys were saying, Bass," she warbled, her old lady voice seeming to cover several keys at once. "Say, weren't Jason and Donald in a hurry?"

"Yeah, Donald went to meet Cristianne," Bascolm said. "Jason's off shooting pool. They loved the steaks. Asked us to tell you so."

"I hope you all did," she said, patting their shoulders like a grandma. "Would you care for any more?"

"The food was wonderful, Mrs. Mancy," Vic said, "but I don't want to make a pig of myself."

She cleared their plates and bustled off toward the kitchen. Vic and Bascolm sipped their fresh drinks.

"Mrs. Mancy told me once," Bascolm said, "when she cooked meals for her family, she used to imagine her dining room was a restaurant. I have a world without crime. So, what do you wish for?"

Vic thought for a moment. "It's like I told you, Bass, I'm an art teacher. I paint after work, on the weekends and all summer. I guess I always hoped my stuff would be recognized, someday. You know, galleries

in big cities selling it so I could make some extra money, if not a living."
He pointed his finger at Bascolm and winked. "And be famous."

Bascolm grinned. "You can paint here. I know where we can get
you everything you need. What kind of pictures do you paint? Landscapes?
Abstracts?"

Vic pushed away from the table and relaxed with his arms crossed.
"Never had the balls to paint abstracts."

Bascolm's eyebrows shot skyward. "Balls?"

"Sure. Look, most people don't know much about art. They don't
know how hard it is to paint a good abstract. They stand in front of great art
they don't have a clue about and say, 'Hell, my three-year-old paints like
that,'" Vic drawled, doing his best Gomer Pyle. "My ego couldn't deal with
that, so I paint realistically. They may not like the image, but at least they
have to admit I'm talented."

"So it takes a big ego to be an artist?"

"Yeah, uh, I don't know. Maybe a thick skin. Thicker than mine,
anyway. Besides, I enjoy realism. I do some landscape, and I like painting
people." Vic paused. He had trouble keeping his focus on painting, his
mind skipping back to the rounds they played earlier that day. He wanted to
put the meaning of his new game in words, but wasn't certain he could. He
decided to try. "But you know what, Bass? I'm a pretty damned good
painter, if I do say so myself. And I was a lousy golfer. I usually carded the
highest score when I played with the guys, and I hated that. I don't like
being second string at anything. So, after the way I was able to play golf
today, I don't know that I really want to paint anymore. Not for a while,
anyway. Painting is something I've been good at for a long time, and you
taught me to be good at something I've always wished I could be good at."
Vic shrugged. "Painting isn't a priority, right now."

"You want to give up your painting for golf?"

"Not give it up, really. Not forever, anyway." Vic leaned forward,
resting his elbows on his knees, his eyes on Bascolm's. "But you can view
golf as a kind of art. You ever hear of performance art?" Bascolm looked
puzzled while Vic scrabbled for a suitable definition. "You take a finely

crafted implement, a club, and use your skill with it to control an object, the ball. You make that ball hit your target." Vic wasn't satisfied with his explanation. The right words dangled there in his head, waiting to be spoken, but as soon as he tried to snatch them and process them through his mouth, they faded away. *It must be I'm tired,* he thought. *It couldn't be the alcohol, since I'm only drinking mentally.* He pressed on. "Not like drawing, or painting. No visual record. Only the memory of the ball's flight recorded in the mind of anyone who sees the shot. To me, that qualifies as art. High quality art, in fact."

Bascolm sipped his beer and rocked back in his chair, clasping his hands across his stomach. "Okay. Yeah, I guess that's how I've come to think of the game, but I couldn't have put it in those words." He nodded. "I love the purity of putting a good strike on the ball. I never thought of it as real art, but I guess I buy into your point. Still, it's hard to believe you could let golf take the place of painting."

Vic rattled the ice in his glass. "I'll never stop painting completely, but I'll tell you one thing, Bass. If I went back and I could play golf in Toledo like I did today; okay, maybe a little better than I did today, things would be different, for sure. I'd kiss off teaching and go professional. Play on the tour. Make some real money. And you! Christ, you could make a fortune with your game!"

Bascolm looked at Vic as though his words stung somehow. "I wouldn't play for money," he said.

Vic felt scolded. "No?"

"It wouldn't seem right to me."

"What do you mean, not right? Why not?"

"Just wouldn't. I love the game. I play for all those who played before me, but for whatever reason, can't anymore. I play for them and for the love of the game, but I'd never play for money." He paused, looking straight into Vic's eyes. "I guess I value the game more than I value anything I could buy with money. Money would cheapen it, the way going to a whore cheapens sex."

Vic's ears warmed with embarrassment, and at that moment the floor suddenly heaved. What the hell was that? He tried to stand. "Did you feel that, Bass?" he asked. His head filled with intolerably loud metallic screeches and squawks. It sounded like the feedback avalanching from the speakers at a Ted Nugent concert. He slammed his hands over his ears to seal out the noise, but it didn't work. He felt himself rolling, on the tablecloth? Did I fall? He tried to see, but the lights went out. "Bass! Bass!" he shouted. He couldn't hear anything over the terrible shrieking. It sounded like someone going at a harp with a chain saw. He saw pinpoints of light, colors, almost like fireworks. He opened his eyes wide, trying to pull in more light, to pick out anything recognizable. The noise stopped as abruptly as it started. In the new silence, Vic thought he heard voices, but he couldn't understand them. The tiny specks of light increased in size, then lost their color. His entire field of vision shifted into a soft, light gray haze. He blinked. Nothing! It was like he was in a heavy fog. He rocked his eyes in their sockets, trying to locate an object of any kind.

Then he felt them. At first, he wasn't certain. He waited, trying not to jump to conclusions. Yes, they were hands. They gripped his wrists and his ankles. Whose were they? He strained to see. His first reaction was to fight against them, but when he did, they tightened their grip. When he relaxed, their hold eased, so he decided to stop struggling. He refocused on the voices. Still unintelligible, they sounded almost like an audio tape running at all the wrong speeds; fast, until they sound like a porpoise's chirps and whistles, then they slowed until they dragged in low distorted rumbles. Suddenly, the tape found its tempo. "It looks like he's stopped seizing," a voice said.

Christ, Vic thought. *I must be going back.*

~ * ~

From the time Vic first awakened into his coma, his thoughts repeatedly returned to his conscious life. He tried to keep his mind off Angie and his life in Toledo because he wasn't sure he would ever get back to them. He was reasonably successful, but in his solitary moments, memories and worries about the life he led in Toledo haunted him like wispy specters. Now that it looked like he was making the transition back to his conscious state, the realization he had to confront these ghosts in the flesh was overwhelming. And scary.

Angie was his utmost concern. While the coma put his life on hold, he missed her and wanted desperately to reclaim the happiness they once had. Now, he felt the crushing pressure of knowing he would have no choice. He didn't have any idea of how to get their relationship back on track, and he didn't know if she would still be rooted in denial. It was impossible to work on a problem she refused to even recognize. In addition, Vic had the feeling he'd lost all his momentum. Dealing with marriage was hard enough before he was whacked on the head. Now he'd have to accelerate back into their relationship from a standstill. He hoped he had the mental and emotional horsepower to do it.

On top of that, there was the issue of his body. Jason knew his was wilted and atrophied, and Bascolm had every reason to believe the same was true with him. But Vic had no idea what condition his mind and body were in. He didn't think he'd been out for long, but it was a gut-level guess. Besides, the amount of time meant nothing if it turned out that shot to the head left him with brain damage.

Vic's fears were heightened by the feeling he hung somewhere between existences. He felt like a passenger on an elevator during a power outage, stalled between floors. He couldn't get back to the one he'd been on, and he'd yet to arrive at the next one. Marooned in an elevator where nothing worked. He waited. It seemed like he awakened into his coma almost immediately. Now, however, he'd been trapped in this nether-world a long time. He wasn't capable of waking in Toledo, or going back to pick himself up off the floor of June Mancy's restaurant.

He thought about the fact that the last thing he did in Bascolm's presence was to make an ass of himself. While Bass spoke in simple eloquence about his reverence for the sanctity of the game, all Vic talked

64

about was turning the golf swing Bass helped him develop into cash. He felt like a jerk.

His musings came full circle. When he was comatose, Vic longed for his life in Toledo. Now, he hadn't even regained consciousness, and already missed Bascolm, Donald, Jason, and Loon's Lair. And his golf game. It would have been so great to stay and play golf, he thought. He could do that when he was comatose. His body was disconnected, but his perception in the coma was he could play golf—better than he ever had. He knew what that state of existence held for him, and he had no idea what lay ahead if he came to. He was sealed inside an unresponsive carcass. Everything was shut down. He couldn't find the switch to reanimate his body, but he couldn't find his way back out of it either. Of course, even if he could find his way back into the coma, would he wind up back with Bascolm and the others? Maybe that was like trying to return to the same place in a dream, after getting up to take a whiz.

Suddenly, Vic got the sensation he was falling; the cable snapped and the elevator dropped into darkness. His field of vision turned black, and he worried he'd lost his sight. Maybe the head-shot on the golf course blinded him. He strained against the urge to cry, but couldn't help himself. Goddamn! What the hell will I do if I'm blind? Teach art? Paint? Play golf? Not likely. How will I run? How will I drive? What the fuck will I do? It felt as though pins were poking at the sensitive skin around his nose and eyes. He wanted more than anything to reach up and rub his face, but his arms didn't work.

Then someone touched his neck. It didn't feel like any of the hands that restrained him earlier. These fingers were gentle and cool. They stroked his neck and slid up onto his cheek. It had to be someone who knew him, someone he was close to. Nobody better be touching me like that unless I know them pretty damned well. Angie, maybe? Something told him it wasn't her. Then he was suddenly overwhelmed with the feeling the fingers belonged to his mother.

"Mom? Is that you? Oh God, Ma, I think I'm blind."

"I'm not your mother," a voice from out of the blackness said.

"Who is it?" Vic asked, as surprised he could speak as he was embarrassed about the fact that he blubbered like a child.

The voice giggled. "I'm disappointed, Vic. You don't remember me?"

"I'm sorry. I remember your voice, but I can't put a face with it. And I'm blind, so I can't see you."

The voice laughed. "You're not blind, silly. I'm the one who's blind. Don't you remember? We spent a lot of time together the summer before you and Angie were married. Does that help?"

"Jillian?" Vic was thunderstruck. Was it possible? "Jillian Reefe?"

She combed her fingers through his hair. "Now I feel a little better. I'd always hoped you wouldn't forget me. But you never called me Jillian."

"Reefer," Vic whispered, overwhelmed with a wave of affection for this woman. He suddenly didn't care it was too dark for him to see her. It felt so good to be with her again; the blind girl who lived in the apartment across the hall from Vic during his senior year in college.

"Reefer, are you still smoking all that dope?"

"No, darling. I finally took your advice," she replied in her lilting voice.

Vic always thought Reefer's voice sounded like music, and he never tired of listening to her talk. When she was high, which was most of the time back in the summer of 1970, she'd tell him all kinds of funny stories about her crazy lifestyle. Vic remembered one, a story about her friend who had an old Cadillac hearse. The windshield wiper motor gave out on their way home from a war protest in Washington D.C. It was raining too hard to go on without wipers, so the guy found a piece of clothesline somewhere and tied it to the driver's side wiper, routed the rope through the vent windows, then tied it to the passenger's side wiper. They continued on their way at seventy miles per hour, with Reefer tugging the rope back and forth to sweep the rain away. Vic was never certain honest-to-God hippies even existed until he met Reefer. She was one of the first to arrive at Woodstock, and one of the last to leave. She sang and played her guitar in bars and coffee houses. The girl may have been blind, but she was fearless.

Wonderful as her adventures were, however, they weren't as captivating as the sound of her voice.

"How's Ziggy?" Vic asked. Reefer's Seeing Eye dog's name was Zig-Zag, after the rolling papers, but Reefer always called her Ziggy.

"Zig died years ago."

"Oh, Reef. I'm so sorry. Shit, I should have done the math." Vic blinked against tears that threatened to overrun his eyelids. Being with Reefer again put him in touch with a raft of long-forgotten emotions, and the death of her big friendly chocolate lab turned them loose.

"No, no. It's okay. Ziggy lived a great life. I miss her, but the memories are good ones. I work with a cane, now. No other dog could replace Zig." She apparently heard him snuffle and wiped her fingers across his eyes. "You cried the first time we went out together. Remember?"

"What was the movie's name? That great anti-war flick with George Hamilton, right?"

"Um-hmm. *The Victors.* You cried when the soldiers shot Peter Fonda's puppy."

"That's right. You asked me to go see it with you because the manager wouldn't let Ziggy in the theater. Remember? You asked me to be your Seeing Eye dog for the day." He chuckled. "Man, nobody could get away with that shit now, barring a Seeing Eye dog."

"No. The world's a more enlightened place today. But I'm glad it worked out the way it did. We had a beautiful summer together."

A bit over five feet tall, with a curvy-cute body, Reefer wore sandals and tie-dyed frocks with scoop necklines back then. Her long, straight, dark hair accented her olive complexion. She wore beaded necklaces and tied feathers in her hair, which made her look like an Indian princess. Her single conceit was her discomfort about anyone seeing her eyes. She wore wrap-around bubble-lens sunglasses, and only removed them if she was alone, or if she was convinced it was completely dark. As close as they became, Vic never once saw her eyes. Although Reefer lived in an apartment right across the hall from Vic, they'd only exchanged hellos in the hallway or at the mailboxes until that summer. The June afternoon at the movies changed all that. Vic never spent time with a blind person before and was uncomfortable being with her, at first. He soon learned if Reefer needed help with something, she'd ask. She seldom did. Between Ziggy and her own self-reliance, Reefer seemed in control regardless of the situation. All through the movie, on that far-away summer day, she seemed to know what happened, and only asked Vic to explain what occurred a time or two.

When they returned to the apartment building, she invited him into her place for some wine, and later they went out for dinner at a Chinese joint. By the time they returned home, an early evening thunderstorm was building.

"I'm afraid of storms, Vic. Will you stay with me tonight?"

"I—I'm getting married in August," he replied, unable to hide his shock.

"But you're not married now. If you can't be with the one you love, love the one you're with," she said, more convincingly than Steven Stills himself.

"You're right, Reefer," Vic said, returning from his memories. "It was a beautiful summer. I've thought back on it many times."

"Me, too. How are things with you and Angie?"

"Ah, they're fine."

"Come on, Vic. It's me. You don't have to tap-dance." Reefer's musical voice melted his reluctance to tell the truth.

"Things aren't great, Reef. It started out so good. I love her so much. I always have. But she's not the girl I fell for back in college." Reefer stroked his cheek and said nothing. Vic imagined her cocking her head and dipping her chin, her habit when someone spoke to her. "I know people change over the years," Vic continued. "Hell, I'm not who I was back when you knew me in Bowling Green. But with Angie, the changes are so dramatic. She used to be so passionate. So happy. We used to play silly word games we made up as we went along." Vic decided that was a lame example of the weave of their life together before it unraveled, but he couldn't think of anything else that wouldn't take too long to explain. "Honest, Reef, she looks like she did the day I met her in the student union. Hasn't changed a bit. But it's like *Revenge of the Body Snatchers,* or something. Like somebody else moved in and pushed the woman I loved out."

There was silence. Vic couldn't even hear Reefer breathing. He was overtaken by the fear she'd gone and he was alone. Then her beautiful contralto came out of the darkness and literally gave him chills. "I understand," she nearly whispered.

"And, I can't believe I'm telling you this, but I've always wondered if it was all because of us."

"Us?" Reefer asked.

"Yeah. Punishment, sort of. You know, like I was unfaithful to her that summer, and this is what I get for it. You and I had a terrific relationship, and now Angie and I don't "

"But you never told her ..."

"Oh, no. She doesn't have the faintest idea about us. No, I mean the karma thing. You know, yin and yang, opposite and equal. The fates evening up the score."

Vic felt Reefer's hand on his shoulder. She squeezed gently. "The universe doesn't operate that way," she said softly, with so much conviction he would have felt foolish if he asked her how she could be so sure.

"Anyway, the main problem right now is Angie and I have been apart. I got hit by a golf ball, and I've been in a coma. Unless you're wrong about it being dark, I'm blind." Again, he slipped toward the verge of tears.

Reefer kissed him on the forehead; her lips were as cool as her hands. She ran her fingers across his cheek. "You are not blind, Vic."

"Then why am I seeing black?"

"You're right, you're *seeing* black. You remember I told you I was sighted until I was six?"

"Yeah. Some kind of cancer? They removed it, but damaged your optic nerve."

"Yes. And I remember colors, so I know what black looks like. I can tell you for certain, if you're seeing black, then you're not blind."

"I'm not? So, what do you see? Gray?"

She giggled. "No, silly. I don't see anything. Hey, look at me with your nose," she said, giving the end of his a tweak. "What do you see?"

"With my nose? Hell, I can't see anything with my nose."

"There. That's what I see with my eyes. There's nothing wrong with yours. You need to open them."

"But they are ..." he insisted, before he felt her cool fingertips exert gentle pressure on his eyelids. Suddenly, he was looking at a light fixture on a ceiling.

~ * ~

The clock on the wall of the hospital room reminded Vic of the one in his classroom at Alexis. 11:46, it read. Time was back. Sun streamed in through the window, and Vic could feel it caressing his arm with warmth, something he'd longed for when he was comatose. The sun was back. Time and sun. Their presence caused a rush of tears that made Angie a soft blur when Vic rolled his head on the pillow and saw her standing by the window. She faced away and didn't know Vic's eyes were open. He was too weak to maintain consciousness, but it didn't feel like he was dropping back into the coma. He smiled and allowed himself to slide into the dusk.

Vertigo. Vic didn't even feel as though he was lying down. More like he was falling, or flying. Or both. Like he was piloting a small plane lost in banks of clouds. No horizon. No idea which way was up. Pulling back on the stick and praying he was climbing, not diving. Waiting. Then the nose of the plane broke through. Sun again. Angie.

"Vic. Vic, can you hear me?" She apparently noticed him looking at her and dashed to his bedside, her face so close, he could feel the heat from her skin, but he couldn't focus. "Are you all right?"

He processed the question and connected with his vocal cords. "Um-hmm," he groaned. It was enough of a response for her to shriek with joy.

Vic was in and out of consciousness during the rest of that afternoon. He couldn't believe how tired he was. Early on, he managed to be alert only a few minutes before slipping back into sleep. As the day progressed, his awakenings lengthened, and the time between them decreased. At first, it was Angie alone. Then, aside from visits from a parade of nurses, it was Angie and his mother, who wept with joy, and held Vic's hand. He tried to squeeze her fingers, but managed only to wiggle his slightly. Still, he fell back asleep awash in her happy laughter.

The next time he opened his eyes, a tall gray-haired man, with a stethoscope draped over his shoulder, was talking to Angie. His posture reminded Vic of Bascolm's, straight as a ramrod. Vic couldn't hear what he said to her, but Angie didn't appear to be missing a word. The man glanced over, noticed Vic's eyes were open, and stopped in mid-sentence.

"Well, hello, Mr. Vickery," he said, his furry dark eyebrows arching in surprise. "Welcome back. I've been looking forward to finally meeting you." He smiled, stepped over and patted Vic's arm. "I'm Dr. Pembrooke. Angie tells me everyone calls you Vic?" Vic tried to nod, but it felt like he was in one of those dreams where he could only move in slow motion. "You had us worried for a while. How do you feel?" Vic moved his lips to form a word, but when he tried to push air through his vocal cords, his throat erupted in pain. A strange croaking sound was all that came out. Pembrooke held up his hand. "That's okay, Vic. I'm sorry. No, don't try to talk. We had to put some tubes down your throat, and it's going to be sore."

Vic's arm felt like it had a heavy weight tied to it, but he managed to raise it and wiggle a finger, inviting the doctor closer. When Pembrooke bent near, Vic forced a whisper. "Dorothy." The doctor and Angie looked at each other in disbelief, then gaped back at him.

"What?" Angie asked.

71

"Like ... Dorothy. Back from Oz," Vic said, his words ending in a cough. Sleep overpowered him before he could inquire as to how long he'd been over the rainbow.

~ * ~

The next time Vic awakened, it was dark outside his hospital room window. Only a small fixture above his headboard lit the room. He rolled his head on the pillow to see what time it was. His muscles, stiff from disuse, weren't very cooperative, but he managed a glimpse at the clock. A little after midnight. He allowed his head to roll back, but he noticed something unusual on the tray next to his bed, or thought he did. He labored to lift his right arm and let it fall onto the cold metal. He couldn't see everything that was up there, but he began to feel around. Tissues or napkins, a pad of paper. Then his finger nudged the object he searched for and heard it roll. Following the sound with his hand, his fingers closed around the familiar shape. It was a golf ball. It has to be the one that hit me, or why would it be here? He lifted it, marveling at how heavy it felt, and brought it to a comfortable viewing distance. He fought for focus and looked it over. It was a Top Flite 3. As he turned it clumsily in fingers, fingers that almost wouldn't respond to the commands he sent to them, he noticed something else. Stamped on the ball in precise black letters was a name:

TOM BAYER

A nurse's aide looked in.

"Oh! You're awake, Mr. Vickery," she said. "How are we feeling?"

"Thirsty," he rasped. The word sounded more like a growl, even to Vic. He heard her footsteps hurrying away, then returning, accompanied by the soft shuffle of ice cubes and water sloshing inside a container. She adjusted the bed so Vic was in a semi-seated position, and poured some water into a cup. She picked up a straw, but froze in mid-task. Vic glanced at her, wondering what was wrong.

"On second thought, maybe we should start like this," the aid said, picking a small ice cube out of the cup with a plastic spoon. She placed it between his lips.

The sensation in his parched mouth was overwhelming, even better than Southern Comfort, he decided. Arching his tongue, Vic formed a warm cradle for the slippery pellet. The chilly meltings ran down his throat, soothing the raw tissues. He closed his eyes and moaned.

"I have a few minutes here," the aide said, pulling up a chair. "I'll take a load off and give you some more. My name's Sarah. Let me know when you're ready."

Vic opened his eyes and grinned at her. She was a heavy-set woman who appeared to be younger than he was. When she wasn't talking, the weight of her cheeks seemed to pull her expression into a frown that belied her kindness. "What's the date?" Vic asked.

"You've been gone a while," Sarah said, smiling. His eyes widened. "No, no," she blurted. "Not *that* long. It's still 1981 and everything. October sixth ah, seventh," she corrected herself after a glance at her watch. "Wednesday, October seventh. You've been gone a little over a week." She fished out another ice cube and slid it into his mouth. "Did you have any dreams?" she asked.

Vic slid the chunk of ice between his cheek and his teeth so he could talk. "Dreams?" he asked.

"Yes. I mean, not that I'm nosy, but I always ask any of the patients who have been out for a while. I think it's real interesting, you know, to find out if they remember anything." She perched another ice cube on the spoon as she spoke.

"And what do most of them say?" Vic asked.

"Not a whole lot, to be honest." She shrugged. "Most of them don't remember much. Do you?"

Vic felt a surge of excitement, but it was tempered by the innate caution hard-wired into his psyche. After all, he could tell the aide something she never heard before, and the temptation to do that was hard to resist. After all, he was a teacher, and he loved opening people's eyes to things they never conceptualized before. However, what he had to say was pretty crazy and weird, by anybody's standard. Coming out of a coma and talking about a world for the comatose might make him seem like a nut case, or brain-damaged, at the very least. Additionally, he'd had so little conscious time to ponder what he experienced, or even decide if he believed what he remembered. Maybe it was all a dream, as the aide referred to it. And, how would he describe anything so strange and wonderful in fewer than many hours and thousands of words? Even though the meltings from the ice were beginning to sooth his throat, the feeling that he'd gargled glass shards didn't promote the idea of talk. He glanced at the aide. She was waiting, and he had to answer her question. All he had to do was say, "no." Or even shake his head in the negative. But, at the last second, he could do neither. "You'd have trouble believing what I could tell you. In fact, I have a little trouble buying it, myself."

"Really?"

"That's right. And I don't know if it was a dream, or a real place, but I met people and we got to be real good friends. It seemed so real. The guys I met were all in comas, too. We played golf, and ate and drank. Had a great time." Vic paused, stiffening against pain that registered upstream of his tongue. "I'll tell you more about it when my throat doesn't feel like hamburger."

Sarah slipped another piece of ice into his mouth. "Oh, I hope that's a promise," she said, winking.

~ * ~

October seventh was the first day Vic felt like he'd officially returned to the world. He awoke around eight o'clock, and the day nurse helped him into the chair next to his bed. Angie arrived to find him there, holding the golf ball he'd found, and watching *Today* on TV. "How are you feeling?" she asked, bending to buss his forehead, close to where Reefer kissed him.

"Not all that bad, to be honest. A little dizzy, but more hungry than anything else."

Angie noticed he held the golf ball, and gentled it from his weakened grasp. "You found it, huh? Can you believe it? Do you know who Tom Bayer is?"

"Isn't he our neighbor? The new one from two doors down?" Angie nodded. "How'd it wind up here?"

"Sal brought it up last week. He was so nice, sat with me a long time. Said he knew you'd want to see it when you woke up. That was back when none of us were sure you ever would. He put it on the tray and said you'd find it when you came around."

"He was exactly right," Vic said. His throat was already feeling less like chipped beef. "Woke up and spotted it around midnight." He paused. "So I got nailed by the guy down the street? How strange is that? And how did the guys do in the scrambles?"

"My God, Vic! They didn't keep playing after you were hit. I told them you'd have wanted them to."

"Shit, yes. They ask me to fill in for Jay, I get hit on the head, and the team winds up not playing, anyway. On top of that, I wasn't even any help. In four holes, we'd only used one of my shots. I really screwed things up."

"It's not like you meant to get hurt."

"Yeah, but it's still hard not to feel responsible." He glanced out the window, then turned back to Angie. "Did Sal say whether I made the putt?"

Angie dabbed at her eyes with a tissue and sniffed. "Now I know you're okay," she said. "Yes, the damned putt went in." She wadded the tissue and tossed it toward the waste basket. She missed. "The Bayers have been really nice," she continued, bending to pick it up. "Ah, not Tom, so much. I think he feels pretty embarrassed about the whole thing. I've only talked to *him* once." She dropped the tissue in the basket and sat back down on the side of the bed. "He seemed really emotional, but I think he was also drunk at the time. I have a feeling he's quite a drinker." She placed her hands on the mattress, straightened her arms so her shoulders rose above her chin, and swung her feet. Something about that gesture made her look like a ten-year-old, Vic thought. "Mrs. Bayer, Roxanne, called a couple of times," Angie went on. "She brought a casserole down, too. It might be she's real nice, but I think she's also worried we're going to sue or something." She looked into Vic's eyes over the top of her shoulder. "I'm so glad we're sitting here talking. I wasn't sure we ever would again."

Vic felt a flush of warmth when he put his hand on hers and she didn't pull away. She usually preferred that he not show affection outside their house.

The atmosphere in Vic's room was lighthearted all the rest of the day. At first, it was only Angie and Vic's mother, but later, her friend Hobart Early joined them. Mr. Early was a homely man. His too-big ears and generously wrinkled face were not what anyone would call handsome. Vic assumed Early made up for his looks by being kind and caring. His hair showed no gray, yet through the limited conversation they had, Vic couldn't imagine Hobart as a man who owned enough vanity to dye it. He smiled often, his thin lips parting to reveal picket-fence teeth that were grayish in color. His skin fit his aging body like a one-size-too-large suit. At rest, he had a feeble presence; but once in motion, his graceful and economical movements implied the rangy strength of a cat. An aging cat for certain, but cunning could come with age. Hobart's sparkling eyes convinced Vic a lot was going on in his head; maybe calculation, or perhaps a zest for life. Vic didn't know which, but he assumed he would find out if his mother kept seeing the man. Hobart seemed somewhat ill-at-ease; at a party for someone he barely knew. Of course, that was close to the truth, but Hobart seemed to warm up as the four of them talked and traded tales into the afternoon. When Angie's parents came up later on, her father seemed genuinely happy to be there and to see Vic. Angie's mother put up a good front, but Vic felt an undercurrent of resentment. She was probably missing a social event back in Chicago, he decided.

As long as he reclined, Vic's dizziness and unsettled stomach were no problem. Then, around four o'clock, a couple of orderlies arrived with instructions to get Vic on his feet. He managed some faltering steps, much to everyone's delight, although the orderlies supported most of Vic's weight. He forced a grin, but was disturbed by his lack of balance and strength. Not only that, he'd lost a noticeable amount of weight. His limbs looked shrunken and frail, even to himself.

Dr. Pembrooke stopped in while Angie and the others were at dinner, and he was unable to say anything to lift Vic's spirits. "Being in a coma is not like being asleep. It's actually quite stressful on both the mind and the body, Vic. You haven't had much, if any, of what we typically call sleep in the past week, and you have to expect to be tired. The lack of strength and balance are both products of being flat on your back for so long. Your inner ears have to become acclimated to you being vertical again." The doctor patted Vic's blanket-covered foot. "Time is the great healer. We need to take it slowly."

"When will I be able to go home?"

"Shouldn't be too long. Early next week, I'd imagine." Dr. Pembrooke smiled like a kindly grandfather. "Oh, by the way," the doctor said, the tone of his voice changing only slightly, but enough for Vic to notice. "The night nurse charted something about a conversation you had with one of the aides. Something regarding your being somewhere when you were in the coma. Could you tell me a little more about that?"

Pembrooke seemed to turn up the warmth when he asked the question, and this change in his demeanor set off warning sirens in Vic's head. The doctor seemed false and smarmy, like a distant relative who would give you a hug so she could pick your pocket. Vic never got those vibes from Pembrooke before, and he questioned their accuracy. Either way, he was going to have to answer the question, and he didn't know what to say. It was hard to back away from a story he already told the aide. Still, as fantastic and wonderful as his coma experience was to him, he had yet to sort it out, or to even ease into the belief it actually occurred. If it did happen as he remembered it, he still didn't understand all the implications. That made him uncertain about how much detail to give up, or even if he should talk about it at all. He was prepared to modify the story if necessary, or even fabricate new portions if he decided the doctor saw it as a negative. "Do you play golf, Doctor?" Vic asked, testing the waters.

Pembrooke seemed genuine. "Oh yes," he said, rolling his eyes like a man admitting he watches afternoon soap operas. "I get out and hack it around a couple times a week." He may have blushed. "I'm not much good."

That answer helped the doctor pass Vic's test. He felt like he could confide in a fellow duffer. *Hell,* Vic thought, *the Doc might be able to shed some light on what happened. He might have encountered something like this before. I might not be an isolated case.* "I'm not much good either," he began, not certain how he would sequence things. "Or, I wasn't. I don't know how it'll be now. See, I played golf while I was clocked out. Of course, it was all in my mind, but that's the point, Doctor. No body to get in my way."

"Nobody," Pembrooke asked, "or no *body*?"

"No physical body," Vic said, nodding. "See, that's most players' problem, getting their doggone bodies to do what their mind tells them to do. I mean, we watch good golfers swing the club, so we know what we should be doing." Vic spread his hands like he held a large book. "The difficulty is making our bodies to do what we want them to."

"I guess so," the doctor said, smiling again. "We have trouble keeping our bodies from doing what we know they *shouldn't.*"

"There you go," Vic said, slapping his leg. "Anyway, I wound up in this place where everyone was unconscious. Lots of people. It was like another world. A lot like this one, but for the comatose. I met some terrific guys there. Bascolm Traskett, he kind of took me under his wing. He explained everything about the place, what it was all about. He'd been a New York State Trooper and was in an accident on the New York Thruway back in the sixties. That's how he got there. Happened so long ago, he was vegetative, not comatose. He knew he'd probably never wake up."

"And you say you played golf?" The skin around Pembrooke's eyes tensed into a squint.

Vic became as nervous as if he would be confronting a five-foot par putt. The change in the doctor's expression did it, but Vic already said what he said. He couldn't back-pedal. He inhaled and plunged ahead. "Ah, yeah. There was this golf course there. Bass put me together a set of clubs in the pro shop, and he showed me what was wrong with my swing. I have a terrible slice, but Bass showed me what I was doing wrong, and I could correct it right away because it was all mental. Like I said, I didn't have to fight my body. Does that make even a little sense?" Vic asked, hoping the doctor would agree.

"Sure. I think I understand what you're saying," Dr. Pembrooke replied, his contemplative frown switching back to a grandfatherly expression. "So this was a real place?" The doctor picked up Vic's charts and began to write.

"I honestly don't have a clue, but it sure seemed real at the time. I mean, if it wasn't a real place, then it seems like I could have manipulated some things, you know, if it was just something I concocted. For instance, there was no sun, only this sort of constant gray light No wind. Temperature was always the same. And there was no time. The hands on my watch never moved. I thought I was dead, to tell you the truth. I argued with Bass about it, but he pretty much convinced me we weren't. And now I'm in Toledo Hospital with you, so he was apparently right," Vic added. "A place for the living, a place for the dead, and a place for the ones who are somewhere in between, was how he explained it. You ever had a patient come out of a coma with a story like that before, Doc?"

Pembrooke shrugged. "I've had patients with various experiences, Vic, but none quite like yours. Of course, we're all different people, so we should expect a variety of experiences."

Dr. Pembrooke apparently picked up on the fact Vic was tiring. He stood to leave, patting Vic's foot as he did so. "But no, nothing similar to yours."

"Anyhow, you're thinking I could get out Monday?" Vic pressed.

Before Pembrooke could answer, a nurse appeared at the door. "Dr. Pembrooke," she whispered, "I'm so sorry to interrupt, but could I see you a moment?" She waved her hands in what Vic believed to be a gesture of urgency. "It's about the gunshot victim from last night."

Pembrooke held up a finger to break off from their conversation, laid Vic's charts on a nearby chair. "Sorry, Vic, I'll be right back."

As soon as the doctor cleared the door, Vic crawled to the end of the bed and picked up his charts. He flipped a few pages until he found the most recent entry. The doctor outlined what Vic told him. Below that, it said, "Possible abnormal confusion."

"Oh shit," Vic mumbled. "Now he thinks I'm a fucking head-case."

Vic fought a new wave of vertigo, dropped the charts back on the chair, and no more than laid back down before the doctor reappeared.

"Sorry about that," Pembrooke said with a chuckle. "Seems my day is going to be a bit longer than I thought. But, where were we?"

"I just want to know what you think about my getting out of here." Vic paused. "Soon, like maybe Monday?"

"I want some fresh pictures of your skull. We have to be certain there's nothing going on that we need to know about. And I want you to be able to get around on your own, although we may be able to offer you some help at home. Maybe a visiting nurse."

Vic grimaced. "Ah, gee Doc. I really wouldn't want a nurse or anything. I want to go home, hole up and heal. That's the problem. I mean, don't get me wrong, everybody treats me great. But I feel like I'm on display. No privacy. I'm going to do much better if I can be on my own. Angie can get me all set up in the morning before she leaves for work, then I'll relax and get better. Get myself together and get on with my life." Vic raised his eyebrows like he answered a question in class and awaited the teacher's reaction. "Make sense?"

Pembrooke smiled. "Monday would be the earliest, assuming the pictures are negative."

"And what about work? How soon will I be able to go back?"

"There's no way to predict that, Vic," Pembrooke said, leaning against the wall. "It'll depend on a lot of things. The truth is you're going to be rather unsteady on your feet for perhaps as long as a month. Dizziness may well be a recurring problem for some time. On the other hand, it may clear up quite quickly." He shrugged. "Over and above that, strength will be the major consideration. That week in a coma was tough on you, more so than you realize. As you'll see, it's going to take some time to bounce back." Pembrooke warmed. Gramps was back. "I don't want to be a wet blanket, but frustration and self-doubt will be your constant enemies." The doctor placed his hand on Vic's shoulder. "To answer your question directly, I wouldn't count on starting back before Thanksgiving. That's only six or seven weeks from now, after all. You could very easily prove me wrong, but I'd rather give you the worse-case scenario and have you pleasantly surprised."

The doctor no more than said goodbye and stepped out before the torrent of what he said joined up with fatigue to push Vic through the threshold of slumber. He dreamed he was running on the country club golf course, near Bittersweet. The grass was lush and the temperature perfect. Obscured by clouds, the half-hearted sunlight reminded him of Loon's Lair. Nonetheless, he knew he was on the thirteenth fairway at Toledo Country Club, one of his favorite places to run. Every stride was effortless. He pumped his legs hard and was flat out flying. Then he spotted a woman up ahead, with long dark hair and a flowing dress, its hem skimming the grass. She swept a white cane from side to side as she moved.

"Reefer!" Vic shouted as he closed on her from behind. She didn't react, so he ran around in front of her, turned, and backpedaled as he talked. "Reefer, I'm so glad to see you." He wasn't winded and had no difficulty speaking. "You were right, I wasn't blind. I can't believe I was so stupid." She didn't answer or change her expression. She continued forward as he ran in reverse, keeping himself outside the arc of her cane. "Reef! It's me, Vic!" He stepped aside. "Please ... "

Reefer never responded, leaving him to stand and watch as she seemed to glide through a cluster of tall pines, the hem of her long purple frock barely touching the blades of grass. Only the sound of a dog barking somewhere in the direction she was headed broke the perfect silence. Vic wanted to follow, to thank Reefer for literally opening his eyes. That thought made him think of Bascolm, whom he also was never able to thank. When Vic no longer heard the barking dog, he realized he'd reawakened into the cool quiet of the hospital room, his fists balled in frustration.

~ * ~

The hours in the hospital peeled away at a pace that tested Vic's patience. He wanted out of the limelight. He wanted to go home, hide out, and heal without an audience of concerned onlookers hanging on his every movement and reacting to every sigh or groan. He was convinced everything would be better back on Bittersweet, and going home would speed his recovery. Not only that, his mother, Hobart, and Angie's parents would feel free to go home, themselves. Although thankful for their concern, Vic couldn't escape the feeling he was somehow responsible for keeping them entertained and happy.

The only good thing about the time he spent lying in his hospital bed was there was plenty of opportunity to ruminate over the coma experience. Did it really happen? Was it all merely a dream, or was there really a place where the comatose existed until they regained consciousness or died? And the meeting with Reefer. Where the hell did that come from, unless it really occurred? He hadn't so much as thought of her for years. For her to suddenly surface in his life, conscious or unconscious, seemed to give legitimacy to the whole of the experience. He couldn't imagine his mind merely manufacturing such a meeting, not after years without a thought of her. And where was she when they met up? She wasn't in the coma world. She came out of nowhere when Vic was on his way back to consciousness. As warm as her feelings for him were, her fingers and lips were so cold. So what did that mean? These were the things that passed through his mind as he whiled away the hours when he was alone in his small hospital room.

Dr. Pembrooke didn't have hospital hours on Thursday. Probably out playing golf, Vic figured, which really put his spirits in a nosedive. It wasn't that Pembrooke played golf and Vic couldn't because he was in the hospital; it was more personal than that. Vic couldn't play golf even if Pembrooke asked him to go. He could barely execute a walking step, much less a golf swing. And how long would it be before he could regain control over his body again? How long would it be before he could try to recreate the swing Bascolm taught him? And, if it turned out he couldn't rise above hacker status, would it be because he couldn't recover his physical dexterity, or because the whole experience at Loon's Lair was a dream his artist's imagination, concocted while he was out cold? He knew it would be weeks before he could even begin to answer these questions, and that fact, along with the reality of being cooped in a hospital room, made him quiet and moody.

"I know I haven't been very good company, today," he finally said. It was pressing toward the dinner hour, and the conversations Angie and the others were trying to maintain, probably as much for their own sanity as for Vic's entertainment, were beginning to succumb to long periods of silence. "Why don't you guys skip the hospital cafeteria tonight and go to a nice restaurant somewhere." He paused to paste on a smile. "I'm buying," he announced.

Angie's father looked like a man who drew aces. "No, I'm buying," he said, jumping to his feet. "Great idea, Vic."

"I don't know," Vic's mother said, but the phone rang before she could complete her protest.

It turned out to be Sal. "Yeah, Ron, Phil and I thought we might stop by, if you're up to it."

Now it was Vic with the hot cards. "Ab-so-damned-lutely," he said, enjoying the use of Bascolm's favorite response. "My family is ditching me to eat at some ritzy restaurant, so I'll be all by my lonesome," he said, smiling at Angie, and winking at his mother. "Can't wait to see you guys."

Vic's mother still protested as they left, but Vic was certain she would enjoy the time out as much as he. Sal and the others weren't coming up until regular visiting hours began after dinner, so it gave Vic time to rest up and get his story in order; what he would and would not explain about the coma. Of course they would ask. What was it like? Did you dream, or was it the big black abyss? I sure as hell would ask any of them, he figured. And at first, Vic worried about what he would say. Then it occurred to him; he really had no choice. Telling them about the experience he had while he was in his coma would be a little like telling them he'd seen a ghost; they might be really interested, or they might conclude he was a club or two short of a regulation set. But the main consideration was if he was going to get out of the hospital anytime soon, he had to distance himself from the abnormal confusion Pembrooke noted on his charts. He couldn't tell the guys anything that would jeopardize his release. In fact, he decided he could use the visit with his friends as a dress rehearsal for the performance he knew he would have to give Pembrooke when he brought it up again, as Vic knew he would. By the time he finished eating the hospital's version of a spaghetti dinner, his story was polished and ready to be spun.

Phil was the first to stick his head in the door. "Hey, Vic," he blustered, "how they hangin'?"

The three of them filed in, and the first thing Vic noticed was the way the happy expressions drained from their faces when they got a good look at him. It was obvious they weren't ready for what they saw. He knew he'd lost some weight and some of his tan, but when he reached out to shake their hands, his movements were labored and slow. He felt like a drunk trying desperately to appear sober, and his three friends looked like funeral-goers trying hard to find something nice to say about a guy in a shiny long box. Vic's family saw his frailty and appearance as a huge improvement over unconsciousness, but the shock on the faces of his friends hit Vic like a closed fist. Regardless, he tried to seem upbeat and put his friends at ease. "Christ," he said, "I'm glad you guys showed up. None of the nurses will arm-wrestle with me anymore." He placed his elbow on the tray that bridged his bed as though he was ready to take on all comers.

That seemed to put his friends at ease. Sal clasped Vic's up-stretched hand in both of his, and gave it a squeeze. "We've all been thinking about you, buddy. I can't get that day out of my mind."

Vic squeezed back, as best he could, and the mood that settled over the room was somber, with gentle humor for punctuation. Vic assured them he was expected to recover completely, that no real damage was done and his diminished motor control was only a temporary condition, attributable to his mind being out of touch with his body for a week.

"I gotta tell you," Sal went on, "it was the weirdest thing. I mean, that ball hit you, and when you dropped, I thought you were dead. Man, you hit the ground like a sack—"

"Of shit?" Vic offered, when Sal's sentence hit a dead end.

Sal laughed. "Yeah, I guess. Then, you kind of came around, remember?"

"Yeah," Vic said, "you mean, when I started joking about milking it for a beer." He chuckled. "Truth is, I didn't think it was serious myself, at that point."

"Neither did I," Sal continued. "Then you went into convulsions. Christ, I didn't know what the fuck to do. You were rubbing your head, and making this terrible gargling sound. It was creepy as hell."

Vic recalled how he checked for lumps or sore spots on his head when he first awakened into his coma. Was that what Sal referred to? The thought gave Vic chills. "I guess the important thing is it's all history, now." He winked, but it felt like slow-motion. "I'm only sorry you guys had to be a part of it, and I'm sorry it fucked up the Open for you. Christ, we were four under with an eagle in the bag."

"And wouldn't you know," Phil cut in, "that eagle held up. We'd have won a skin on that one; about fifty bucks apiece."

Ron awarded Phil a shot with his elbow. "And what's a coma like?" Ron asked. "Did you, like, dream or anything?"

Vic remembered the almost identical question from the aide, the answer to which had him labeled a victim of abnormal confusion. "Ah, shit," Vic began. "I don't know what to tell you. I did have some dreams, and when I woke up, I could remember them like they just happened. But, like with a lot of dreams, I can't remember any of it, now. I actually think I dreamed about playing golf, but I couldn't tell you any more than that." He chuckled. "Hope I shot well," he added, enjoying his inside joke.

They talked for almost half an hour longer. Idle chit-chat, and the latest rumors that were circulating at Alexis High. Who was on who's shit list. The latest on contract negotiations. Normal day-to-day kinds of things that were no longer part of Vic's world. He was still interested, and was anxious to be a teacher, again.

"So, any idea when you'll be coming back?" Phil asked.

Vic blew a column of air through his nose. "Main thing, right now, is to get the hell out of this joint, early next week, I hope. But I won't be back at work 'til at least around Thanksgiving, anyway."

His friends could see Vic was tired. After they left, Vic thought over what he'd told them, and gave himself high marks for the way he handled the coma experience with them. He felt he was ready to take on the doctor, and that fact bought him a good night's sleep.

~ * ~

Friday morning, Pembrooke stopped to say he'd scheduled Vic for another CT scan later that day. "If it looks the way we hope, we'll have you on your way home early next week," he answered, when Vic asked again about being released. The doctor never mentioned anything about the coma, which surprised Vic, but he was confident he would be ready when the time came.

Meanwhile, he worked on building his strength, making endless loops of the ward, and answering "no" if anyone asked him about dizziness or fatigue. The truth was, he did feel better, but every step required as much concentration as a good golf swing, which slowed his gait to about that of an elderly man. Much of the time he spent walking, he thought about Angie and wondered what effect his injury might have on the future of their marriage. He hoped the fact she thought she'd lost him might give her a push toward becoming the warm, loving lady she once was. She seemed so genuinely happy to have him back. Vic hoped that might translate into a desire to renew the companionship and passion they'd lost. A new beginning for both of them, he hoped.

After Vic's CAT, Angie's parents left for Chicago, and his mother and Hobart decided to leave as well, to beat the weekend traffic. Angie stopped in at the law office for a few hours Thursday morning, and she made Friday her first full day back. As much as Vic wanted everyone to return to live their own lives, he couldn't help but feel deserted when they did. Saturday and Sunday were worse than the weekdays. The populations at the hospital reversed, with the number of visitors increasing and the number of medical staff, especially doctors, taking a nosedive. Vic knew the scan wouldn't be read until Monday, so there was no hope of being released.

Angie sat with Vic most of the afternoon on Saturday. They chatted in fits and starts, but it was hard to find anything new to talk about. Angie looked at some doll house magazines she'd brought along while Vic watched golf on TV. He toyed with telling her about Bascolm and Loons Lair, but he was afraid she might slip and mention it to Dr. Pembrooke. For all Vic knew, Pembrooke might have already told her about his "abnormal confusion." *I'll tell her after I bust out of here,* he decided.

Angie returned Sunday morning, and she and Vic walked to the hospital cafeteria for a late brunch. "Come on, Ange," Vic said, when they walked into his room. "You're working tomorrow. Go home and spend some time on your miniatures. Hell, I should be coming home tomorrow. I'll rest up this afternoon and watch some golf." She stayed another half hour, then kissed him on the forehead and accepted his offer.

Later that afternoon, Vic dozed and dreamt a replay of Reefer vanishing into the trees, heading toward the far-off barking of the dog. When he awakened, Vic couldn't help but wonder if it was Ziggy. Since Ziggy was dead, did that mean Reefer was, too? He spent a long time wondering what life would have been like had he married Reefer instead of Angie. Would Reefer have changed the way Angie did? Is it my fault Angie is so different from the girl I married? Vic wondered if it was some inherent flaw in his make-up that made Angie morph from the amorous, fun-loving

87

woman he fell in love with, to who she was now. He contemplated these questions until he finally drifted off again.

Monday morning, Dr. Pembrooke strode into Vic's room. "How was my scan?" Vic asked him.

"Very good," Pembrooke replied. "I don't think we have any physical problems to worry over." Then his brow furrowed. "But I did have one more thing I wanted to ask you relative to your coma experience."

"My what?" Vic asked. He was sure about where the doctor was going, so he scrunched his face into his best impersonation of a man who was asked what size pantyhose he wore.

"About the time you spent with … " Pembrooke flipped through the sheets of paper on Vic's chart, "ah, with Bascolm and the others."

"Gosh, Dr. Pembrooke, I'd like to help, but I really can't."

Pembrooke appeared stunned. "Why not?"

Vic shook his head. "Those weird dreams, I remembered them clear as a bell when I first came back, but I can't now." He turned up his palms and splayed his fingers, trying to look as vacant as possible.

"Nothing at all?"

"Sorry. It's kind of like when you wake from a great dream, and you think, 'Boy, no way I'm gonna forget that.' Then ten minutes later, it's gone." Again, he shook his head. "Took longer than ten minutes, but I can't remember any of it, now. Can't remember who Mr. Bascolm was."

"No, it was," Pembrooke flipped pages again, "Mr. Traskett. Bascolm Traskett."

Vic shrugged. "It sounds like a name I've heard before, but I really don't know any more."

Pembrooke wrinkled his forehead in what appeared to be an indication he was satisfied Vic's "confusion" was behind him, and he dropped the clipboard on the bed. "They tell me down at the nurse's station you've been lapping the ward like a racehorse," he said, smiling.

"I wish. I sure don't feel like a racehorse, but I'm getting around okay. You say my CAT was good? Can I go home now?"

"Anxious, are you?"

"Yeah, Doc, I really am. I need to be back in my own house. Any reason why I can't get out today?"

Pembrooke performed his grandfatherly smile. "I'll talk to the nurse in charge and see if we can expedite things." Then, every trace of warmth drained from his eyes. "Vic, I'm as serious as I can be now. *No* strenuous exercise of any kind for the next three weeks. I'll set up an appointment for you at that time, and we can reevaluate your condition. Until then, nothing that elevates your resting pulse. No walking for any distance. No lifting." The doctor leaned close, as though he was about to deliver an off-color punch line in mixed company. "No sex," he whispered. "I absolutely do not want you to do anything to put yourself at risk. This period is critical. The quality of your life from this day forward depends on your following the instructions I'm giving you now. Do you understand?"

Vic nodded. In the past, he often minimized warnings from doctors. Directives like, "Make sure you stay off this sprain for several days," or "be certain you take these pills until they are gone," often went unheeded, or were modified to suit Vic's schedule. But Dr. Pembrooke sounded very sincere, and Vic took his instructions to heart. "I understand, sir," Vic said.

"One last thing," Dr. Pembrooke said, reaching to clasp Vic's shoulder. "You may find yourself to be highly emotional for a while. Mood swings. You may cry easily. All that is normal in the case of closed head injuries. Oh, and be careful not to make any big decisions for a while. Nothing financial, or even personal. People who have experienced head injuries need some time to stabilize." He picked up his clipboard. "One of the doctors in our group had a patient who came out of a coma, sold his house, bought a Volkswagen bus, and went off to follow The Grateful Dead … what do those people call themselves?"

"Deadheads?" Vic offered.

"That's it. Yes, he became a Deadhead." Pembrooke winked. "Make sure you give yourself some time. Any questions?"

"What about alcohol?"

The doctor's eyebrows jittered like nervous caterpillars. "Do you have a drinking problem?"

"No. I enjoy a drink in the afternoon if I'm working around the house. Maybe one in the evening before I hit the sack, is all."

The doctor stared at him. "Two beers, or one hard drink a day, at most. No more."

Vic nodded again.

"You understand how important it is that you do what we're talking about here, Vic? You're not a person who was comatose and is well. You're a person who was comatose and will *soon* be well. We need to proceed slowly. Head injuries are nothing to take lightly." The doctor's face softened and Gramps returned. "What will you do to keep yourself busy?"

"I paint. And I do photography. I have my own darkroom. I have plenty of negatives I can print."

"Splendid!" Pembrooke said, patting Vic's shoulder. "That sounds both interesting, and suitably sedate. Remember, take it slowly."

After the doctor left, Vic couldn't help but feel he'd betrayed Bascolm and the other friends he'd made when he was comatose. They were real people and deserved to have their stories told. He tried to reason disavowing his coma experience was the only way to gain his freedom to go home; but the idea he did it at the expense of his friends haunted him like a persistent ghost.

Regardless, at 5 P.M. on Monday, October 12th, Vic passed through the automatic sliding glass doors of Toledo Hospital and out into early autumn. For the first time in over two weeks, he savored a deep breath of air that hadn't passed through electronic air filtration units and air conditioners. His first breaths of fresh air nearly overrode his embarrassment at being rolled out of the hospital in a wheelchair, and a vague feeling that he'd somehow sold out Bascolm and the others.

Chapter Four

Vic was home. Angie turned into the driveway, and their house on Bittersweet never looked as wonderful to him as it did at that moment. *I came so close to never seeing this place again,* he thought. He let his eyes slide across the image in the windshield, from the garage to the dormer on the far end of the roof. One detail caught his attention; little Freddie's glider was still caught in the eaves trough. He looked up at the little plane and recalled how different it looked when he viewed it from above. The garage door yawned open, Angie pulled in and came to a stop next to his Mazda. The light glinted on the sensuous curves of the little coupe until the garage door closed again, like a slow-motion shutter, to seal out the sunlight.

"How'd you get the Mazda back home?" Vic asked, pushing open the passenger door of Angie's Honda.

She hurried around to help him get out. "Oh, somebody from the golf course drove it over. They all were so nice," she added, reaching to take his arm.

An elderly man would have bested Vic in getting out of the Honda, and Angie, carrying the small bag of clothes and medications he brought home, followed him closely as he made his way to the entry door. "Careful, now," she must have said half a dozen times. When he opened the door, the smell of their house hit him like a familiar song. Day to day, he never noticed it; but after the long absence, the aroma of their daily life filled his nostrils like perfume. He made his way to the recliner in the den, collapsed onto its familiar comfort and immediately fell asleep.

The next few days, when Vic wasn't sleeping, he spent his time reflecting on the coma. In the midst of the physical reality of his house and other trappings of his life, what he experienced seemed as vaporous as smoke. Yet, like smoke, even though it had no substance, the effect of its presence was indisputable. Vic couldn't prove what he recalled actually happened, but each day he became more positive the coma experience and everyday life would entwine in some way, and each would somehow strengthen the other. Whether the coma experience really happened or was fantasy, Vic believed he would benefit from what he remembered. That belief comforted him.

As uplifting as this spiritual side of Vic's life was, the cold truth regarding his marital relationship was crushing. It didn't take more than a day or two for him to realize nothing changed. Angie seemed to vacillate between Florence Nightingale and an aloof acquaintance, reminding Vic of Soozy MacJacobs, the hottie who lockered next to him in high school. All smiles and hellos, but vague and evasive when Vic tried to get beyond an adjoining-lockers friendship.

"Anything you need? Feeling okay?" Angie asked. They were standing in the kitchen on the Friday morning after Vic came home from the hospital. In the intervening days, Vic's energy level and stability improved two or three-fold. She slipped into her coat and picked up her purse. "You need me to pick up anything for you on my way home?"

"Sure," Vic answered, firing off his best winning smile. "How about some steaks and a bottle of wine? As I remember it, we missed our romantic dinner from the day of the Chili Open," he said, punctuating his offer with a wink. "I'll grill them up."

"Uh, the thing is, today is Penny Bolster's last day before her maternity leave." Her face did what looked like an apologetic grimace. "I guess I forgot to mention it. The other secretaries and I are taking her out for dinner after work," she said, scraping a quick kiss across his cheek.

"Besides, the doctor said none of that 'til after he checks you out," she said, pressing her finger reprovingly against Vic's chin.

"He said no sex," Vic replied. "I was talking romance, Ange. Candlelight, and maybe some cuddling."

"I'm sorry," she said, raising her eyebrows for emphasis. "I won't be late."

"That's okay," he said. "Maybe tomorrow night, then."

"Yeah," she said, turning for the door. "We'll see."

Vic stood in the kitchen for a long time after he heard the garage door close, the "we'll see" bomb blast ringing in his ears. He wavered between hurt and anger. The question he faced was, could things change? Could he somehow find a way to get Angie to realize the depths of his anguish?

As he began drying the dishes resting in the strainer, his thoughts turned to telling Angie about the coma. It felt like it was sorted out. He believed he understood it and its ramifications about as well as he ever would, but he hadn't told her any of it yet. He may have waited too long, he feared. The amount of time that passed could be an issue. Still and all, he had to feel right with it himself before he could share it with her. It had only been a few days that he'd been home, able to really focus on what happened without interruptions and the need to keep it secret. Now he probably could tell her, but there was a part of him that didn't want to. It wasn't that he wanted to punish her for her cool distance, but trying to explain something as amazing and otherworldly as what he experienced when he was out cold seemed insurmountable. What he blurted to the nurse's aide the night he awakened didn't do the coma justice, and he wanted Angie to understand what he'd taken away from his experiences. Doing that would be difficult, especially when he really didn't feel all that close to Angie, not right then, at least. They only shared adjoining lockers.

Vic spent the next two days watching TV, napping and painting as much as his energy would allow. How and when to tell Angie about the coma experience filled in any available cracks.

~ * ~

Saturday evening, Roxanne Bayer called to ask if she and Tom could come down for a visit. Angie made certain he had the gist of the request from her side of the conversation, and looked over at him with raised eyebrows. He gave the thumbs up. "Yes, tomorrow will be fine. Why not give us a call around noon and we'll see how he's feeling."

Sunday afternoon, Vic came out of a nap when the phone rang, then he heard Angie's rapid steps on the staircase. He blinked several times, and managed to clear the smudge from his vision. Angie's blonde curls continued to float and bounce after she came to a stop in the bedroom doorway. She wore a yellow blouse that emphasized what remained of the tan she'd nurtured at their backyard pool.

"Oh, you're awake," she said.

"I am now. That was the Bayers on the phone?"

"Roxanne, yes," she replied, walking over to sit on the edge of the bed. "They'll be down in about an hour. How are you feeling? If you're not up to this, I can call back and tell her today's no good."

"'Let's get it over with. Let Tom come down and make his 'I'm sorry' pitch. I'm all right. No headache or anything, but I can't shake the feeling I'm wearing a lead suit."

"Dr. Pembrooke said it would be like this. Don't forget, two weeks ago, they hauled you off the course and into the ICU." She fluffed his pillow. "You're home and making progress. You have to be patient."

"You know me. I'm not very patient. And, I've found out I'm not a very good patient, either."

"Well, be patient with the Bayers." She winked. "I'll make sure their visit's short."

"Good. I mean, we don't even know these people, which makes me feel a little guilty. We never went down to meet them when they moved in."

Angie thought a moment. "True, but it's not like they live right next door. I don't remember neighbors from two doors down running over here when we moved in, and I didn't feel slighted." She paused. "You going to rest some more? Want me to make sure you're awake in a half hour or so?"

"No, think I'll take a long steamy shower. Maybe take a cold beer in there with me. If that doesn't shore me up enough to face the Bayers, nothing will."

An hour later, clean, shaved and combed, Vic sat on the living room couch while Angie greeted Roxanne and Tom Bayer in the foyer. Vic squirmed, self-conscious about meeting strangers in his bathrobe.

"Here he is," Angie announced, leading them in.

Vic was taken aback by what an odd couple they made. Tom Bayer was huge, well over six feet tall, and meaty. Vic couldn't decide if he was muscularly chubby or the reverse. He wasn't a bad looking man, but middle age had busied itself, pushing his hairline north and working wrinkles into his face. Vic decided Bayer looked like he'd tasted vinegar. He had the slump of a laborer; not so much a slouch from the weight of the work itself, but from the weight of being a man who labored at the pleasure of others.

Roxanne, although tall for a woman, appeared small next to her husband. She was sleek and attractive, with a hair-trigger smile, and green eyes that flashed like high beams. She moved with a crisp bounce that reminded Vic of the teenage girls in the halls at Alexis. As out of place as she must have felt in the home of the man her husband accidentally injured, she still exuded a radiant self-confidence. Even though she was probably a good ten years older than Angie, she wore the decade well. Her hair showed a gray strand here and there, but not many for a woman in her forties.

They stood back-lit against the picture window, and Vic smiled toward their silhouettes. "Tom, Roxanne, nice to ... well, meet you, I guess," Vic said, leaning forward to extend his hand. "I'm sorry we never came down to introduce ourselves, but at least Tom found a way for us to finally get together."

Vic's joke provoked a nervous chuckle from Mrs. Bayer, but her husband remained solemn. He shuffled forward clumsily. Vic watched his hand disappear into the big man's two-handed grasp. He didn't speak, but shook Vic's hand like he was trying to wiggle his arm off.

Angie came to the rescue. "Can I take your jacket, Tom?" She'd already harvested Roxanne's. Tom released Vic's hand and was out of his coat in an instant, holding it in Angie's direction without taking his watery, red, and rapidly blinking eyes off Vic. The odor of stale beer rode on his breath.

"Nice to finally meet you, too," Roxanne said, stepping to Tom's side. "It's great to see you're doing so well. You're feeling okay?"

"Feeling pretty good, thank you." Vic smoothed his robe. "Still moving slow. Dizzy sometimes. A few headaches, but no seizures so far."

"Seizures?" Roxanne grasped Tom's arm and guided him backwards to the loveseat.

"Yeah. According to the doctor, they're fairly common with head injuries, but the chances diminish with time. So far, so good."

"He's really doing terrific," Angie said, back from hanging up their coats. "The hospital would have arranged for a nurse to look in on him, but we decided to go without. He hasn't had any problems, yet. He spends lots of time sleeping, but that's what the doctor ordered. Could I get either of you something to drink?"

Tom's arm shot up like he'd heard last call, but Roxanne answered for both of them. "Thanks, but no. We don't want to stay too long and tire this guy out," she said, tipping her head toward Vic as she grabbed Tom's arm and pulled it down. "How soon will it be before you can get back to work?"

"Not sure. The doctor said maybe not until after Thanksgiving, but nothing's written in stone. Have to play it by ear."

Roxanne grimaced. "Thanksgiving? My God, what will you do for money?"

Vic winked. "Oh, money's not really an issue. A lot of jobs pay better than teaching, but we have great benefits. I have lots of sick days accumulated." He winked. "The checks'll keep on coming."

Tom suddenly slid forward, his knees making dull thuds when they landed on the carpet. He'd dropped off the loveseat so quickly, he lost his balance and wound up on all fours. He stayed in that ridiculously awkward position, looking up into Vic's eyes. "I'm ... I'm so sorry," he blubbered. "Jesus! Forgive me!"

With that, Tom's head dangled toward the floor. He began to sob, heaving as though he'd just finished the Boston Marathon. Vic was caught completely off-guard and didn't know how to react. Roxanne rose to a hunched kind of squat, grasping one of Tom's arms. It looked like she might be trying to lift him or encourage him to stand. It was the first time she'd looked off-balance or uncomfortable since they arrived. Vic started to get to his feet, but Angie was already on her way, gesturing for him to stay seated while she clutched Tom's other arm to help Roxanne. Whether or not the two women did much to lift the huge man, Tom did wind up back on the loveseat. Vic was shocked. He'd assumed Tom was there only because Roxanne dragged him down to try to blunt the possibility of a lawsuit. The wet streaks on the big man's cheeks said otherwise. Even if Tom was drunk, the depths of his regret were touching.

"Tom. TOM!" Vic said, almost shouting to get the man's attention. Vic slid further forward on the couch, and even began to stand, but a wave of dizziness dissuaded him. Bayer slid his hands down from his eyes, his mouth and chin quavering. "It's okay, honest," Vic continued. "Look, you yelled. I *heard* you. Hell, your whole foursome yelled." Vic grinned. "I never figured I'd get hit. I mean, how often do you hear somebody yell 'fore' out on the course and the ball doesn't even come close? Right? I chose to ignore your warning. You did what you were supposed to do. I didn't."

Vic paused and swigged the ginger ale Angie had brought for him. He teetered over the decision about whether or not to go into the story of the coma, and taking a drink gave him extra time to decide. He'd told no one about his coma adventures except the nurse's aide and Pembrooke, and nothing good came of that. The other sticking point was he hadn't told Angie. After the reaction he got from Pembrooke, Vic didn't want to tell her while he was still in the hospital. He could have told her when he came home, of course, but by then, he decided he wanted to wait until he sorted out what happened. Was it a dream, or was it rooted in some huge cosmic truth? All the same, Tom needed to be comforted, and Angie needed to know what Vic experienced. Telling the story suddenly seemed like a logical, if risky, move. *I could kill two birds here,* Vic thought. He put the ginger ale down and prepared to spin his tale.

At the last second, Vic gagged back the sentence he was about to speak. Angie would be beside herself if she found out about the coma experience with two neighbors they barely knew. Not only that, trying to convince Tom he'd done no permanent damage by telling so wild a tale was probably self-defeating. So, Vic did the mental equivalent of veering across two lanes of traffic to catch an off-ramp. "Number two, ah, look, I'm doing fine. The doctor says there's no permanent damage. None whatsoever, Tom. I know, I look a little shaky, right now." He chuckled. "God's truth, I feel a little shaky. But, I have no doubt that I'll recover fully and be able to do everything I used to do the way I've always done it, in only a couple weeks." He fired off a huge smile. "Meanwhile, I'm home on paid vacation. I can paint, catch up on some reading, and have dinner waiting for Angie when she comes home from work. What could be better?

"So, there's no blame. Ain't gonna be no lawsuits. You didn't intend to hit me, and I believe it'll eventually turn out to be a positive, not a negative. The only thing that bothers me is that you're feeling so bad. Hey, check this out." Vic reached into the pocket of his robe. He pulled out a golf ball and tossed it to Tom. "Look familiar?"

Tom rolled the ball in his fingers and began to look relaxed for the first time since he'd arrived. "This is the one, huh?"

"Yup. One of the guys I was playing with brought it to the hospital. If it's okay, I'd like to keep it. Kind of like a good luck charm."

"Good luck?" Tom asked. Disbelief wrinkled his face.

"Sure. The ball didn't kill me, and it could have. So, it might be like a, what's the word?"

"An amulet?" Angie offered.

"That's it. An amulet, or talisman, kind of. Who knows, I'll carry this ball in my bag, from now on, and it might even make me a better player." He smirked, enjoying the inside joke. *This is actually fun,* he thought.

"Sure, you can keep it." Tom half-stood to give the ball back. "The least I can do."

"We really should be going," Roxanne said. She stood and grasped Tom's arm, apparently to keep him from sitting back down. Tom turned his palms up in a "what'cha gonna do?" gesture. They exchanged goodbyes, and Tom shuffled off with Angie and Roxanne in the lead.

The Bayer's visit wasn't as uncomfortable as Vic feared it might be, but as soon as he heard the front door close, Angie swept back into the living room like a gust of October wind. A strange half-smile Vic couldn't remember seeing in a long while pulled at the corners of her mouth.

"What went on there?" she asked.

"There? Where? What do you mean?" Vic asked, stalling while he tried to read her frame of mind.

"Right here. When you were consoling Tom." She squinted and turned her head askance. "You changed directions, all of a sudden. What were you going to say?" She walked over and faced him from the other side of the coffee table.

Vic sniffed. "You know me too well." Before he began to relate the coma experience, he wanted to see if there was a foundation to build the story on. "Did Pembrooke ever mention anything to you about something he called abnormal confusion?"

Angie looked stricken. "Abnormal what?"

"I guess not. I thought he might have. Here's the deal," he began, looking up into her eyes. "I didn't tell you any of this earlier because I didn't have it all sorted out."

"Tell me what?" she asked, her voice beginning to rise. "What's abnormal?"

"That's a medical term. Nothing's wrong. I'm fine. But see, what everyone calls a coma turned out to be an incredible experience. A learning experience," Vic leaned back and looked up at her. "I wasn't merely unconscious when I was in that coma. I *was* someplace. I don't know where the hell I was, but it was a real place, Ange." He splayed his arms outward. "As real as this place. And there were a bunch of other people there, too. Nice people. I made friends with three guys who were also in comas. It was like an afterlife for the unconscious. An after-conscious, you might call it. I don't know." He hoped he was saying everything the way he wanted to, so Angie could get a clear picture of what he tried to convey.

She looked wary. A blush of pink flushed across her cheeks. "And what did you and these three guys do?"

"We played golf. There was this gorgeous course called Loon's Lair. I've never played a course like it. It was amazing. Really tough. Lots of uphill and downhill lies, trees, and lots of water and bunkers. I met a man named Bascolm Traskett and he showed me what was wrong with my swing. He helped me cure my slice, then we played golf. We only were able to play a couple rounds before I came back, but with what Bascolm and the other guys showed me, I shot six over par on the first round, and two under on the second one. Two under par! Not only that, I could have easily been three or four under if a few more putts dropped." He paused to try to gauge the effect of what he said. Her face was impassive. "I learned things I'm sure are going to work for me as soon as I can get out and practice. I'm going to be a much better player now, with some hard work. I can't wait to get a club in my hands."

Vic watched a flush of blood percolate up Angie's neck and across her face, taking her complexion through red to ripe plum. Without a word, she spun toward the door and was on her way, like a woman responding to an alarm.

"Angie," he called to her, calmly. "Where are you going? What's the matter?"

She pirouetted like a dancer. Tears flew from her eyelashes when she blinked. "The matter?" She was almost shouting. "Why am I hearing about all this now? For almost a week, my husband is unconscious, near death, as far as I know. I'm at the hospital every day, watching him quiver and twitch, when he's not laying there drooling. So, he finally comes out of his coma, and two weeks later he tells me he was actually out in

Looneyville somewhere, playing golf with some new friends while I was afraid he was dying." Again, she began to turn away, but instead she came closer, her knees banging the coffee table and nearly dumping the ginger ale. "Not only that, but you almost spilled it all to Tom Bayer and his wife, without telling me first."

"But I didn't." He slid forward on the couch. He intended to stand up, but he was afraid he'd get dizzy. "That's the important thing, isn't it? Yeah, I thought about it, but I didn't do it. And if I did, it would have been to make him feel better. The man cried, for Christ's sake."

"The man was also *drunk*, for Christ's sake."

"Drunk or not, he was fucking beside himself. I thought about telling him so he'd know there was a good side to the whole thing."

"And why wouldn't I have cared to know that? You never told *me* about the good side of it." Angie paced in front of the couch. "Not until now, after I pressed you on it."

"But Angie, I couldn't tell you at the hospital. Dr. Pembrooke heard about it after I told the night nurse when I first regained consciousness, and thought I had the abnormal confusion thing. He wasn't gonna release me until he was sure my head was on straight, so I had to be careful. I was waiting for the right time, and we were practically never alone. Doctors and nurses, our folks, were always around. I wanted to tell you when we were by ourselves." He stood, felt tipsy, and sat back down. "Then I came home, but I didn't want to try to explain it until I sorted it out for myself. And for all I knew, Pembrooke might have told you about it already anyhow. So, when Tom started carrying on, it really caught me off-guard. I never thought he'd be that upset, and I felt sorry for the guy."

She paused in the doorway. "Yeah, and wouldn't it have been nice if you'd have felt that sorry for me? It happens all the time. I find stuff out when you're talking to someone else. You never tell me."

"I try to." He spoke barely above a whisper, still hoping she'd calm down.

"What's *that* supposed to mean?" It came out like an accusation, not a question.

Fatigue and vertigo were sitting on Vic like a Sumo wrestler. His head ached. He wanted to close his eyes. "Let's let it go for now, Angie."

"No. I'd like to know what you mean."

Vic looked out the window and squinted against the light. "You used to tell me what you were doing. You used to ask me what I was up to." He trained his eyes on her. "We lost that along the way. We used to laugh and joke around. At the hospital, after our parents left, we sat for two days without anything to say. You work on your miniatures. I paint. We used to offer each other suggestions and compare notes. Do you even know what I have on the easel right now?"

Angie's face broke into a "gotcha" grin. "That landscape. The one with the barn on a hill."

Vic shook his head slowly. "I finished that months ago." He picked up the ginger ale, but the ice was gone and the glass felt warm, so he put it back down. "I don't remember exactly when, but I know I finished it around the last time we made love."

Angie's face registered genuine surprise. "What does *that* have to do with this?" She stepped forward.

"A lot, goddamn it." His voice began to rise. He felt like he'd exposed a nerve, and Angie poked it. "Talking and making love are two different kinds of intimacy, but they're both important. And we don't have either one. Did we make love in August?" Angie appeared to freeze, but Vic wagged his head. "No, I'm pretty sure we didn't. I don't know if we made love in July, for that matter. I mean, even if you're right, and it's my fault we don't talk, all I can say is it's hard to open yourself mentally to someone who's physically closed to you."

Angie stared at him. A tide of tears began to rise, and she didn't even try to blink them away. "You were on the verge of 'opening yourself' to Tom Bayer," she hissed. "When's the last time you got it on with *him*?"

She whirled and stomped out of the room, leaving Vic angry with her, angry with himself, and with a banging headache. He slumped against the throw pillow, closed his eyes, and folded his hands across his stomach. "Take Me," he whispered.

Take Me was a game Vic played since he was very young—so young, he couldn't remember for certain when he started, but he'd have bet the onset revolved around the time his father became The Old Man. Whenever life overwhelmed him, he'd challenge God or the gods to kill him, to "take" him. Vic called it a game, but he was always a hundred percent serious. He'd speak those words, believing the outcome could very well be his death. When the challenge went unanswered, he experienced a surge of exhilaration rooted in the belief, since his request was denied, there must be a reason for his life to go on. Even after he came to question the existence of a god, Take Me still seemed to work.

As usual, it did again. Vic relaxed and fell asleep, not awakening until a little before eight that evening. His headache was gone, but his new companion, dizziness, accompanied him as he shuffled to the picture window. Fallen maple leaves in the front yard glowed in the silvery moonlight. He stood for a long while, wondering how he might paint the scene. Nighttime was hard to capture on canvas. It was difficult to show enough detail in the shadow areas without it looking merely like an overcast day. He decided he'd try a nightscape after he finished the painting he began before his accident.

It felt strange to not confront work in the morning. Sunday nights often found him dog-paddling in a pool of melancholy. He loved teaching, but he also treasured his free time to paint, to work around the house, and to play golf. Even though most of those activities were out of the question for the next month or so, weeks of unstructured time was pleasant to contemplate. Every night was Friday night, and every morning was Saturday. Seven day weekends, at least for the near-future.

Vic walked into the front hall and looked upstairs. The light was on in Angie's workroom. He considered going up, but he figured she was probably at work on her house. He was happy she was building again, and decided not to interrupt.

Instead he made a ham sandwich and poured his one Southern Comfort for the day. He ate bachelor-style, standing over the kitchen sink.

The sandwich was delicious. He rinsed the plate and carried the rest of his drink into the den. He no more than turned on the TV and settled into his recliner when Muldoon, their house cat, jumped onto his lap and stared at him with his vigilant yellow eyes. Vic sipped his drink and stroked the cat's shiny black coat. *CHiPs* was on, and Ponch and Jon pulled over a suspected drug dealer. Muldoon drifted off before they put the cuffs on the bad guy. Vic wasn't far behind.

~ * ~

Vic awakened the next morning and heard Angie stirring in the upstairs bathroom. He was a bit surprised she hadn't awakened him when she turned off the TV. He struggled to get off the recliner. His body was stiff. *At least I'm back in my body and can feel it,* he thought, stretching his arms and legs straight.

He shuffled into the kitchen, started the coffee and spooned some cat food onto a saucer. While he did that, he replayed the blowup. *Everything will be nice as pie this morning,* Vic thought. He planned to apologize, needed to apologize, but there would be no reason. Angie would alibi for him, deny there was a transgression. That was her way of maintaining the status quo. If she had no complaints, then how could there be any problems in their marriage? Angie apparently didn't want to change the way things were. Was it because change required effort? Because working on it pushed a relationship into unknown territory? Or, maybe it was the power she enjoyed. After all, when two people are involved in a decision, if one votes no, the answer is no for both. Vic hoped power wasn't her motive.

By the time Muldoon finished his Savory Stew, the coffee was ready. Vic poured two mugs and lumbered upstairs. The door to the bathroom was cracked a few inches. "O-o-o, cold!" Angie said, when Vic nudged it open. Fresh from her shower, she was wearing only panties and a towel she'd wrapped like a turban around her head. Vic used his foot to push the door closed behind him.

"Sorry, Ange, wanted to bring you some coffee."

"Oh, thanks. That's nice." She sipped it and went back to applying her makeup. As Vic anticipated, there was no hint of lingering anger after yesterday's verbal dustup. "Feeling okay? Dizzy at all?" she asked.

"Not so far today. A little stiff from sleeping in the chair," he replied, leaning against the countertop and taking a sip. His coffee was bitter, Angie's was always smooth. "We need to talk."

Her eyes flicked nervously in his direction. "I didn't wake you to come upstairs because you looked so comfortable. I put a blanket over you and you never stirred."

"No," he said, waving her off. "It's not that. Look, I was wrong. I should have told you about the coma thing sooner. I'm sorry I didn't. That wasn't right. I feel really bad about it. I was a jerk."

She put down her eyebrow pencil and made a move like she would touch his shoulder, but her hand didn't complete the landing. "No, I'm sorry I made such a big deal of it," she said. "It's nice of you to apologize, but you don't need to." She unwrapped the towel and began to arrange her thick, wet curls, her fingers splayed like tines on a rake.

"Look, having people around was part of the reason, but like I said yesterday, there was that other thing," Vic said. Angie's arms fell to her sides, and she looked at his reflection in the mirror and raised one of her newly accented eyebrows. "I wanted to wait before telling you what happened in the coma so you wouldn't think I was fucking nuts or something." She started to laugh and he joined in. "So, doesn't that make even a little sense? I mean, it's a pretty wild story, right?" She nodded, still laughing. "I figured if I spun a yarn like that too soon after coming around, you'd chalk it up to brain damage. That's what Pembrooke thought, that abnormal confusion bullshit he wrote about on my chart. I had to convince him I forgot my 'dreams' so he'd let me out of the goddamned hospital."

"That makes perfect sense," she said. She gave him a brief hug, but Vic couldn't get out of his mind that it was a social embrace, with no contact below their collar bones. He pulled back to ease the discomfort for both of them. "I told you," she went on, looking at him in the mirror, "I lost it and I shouldn't have. I understand why you waited to tell me. The important thing is, you did tell me, and that's all that matters now."

"But what's also important is we have work to do, Ange. Both of us. We have to be more sensitive to each other's needs. We both have to be more communicative. And we have to work on the physical part of our marriage. I want it to be like it used to be." He reached to touch her wrist. "We used to have so much fun. We used to joke and play stupid little games." He paused. "And make love."

As she continued with her hair, her arms appeared to move in closer, to shield her breasts from his view, as though she'd suddenly become aware of her nakedness. She smiled, but it appeared to be forced and looked more like a scowl. "Oh, we will. And, when I'm not in such a hurry, I want to hear more about what happened in, I don't know what you'd call it, 'coma world,' I guess?" She looked directly at him. "In the meantime, we need to get you nursed back to health." She turned away and slipped into her bra. "And thanks for the coffee," she said over her shoulder.

"Your coffee tastes better," Vic replied, pulling the door closed as he stepped into the hallway. Cool and dark as it was, the hallway didn't begin to match the gloom he felt deep inside. Angie made it clear, once again, as far as she was concerned, there were no problems. Things would remain the same.

After she left for the office, Vic feasted on fried eggs, then made his way up to the room above the garage, adjacent to their bedroom. He'd made the former attic space into a studio, and it was his refuge. He insulated it so it would stay warm in the winter, and as a result, he could listen to the radio or watch TV as he worked late into the night, even if Angie was asleep in the bedroom a few feet away. As with his golf, painting helped to erase the other cares in his life. When he painted, his universe shrank to where the tip of his brush met the canvas, and there was no room for any other awareness.

He started right to work on a painting he started before the accident. The idea he almost didn't get the chance to complete it made him anxious to finish. He wetted his brush and worked water into the acrylic paint he squirted from several tubes onto his palette. He made subtle adjustments, deepening shadows and brightening highlights with translucent glazes of color. "Tickling," is what he called it, putting on the last bit of finish. The brush assumed its familiar set as he smoothed a translucent film of pigment onto the canvas. He twisted around to look into the large mirror positioned on the wall behind him. The reflected image told him the film of color worked the way he wanted it to. When the phone rang, dizziness overcame him as he rose to answer it. It subsided as he shuffled into the bedroom and to the phone on the nightstand.

"Hello, Vic? This is Roxanne Bayer."

Vic tried to mask his surprise. "Oh, Roxanne. Hi ... how're you?"

"Great! I didn't wake you or anything?"

"Oh, no. Early riser, here. In fact, I was just sitting down to paint."

"That's right! You teach art. I should have figured you were an artist yourself. What's it a painting of?" she asked.

"A landscape. Kind of hard to describe. The central image is a pumpkin smashed on a road."

"Sounds neat. I'd like to see it sometime." She paused. "I called because I have a few errands to run. You're kind of a shut-in, right now. Can I pick anything up for you? Anything at all?"

"Gee, Roxanne. It's nice of you to offer. I can't ... no, I can't think of a thing."

"Do you get the morning paper?"

"No. We used to, but we cancelled because we never had time to read it before we left for work."

"If it's okay, I'll bring ours down. There's a story on Jack Nicklaus Tom thought you'd like to read. He said it was interesting. Thought you might enjoy it."

"Oh, gosh, you don't have to do that. I hate for you to go to the trouble."

"No trouble at all. I'm on my way out the door to pick up some things anyway. Have to drive right past your place. See you in a few."

She must really feel guilty, or still be worried about a lawsuit, Vic thought, walking slowly back into his studio. He looked at his painting straight on, then in the mirror. The reflection not only allowed him to see the painting from a distant perspective, but it reversed the image, giving him a differing slant.

What Vic longed for was a fresh look at his marriage. His life. He loved Angie as much as he ever did, but he couldn't help feeling he'd lost her. In every important way, other than her appearance, the changes in her were dramatic. He longed for the playful, warm, and sensual woman he'd married. How could she not understand weeks without lovemaking pointed to serious trouble in a marriage, unless she didn't want to know? Her state of denial made Vic feel even more discouraged and estranged. He felt like they were caught in a storm, but she had an umbrella that shielded her from the rain.

Talking didn't work. She always cried and promised things would change, but they never did. Vic's latest strategy was to find as many ways as he could to make Angie happy in hopes she would do the same in return. Remodeled the kitchen. Put in the pool out back. When his plan didn't work, he became angry, but managed to sublimate his feelings. He was good at it. He wanted everyone to believe he was a good husband who made his wife happy, and received happiness in return. But holding the lid down only amplified the pressure of his anger and confusion.

Vic stood and walked to the window. No dizziness this time. The progress was slow, but he was beginning to find harmony with his body. He still walked like an arthritic old man, but his movements felt less jerky and contemplated, from the inside anyway. Plus, his sex drive was back, its return heralded when he awakened a few mornings before with his first hard-on since the accident. Of course, that was both good and bad. Dr. Pembrooke gave "the talk" to Angie as well, so sex was more out of the question than usual. Gazing at his painting, Vic thought about how easy it was for him to "tickle" the colors into harmony. He wished he was skilled enough to find a way to tickle his life. The difference was painting was a solitary pursuit. Married life was a product of interaction. He couldn't find harmony with Angie unless she cooperated.

The doorbell rang. Vic plodded carefully downstairs and opened the door. "Hi, Roxanne," he said, stepping out onto the front stoop, enjoying the warm October sunshine on his face. "Man, that sun feels great. I haven't been out much. Miss it."

Roxanne smiled, but with a hint of what looked like embarrassment, as though someone reminded her she owed money. "Hope you can get out more before winter hits. Not many days like this left," she said, her arm arcing toward the powder blue sky.

Vic nodded, but his mind was empty of anything else to say, so they stood, smiling and looking at each other. "Uh, so that's the paper?" Vic finally asked, pointing with his chin.

Roxanne looked like she'd completely forgotten she had it with her. Her face morphed into another embarrassed expression. "Oh, yeah," she gushed, pressing the newspaper into his hand. "The article is in the sports section. The one on Nicklaus. Tom really liked it. He used to be an Arnold Palmer fan."

"Who wasn't?" Vic asked, glancing at the front page, then folding it over. "They didn't call it 'Arnie's Army' for nothing. Poor guy's over fifty now. Everybody's looking for a new young hero. Heck, Nicklaus is no spring chicken, forty or thereabouts."

Roxanne exploded in laughter. "Careful now, sonny," she said when she regained herself, her eyes widening. "You're talking to a gal who's pushing forty-three." Like a splash diminishing to ripples, her mirth reduced to a giggle. "I hope I have a few good years left in this old bod."

Vic felt the flush as his face reddened. "No, I meant for an athlete, you know, he's getting older. You, you look terrific," he said. Too embarrassed to maintain eye contact, he let his gaze drift down the length of her body. When he looked up into her dark green eyes, he saw she'd noticed. Vic had the impression she was enjoying his discomfort. She laughed again, but it seemed like a product of honest emotion, not social grease. Then she lowered her chin and looked up at him like someone who'd just heard a secret.

"Compliments like that will get you anywhere," she said, her voice a soft lilt. She waited a beat, then gave him a gentle push on the shoulder, as if to defuse what she said. Her voice went back to the friendly neighbor tonality. "So, your painting is going well? The pumpkin one."

"Ah, yeah. I, ah, I should finish it today," he said, tilting his head in the general direction of the stairway.

"You paint upstairs, do you?"

"Uh-huh, in a room above the garage," he said. "That room," he added, leaning to point out the studio's window on the gable over the garage. Roxanne didn't step back and Vic realized their heads were very close together. Vic noticed her skin was flawless, except for a tiny spot on the right side of her nose. Maybe the remnants of a childhood case of chicken pox, he decided.

"You'll have to show me sometime. I'd love to see some of your work. And your studio," she added, raising an eyebrow.

"That's one of mine right there," Vic said, stepping back into the entryway, reaching to hold the storm door open with his arm.

Roxanne moved forward and leaned in next to him, looking at the painting that hung on the wall over the first flight of stairs.

"Oh, God. That's beautiful, Vic. I saw it yesterday when Tom and I came down. I love the way the sun shines on the old farmhouse with the dark purplish sky behind. I can feel the storm coming, like that big one last

August. The sky was like that then. Real dark clouds, but the sun still bright. The contrast." She looked up at him and he thought he could feel her breath on his neck. "You're very good," she concluded, looking up at him again with the curious demeanor of a little girl. She seemed to hover there for a moment too long. Then a tiny smile wrinkled her cheeks before she stepped back out onto the front stoop. "I used to do the paint-by-number kind when I was a kid," Roxanne continued. "Craft Master, I think. Yeah, that was the company."

"That one's a paint-by-number." He watched the surprise take over her face before going on. "The difference is I make up the numbers."

Roxanne shook her head in mock disgust. "Will we know you're recovered if your jokes get funnier?" Her eyes twinkled, and she had a way of looking at Vic that made it seem no one else existed. She unnerved him, but it was a good kind of edginess, the kind he felt when he was a boy, standing in line for a rollercoaster.

"It was really nice of you to go to the trouble to stop with the paper," Vic said.

"I'll bring it again tomorrow," she offered, turning to walk to her car. The wale of her snug corduroys clung to the fetching contours of her bottom and legs. Vic allowed himself another eyeful.

"Oh, that's okay, Roxanne. Maybe I'll call and have it delivered, since I'll be home for a while."

"Do that and I'll lose my only customer. Tom doesn't let me work. This paper route's the first job I've had in years." She let that great laugh of hers roll.

~*~

Roxanne kept her job. Each morning, she stopped by with the *Toledo Times.* Vic buried each issue in the trash so Angie wouldn't see them. He wasn't worried she would be jealous if she knew Roxanne brought them over; in fact, a little possessiveness on Angie's part would have given

111

his self-esteem a shot in the arm. No, his concern was she would insist they subscribe, which would end the reason for Roxanne's visits. Vic looked forward to them. He began bringing out a cup of coffee for her, and they sat or stood on the front stoop and talked. Always outside. He never invited her in, but more and more often, he fantasized about it. Roxanne began to phone regularly as well. They chatted and joked. It was harmless fun, Vic convinced himself, that kept the day moving at a time when he still wasn't moving very well.

As time passed, they began to share the details of their lives. Roxanne was a lonely woman. Tom worked a lot of hours at the Toledo Jeep plant. He played golf in the warm months, bowled the rest of the time, and drank *all* the time. She had friends in their former neighborhood, but the neighborhood had gone downhill. Bittersweet was much nicer, but she hadn't found anyone to connect with. And Tom was old-fashioned. In his house the man was the provider, the wife stayed home.

Tom changed from the man Roxanne fell in love with years ago, so she understood Vic's predicament with Angie. Vic felt a kinship with Roxanne as well. Besides, having a woman friend to confide in was different than talk with the guys. Men play unspoken macho games and an admission of emotion can be used later, say during a round of golf, at the card table, or even in the teacher's lounge, to get one-up on another guy. Vic was a pro at protecting his vulnerable spots. Life with The Old Man taught him to never let his guard down. When he exposed his underbelly to Roxanne, he didn't have to worry about her using what he said against him. On the contrary, she seemed to understand and care he was unhappy in a way none of his friends could have. Additionally, he hoped her woman's perspective might give him better insights regarding what to do to save his marriage.

"There's something I have to tell you," Vic said, one morning as they sat on the front stoop with their cups of coffee. "I've been wanting to, and when I do, you'll be in a pretty exclusive group. Only three or four people have ever heard this."

Roxanne gave him a quizzical look and put her hand on his. "Fire away".

"When I was in that coma, well, it wasn't what you'd think or ever imagine it was like." He went on to tell her about the entire comma episode. She listened attentively, occasionally asking questions while he told her about how he awakened into the coma, about the people he met, Loon's Lair and the way he played golf after Bascolm taught him how to hit the ball. He even told her who Reefer was, and how she helped him awaken in the hospital.

When he finished, there was a long silence. "Damn, that's the most amazing story I ever heard in my life. That ranks right up there with ghosts and men from outer space. I'll be honest, if it weren't you telling it, I'm not sure I'd believe it." Then Roxanne hit him with her mischievous grin. "And that's what you almost told us that Sunday we stopped over, right?"

"Shit," Vic said. "You picked up on that, too. Christ, Angie knew I detoured, and she gave me hell because I almost told the two of you. I hadn't even told her yet."

"But you didn't tell us," Roxanne offered.

"Yeah, but I didn't tell her sooner, either. She was pissed because she thought I should have, instead of waiting two weeks." He shrugged. "Probably true, but I didn't have it all sorted out for myself. And I didn't want her, or you two, to think I was brain-damaged. I mean, you're right. The story is right there with ghosts and little green men."

"And you have it sorted out now? You honestly believe it all happened?"

"As much as I can. I'll know more when I hit some balls and see if what Bass showed me makes a difference." He playfully slapped her knee. "Hey, I might wind up being the first guy you know to play on the PGA Tour with Jack."

"And what if you can't play better? Does that mean it was all a dream?"

"Not necessarily," he said, shifting on the tile surface of the front step. "It might mean I can't make my body do what I could when I was in the coma. I didn't have to control my body when it was all happening in my mind. In that case, I'll figure out some other way of validating whether it happened or not," he said. He looked into her eyes. "But, yes, I believe it happened. I wish I could let Tom know about it. He still feels really bad, doesn't he?"

Roxanne grimaced. "He hasn't played since the Chili Open. Took the clubs out of his car."

"After I get off the short leash the doctor has me on, I'll invite him out for a round. Hell, if I'm hitting them like I think I will, he won't have any reason to feel bad anymore." Vic laughed hard. "And he won't be able to hit me again if I'm standing behind him on the tee box."

~ * ~

There was probably a time when Vic realized his friendship with Roxanne was evolving in ways he'd never anticipated, but the boundary lines of relationships are nebulous and difficult to chart. Even though most of the neighbors on Bittersweet worked, Roxanne soon began cutting through their shared neighbor's back yard instead of coming to the front door. They never discussed it. Roxanne showed up at the back door one day, and Vic accepted it at face value. After all, it was getting too cold to sit on the step and talk, and with as much time as they were spending together, neither of them wanted the tongues of the retirees on the street to wag. Rumors travel quickly anywhere, and especially on dead-end streets. So, Vic would meet her at the back door to usher her inside. They'd drink coffee and talk.

It was all innocent enough at first, but by the time Vic was willing to admit to himself a flame was struck, the heat felt too good for him to even consider putting it out or moving away from the fire, especially after years of frigidity. The Friday before his appointment with the doctor, as Roxanne slipped out the door to leave, their orbits were suddenly on a collision course. The gravity was overpowering, and Vic's lips crashed against Roxanne's. He closed his eyes, but reopened them, as if to confirm he was kissing someone other than Angie. Roxanne's indigo eyes were peering straight back into his. He pulled away. "Oh no, you don't," Roxanne said, playfully yanking his face back toward her. This time the kiss was a bit off center. Her lips were moist and soft. Her nose felt cool against the side of his. Vic sampled a stew of sensations—guilt, desire, longing and craving. He even felt the stirrings of an erection, something a mere kiss hadn't produced since junior high school. It all made for a delicious mixture that was difficult to resist, but he did his best.

"We shouldn't do this," Vic whispered.

"We probably shouldn't. But we *could.*"

"No. We *can't.* The doctor said no excitement until after my checkup on Monday. He was very serious, and so am I."

Roxanne knocked the glower off Vic's face with her impish grin. She brought her index finger to her mouth and kissed it, then brushed it softly across Vic's cheek.

"What was that?" Vic asked.

Roxanne shrugged. "I gave you a kiss by proxy. Or maybe I gave you the finger." The edges of her teeth glistened in the sunlight when she giggled. "You decide."

That night, Vic wasn't able to fall asleep. He didn't know if it was due to excitement over the kiss, or because of the guilt he felt. Probably some of both, he concluded. Hours passed with him lying very still, listening to the rhythmic cadence of Angie's breathing, while he watched the illuminated numbers change on their digital clock. 3:03, it read. Angie was off somewhere, dreaming a world for herself he would never know. He wished he could see the images. Were they as clear and realistic as the ones from his coma? Were they rich in color? Did she dream of him? Was he even a part of her dreams anymore? Christ, I'm barely a part of her waking life. Maybe she dreamed of her doll house. He was close to slumber, and in the foggy logic of a mind drifting toward the edge of its subconscious, he wondered if he could find her somewhere inside the colonial mansion. He'd helped her draw the plans, back when they were still involved with each other's pursuits, so he knew every room. Could he put himself in there and track her down?

Vic pushed open the front door and stepped into the foyer. "Angie?" he called. His voice reverberated against the unfinished walls. He called out again, but there was no answer. He walked into the living room. The walls were yet to be papered, but he was amazed at how beautifully she'd laid the tile. The grout-filled spaces between each piece were nearly perfect in alignment, but most shocking was how level she was able to lay a floor comprised of tiles that were only one inch square. It was so easy to walk on, each tile smoothly abutting the next. Then, a phone began to ring. "Angie," Vic called. "Should I get it?" He stepped into the study where a phone sat on the roll-top desk he bought for the doll house on her birthday. He stood, not certain what he should do, but decided to pick it up. "Hello?" he said into the receiver.

"Hey lover," Roxanne said. "We probably shouldn't. But we *could.*"

Vic's eyes snapped open. Angie groaned softly as she shifted in her sleep, pulling the covers up to her chin. The clock read a few minutes after three-thirty.

Saturday and Sunday dragged, as usual. It seemed anytime Angie went somewhere, Tom Bayer's car was parked in their driveway, and vice versa, so even a quick phone call was out of the question. But Monday, the day of Vic's appointment with Pembrooke, finally arrived.

"I'm going to try swinging a club," Vic said, as he followed Roxanne to the utility room door, at the end of her daily visit.

She whirled like a dancer. "What?"

"I can't stand it," he said. "I have to see if what Bascolm taught me in the coma really works." He paused. "If I can even do it."

"But the doctor said—"

"I feel great," he cut in. "Hardly any dizziness, and I really feel like I own my body again. Like it's really me in here running things. He's going to okay me for normal activity today, but I can't wait any longer." He mugged. "And, I've been a good boy."

"Too good, if you ask me." She gave him a slo-mo wink and raised an eyebrow. "You going to be ready to misbehave a little after the doc signs off on you?"

Vic answered her with a long, opened-mouth kiss, then pulled away. "You bet."

She ramped up a lascivious smile. "Don't let your mouth write any checks your body can't cash."

"Stealing Flip Wilson's material, now?"

She gently slapped his cheek. "No, Geraldine's."

"Don't you worry yourself. I've got sufficient funds."

"Be careful. I bet I could drain your account." She pushed her lips into a sensual pout, then said, "I'll call you later."

Vic watched Roxanne slip through to the neighbor's yard. She was so hot. And she left him feeling hot. But he was also hot to get a hold on a golf club, so he shut the door and started for the garage. Could he recreate the golf swing Bascolm helped him develop at Loon's Lair? He often laid awake at night firing shots into his imagination, until he finally drifted off. He'd followed Pembrooke's instructions to the letter until then, but he simply had to find out if what Bascolm taught him would work, or if it was all merely rooted in dreams. The appointment was only hours away. He felt great. And he *had* to know.

In the garage, Vic pulled out his five iron and ran his hand over its head. The chilly stainless steel warmed in his fingers like a lustful lover. He placed the doormat in the middle of the empty stall where Angie parked her Honda, dug out a handful of Wiffle balls, and dropped them on the mat's bristly surface. Rolling one into position, he picked a knot in the garage door that would serve as a target. After a couple warm-up swings to loosen his muscles, he lined up, paused to go through the catechism Bascolm ingrained in him, and triggered his swing. The club came through and dug into the mat. Only the toe of the clubface caught the ball, and it veered right, ricocheted off the lawn mower and pirouetted over Vic's head before hitting the front fender of his car.

"Shit!" he growled.

It wasn't the swing. The problem was the mat. Vic hadn't allowed for its thickness. He pulled another Wiffle ball over and slid his hands further down the grip, effectively shortening the club. Again, focusing on the target, he executed his swing. The ball hit the door, narrowly missing the knot. A stab of dizziness passed through him, and Vic used the club for support until the rush of vertigo passed. As soon as the unsteadiness ebbed, he gathered another ball. That one also flew true to its mark. For almost half an hour, Vic hit balls against the door. Exhausted, he didn't hurry a steamy shower, and dressed for his appointment. Then went back into the garage, to see if the time away from hitting balls made any difference. It didn't. The balls flew true to his target, with only an occasional mishit.

When he heard the phone ringing, he knew it would be Roxanne. "Hey, buddy. How's the swing?" she asked.

"You wouldn't believe it," he said. Even to himself, he sounded like a kid at Christmas. "I've been pounding Wiffle balls at a knot on the garage door. Oh, baby, was I ever hitting 'em good. Like back at Loon's Lair. Honest, I haven't forgotten a thing. I've wondered so long, hoped and prayed I wasn't a nut-case who dreamed up all the stuff about the coma. That I could connect with what Bass taught me. I'm not kidding you, I really think I remember it all. I mean, it's hard to be sure, hitting plastic balls in a damned garage, but I was hammering them right at a knot in the garage door. I can't wait to hit some real ones."

"That's great, Vic. And, how are you feeling?"

Vic was surprised Roxanne didn't sound more excited about his being able to connect with the swing he remembered from his coma, but he was so elated, her lack of enthusiasm didn't bother him. "Great. I'm feeling great. I was a little dizzy once, but that's all. I know the doctor will tell me I'm okay. I *know* I'm okay."

"Angie turned off River Road," Roxanne said. "Call me soon as you can?"

"Sure. Yeah. I'll talk to you later."

Vic made it into the garage as the door opener began its work.

"So, what's this?" Angie asked, getting out of her car. "Somebody's opening a driving range?"

"I was going to have it all picked up before you came home, but the phone rang. You should have seen me hit, though." He stooped to gather the balls.

"I wish you'd wait until Dr. Pembrooke says you can do this stuff," she muttered, bending to help pick up balls. "Who called?"

"Siding salesman," Vic answered, amazed at the ease with which the lie rolled off his tongue. "Hey, do I get to drive?"

"Vic ... "

"Ah, come on, please, Mom?" he whined, trying to ape Beaver Cleaver. Angie giggled and shook her head. "Seriously, Ange. I haven't driven in almost a month! Was tempted to go for a spin plenty of times, but I never did."

"I know," she said. "I checked the odometer."

"You little shit!" Vic said. He grabbed her and spun her into his arms. "Hey, you really are turning into my mother! But today, the doctor's gonna release me, and then I'll be able to run. And play golf. And ... " He finished the list with a kiss that didn't quite find the center of Angie's lips.

Vic prayed she'd reciprocate. Prayed Angie would open her lips and revert to the woman he remembered, the lover she once was. The Angie who used to leave a note with a riddle on the kitchen table, so when Vic came in from cutting the grass or from golf, he had to decipher it to find her hideaway. His reward—no, *their* reward—was always a hot round of lovemaking. Vic missed those riddles, and missed the way she laughed at his inferior attempts to mimic them in return. He hoped the coma episode would shock Angie into seeing the difference between who the two of them once were versus who they'd become. The Angie of old could easily extinguish the flame that drew Vic, like a moth, to Roxanne. He prayed Angie would hold him and kiss him the way she used to now while he and Roxanne were friends who'd traded a kiss and some vague promises. Now, before it was too late.

"Cool off, Oedipus," she giggled, pushing him away. "He may not release you, so we'll have to see."

"He will," Vic said, fighting to hide his disappointment. "But, I'm driving to the doctor's."

~ * ~

Vic savored the smooth snick he felt through the gearshift lever as he pulled it into second. When he let out the clutch and he nailed the gas, the coupe swung a little sideways as it shot forward.

"Vic," Angie shouted. "Take it easy."

He side-glanced. She looked like a woman riding the first big drop on a rollercoaster. He eased off. "Sorry, but it's been a while."

The RX7 was powerful, fast and nimble. Especially now, Vic was none of those, except when he was in the driver's seat. He loved driving from his first spin in a pedal-car The Old Man brought home for Vic's third birthday. He enjoyed controlling that machine, even if he was the only power source. And one kid-power was nothing compared to the couple hundred horsepower in the Mazda.

"Don't tell the doctor I let you drive," Angie said, looking out the passenger-side window and shaking her head. "He probably assumes the streets are still safe."

"He's safe in his office," Vic said, stinging from Angie's assertion she "let" him drive. He almost pursued it, but decided to let it drop. It wasn't worth the hassle. Besides, he didn't want anything to diminish the pleasure of driving.

And Pembrooke didn't care. "I don't want you over-doing," he said, training his scope's light into Vic's pupil, then moving it away. "All your vitals and your reflexes look good." He shifted into his grandfatherly mode. "Honestly, how do you feel?"

Vic looked him back. "No where's near one-hundred percent, but about a hundred percent better than I did last time we crossed paths," he answered. "Big thing is, now I'm dying from inactivity. I've been hobbling around like a sixty-five year-old man."

"Careful, Vic. I'm turning sixty-four in a month."

Vic felt a blush. "You know what I mean," he said, looking up at the doctor. "I'm half your age, and I feel like some of those old goats who can barely move. You're no old goat. But, I really need to get back to my life."

The doctor smiled. "And I want you back to your life, but I want you to ease your way in. You're a runner. You know how to listen to your body." He squeezed Vic's upper arm. "No restrictions but pay attention to what your body tells you."

Vic winked. "And what about work?"

"How many days of school do you have on Thanksgiving week?"

"Only Monday and Tuesday."

"Let's hold off until then," Pembrooke said, sitting down to write. "Only a couple days of work, and five days to rest up before getting back in the saddle. Think you can handle that?"

Vic grinned. "With no restrictions? You bet I can."

As soon as they came back home, Vic put on his sweats and running shoes. He couldn't remember the last time the country club's golf course looked as beautiful, or the last time a run felt as lousy. Part of it was he usually ran in the morning, not in the late afternoon. But, after Dr. Pembrooke released him to his normal activities, Vic couldn't wait for the next day. Even though he jogged at a pace that was only slightly faster than a walk, he was still fighting a side stitch, something he knew came from breathing with the chest rather than the diaphragm. *My God,* he thought, *not only am I completely out of shape, but I've even forgotten how to breathe!*

He ambled back to Bittersweet, and as soon as he ducked out of the woods, he saw Roxanne hosing down some window screens she'd leaned against the side of the garage. Her faithful mutt was tied nearby, barking and snapping at the spray the chilly breeze blew his way. In spite of the cool temperatures, Roxanne was barefoot and wearing short shorts. Her only concession to the season was a big loose sweatshirt.

"Hey, neighbor," he said between breaths, doing his best to hide his panting as he walked up the Bayer's driveway.

She dropped the hose. "Hi," she said, smiling at first, before her expression became one of a person who just witnessed an accident. "You look like shit. You're not gonna vapor lock on me, are you?"

"A little out of shape, but that'll change," Vic said with conviction.

"The doctor may have okay'd running, but I bet he didn't mean marathons."

"I only did two miles. I used to go that far before I'd break a sweat." He tried not to sound whiny.

"Men," Roxanne said, tossing her head. "How long 'til you can go back to work?"

"The week of Thanksgiving," Vic replied. "It's a two-day week, and the doctor and I decided it's the perfect time to ease back into it."

"Good idea. So, what's the plan?" Roxanne asked, cocking her head and giving him a look that said she already had the answer.

Vic wrinkled his forehead. "Wait 'til Thanksgiving," he said.

"No, silly," she said. "I mean for the *near* future."

"First, I'm gonna shower up and go out to hit some balls. Real golf balls. Out there," he jerked his head toward the fairway on the other side of the Bayer's house, "on a real golf course. I feel like I'm back from the dead. There are so many things I want to do, so many things I've been missing."

"Any plans for tomorrow?" she asked.

"Tomorrow?" Vic repeated, searching out the answer she apparently wanted. Roxanne pushed her lower lip into an exaggerated pout that made what her point obvious. "I'm sorry," he said, taking hold of her arm, then releasing it and glancing around to confirm no one saw him. He looked into her eyes. "You know I do. I wasn't thinking past today."

"So, now that you are, will you be needing a paper tomorrow?"

"Ab-so-damn-lutely!" The fact he used Bascolm's signature phrase caught him by surprise. The memory of his friend's face flashed through Vic's mind. His thoughts were mixed. He missed his old friend, but

Bascolm was devoted to his wife. Vic was in the midst of plotting a rendezvous with Roxanne.

"Are you sure? 'Cause I told you before, buddy, you can drop your subscription anytime." She gave him a searching look. "I mean it."

Vic teetered. All he wanted was the love and closeness he craved with Angie. He wanted his wife. He wanted to be loved and desired. He wanted to feel like he was in bed with someone who wasn't a kid handing lunch money over to the class bully. He didn't want to be like The Old Man he hated for the very thing Vic knew he was damned close to committing; adultery. Even what the doctor said, about caution in making long-term personal decisions, shot through his head, but Roxanne's eyes smoldered with desire when he looked into them. Roxanne wanted him. Roxanne needed him. And Vic longed to be wanted and needed. Years of hunger made him ravenous for a feast of wanting and needing. "We can't get caught."

"We won't. No one will ever know about us. No one." She fished her cigarettes from a pocket in her shorts and lit one. "We're neighbors," she continued, exhaling. "Not even next door neighbors." She started back up the drive, gathering her sweatshirt around her waist as she walked. He watched the tiny wrinkles on the seat of her tight yellow shorts shoot from one side of the center seam to the other with each of her strides. She stopped and fired him a seductive look. "So, the paper girl will be over in the morning," she said. "To collect. Have that check ready."

Vic went home, showered, dressed, and heated dinner. He and Angie ate an early supper, and Vic headed back out on the country club's course, but this time, he carried his clubs. When he ran on the course, he always made a point of stopping to talk to Joe Miller, the greens keeper. Over the years, the two of them became friends. Joe didn't mind if Vic practiced as long as it was late in the day, when no members were around.

Walking out onto Toledo County Club's course that evening turned out to be a powerful emotional experience. Although he was never much good at it, Vic loved golf. Even without the promise of a better game, carrying his clubs onto the course would have been overwhelming. He couldn't wait to finally hit a real golf ball toward a real green. He'd spent every day since coming out of the coma thinking about hitting a ball, and the fact he was physically able was exhilarating. Still, the fear his coma experience was a dream, or it would in no way improve his golf game was worrisome. He put a lot of stock in the belief he'd met a man who showed him the right way to swing a club. If it turned out he couldn't hit real golf balls any differently, wouldn't that disprove the memories he clung to? He gazed around, pausing to notice the low sunlight painting the trees and casting deep green shadows in its lea. The west-facing bunkers glistened like brown sugar, and the pins and flags shown bright as neon. Good swing or bad, this is going to be great, he decided. He dropped his clubs on the fairway about one hundred thirty-five yards from the tenth green, and emptied his shag bag. The balls scattered into a loose pile, and the sound of them bouncing off one another was shear music.

Vic pulled his eight-iron and warmed-up his swing. Closing his eyes, he pictured Bascolm's swing and ticked off the elements of the move he'd learned from his mentor. After half a dozen practice rips, he decided it was show time.

He pulled a ball out of the cluster and lined up on the right side of the green. There was a bunker to aim at, and if he hit the draw Bascolm taught him, the ball would draw left of the sand and find the green's surface. He inhaled deeply, let half of it out, and swung. After the club head strafed the grass, Vic looked up to see the result. It was mixed. He'd put a great strike on the ball, and it was rocketing toward the green, but it drew only a smidge. "Come on," he hissed through his clenched teeth. When it dropped out of the sky, it landed on the slender margin between the bunker and the putting surface, bounced right, and rolled into the bunker. "Crap," he said, then looked around to make sure no one was within hearing distance. He was alone, and he was heartened by the way he'd hit the ball. It didn't draw the way he wanted it to, but it certainly was a better shot than he usually made. He tried again and once more, the ball showed an inkling of wanting to draw, but it flopped into the bunker, on the fly, this time.

Okay, he thought, *I'll go right for the pin, then.* He did, and the next shot landed short of the hole, and spun back toward the front of the green. "Christ, that's the first time I ever spun one back," he said. He literally giggled, both in delight, and also because he usually didn't talk to himself aloud. He hit another at the pin, this time putting a bit more snap into the ball strike. Sure enough, the ball landed beyond the pin, and spun back toward it, coming to rest close to the hole.

He was excited. What Bascolm taught him really did work, but he hadn't been able to make the ball draw, yet. He hit balls until only a few were left, and he glanced at his watch. It was close to sunset. Time for one more, he decided. He set up to hit a ball, looked at the bunker, and began his backswing. On the follow-through, the shaft sliced the air as his wrists un-cocked and delivered the club head to collide with the ball. He locked his eyes on the brilliant white Titleist as it rose like a rocket in the fading glow of the golden October sunset. But as before, the draw that was supposed to curve the ball's flight toward the flag didn't materialize, and the ball bivouacked in the green's right side bunker.

"Shit!" he grumbled. He picked up his shag bag and clubs, and started for the green. His swing was ninety-nine percent there, but some tiny element was missing. The balls started out in the direction he aimed them, but they wouldn't draw the way he wanted them to, something that never showed up in the short distance he hit the Wiffles in the garage. He replayed what Bascolm taught him while he retrieved his balls and raked the bunker. He could hit the ball straight at the green, but the natural draw Bascolm helped Vic develop wasn't there. Regardless, he was convinced his memories from the coma were spot-on. "I'm finally going to be good at this," he said. "I've got a game."

He started for home, and as he walked out of the woods at the dead end of Bittersweet, he glanced toward the Bayers' house. The memory of Roxanne's image, raising her sweatshirt to playfully flaunt her pretty bottom, replayed in his mind. Then it struck him: hips.

He hurried back to the fairway. The scene there reminded him of an Edward Hopper landscape. The waning sunset slathered the course with yellow-orange light and left long purplish shadows. He dropped a ball, pulled out his eight iron, and lined up on the bunker like before. This time, he turned his hips an inch or so clockwise, closing them to his intended line of flight. When he made his swing, it was as though he was back at Loon's Lair. This tiny correction in his setup caused the shiny ball, its spin pulling it left, to drop and roll to rest near the pin. "Yes," Vic barked, thrusting his club into the air. "I did it, Bass." He got a prickly feeling around his nose, like before a sneeze. His eyes watered as he picked up his equipment. He proudly left the ball he'd hit to sleep on the green.

When he returned to the house, Angie was upstairs working on her dollhouse. Vic vaulted the steps two at a time. When he walked into her workroom, she was using tweezers to put a piece of bass wood in place and didn't look up. "How'd it go?" she mumbled.

Vic couldn't hide his excitement, nor did he want to. "I still have it," he gushed. "The swing Bascolm taught me. It took some doing, but I have it."

Angie stopped, and turned toward him with an expression he'd never seen before. It almost looked like she was near-sighted and couldn't focus. "That is so strange," she murmured. "The story itself is weird enough, but the fact that you can hit the ball better now, it kind of creeps me out." She picked up another piece of wood in her tweezers and began to apply glue to the ends. "Anyway, I'm happy for you. I know it's what you always wanted, a good golf swing." She reached to put the piece of trim in its place above the front door. "I'll be down in a bit," she added.

Vic hoped she would be excited for him and would want to talk more about what his new ability at golf implied. He found it difficult to grasp the entirety of what happened out on the course, and he hoped Angie would be an interested participant in a conversation about it.

He trudged downstairs and by the time he made it to the den and turned on the TV, the sum of all the day's activity overcame him and he quickly fell asleep. When he awakened, it was 11:28, and the weatherman summed up the outlook for the next day. When Vic stood, he literally felt beaten. The muscles in his legs, arms and even the ones in his back and chest were sore, and they protested his movements as he lumbered into the kitchen. *I feel like an old man,* he thought. He fixed himself a ham sandwich, dropped ice in a glass and washed the cubes in Southern Comfort. He checked: it was dark and quiet upstairs. When he returned to the den, Ed McMahon finished listing the guests on that night's show. "And now—he-e-e-e-re's Johnny!" Carson stepped through the curtain wearing his engaging grin, tugged on his shirt cuffs and bowed to the audience. The music reached its crescendo, and Carson brought it to a stop with his classic smirk and a wave of his arm. His monologue was amusing, but Vic's mind wandered to Roxanne. "The paper girl will be over. To collect." He replayed her parting words again and again. Someone wanted him. After years of being kept at arm's length by the woman he loved, someone found him sexy and attractive. It had been a long drought, and Vic was thirsty. Not just for sex. For acceptance. Attention. For conversation. He yearned for someone to initiate a kiss, an embrace. Someone to talk to. Roxanne's smiling face appeared in his mind. Thoughts of her were more intoxicating than Southern Comfort.

The sandwich was delicious. He thought about going to get a bowl of potato chips, but his aching body voted no. He sipped his drink, and was asleep again before Johnny could perform the golf swing he used to close his monologue.

When he awakened, Vic could hear Angie humming softly to herself as she washed her breakfast dishes. He was still in his recliner, but the TV screen was dark.

"G'morning," he said, walking stiffly into the kitchen and rubbing his eyes. Angie's business suit made her look every bit the proper legal secretary, but the gray tweed skirt fell short of covering her shapely calves.

"Oh. Good morning! I'm sorry, I tried to be as quiet as I could." She flashed a smile. "You must have been as tired as me."

He poured some coffee. "Not a problem. I've slept enough."

"I didn't want to wake you. The TV was still on when I came down this morning. How do you feel? Think maybe you overdid it yesterday?"

"Oh, I think I can safely say I did." He stretched his arms. "I feel like I fell down a flight or two of stairs, but unlike with Jay Carlin, it's a good soreness. Like I used to get when I overdid it with the exercise; you know, when I run ten miles or water ski, or do anything out of the ordinary. It hurts, but it's short-lived. I'm glad to be doing things, not just sitting around."

"So, what are you up to today?"

"I'm going to run, again," Vic said, leaning against the counter. "Other than that, not really sure. Might hit some balls if it isn't too windy. It's not supposed to get out of the forties, though."

"I heard," she said, picking up her shoulder bag.

"Halloween isn't until tomorrow, but I might drive out to the cemetery anyway, for my yearly audience with The Old Man."

"Oh, it *is* that time already, isn't it?" She kissed him on the cheek and started for the door. "Hey, have a great day." She stopped, gripping the knob. "And try not to make yourself too sore in the process, okay?" Vic nodded. "My Friday to pick up the lawyer fuel at Dunkin' Donuts." She opened the door. "Bye."

"Bye," Vic replied, eyeing her calves before she disappeared into the garage.

Chapter Five

A log in the fireplace burned through and the two halves fell into the coals. Vic was almost on his feet before he realized what caused the noise.

"Jesus, buddy!" Roxanne said, shaking her head. "You *are* nervous. Do you want me to go?"

He answered with a long, opened-mouth kiss, during which he slid his hand up from her stomach and gently palmed her breast. She made a soft cooing sound deep in her throat, reached up, and put her hand on his. "I'll give you one hour to cut that out," she moaned. They kissed again. "I'm sorry things didn't work out, you know ... with my period starting early. I can't frickin' believe it. I figured the day before would be perfect." She arched an eyebrow and gave him a lecherous grin. "We could have gone bareback."

"Not a problem, there's no hurry." There wasn't. Vic didn't want their relationship to be only about sex. At some level, not making love the first time they were together without the doctor's restrictions made him feel better about being with Roxanne, as though that would make him less of a cheat. He looked into her eyes, amazed at how many flecks of brown there were in her emerald irises. "I like making out. Haven't done it in years."

"There's no reason why I can't take care of you," she said, with a libidinous wink. "I'd love that, buddy."

Vic's erect penis strained against his Levis. She smiled, and let a bit of her tongue show as she licked her upper lip. It had been years since Angie gave him oral sex, and Vic was nearly certain that was her offer.

Even the thought of a hand-job was exciting. He wavered. He wanted to say yes. Was dying to say yes. But, saying no to sex bought more time for Angie to come around. In Vic's mind, an actual sex act with Roxanne would cement a commitment to her, and he still hoped Angie might change. He forced himself to shake his head. "Let's wait. I meant what I said. There's no hurry."

They kissed once more, then she sat up.

"You just turned down the best offer you'll get today," she said, chuckling.

"Christ, it's the best offer *I've* had in years."

She reached under her sweatshirt to hook her bra, clasping it before he could attempt to assist.

"So, what are you going to do with the rest of your day?" she asked.

He looked out the living room window. "I think I'm gonna go visit The Old Man."

"Your father? Didn't you say he was—"

"Dead. Yes, but tomorrow is Halloween, my dear," Vic answered, trying for some Boris Karloff in his delivery. "He's buried over in Ottawa Hills Cemetery. I drop by this time every year."

"Okay, I'll bite. Why Halloween?"

"Because my most vivid memory of The Old Man is from Halloween. I was about ten. Fifth grade, I think. Some big kids jumped me and stole my candy, pushed me down on my fat little butt and made off with my whole bag of goodies. When I went home crying, The Old Man tossed me in his car, tracked 'em down, and beat the shit out of them." He leaned against the sofa and shook his head. "Three lettermen from Libby High. The Old Man rammed their car from behind, kicked their asses when they got out, and had me load all the candy they'd looted into our car. My parents were going to a costume party that night, so he was wearing a devil's outfit. Long underwear my mother dyed red, and one of those little plastic headpieces with horns. The kind with the little elastic strap that goes under your chin."

"You're kidding."

"No ma'am. When we started out, I prayed we wouldn't find those guys 'cause I figured they'd beat the crap out of him, three on one. By the time I spotted their car, he'd whipped himself into such a fury, I'll never forget it. I was delighted to point them out because I knew that anger was gonna get unleashed somewhere, and I was the only other one around."

"So, you go to the cemetery every year?"

"Only the last few. I pass out candy to my classes on Halloween. One year, some kid started mouthing off about stealing little kids' candy, and I found myself telling him what I told you, to make him think twice about doing it. On a whim, I swung past the cemetery on the way home after school. Haven't missed a Halloween since. This year, it's on Saturday, but today's close enough. One of the guys called and we're playing golf tomorrow, if the weather's as good as the forecast."

"How long has he been dead?"

"Since '65. I was a senior in high school. Fifteenth of October, 1965. The Old Man didn't make it to Halloween that year. He picked a fight with a guy in a bar in Redlands, California. The guy was with three or four friends The Old Man didn't know about."

Roxanne winced.

"Hey, he who lives by the sword ... " Vic said.

"Can I come with you?"

"What?" The word came out almost an octave higher than normal.

"I'd like to come along with you to the cemetery. Could I?"

"Are you crazy?"

"Maybe." She shrugged. "I'll slide down in the seat. Nobody'll see me. Once we get out of the neighborhood, we have nothing to worry about."

"Lady, you are a lunatic!"

"Maybe. But if you'd rather go alone ... "

"It's not that. What if we were in an accident or something?"

"That won't happen." She stood and slipped into her penny loafers. "Let's go."

"You *are* crazy," Vic said, grinning.

She winked. "Probably. Ain't it great?"

On the drive to the cemetery, Vic worried someone he knew would see them together. His nerves let him alone once they pulled through the gates. Then, as he stood at The Old Man's grave, heavy gray clouds barrel-rolled across the sky. A chilly wind made the fallen leaves skitter among the grave markers like a hoard of multicolored mice in the gloom of the dark afternoon. He glanced over at Roxanne. She sat in the Mazda, holding her cigarette outside the partially open passenger window, looking off at another part of the cemetery.

Vic always got a strange feeling at The Old Man's grave. He imagined his father's body lying below and remembered all the times he looked up to see him. Now, try as he might, Vic couldn't envision the man at all. At the funeral, the sallow face of the wasted alcoholic in the coffin was in such complete conflict with the looming volatile beast who prowled Vic's memories, the two images canceled each other out, leaving Vic with no mental picture of him at all. Vic couldn't even remember much about the funeral, anymore. Vic's Uncle Bill brought his wife, Marge, and Vic's young cousins, Bill Jr. and Nancy Ann. Understandably, Vic's mother didn't go, so it was the five of them, and the minister.

After close to ten years with little contact, Vic was amazed at how much they'd all changed. Making small talk was difficult. It was a stressful situation, but Vic remembered his uncle seemed unusually friendly and caring, working overtime to make everyone feel at ease. Vic couldn't help but wonder how different life would have been had his mother married Uncle Bill instead of The Old Man. The day of the funeral was cold and rainy, so the graveside service was cancelled in favor of a short ceremony in the cemetery's chapel conducted by a pastor Bill hired, a tall, glowering man who obviously never met Vic's father. Vic remembered thinking if the minister ever met The Old Man, he would have had a hard time saying the positive things he managed to come up with.

When the service was over, Vic's cousin, Nancy Ann, walked over and grasped his hand. She was fourteen, only a few years younger than Vic, and very pretty. Her face seemed almost to shine with a radiant warmth, in distinct contrast to the weather outside.

"Do you remember the trick you used to play on me, Allan?" she asked. Vic searched his memory and, try as he might, he couldn't figure out what she was talking about. He looked into her eyes and shrugged. "You used to pull quarters out of my ear when I was four or five. Remember?" She began to giggle. "You were so good at it, I really believed you could do it, that you were magic." Both of them smiled, then she leaned close. Vic thought she might kiss his cheek, but she only whispered, "Have a wonderful life." It was not until that moment he realized they would undoubtedly never see each other again, there being a hundred-twenty miles and an equal number of ambivalent feelings between the two families. Vic looked over toward the funeral chapel, and the memory of that long ago day dampened his eyes.

"You okay?" Roxanne asked, walking up to put her arm around his waist.

Vic snuffled and pointed to the bronze plate that marked the grave. Its edges were being overrun by the encroaching turf, as though the Earth was trying to slowly swallow it.

THOMAS ALLAN VICKERY
Cpl., U.S. Army Air Corps.
1926-1966

"Jesus, buddy. You never told me *his* name was Tom."

"Tom the Atom Bomb. That's what his friends called him. He was really something."

"Sounds like it. And you're Allan Thomas Vickery?"

Vic nodded. "After he became The Old Man, it made me feel good to know my name is the reverse of his, like I was his antithesis. Now I try to ignore the whole issue, until some little shit reminds me." Vic chuckled, and gave her a gentle shove.

She started to smile, but it looked as though a thought interrupted. "Do you hate him?"

"I used to hate what he became, but it's hard to hate a ghost. I hate the way he treated me, and the way he cheated on Mom. Of course, here I am with you ... "

Roxanne turned and slugged Vic hard on the arm. He was certain she was doing some acting, but the fisted blow hurt. He gave her a look like she'd hurled an insult. She glared at him. "Is that supposed to be funny?"

Her reaction shocked him. "No, but it's true."

"It was a cheap shot."

"If it was, I directed it at myself, not you."

"Listen, buddy! I swore I'd never hurt you. Don't *you* use me to hurt yourself. And like I said before, one word from you, and we'll end the whole thing."

Vic looked into Roxanne's eyes. "Why did you risk coming out here today?"

Roxanne did a visual sweep of the cemetery, then looked Vic in the eye and shrugged. "I don't know. You think this is a huge risk, coming out here?" She didn't give him time to answer. "I mean, who's gonna see us at a cemetery? Sure, we could have had an accident on the way out here, or on the way back, for that matter, but I figured you're a good driver." She cocked her head. "Besides, what's wrong with a little risk? Makes life interesting." She gripped his hands. "Anyway, we're friends first. Anything else comes second. Seemed like something a friend would do."

"Angie's never come here to the cemetery with me. Not once," Vic said.

"You know, I gotta come out and say it. I don't understand the deal with Angie."

"What deal?" Vic asked.

"Look, you're a handsome guy. In good shape. Smart. Sensitive. Artistic. I could go on." A smile pinched her face.

"I wish you would," Vic joked.

She lifted her arms and let them drop. "So, what's Angie's fucking problem? Speaking as a woman," she continued, giving Vic a wink, "you're hard to resist. I can't understand what you tell me about her, about the two of you. You have no idea what the problem is?"

"I've racked my brain. I have no clue." The air was chilly, and he crossed his arms over his chest and rubbed his upper arms. "I'm telling you, Rox, it used to be so good. Fantastic. She was the most unbelievable friend, lover. I never looked at another woman. Never would have. And I was so goddamned sure it would be different after my injury. Maybe she'd realize she almost lost me and want to get back to what we once had." He shrugged. "Nada."

"It doesn't make sense. Something must have changed before she did," Roxanne said, shaking her head.

"I've wondered if it's the pill she takes. I mean, neither of us ever wanted kids. Not at the same time, anyway," he added, smiling "She loves her job, and I get plenty of parenting in, as a teacher. Enough to suit me, anyway. By the time we were financially set and could afford kids, I had little enough of her attention as it was. I sure as heck didn't want to share it. So maybe it's the birth control. That's the only thing I ever came up with." He clicked his tongue. "Ain't that the shits? The drug that's supposed to make your relationship more carefree ... "

"Now it may be your turn to punch me, but I have to ask. Any chance *she's* having an affair?"

"Angie? No fucking way." He looked down, then locked on Roxanne's eyes and grinned. "And that's not just ego talking, like I believe I'm smart, sensitive, and what were all the other things you listed?" He smirked. "No, there's no way in hell. She goes to work, comes right home, and she's up in her miniature room the rest of the night. That's it. Oh, very occasionally, she stops for a drink after work with the other secretaries or some girlfriends, but not more than a few times a month. Not often enough to be having an affair, anyway."

"You're not pissed that I asked?" Vic shook his head. "I mean, you have to look at all the possibilities," Roxanne said. "I even wondered about Tom at first, when he stopped coming on to me."

"Yeah?" Vic asked, then he broke out in a huge grin. "Hey, wouldn't it be a hoot if Tom and Angie had a thing going? God, wouldn't that be nuts?"

Roxanne managed a laugh, but with little true mirth. "It's worse than that. Maybe, just maybe, I could compete with Angie or some other woman. But Tom's lover comes in a bottle. I think he even drinks before work, now. It's gonna ruin his liver, if it hasn't already. Time he gets home, he couldn't get it up with a blast of helium." She looked at the sky. "He used to be something. A really great husband."

Vic looked at The Old Man's grave marker. "Sounds like another Tom I knew." Vic stepped forward and wrapped Roxanne in his arms. "When he was my dad, this guy was pretty great, too," Vic said. "Then he turned into The Old Man. The last time I saw him alive, I was twelve." Vic murmured into her ear, a blip above a whisper. "He came over to the house one afternoon and asked if I was alone. I said yes." Vic stepped back, but held one of Roxanne's hands. "He was driving a new red Bonneville convertible, and I could tell he was in a hurry. He got out, walked real fast to the trunk, opened it and yanked out his favorite shotgun, a twelve gauge Remington over and under. He pulled it out of its case, and for a second, I thought he was going to shoot me. He could see I was scared, but didn't realize why. He said, 'Don't you be afraid of this gun. I'm giving it to you so you can hunt when you get older. Don't let your mother take it.'" Vic smiled at Roxanne. "It's still in its case, leaning against the wall in a closet off the den. I'm not into recreational killing. Then he pulled out his golf clubs and gave them to me, too; the same ones I use today. He got back in his car, pulled out into the street, then yelled for me to come out there. I walked up and he said, 'Have you ever thought that if you dug a hole to China, you'd come through feet first?' I looked down, you know, to try to form a mental picture. When I looked up, he'd already driven away. He headed for California and never came back. Not until his funeral." Vic put his arm around Roxanne and guided her toward his car. He chuckled as he opened the door for her.

"What?" she asked.

"The son-of-a-bitch is six feet closer to China than we are."

~ * ~

That night proved to be a long one. Vic got little, if any, sleep, although there were some times when the numbers on the digital clock did an unexplained fast-forward. Regardless, the events of the day played in Technicolor as he tried his best to remain still and not disturb Angie as she slept.

Roxanne. Roxanne's mischievous look as she came through the back door that morning. Their banter as they drank coffee. Vic wondered if she was as nervous as he was. He was jittery because he believed they would probably make love that morning, but Roxanne knew she would have to tell him her period started early. Having to reveal something like that would have made him nervous, he decided. Until she did tell him, Vic felt like a high school kid, wondering how or when to initiate a kiss. He hoped he would read her cues correctly, although her seductive and suggestive talk led him to believe she was as eager as he to let go. Her lips were soft and yielding, but she pushed her tongue between his lips and teeth with an ardor that surprised him. Then, as surprisingly, she pulled back, cradled his face in her hands, and grimaced. "I have bad news," she said. The idea she may be having second thoughts cart-wheeled through his mind, but what really caught him off-guard was the rush of relief he felt in the seconds after she explained her period's early arrival. Even though he ached for the woman who made it so clear she wanted him, or seemed to, the voice in his head was persistently negative. The Old Man. Do you want to be The Old Man?

137

With her revelation came a wave of relief. They would not have intercourse. Some necking and petting. Kiss, and cop a good feel. That didn't seem so much like adultery. Not real adultery. Kissing. That wasn't sinful. Okay, maybe. And touching her breast was worse, but still not like getting it on. "No, it's okay," he told her. "Really. I want to hold and kiss you today," he'd said, emphasizing his voracity with another open-mouthed kiss.

His mind made the shift from reality to fantasy. What if her period hadn't started? What would it have been like? Would she be as good a lover as she led him to believe? Vic knew enough of the map of her body to form a realistic image of her naked. He could envision her thighs spread for him. The warmth of them as they wrapped around him. Her heat. Her wetness. Would he have used a rubber? It would have been, after all, only a day before her period? Probably safe. The thought of her period brought him back from that fantasy, but his mind was persistent. It drifted to another one, just as exciting. What if he had taken her up on her offer? "There's no reason why I can't take care of you." He replayed those words. Even the memory made him so hard, it felt like he was going to hemorrhage. He was dying to say yes, to feel her hands on him. And would it have been a hand-job, or would she have used her mouth? He was pretty certain a blow-job was what she offered. Years. It had been years since Angie did it. And only once. He didn't ask her to, and he warned her when he was about to come, but she didn't pull away. He remembered how she jumped off the bed, ran into the bathroom, and spit his semen into the toilet. It sounded like she was going to retch.

That memory softened his erection. He looked at the clock. 5:56. *May as well get up*, he thought. There were things he wanted to do before he met the guys to play golf at Heather Hills. The thought of being with the guys who were with him when he was hit by Tom Bayer's golf ball brought on another barrage of questions. If he still had his "new" golf game, something he constantly feared might slip away, what would he tell them when they asked what the deal was? How much would he let them know?

They were his friends, and he didn't want to lie to them. But was leaving selected bits of information out really lying? He decided he'd fashion a tale about his mind having a better connection with his body now, since he came out of his coma. Nothing about Bass and playing golf at Loon's Lair. They'd think he was nuts, for sure.

He wasn't even certain of the read Angie and Roxanne had on the entire episode. Strangely, neither of them ever brought it up, almost as though they hoped he might forget about it, and the entire embarrassing idea might all go away. Neither of them ever saw him play golf before or after the coma, so they could be assuming he exaggerated the difference "coma world" made in his game. For Vic's part, he was happy to let it all drop. That freed him to sort it out for himself at his own pace. Admittedly, the progress was slow. Maybe I shouldn't try to understand, he thought, like Bascolm kept telling him. Accept what happened, and toss what didn't make sense into the category of the unknowables.

That soothed him, and the next thing he knew, it was 6:45. He was surprised that he'd fallen asleep, or that he was still drowsy. When his mind skipped to the fact that, in a few hours, he would be on the fourth hole at Heather Hills, where his weird journey began, he snapped fully alert. There would be no more sleep.

After breakfast, that Halloween Saturday, Vic did some odd jobs around the house, but thoughts of the fourth hole wouldn't leave him alone. What would it be like to stand where he stood the day his world went spinning wildly out of his control? He finally came to the conclusion that he was eager to confront the hole where destiny interrupted his life.

So later, along with his partners from the Chili Open—Sal, Phil, and Ron—Vic played golf at Heather Hills. From the opening tee shot, his game was spot on. His three friends were unable to hide their astonishment.

"Jesus," Phil said loudly to Ron and Sal while Vic readied himself to hit his drive on the third tee, "this is like watching one of those seven-year old kids who play Chopin concertos without taking a lesson." Vic wondered if Phil was trying to put pressure on him to see if Vic would cave in.

"Nothing short of otherworldly," Ron said.

Vic rocketed his shot a good two hundred-fifty yards. It dropped and rolled to a stop in the middle of the fairway.

"Damn," Sal said as Vic stooped to pick up his tee, "you're hittin' it almost as far as me, except you know where yours is going." He traded an open-handed five with Vic as they passed each other. Sal walked up and teed his ball, started to address it, then turned and leaned against his driver with his forearm resting on the butt end of the club. "I'm not shitting you," Sal said through a wide grin, "I can't even concentrate on what I'm doin' here." He gave Vic a look like an arresting officer. "You're eventually going to have to try to explain all this."

Vic shrugged and raised his eyebrows. "Maybe over some beers when we're done."

It was warm for Halloween, and the course was crowded. With so many groups playing, the round lasted almost five hours. That included some extra time on the fourth hole, where Vic's head once stopped the forward progress of Tom Bayer's Top Flite.

"Christ, that's almost exactly where your ball landed in when we were playing the open, kid," Phil said when they arrived at the green.

"That's right," Ron said, raising his eyebrows. "Talk about a weird—"

"Yeah, especially since this's the first one of your iron shots that's missed a green," Sal said. "Come on now, admit it. You're a little spooked, right? Or did you hit it there on purpose to show us you can pitch it closer than you did then, with this new game of yours?"

Vic winked and laid on the sarcasm. "Yeah, right. I missed the green on purpose." He tried to appear nonchalant, as though hole number four hadn't been eating at him all morning. In fact, it shouldered past thoughts of Roxanne and was the last thing Vic remembered thinking about as he tossed sleeplessly the night before. As it turned out, he was happy to confront the hole where his life forever changed. *Maybe facing down number four at Heather Hills will help me get a grip on myself,* Vic thought. *On my life.*

The irony of the whole situation had him shaking his head. He could control his body in a way he'd never been able to before, and repeat a golf swing with the regularity of a clock's swinging pendulum. But he couldn't control his mind; he couldn't suppress the desires and urges that were making his personal life swing in directions he'd never imagined. Never wanted. At the same time, he couldn't seem to make himself draw away from them. Like years before, when he used to smoke cigarettes, he told himself over and over as he lit up he was killing himself, but craved the hit of smoke that would settle the gnawing ache inside. Getting beaned on the fourth hole set events in motion that gave him the game he always wished for, but the backside of the bargain was an inability to stay on the course of a life he could be proud of, unhappy as that life was.

"But seriously," Phil asked, "what the hell's the deal? You get smacked and, all of a sudden, you're the best player I know. How can that be?"

"Like I told you guys, after the round, over some beers. And remember, it's only the fourth hole. I had happy streaks in the past, too. My game could head south at any moment," he said. He was glad he'd thought to put that in. It relieved some pressure, like admitting to an audience you're nervous at the beginning of a speech.

While he got ready to hit his pitch shot, the idea of actually coming clean with the guys worked on his mind. At one level he wanted to explain the huge change in his game to his friends. Still, another part of him wrapped itself around the whole coma experience and wanted to keep it a private matter. There wasn't much about Vic's life he wouldn't share with people he knew as well as his golf buddies, but there was a part of him that didn't want to discuss it. Almost like Bascolm's concept of how playing golf for money cheapened the game, telling his friends about something so life-altering would degrade the coma experience. There was no way he could put into words the monumental rush of emotion he experienced when he thought back to Bascolm and the others at Loon's Lair. So why try?

Vic's final reason for not telling them was pure ego. He worried spinning the yarn about 'Coma World,' as Angie liked to call it, would make them wonder if he was half a bubble off. Telling the nurse's aide was easy; he was still groggy, and didn't care what she thought of him anyway. But telling close friends something that hard to believe was frightening. Something he would not do, he decided. Besides, he thought, telling them wouldn't explain anything because what I know doesn't account for everything, even to me.

With these thoughts running through his mind, Vic couldn't concentrate on the shot and wound up chunking the pitch on number four. His ball rolled past the hole and almost off the green. "Not a hacker anymore, eh?" he joked as he slid his pitching wedge into his bag and pulled out his putter. None of his friends responded beyond a chuckle. They all were involved in finding the hole with their own golf balls. Vic needed two putts to sink his, and that bogey turned out to be his only one that day.

When they finished the round, they went into the clubhouse and Vic sprung for the beer. Walking back to the table with a pitcher and four mugs, he still wondered what he would tell them. As he poured the beer, an idea occurred to him. "Here's to being back and playing golf with you jerks again," he said, raising his mug in a toast.

Ron raised his mug to tap Vic's. "We may be jerks, but we're the best jerks you have."

Everyone laughed, then Vic gave them a look that said he wanted to be serious. "All right," he began, "let's put the 'new game' thing to bed. If I could tell you exactly how it happened, I would. But I can't. Like I can't tell you how I paint a landscape. I mean, come on, guys, don't you think I wonder about it myself? The only difference between the golf thing and my artistic skills is the golf game came all at once, the artistic stuff was gradual and took a lot of effort. So yeah, the coma obviously had something to do with it." Vic stopped to take a drink of beer and invent more story. "The only theory I can come up with is maybe it's because I was disconnected from my body for a while. I came out of the coma, and maybe the hook-up between my mind and my body is stronger now. I always knew what I

142

wanted my body to do. Actually doing it was the problem." Vic shrugged. "Now it's not, I guess." A story he'd heard on the radio spun through his mind, and decided he could use it. "Or it could be magic," Vic continued. "I was listening to that guy on some oldies station ... what's his name ... Kase something?"

"Casey Kasem?" Ron ventured.

"Yeah, that the guy." Vic topped off everyone's beers. "American Top Twenty, or Forty, I don't remember. Anyway, he was going to play *Monday Monday*, but first he told this really cool story about how *The Mamas and The Papas* formed. He said Doherty and Michelle Phillips wanted Cass Elliot in the group, but John Phillips wasn't so sure. Didn't think her voice fit, or something." He sipped his beer. "Anyhow, according to Kasem, Elliot walked past a construction site and somebody dropped a piece of pipe that hit her on the head. She didn't go comatose or anything. Wound up with a concussion and a bad headache, if I remember correctly, but according to Kasem, she gained some notes at the top of her vocal range."

"For real?" Sal asked.

Vic raised his hands like he was getting robbed. "Hey, I don't know. I'm just repeating what that Kasem guy said. Anyway, guess when John Phillips heard she could hit the higher notes, he gave her an audition and that's how she became a Mama. Elliot even went back to the job site and found the pipe. She called it her 'magic pipe,' and Kasem said she kept it." Vic smiled, put his hands next to each side of his head, and wiggled his fingers. "I still have the ball my neighbor smacked me with. Maybe it's my 'magic ball.' Abracadabra," he intoned, making his eyes open until they bulged.

"Man, I wish somebody would clobber me," Phil said, looking around to see if the others thought he was as funny as he apparently did.

Vic shot Phil a look like he'd farted. However, what Phil said gave Vic a chance to make a point out the trade-offs that came with the new territory. He slugged down the rest of his beer, then all the humor drained from his voice. "Well, here's some truth to chew on, so pay close attention,

Phil. Nothing comes for free." He raised an eyebrow. "I've been through some real heavy shit since the Chili Open, both mental and physical. Depression over being puny and weak. Not able to teach, run, or even play golf. And, worried I might never be able to do the things I love again. It's a dream come true, being able to play golf as well as I can now, but in reality, shooting par or better isn't going to change my life in any significant way. For a teacher from Toledo, a good golf game is like having a great sound system in your car. Cool to listen to, but it doesn't really help you get down the road."

Ron and Sal both grinned. Phil stared into his half-empty beer glass and didn't look up, apparently feeling some sting. Vic enjoyed that, in the way only one who has been stung could. He clapped Phil on the back and topped off his mug.

~ * ~

The whole next week, Vic and Roxanne spent as much time as they could together, merely necking and petting like teenage lovers. Vic believed it deepened their friendship, and he enjoyed their playful sessions together. All the while, he tried his best to melt Angie's chilly demeanor, but try as he might, the results were never what he prayed for.

The following Monday, Roxanne was at the back door minutes after Angie left for work. Vic tried to be casual, talking and drinking coffee with her as they usually did, but both of them knew it was all a charade. They were going to get naked. Her period was over and they were going to make love. Vic stood before they'd downed more than a few sips of Maxwell House, clasped Roxanne's hand, and led her into the living room. In seconds, they collapsed onto the carpet's soft pile. Vic knew for certain they weren't going to stop. This was going to happen. The realization he would soon be making love to a woman other than Angie was every bit as scary as it was exciting. An image of The Old Man grazed his cortex, but Roxanne made the thought ricochet when she unfastened his belt and pulled down the zipper. "You should have stayed in your pajamas," she rasped, pulling his jeans over his hips.

Vic slid his thumbs under the waist-band of her slacks. "Keep taking my clothes off, you'll eventually get to my jammies."

"O-o-o, the boy sleeps in his all-together," she said, smirking. They locked into a kiss as they continued to pull at each other's clothes. Vic peeled Roxanne's sweater off, and found she hadn't bothered with a bra. The buttery light from the window painted her skin, and Vic savored the glow the sun put on the curves of her lithe body. She was firmer than Angie. For a woman who claimed she never exercised, she was amazingly trim. Her skin lay taut over the structures it covered, and he found her body almost magnetic. He had to touch her. He slid his hands into the close-cropped hair on the sides of her head, then ran them onto her shoulders, and across her back. Gripping her hip bones like handles, he eased her onto her back and crawled over her like a starving predator. He was filled with a blur of sensations and feelings. All of his senses channeled simultaneous sights, smells, flavors, sounds, and textures that overflowed his conscience, leaving him bobbing happily in a flood of sensory thrills and delights. His mind zinged from nipple, to moan, to musk. The tickle of pubic hair. Salty-sweetness. Coupled with the intensity of emotion he felt, he was a starving man at a banquet. Roxanne's hands heated his body as she touched and stroked. Her mouth felt like a soft furnace. The familiar pleasure of tightness began to build, low in his groin while he enjoyed her wet suction. He knew it would be soon, and Roxanne's lips made a popping sound when he pulled out. "Let yourself go, lover," she cooed. "And don't make me do all the work," she added. She pulled rhythmically on his hips. His orgasm soon exploded, ripping through his body. He was blind. Deaf. For an instant, it was like he ceased to exist, except for the waves of ecstasy crashing around inside him. The collisions slowly came to an end. He rolled over, lifted her, and wrapped his arms around her.

"Sweet Jesus," he managed to mumble in her ear.

"Glad it was good," she said, pulling her head back to give him a wink. "I wasn't sure I still remembered how." She giggled. "My doctor says us older gals need extra protein in our diets." She gave him her patented smirk. "Thanks for the supplement."

Roxanne's bawdy sense of humor never ceased to make him happy and comfortable. Then he rolled Roxanne onto her back, and began a slide of his own, his tongue tracing a circuitous wet path. He paused at her navel, nipped at and licked the bud-like whorl of flesh, and continued his descent. Roxanne's knees rose toward her breasts, and she began to rock her hips. When Vic heard her moan, it was as though he was underwater, feeling the sound as much as hearing. Guttural. Throbbing. Increasing in tempo and intensity. He relished every moment, but time ran out too soon. Roxanne locked his head in her thighs, and her final moan reached its crescendo.

The two of them lay, their bodies entangled. They didn't speak. Vic listened to her breathe, and thought about what they'd done. He tried to block Angie from his thoughts, but it was impossible. He had sex with someone other than his wife, the woman he vowed to love, honor, and cherish. Until death. Until the end of time, he thought, remembering the lyrics Meatloaf bellowed in *Dashboard Lights*.

"What?" Roxanne asked, quelling the silence between them. "I can tell your mind's working overtime."

"Paradise by the dashboard lights," Vic deadpanned.

"What's that got to do with your living room?" she asked, the impish grin turning the corners of her mouth northward. "You want round two to be in your car or something?" She shrugged, her breasts jiggling pleasingly. "I'm game," she allowed, then her face became serious, all the mirth draining away. "You going to be okay with all this?"

"Are you?" Vic countered.

"I asked first, but for your information, yeah. I'm fine." She sat up, cross-legged. Vic marveled over how at ease she was with nudity. "Look, tonight, Tom's gonna get off work, go bowling, and roll in about ten or so. I'll give him a smooch, heat up his dinner, and go read. He'll eat, sit down in front of the tube, drink more beer, and pass out." She rocked backward, using her arms for support. "He'll wake up about two or three, stumble into bed, and I won't know he's there until I wake up in the morning." She kept her legs crossed, but rolled up onto her hands and knees, and gave Vic a quick kiss. "Net result of our little session this morning on my marriage? Zilch," she said with finality. She rocked back and sat down hard, and her breasts taking another arresting bounce. "How 'bout for you? Anything going to change tonight?"

Vic slowly shook his head.

"So see? No difference in their lives, at all." She crawled over and gave him a long hug. "But big change in ours, buddy," she whispered, her breath hot against his neck. She pulled away and looked straight into his eyes. "Our lives will be a lot happier. Mine will, at least." She stuck out the tip of her tongue. "Already is."

Everything Roxanne said made sense. Vic wanted it to. Needed it to. He wanted to be okay with all of it, because he needed her. He experienced feelings of closeness with Roxanne he hadn't felt with anyone in years. And she was a true sexual *partner*, unflappable and unblushing in her relish for erotic pleasure. Vic had what he longed for, someone who wanted him. Someone to talk with and to make love with. Someone with whom he didn't need to censor his impulses. He was not about to let go of her.

They chatted for quite a while, light conversation that seemed entirely incongruous between a naked man and woman lying on a living room floor. Then, Roxanne looked at the clock on the mantel. "It's almost ten, buddy. We better get on with round two, because I have to get some wash done." She put her hand on his. "The regular way, this time, doll. But it doesn't have to be a regular position." She raised her brow, and motioned toward the garage with a tilt of her head. "You want me in your car?"

Vic found the thought of making love in his Mazda strangely titillating. How long had it been since he'd had sex in a car? College maybe? Probably high school. It was an exciting idea, but not, he decided, what he wanted that day. For their first intercourse, he'd have preferred a bed, but the carpet on the living room floor was his second choice. "I like the way you think, but not this time," he said, pulling some hidden condoms from under the couch.

"Now that's a novel spot for them," she said, her laughter spilling between them.

Not since the summer with Reefer had he felt so at ease with, and desired by, a woman. Roxanne hit his system like a strong drug, and the resulting rush left him awash in euphoric addiction. No junkie could match the high Vic rode that day, and for the rest of that week as he and Roxanne attended to each other's mental and physical yearnings. When she left to go home, however, Vic discovered although the exhilaration when they were together was exquisite, the downside was as extreme. As with any addict, the mere thought of the unavailability of his "fix" agitated and upset him. When he watched her walk through their neighbor's back yard on her way home, it felt like vermin were clawing their way around his insides. The weekends were worse yet. Saturday and Sunday seemed endless. Vic saw her drive by Saturday morning, and it was all he could do not to run out into the street.

Additionally, he felt like he was crossing a pond thinly skinned with ice when he was around Angie. His relationship with Roxanne changed everything about his life and his outlook on it, yet he had to keep every interaction with Angie the same so she wouldn't suspect anything. He had to keep his attitude and demeanor around the house as it had been, and the more he tried to remember how he usually acted, the harder it was to feel confidence in his recollection. Acting. That's the way it felt. He was like an actor who couldn't exactly remember the lines, so he improvised and hoped that was good enough. It finally occurred to him that if Angie did sense any difference, he could merely point out how the coma and his new golf game affected him. That idea defused his worries.

Still, another problem reared its head. Regardless of how hard he tried to block them, Vic was soon haunted by visions of himself as The Old Man. He could no longer claim to be the reverse of his father. And, for the first time in Vic's life, he found himself wondering what drove Tom Vickery to cheat. Vic's mother was a wonderful mom, but what kind of wife was she? What kind of lover? Friend? Did the man Vic hated over the years for philandering find himself in the kind of marriage Vic was in? He'd heard of men "marrying their mothers," but he'd always discounted that as Freudian bullshit. Now he wondered if his own mother and Angie shared some of the same traits.

No matter, cheating on Angie didn't conform to Vic's image of who he was, or ever wanted to be. He tried to stay attached to Roxanne's rationale, telling himself what he shared with Roxanne was what Angie didn't want anyway; that the other parts of their marital relationship weren't affected by the affair. From that standpoint, Roxanne was actually performing a service for Angie. Doing her a favor. For short periods, he could bluff himself into believing a little of that, but, in his soul, he believed he was a double-dealing bastard. Like The Old Man.

The illicit relationship with Roxanne proved fertile soil for a bumper crop of self-loathing. Vic was guilt-ridden over what he was doing, but he knew the pain of ending the affair would be excruciating. Not only that, but in a way that even Vic recognized as convoluted, he started to think of recommitting to his marriage as cheating on Roxanne, making him guilty of cheating on two women, not one. In moments of lucidity, that made no sense. Of course, very little of Vic's life did make any sense, at that point. His every waking hour was spent thinking about the situation at some level—trying to talk himself out of seeing Roxanne, or waiting impatiently for their next meeting. Often simultaneously. Vic thought back to the warning Dr. Pembrooke gave him, about not making life-altering decisions for several months, until his psyche was completely healed. Ultimately, asking himself if the head shot had anything to do with his feelings for Roxanne was like asking a drunk if he was okay to drive home.

By the week before Thanksgiving, Vic believed he would lose his mind if he didn't settle on some course of action and take it. Ending the affair with Roxanne was not on the table, so Monday morning, after Roxanne left for home, he began looking at ads for apartments in the newspaper. He almost hoped taking that step might dissuade him from doing anything more, but that afternoon, he found himself in the parking lot of an apartment building a few miles from Bittersweet, waiting for the manager to arrive. Vic glanced, again, at the page from the newspaper folded in his lap, against the steering wheel.

FOR RENT. Nice furnished 1 bedrm garden apt. Good
area. Utilities inc.
Cable. $145 per mo. Refundable deposit.

The man who answered the phone when Vic called seemed hurried, and didn't offer much information. "Just come out and see it," he said in answer to the questions Vic asked. The building was in Maumee, probably a five-iron shot from the turnpike, and Toledo. Vic knew he needed to shovel snow that winter, and cut grass in the spring, which dovetailed into his other requirement, not too close to Angie, but not too far from Roxanne. This place seemed like a compromise that would fill all the bills.

Vic sat in the parking lot that Monday afternoon, fighting to make himself drive away. "What the fuck am I doing?" he said aloud. There were times he felt like a passenger in his own life, and this was one of those. *Allan Vickery,* he thought. *Vic. Mr. Stable. The happily married, happy-go-lucky, mild mannered art teacher was leaving his wife because he became involved with the older wife of the man who accidently hit him with a golf ball and put Vic into a life-changing coma. Vic, a guy who spent most of his life loathing his father because he played around with ladies and broke his wife's heart, was doing exactly the same thing. To Angie. To his mother; putting her through another round of infidelity-once-removed.* "You couldn't write this shit," he said, aloud. And yet, try as he might, he couldn't make himself key the ignition and go home to Angie. Not the Angie he lived with now. If she was the Angie of old, Vic wouldn't even be sitting there.

The black pickup the manager told Vic to look for appeared. The driver was burly, with red hair and an even redder flush to his skin. Vic grabbed a big breath for courage, climbed out of his car and hurried to meet him at the door.

"You're the guy?" the man said, before Vic could speak.

"Yes, sir," Vic said, extending his hand. "Allan Vickery. I called this morning."

"Ames," the man growled. He gripped the handle of his lunchbox with his right hand like he feared Vic might snatch it, so he made a clumsy semi-effort at shaking Vic's hand with his left one. "It's down here," Ames barked, at drill sergeant volume, and started down a short flight of stairs tucked inside the building's entrance. The carpet pile was worn on the steps and in the hall. The smell of food was strong, but Vic couldn't have named any particular dish. "This's the one," Ames said, pushing open the unlatched door. Vic thought that strange, but he followed the big man inside.

"Garden apartment" apparently referred to the fact the floor was four or five feet below ground level. The windows provided a view of the parking lot through scraggly bushes and flowerbeds overrun with dandelions. The place smelled of cigarette smoke, and an unidentifiable damp must. Off-white walls defined the living room, the kitchen, the bathroom, and the bedroom, each smaller by half than the corresponding room in the house on Bittersweet. Every switch plate was surrounded by a dark halo of the finger-smudges contributed by past residents. The brown carpet wasn't as worn as its counterpart in the hallway, but Vic wouldn't have laid on it to watch TV. Not without a good vacuuming, at the very least.

"Gonna get the gal to do some sprucin' up," Ames volunteered. "Front me the deposit and the first month's rent, you can go ahead and move in." He looked at his watch, apparently to double-check the date. "Close enough to the first, far as I'm concerned. Deposit and rent's both the same, one forty-five. Two-ninety total. Look around. I'll be upstairs, the apartment right above this one." He started for the door, but turned. "Floors is concrete. You won't hear no noise from me. Oh, an' don't lock the door. Last asshole lived here lit out with the key." Ames walked out. He gave the door a pull, but it didn't close all the way.

Vic walked over and turned on the TV. Sure enough, the reception was cable-clear, but the tube was obviously color-confused. He fooled with the tint and color level knobs, eventually getting the pigmentation of a woman's face out of lizard-range. "Jesus fucking Christ," he said aloud, snapping the set off, wondering if he would be able to handle living there. *The house on Bittersweet is a mansion compared to this,* he thought, looking around. On Bittersweet, he had a garage. A yard, with a swimming pool. He and Angie both kept their house clean and tidy. Even though the apartment was bare except for the furniture, it had a disheveled look. He sat on the sofa, then bent to smell one of the other cushions. Nothing distinct, one way or the other, he decided. The bathroom had a shower/tub, a stool, and a small sink. There was a mirror, but no medicine cabinet, and the shower curtain was ripped and scummy. The bedroom had a closet with two hangers lying on the floor, a bed with a nightstand, and a dresser. The mattress was still encased in its shipping plastic, yellowed and milky with age. He checked to make sure the surface wasn't dirty, then lay down. Not bad, he thought. "But the fucking plastic's coming off," he mumbled. The curtains weren't attractive, but they were opaque and covered the window completely, important in a ground-level place. There was a small closet in the hall that housed the hot water heater and the furnace. Vic turned the thermostat up and heat came on, the blower squawked briefly, then quieted itself. *Gas forced-air,* he thought. *Place will heat up quick. And air conditioning in the summer,* he noted. The kitchen had a small refrigerator, electric stove, and a sink imbedded in a counter with a chipped Formica surface. A small dinette with two chairs sat under a hanging light in a small nook, which opened to the living room. *I'll put my easel right here,* he thought. Vic opened the 'fridge. It was good and cool inside, and a jar of maraschino cherries resided in the rack on the door. The freezer held two ice cube trays, both empty, and a frozen green bean.

Vic slapped at the freezer door, slamming it shut. "The fuck, Ange," he said. "If you could have stayed with the program. Stayed the way you used to be. Goddamned bait and switch." *Or if I could be a duplicitous motherfucker like The Old Man,* he thought. *I could live at home, and see Roxanne on the side.* There were tears that wanted out, but he blinked them back. He walked into the living room and looked out at the slate sky. He never in his wildest bad dreams would have imagined himself living in a place like this one, not at the age of thirty-three, anyway. Not a successful art teacher. A college grad. A guy who sold paintings, and had some stature in Toledo's art community. *Hell, my stuff's even been in some state and national shows,* he thought. He looked around. The apartment did have two things going for it, he decided. It wasn't going to over-stretch his finances, which would be strained with the cost of this place on top of his usual expenses. And, it was close enough to Bittersweet without being too close. "I sure as hell hope this isn't a fucking mistake," he muttered.

He trudged up the stairs to the apartment above his. On a piece of masking tape, scrawled in child-like looking script, it said: G. Ames. Below that, it said "Maniger." Vic scoffed and knocked.

The door flew open like Ames was waiting with his hand on the knob.

"Well?" he boomed. "Whatcha think?" Before Vic could say a word, Ames cut him off.

"Wifey trying to steal your ass in the divorce?" he asked.

"Divorce?" Vic parroted, caught completely off guard.

"Yeah. Looks like that's the deal. We get a lot of divorces. Women sometimes, but mostly guys," Ames added, as though what he shared was top secret. His voice dropped to a near-whisper. "She givin' you a lot of shit?" he asked, his eyes twinkling in the shadows created by his cliff-like forehead. "She starts getting to you," he went on, his hand cupped for privacy, "just say the word." He winked and mouthed the words, "I know people." He waited several beats, then exploded in laughter. "You should have seen your face, boy. Thought your eyes was gonna cross." He opened the door and waved Vic in.

When Vic did, the sight that met him almost did skew his vision. The walls were lined, floor to ceiling, with bows, crossbows, and arrows. There wasn't a space big enough to put an open hand against the wall without touching a weapon or a projectile.

"Competition archer," Ames said, apparently reading Vic's surprise. "Done it all my life. Pretty damned good. Got a lot of ribbons and cups," he said, absently waving an arm toward the myriad awards littering every horizontal surface in the room. "Sagittarius," he explained. "Eighth of December. Natural archer." The big man's smile revealed yellow teeth, and gums nearly as red as the cherries Vic remembered in the refrigerator. "So," he said, reaching over for an Old Milwaukee sitting on his desk, "you going to take it? Like I said, I'll have 'Livia give it a once over. I'll give her a little of this," he said, slamming his fist against his open palm and leering. "She ain't great in the sack, but she cleans a good apartment."

"I have to sign a lease or anything?" Vic asked, thinking he could use that as an excuse to decide against moving in.

"Nah," Ames boomed. "Us divorced guys can't be making commitments like that. Peel me off a check for the two-ninety, and we'll be good 'til January." He gulped down some beer. "Due on the first, but make sure I get it by the tenth. Shove it under my door." He swept his arm in the direction of the desk and burped. "You can write the check over there."

It was then that Vic realized the wall space wasn't exclusively covered with archery equipment. A framed print, one Vic had seen before, adorned the space above the desk. At a distance, the image appeared to be of a skull. Closer in, the skull became a woman sitting in front of a mirror, surrounded by brushes, combs, and cosmetics. "All is Vanity," was printed across the bottom. Charles Allan. Vic was poor at remembering names of artists in his art history classes, but he remembered Allan because the spelling was like Vic's name, not the more common "Allen."

Vic pushed some award ribbons out of the way, leaned over, and began to write. He trembled and he wasn't certain if it was from nerves over whether he was making the right choice, or because Ames was behind him, out of his line of sight. Vic finished, turned, and handed Ames the check. "Any chance I could have a cat? Living with me in the apartment, you know," Vic added.

Ames shrugged. "Don't know, tell you the truth. I'll ask the guy who owns the place. Main thing would be, ya don't let it stink up the joint," he said, before taking another huge gulp of beer. He belched again. "And don't let it roam any. I put a bolt through a stray out back the other day."

"Bolt?" Vic asked.

"With a crossbow." Ames smirked. "People call 'em arrows, but a crossbow fires bolts. That's the actual correct terminology," he advised. Vic made a retreat for the door, and Ames followed. "An' I'll get that lock changed over. Key will be in the mailbox tomorrow, along with the key to the mailbox, so you can lock that up, too. Keep nosy assholes out of your business." Vic made it into the hall and turned to say goodbye. Before he could, Ames had one more piece of advice. "'Nother thing," he said, back in his confidential voice. "Things get too bad, you know, pressures start building," he said, pointing at his crotch, "Yohoko Health Spa, out on Centennial Road." He grinned again, and Vic wondered how far gums could recede before teeth started falling out. "Them little chink gals, they give a good blow job. Not too expensive, either." He winked. "Be sure to tell 'em Gilly-san sent you."

That last little tidbit cemented Vic's dislike for Ames. Weapons nut. Animal killer. Misogynist. Did he cheat on his taxes, too? Regardless, Vic extended his hand as formally as he could make it seem. "Thank you very much, Mr. Ames. I appreciate the tip."

"Gilly, to you." This time, he grabbed Vic's hand and shook it. "Think you'll like it here."

What the hell did I do? Vic wondered, as he walked to his car. It seemed his life kept getting stranger and more complicated by the day, but he didn't feel like he could blame anyone other than himself. Sometimes it almost felt like he was an outsider, part of an audience watching this guy named Vic muddle along. He stopped and looked back at the building, at the windows belonging to the apartment he paid a month's rent for. "My new place," he said, dropped into his car, and drove back to Bittersweet.

Vic still wasn't sure he would ever move into the apartment. There was no lease, so at worst, he would be out three hundred bucks. Angie wouldn't know, because they kept their money separate. The mortgage, the Edison bill, every debt they had in common, was paid with two checks, half from each of them. The deposit and first month put a sizeable hole in Vic's account, but he'd spent practically nothing during his convalescence, so he was actually about even after writing the check. Best case scenario, he could take his new "friend," Gilly, a six-pack of Old Milwaukee, explain things had changed, and maybe sweet-talk him into retuning the month's rent, if not the deposit, too.

That evening, Angie was uncharacteristically chatty, and Vic had a hard time maintaining a conversation with his mind preoccupied, shuffling through the rooms of the apartment.

"Are you listening?" Angie asked, while Vic picked at his chicken pot pie. He didn't like them. The crust was always dry, and the filling that immersed the meat was too viscous to counter the situation.

"Sure," he said. "Molly's husband, Fred."

"Don't you even feel sorry for him? I mean, I know you don't like him all that much, but what a blow."

Vic saved himself on the name of who she talked about, but he missed what the blow was, so he homed in on his dislike for the man. "The last time we went out with them, he practically hijacked us into going to that comedy club. That would have been fine, but when he wound up drunk and practically got us thrown out for heckling the comic, Jesus, how embarrassing." Vic moved a piece of crust out of the way so he could get a fork-full of chicken. "But, yeah, that's terrible news," he offered, going for a comment he hoped would make it sound like he knew what she was talking about.

Angie wagged her head. "And they say it's metastasized," she added.

Cancer. So, that was the blow he'd suffered. "Sure, I feel bad for him, but he does smoke like a chimney," Vic said, convinced he was up to speed.

Angie gave him a strange look. "But, Vic. It's not lung cancer."

Vic shrugged, as though he'd known that all along. "I'd still bet smoking didn't help," he said. "I'm glad I quit when I did."

The same was true the next morning when Roxanne arrived. She picked up on the fact he was distracted, and even asked if something was wrong several times. Vic managed to convince her everything was fine, and they made love in the Mazda, this time. "Man," she said, as they cuddled afterward, "either cars were bigger, or I was more limber back in the fifties."

"Maybe some of both," Vic replied, "but you're awesome, no matter where we do it."

"Yeah? Someday I'd like to try it in an actual bed," she joked. Vic thought of the apartment. He still wasn't positive he was moving in, so he wasn't about to mention it. He actually enjoyed having a secret, and he wondered how and when he would reveal it. Or if.

After she left, Vic drove over to get the key out of the mailbox. When he went downstairs, the apartment door stood open, and the sound of a vacuum roared inside. Vic peeked in, and a statuesque black woman, in jeans and a sweatshirt, ran the sweeper. She happened to see Vic, and shut the machine off. She didn't seem startled. "Help you?" she asked.

"Stopped by to get the key," Vic said, smiling. "Heard the vacuum, and ... "

She smiled broadly and wiped her brow with the back of her hand. Being a teacher, Vic believed he was a quick read in sizing people up. Her eyes struck Vic as those of a kind, engaged person. "So, you're the new resident," she said, reaching to shake his hand. "I'm Olivia. I clean up 'round the place." She held a cupped hand to her mouth and whispered, "Gets me a reduction in my rent." Then, back in full voice, "I'll make it nice for you." She paused and looked around. "Don't mind saying the man who lived here before you was a p-i-g pig." She giggled. "I'm putting in some hours, here."

"I appreciate your efforts."

"Have it ready for you tomorrow. Clean as a whistle," she said, firing off another gleaming smile.

Vic thanked her, and left her to her work. On the way to his car, he thought about what Ames said, and decided there was no way that big jerk was banging her. Olivia was too centered and too classy to be involved with Ames on anything but a professional level. Vic knew he wouldn't be sneaking out to the Yoho-whatever spa anytime soon, but even if he did, Ames's name would be the last one Vic would think to drop. One thing was for certain, the fact that Olivia was in charge of cleaning the apartment made him feel better about moving in. She was right, it was a pig sty, but Vic believed her when she said she would make it livable. At this time in his life, livable was enough.

Nothing happened Wednesday or Thursday to make him decide against the move. He flip-flopped a time or two, but never definitively. Friday morning, he and Roxanne were in the mists of afterglow. Their clothing surrounded them like relief maps of unusually colored islands on the deep blue carpet of the Vickery's den. Her head rested on his stomach. "I can't believe you let the air out of her tire," Roxanne said. "When did you do that?"

"Last night, after she went to bed," Vic answered. "I didn't want her coming home unexpectedly. Sometimes, if he's not at trial, her boss lets her leave early. This way, we know she won't be coming home until I pick her up."

"Oh God, Vic. What are we going to do when you start back at Alexis? When will we be able to see each other?"

Vic didn't answer. Roxanne crawled on top of him on her hands and knees, straddling his torso. It looked like she might kiss him. "I'm moving out," Vic said, in the same tone of voice one might use to say, "Pass the ketchup." He watched closely to gauge her reaction.

Her head dropped like someone hit her, then it snapped back up, her eyes bulging in disbelief and locked on Vic's. "What?" she barked. Her voice reverberated off the wood-paneled walls.

"I rented an apartment Tuesday, a furnished one-bedroom job about a couple miles from here. It's just across the turnpike, in Maumee." Roxanne's wide unblinking eyes began to ricochet back and forth. "The rent is for December, but it's empty now, and the guy says I can move in anytime." He paused. "I'm outta here."

Roxanne's wild eyes stopped twitching, and she retrained them on Vic's. "But why?"

"Because I can't stand it. I can't stand the lies. I don't love Angie anymore, at least not the person she is now. I can't love somebody who doesn't give anything back. But, I *do* still care about her. And damn it, I care about myself. I can't go on like this, playing house with her like there's nothing wrong, and seeing you on the side."

Roxanne grabbed Vic's chin like his grandmother used to when he misbehaved. "What are you going to tell her?"

He gently grasped her wrist and pulled it away. "The truth. That I hate the way she and I are living. Our relationship isn't like it used to be, and she knows it and won't do anything about it, which tells me my happiness isn't important to her. I can't live with someone who doesn't care about me." He paused. "Something like that."

"That's all?"

"I'm not going to tell her about us, if that's what you mean."

"So, what's the plan? You're really going to divorce her, or is this just a pressure play?" Roxanne leaped to her feet and began to snatch up her clothes, islands disappearing from the deep pile ocean. "Because she's gonna promise you the world ... anything you want. Breakfast in bed and sex until you can't get it up anymore." She dropped all of the clothes she'd picked up, except for her panties, which she clumsily, almost frantically, put on. She didn't get them centered and a tuft of her pubic hair stuck out on one side. She didn't notice.

"Dissolution," Vic intoned.

"What the hell is that?" Roxanne asked.

"It's basically a divorce with no fighting. No adversarial crap," Vic said calmly, still lying on the carpet and watching Roxanne's reverse striptease. "We agree to a settlement without lawyers getting into it. Lets us keep control ourselves."

"Fat chance of that," Roxanne shot back. "Angie works for a damned lawyer. Think he's going to stand by and let you two work it out? Think Angie's not going to go to him for help?"

Vic puffed his cheeks and went for some Marlon Brando. "I'll make her an offer she can't refuse," he said, his voice low and reedy. Roxanne shot him a look like he cut a loud fart in a quiet theater. "Why are you so upset?" Vic asked, suddenly feeling very silly, sitting naked on the carpet. He stood and held out her blouse. "Here, I think this goes *under* your sweater." She snatched it from him. "My getting a place solves a lot of problems for us. Why are you so pissed off?"

"Because you're a head case." She peeled off her sweater. "You think this is going to be easy, that she's just going to let you go?"

"All I want is my car, my clothes, and my art stuff. Maybe Muldoon. The manager said he'd ask the owner about a cat. She can have the rest. If she wants the house, she can pay me my half in installments. If not, we'll sell it and split the profit."

Roxanne put on her blouse and sweater, in the correct order this time, and looked Vic straight in the eyes. "I'm not leaving Tom," she growled.

Vic put a vice grip on Roxanne's shoulders. "So that's what has you all bent out of shape. Look, Rox, this is not a 'pressure play,' as you call it. Not for Angie, not for you. I love you. If you and I wind up together, terrific. But if you don't want to leave Tom, I'm not going to try to change your mind." He wrapped his arms around her, and wondered how much of what he'd told her was true. "Whatever else can be said of us, you've shown me there can be more in a relationship, more to life, than what I have now. I'll always owe you for that." Vic stepped back and Roxanne slid into her loafers. "Pretty obvious you're leaving."

"Yeah, I guess. I don't know what to do."

He shrugged. "Do what you want to do. What you need to do. I am."

Still naked, Vic followed as Roxanne marched through the kitchen to the utility room. She turned to face him when she reached the back door. "Are you sure you're doing the right thing?"

"I told you, it's what I need to do. It's what I'm *going* to do." He kissed her, but it was brief and chaste. "I love you, Roxxie."

It looked like she tried to suppress a tinge of a smile. "Put your clothes on. You're really goddamn goofy." With a slam of the door, she was gone.

Vic twisted the deadbolt. The wind came from the northwest, and a frigid blade of air sliced through the crack between the door and the jamb stabbed at him. Regardless, he stood there for a long time, looking out the window, with Roxanne's words echoing in his head. Her reaction to his plan surprised the hell out of him. Vic was so certain she'd be excited and happy, but she'd taken it as pressure on her to follow his lead. Now he felt twice as low as he usually did on a Friday. Not only would they not be together again until Monday, but her tirade confused and disappointed him. Sure, he had deep-down hopes she might follow his lead, but that didn't seem to be anywhere close to happening. Not anytime soon.

He looked out at the pool. It stretched their budget back when they put it in, but Angie was adamant. "A built-in," she'd said, "not the cheap above-ground kind." She made it sound like it would be so much fun. "We can have our friends over for parties." She gave him a seductive wink. "We could even make love in it." Vic knew he would let Angie have her way, but that final suggestion sealed the deal. *That was back when we still made love,* he thought.

One of the tie-downs for the pool cover had come loose, and a corner of the royal blue cover flapped in the wind. The wrought iron patio furniture was stacked on the far side of the deck, and the vacuum and other equipment were locked in the small pool house he and Angie built together. It came as a kit, but it wasn't an easy project. One hour into the build, Angie banged her finger with a hammer. "Oh, fuck!" she yelled. As soon as Vic saw it wasn't serious, he shouted, "Alright! Swearing like a union carpenter." She grinned and flipped him off with the finger she'd smacked.

161

After dinner that evening, they poured wine and christened the structure with some passionate lovemaking. The memory teased Vic as he appraised the cold deserted backyard. The barren late-fall gloom cast itself across the pool the way the current state of their marriage choked Vic's happy memories of the past. He walked back into the den and picked up his clothes, returning the carpet to a featureless sea.

As he often did when he needed to think problems over, Vic left the house and drove lazy loops of the beltway girdling Toledo. The RX7's engine loped while his mind raced. He was moving out. The only question was when. Should I wait until after Thanksgiving? He was going back to work on Monday. Moving out right away would make an already difficult week a lot tougher. Part of him wanted to postpone everything until the following four-day weekend. Selfish asshole, he thought. Sure, turn Angie's life upside down, but heaven forbid you should inconvenience yourself. But why ruin Thanksgiving? If I move out the following weekend, at least she'll have a nice holiday. Very thoughtful. And, a month after Thanksgiving, it'll be Christmas, shithead! What about that?

Even without the "when" decided, Vic wondered how he'd inform his wife of eleven years he was abandoning ship, that he already signed the lease on a one-bedroom lifeboat. How would he chart a conversation that would get to the point where he'd announce his mutiny?

With all of these unresolved questions swirling in his head, he eased his car onto a downtown exit ramp. Dusk slipped over the city like a gray silk veil. He switched on the headlights and, in minutes, came to a stop in front of the law offices, amidst the drivers and pedestrians whisking along with the scent of a weekend in their nostrils. "Nathaniel Fairchild, Esq., Attorney at Law," the gold lettering on the glass doors announced. Angie was waiting. "Hi!" she said, grazing his cheek with a dry little kiss as she climbed in. "Did you get my tire fixed?"

"Yeah," he answered, pulling back into traffic. He shifted into second, and Angie's head jerked back as he let out the clutch and accelerated. Vic knew she didn't like riding in his car, and believed she played up the forces it exerted on her.

"What was wrong?" Angie asked.

"A bad tire valve. It's all taken care of."

"Tire valve," she echoed, almost to herself. "Where you put in the air?"

"Yep."

"That's strange, isn't it? I've never heard of that before. I thought it would be a nail or something."

"That's what it was. It's all fixed, now."

They drove in silence for several blocks. "Mother called. She wants to know if we are coming out for Thanksgiving."

"What did you tell her?" Vic held his breath. He didn't want to be that far from Roxanne, even if it was a holiday weekend and the chances of seeing her were zilch. Then, he noticed Angie's arms were wrapped snugly across her stomach. "Don't you feel well?"

"I'm retaining. You know, that time of the month. Your car's like a buckboard on these rough streets. Makes my boobs hurt." Vic saw her cinch up her forearms, probably for more support. She fell silent until they were cruising smoothly on the Anthony Wayne Trail, the main westbound surface artery out of downtown, then she let her arms slide onto her lap and continued. "We really didn't discuss it, I guess. We usually *do* go. I said I'd call back after I talked to you."

"I don't know, Ange. It's going to be a tough first week. I'm going to be pretty worn out by Wednesday. Then drive four hours to Chicago?"

"But I could drive, Vic. You could ride and rest. Sleep, even."

Waiting for a light to change, Vic moved the shift lever back and forth, in neutral. "Look, Ange, I don't want to keep you from being with your folks for the holiday. Why don't you go by yourself? You can be with them, and I can collapse at home and build my strength for the next week at school." And maybe sneak some time with Roxanne, if he had the house to himself.

"But how would I get there?" she asked.

"Drive?" He used a tone of voice that implied the answer was all too obvious.

"I can't drive to Chicago, Vic."

"You just said you'd drive to Chicago."

"Yeah, together. But I couldn't drive alone."

"Why not?"

"I'd be scared. What if something happened? What if I had another flat tire?"

Vic shook his head at the irony of the tire ghost's resurrection. "How long have we owned that car? Five, six years? And this is the first time we've ever had a problem."

"I know. So I never thought about it before. But now ... "

"Okay, you could fly." He made the turn onto River Road.

"It's too late to get tickets. You have to make reservations way in advance for a holiday. And I don't want to go without you. Flying or driving."

Vic thought of all the days when she never spent ten back-to-back minutes with him, and now she claimed she couldn't be without him. "All I know is I don't want to keep you from being with your folks, but I don't want to travel all that way." He braked to turn onto Bittersweet. "I think you should go. You'll be fine. The Honda's as reliable as a damned bowling ball." He pulled into the garage and pressed the remote to close the door.

Angie stopped him when he made a move to get out. "Is something wrong?"

The door opener light showed on her soft blonde curls through the sunroof, painting yellow light on her cheeks and the tip of her nose. Her eyes glistened in the shadow her brow created. The soft crinkle of the vinyl seat cover, under Vic's weight, leached into the silence as he contemplated his next sentence. Maybe Angie could change, he thought. Maybe Ames would come across with the deposit. "Nothing's wrong."

"Vic ... "

The light from the opener flickered out, leaving the spare illumination from the door to the house. Vic noticed Muldoon stood with his forepaws on the lower window. The cat looked like a hand puppet. "I'm miserable." The sound of his voice surprised him. "I've been miserable for a couple years. I'm tired of being miserable, and I don't want to be miserable anymore."

"Miserable? But why?"

"Because of the way we live." He turned and faced her. "Angie, you used to be my wife. My lover. But for some reason, you've changed. Except for once every few months or so, we could be brother and sister." She began to blink against her tears. "I can't take it anymore, Angie. I can't live with someone who doesn't want me."

Her eyes strayed off, then snapped back, still tearing. "Miserable?"

"I'm moving out." He was mesmerized by the sound of the voice he could scarcely believe was his.

"Oh, no." She rocked back until her head hit the passenger window, then she pitched forward, her hot wet face grazing his. She wrapped her arms around him, her body convulsing in heavy sobs. "NO! Nonono, please no."

Vic was amazed at how detached he felt. Her face was hot against his skin, and her huffy breaths hit his lower neck like moist hot sauna air, while the sound of her breathing nearly made his ears ring. But in the cool cellar of his soul, Vic felt only a calm numbness. He even tried to absorb her agony, but the only discomfort he could muster was from the twist in his spine to accommodate her embrace. He noticed the windows were beginning to fog. Muldoon was little more than a black smudge.

Angie pulled away and began to wipe at her eyes. Her breath began to rasp in ragged hiccup-like gasps. "Please, Vic." *Hiccup.* "Please don't do this." *Hiccup.* "You never told me you were miserable." *Hiccup.* She looked into his eyes. "You still love me, don't you? You still want me?" *Hiccup.*

He sank into the seat. "Why should I have to tell you I'm miserable?"

"Because I didn't know." *Hiccup.*

"Like hell!" His surge of anger surprised even him. "Don't give me that shit. We used to make love two or three times a week. Now I can't remember the last time."

"But, your accident—"

"Forget the damned accident. When was the last time before that? You never gave me a straight answer when I asked you after the Bayer blowup."

"In August?" It sounded like a squeak.

"Yeah? You sure it wasn't July?" He thought for a moment and began to shake his head. "Yes. I think it was July."

"So that's what this is really about. Sex!" She spat the word like it was a big loogy.

Vic met her gaze. "Yes, to some extent, I guess. Uh, no, it's actually not about sex. I have all the sex I want, sex three or sometimes four times a week." He watched her mouth fall open.

"What?"

"I jerk off, Angie. I jerk off more now than I did in junior high. Anytime I feel like sex, I take care of it myself. Alone. Sex is not the problem. Closeness is. Intimacy. The love of another human being. Touching. Caressing. No, being married to someone who has no desire for me, *that's* what this is truly all about."

She fell back against the window again. Hiccups apparently gone, she panted in irregular gasps, her hands lifeless in her lap. She'd given up on tear management. Her head lolled from side to side. "I'm so sorry. I never meant ... I didn't know things were that bad." One of her hands reanimated to touch his cheek. "Honest."

"Yes, you did. You do. You know how things are. How could you not? A married couple goes weeks without sex and you don't see a problem? You choose not to know, to ignore it." He paused. "Ignore me. You ignored me when I apologized after the Bayer deal. Remember? That next morning, I said we should work more on our marriage. What did you say? 'Oh, we'll be okay.' The queen of denial." He climbed out of the car and started for the entry door. Angie followed. "You always say we're okay, because if we are, there's no reason to change. We're not okay, Ange. We haven't been okay for years, and we'll never be okay. And I'm leaving."

"But where will you go?" She was on his heels like a puppy.

"I rented an apartment."

"An apartment! You already rented one? When?"

Muldoon cried and arched his back when Vic opened the door. Scooping the cat up, he walked into the kitchen. "Monday."

Angie pulled on his shirt. "You never answered me. Do you still love me?" Her words hung between them like a noose.

"I fell in love with someone who doesn't exist anymore. You look like her, but the girl I loved left me a long time ago."

Angie stumbled to the table, collapsed onto a chair, and buried her face in her arms, sobbing. "I think there's someone else." She moaned. "There has to be, or you'd be willing to work on this."

He spooned out some Savory Stew and pushed the dish toward Muldoon. "Willing to work on this? I've been willing, *you* weren't. There's no one else. This is about you and me. That's all."

"I don't believe you. Otherwise you wouldn't do this to me."

"To *you*. Do you hear yourself? You think this is about you, but it's really about me. I'm finally doing something for myself. For years, you've run our marriage to suit yourself. You had final say on everything. Money. Vacations. Friends. The house. And, of course, sex. Nothing happened without your say-so. I went along to get along, but I finally decided I can't take anymore, and you accuse me of doing this to *you*? Of having a girlfriend? When the hell would I have time to do that, Angie? I'm always here with you, all by myself!"

He regretted the words, even as he shouted them. Sliding from the chair to the floor, Angie rocked on her knees and cried harder than ever. "I'm sorry. I'm sorry, please give me one more chance." She knee-walked across the floor, pitched forward, and wrapped her arms around Vic's legs. Not knowing what to do, he reached out and almost touched the crown of her head, but stopped short. He wanted to comfort her, but he wasn't about to give in. That's what he'd done in the past. Time after time, he wanted to believe she was serious and she would go back to being the Angie of old. The sweet girl he'd fallen in love with. The fun-loving girl who once tried to start a water fight by spitting a mouthful at Vic. It was back when they lived in their first apartment in Toledo and were just-out-of-college poor. He ducked and the water destroyed a watercolor someone already paid him fifty dollars for, back when fifty bucks bought two weeks' worth of groceries. They both lay on the floor and laughed until their sides hurt. Then they made love. That Angie was gone, and Vic was convinced she would never resurface. There's no turning back now, he decided. No, patting her head would send the wrong message. Instead, he helped her to her feet and back onto a chair, then sat across from her. Her crying eased after several minutes, so he went over and poured himself some Southern Comfort.

"You're leaving?"

Vic leaned against the countertop and nodded.

"You could go right now?"

"Yeah. I can move in anytime."

Angie walked to the counter, pulled off a sheet of paper towel, and blotted her eyes. "Then go. If you're going to that apartment, and nothing I can say now will stop you, then go." She started for the door, then paused. "But I think you're going to be sorry you did this. You'll realize how good this is. And when you do, I'll be here, waiting for you." She whirled, and ran out of the room.

Vic stood against the counter, sipping his drink, but a strong ache started in the pit of his stomach and radiated outward from there. He found himself wishing the earlier numbness would return. He splashed the rest of the liquor into the sink and cautiously went upstairs. Angie had closed herself in her work room, slivers of light escaping from around the edges of the door. Vic headed for the bedroom.

In less than an hour, Vic packed his car with as many of his belongings as he could. He surveyed the interior for open space, but aside from the driver's seat, there was none.

Angie appeared in the doorway to the garage, holding Muldoon in her arms. "Dooner's staying with me."

The screen prevented a clear view of her face, but he could hear her soft snuffling. "I'm not sure I can have a cat in the apartment anyway."

"Where is it? Do I even get to know?"

"Sure. It's on Valley Side. A block north of the Trail, in Maumee. 914 Valley Side, apartment six."

Neither of them spoke. The silence scratched at him like cat's claws.

"And if you don't come back, what will we do with our house?"

Vic tried to sound as though the thought never crossed his mind. "I don't know, I guess we'll have to sell it."

She disappeared from the door. Vic followed her as far as the kitchen and could hear her running up the stairs. He grabbed his bottle of Southern Comfort and walked back to the car. When he backed out into the street, Vic looked at the house. Warm yellow lights made it look cheery and welcoming. *Anyone passing by would think it was the perfect home,* he thought. Then he remembered the way The Old Man backed into the street and had driven away, all those years ago. He glanced down at the Bayers' house. He couldn't see any lights from his angle. *I am The fucking Old Man,* he said to himself as he let out the clutch and nailed the gas.

At the nearest phone booth, Vic brought the Mazda to a skidding stop, and got out. After the tantrum she threw that morning, he didn't know if he wanted to talk to Roxanne or not. He understood. She didn't want to move out, and now she felt pressure, even though Vic didn't mean to apply any. Not directly, anyway. He knew his leaving Angie put pressure on her to leave Tom, but did she honestly expect to sneak back and forth between houses, depending on which spouse wasn't home? So, of course, she probably felt like she'd struck a match for warmth, and wound up starting a house-fire, he figured. She had to be worried the blaze would spread. The phone rang twice before she answered.

"Is this a wrong number?" Vic whispered.

"No," she replied. "He's not even home yet. Where are you? Why are you whispering?"

"I'm out." He ramped up to full voice. "I'm at the pay phone on South Detroit at the Trail."

"Out?"

"Yeah. Out. On my way to the apartment."

"You're shittin' me!" she shouted. "I didn't think you were going *tonight*."

"I wasn't. That's how it worked out. Anyway, I'm heading for my new place." He paused. "Just wanted you to know." His jaw muscles tensed while he waited for her response. There was a pause.

"I can't believe it."

Vic tried to read her tone for clues to how she felt. He came up empty. "Look, I know all this is a shock. You never expected it. But I had to do it, Rox." He paused. "I couldn't stand it anymore, seeing you, getting it on with you and going along with Ange like everything was still chicken noodle.

"I thought we'd ... "

Vic waited for her to complete the sentence. It was obvious she wouldn't. Or couldn't. He let it go. "I couldn't stay with the charade. Of course, she doesn't know about us, so from that standpoint, it's all still a big lie. But at least I served notice. She knows it's over."

"What did she say?"

"Most of what you predicted," Vic said, reflecting on Roxanne's tirade that morning. "She didn't *know* there was a problem. There *must* be another woman. Everything I expected, and a few things I didn't. She said she thinks I'll regret leaving, that I don't know how good I had it." He heaved a breath. "She's that delusional. But she cried *so* hard. It was more horrible than I ever imagined. Much worse."

"God, I can't believe it."

"I won't have a phone until next week sometime, so I'll call from school or a pay phone when I'm pretty sure he's not home."

"Wait! Where's your apartment?"

Vic gave her the address and directions, but he wanted to stop talking. To stop thinking. He wanted to go to the apartment, curl up in a ball, and be numb. "I've *got* to go." The phone booth's windows were fogging, and the Mazda's parking lights looked like fuzzy amber eyes through the haze. "I'll call. Bye." It came out more like a breath than a word. He hung up.

The folding doors of the booth clattered open and the cold air slapped Vic's face. For a moment, he wondered if he should turn around and head for Bittersweet. Maybe his leaving would shake Angie up and make her believe something had to be done about their relationship. Maybe now she would understand how serious he was about wanting more than they had, something approaching what they once had. He wavered, then walked to his car. Nothing changed since he came back from his coma. Nothing was going to change. He was suddenly certain of that. He scanned the area, and as he stood at the open door of his car in the November night, a thought more chilling than the evening air hit him.

Nothing about his life would ever be the same.

Chapter Six

Vic wondered how long had it been since he'd lived alone. Years. Probably since the summer before he and Angie were married. Alone. Now he found himself in a tiny basement apartment. Olivia did a wonderful job of cleaning the place, but regardless, as he lay on the bed, awash in the stark light and shadow created by the security lights outside, he couldn't keep his mind from meandering back to Bittersweet. Like a ghost, Vic slipped from room to room. The garage where he spent so many happy hours puttering amongst his tools and on his car. Through the entry door and into the utility room. The door Roxanne used to sneak through, to and from the backyard. In his memory, the sunlit pool outside sparkled as though it was July, then the reality of early winter inserted itself into his reverie. He recalled the rumble of the furnace and the reflection of the flames from its gas burner dancing on the surrounding linoleum. Then the kitchen, bright and smelling of the fruit Angie always kept in the bowl on the enameled table with chrome legs. Instead of whole rooms, Vic began to revisit items and areas. The place where he'd spilled a quart of paint near where his easel stood. The shotgun The Old Man gave him, sequestered in a small closet off the den, unused because Vic wasn't a hunter. And the small area in the backyard, behind the pool, that was so hard to get to with the lawnmower. A car door slammed outside the apartment and brought Vic back to reality. He'd neglected to bring sheets or blankets, so he was curled on the bare mattress, stripped of its plastic packaging, under a parka and a jacket. No pillow. Alone in his apartment. His apartment, replete with dingy furniture he didn't even own.

Saturday morning, he went for a run and spent the miles rehearsing what he would tell his friends at school on Monday. He never settled on an explanation he really felt good with, instead deciding he'd wing it when the time came. He returned to the apartment, and was standing in the shower's spray when he realized he'd forgotten soap. When he stepped out onto the curling-at-the-corners linoleum, he found he also failed to remember towels.

He put away what he did bring and made a list of essentials he missed. Saturday afternoon, after lunch at McDonalds, he called from a phone booth to ask Angie if he could come by to pick up what he needed. The phone rang and rang. At first, he was alarmed, but figured she was probably out with one of her girlfriends, telling her story and seeking solace. If she isn't at the house, so much the better, he decided.

Sure enough, the Honda wasn't in the garage, but on the kitchen table was a note saying she'd gone to Chicago. *Driven.* She called her boss, explained the situation and requested some vacation days. She wasn't returning for a week, the Sunday after Thanksgiving, so she left plenty of food and fresh litter for Muldoon. The spot on the driveway where Tom parked his Pinto was vacant, but Vic didn't feel much urge to call Roxanne. He felt needy, which he didn't like. Weakness. Still, he wanted some validation, but in order to supply that, Roxanne would almost have to admit she should move out as well. That wasn't in her plans. He didn't want to tightrope walk with her on the phone line, and she apparently felt the same—his phone didn't ring. It required several more trips to transport the rest of his necessary belongings. On the last one, he kidnapped a yowling and agitated Muldoon, along with his litter pan, and a week's supply of cat food.

Vic slept much better on sheets and a pillow, with Muldoon cuddling next to him. Sunday morning, he went for a short run, showered, and made an early trip to Kroger's. He cooked breakfast, using his old Boy Scout camp-out kit, a forgotten relic he ran across in the Bittersweet attic.

Eggs on a paper plate and bread toasted in the oven broiler never tasted better.

It was a day of mixed emotions. The anticipation of going back to work the following day was entwined with the funk of returning to the unbending schedule, the administrators, and an ever-increasing number of students who expected everything of their teachers and virtually nothing of themselves. To keep himself busy, he set about turning the apartment into something resembling a real artist's studio. One end of the small kitchen area had a view of the TV and living room window, so that's where he set up his easel. A small table from the living room worked perfectly to hold the sheet of glass he used for a palette, along with his tubes of paint. In no time, it looked like an actual painter lived there.

He spent the rest of the afternoon painting and watching football on the hallucinating TV. It had developed a band of blue-green that meandered from the bottom of the screen to the top, then back again, in no particular rhythm or cadence. At least the cable hookup is free, Vic grumbled. After putting the finishing touches on the smashed pumpkin painting, he began a sketch for another on a canvas he'd stretched before his accident. When he finished that, he opened a beer, and lay down on the couch to watch the Bears get beat up by the Lions. He drifted off wondering if Angie was there, watching with her father from his company's private box on the forty yard-line.

Loud banging ripped him from his slumber. Muldoon leaped off the couch, and Vic stumbled sleepily to his feet, struggling to pull some reality together. More banging made it clear someone was at his door. Had he been thinking clearly, he would have taken a look through the peephole first, but he swung it open wide, hoping it wasn't Ames, the manger. Roxanne stood in the hallway.

"Got a beer for the Welcome Wagon lady?" she asked, kissing him on the cheek as she brushed past. She carried a large cardboard box that rattled when she set it down. She peeled off her jacket and tossed it onto the chair by his easel. "Because if you have a beer for the Welcome Wagon lady, the Welcome Wagon lady has something she knows you're gonna like." She paused, staring at Vic while the humor drained from her face. "What's wrong?" she asked.

"It's ... Jesus, I don't know. You were so pissed off about my moving out. Now, all of a sudden, here you are like, 'this is great.'"

Roxanne stepped closer and rested her hands on his hips.

"Look. When you first dropped the bombshell, I figured you expected me to move out, too. I told you I wouldn't, but you went ahead on your own." She shrugged. "So, you convinced me you did this for yourself. You were going to do it no matter what. And that's the deal. I'm not leaving Tom." She paused, let her arms hang at her sides, and gave Vic a look like she'd locked herself out of her car. "Maybe it's the old Catholic thing. I don't practice anymore, but all those years in Catholic school took their toll." She raised a scythe-shaped eyebrow. "Probably the way it's supposed to work." She flashed her thousand kilowatt smile. "So, I thought you might enjoy it if I came over to throw a little house-warming. I know I will," she added, winking at him.

Vic smiled back. "And the welcome lady wants a beer?"

She let loose with her throaty laugh. "Are bullfrogs waterproof?"

Vic pulled two cold bottles of Pabst Blue Ribbon out of the refrigerator while Roxanne peeked into the living room. "To my new beginning," Vic said, handing her a bottle and raising his own.

"New beginning," she repeated, tapping Vic's bottle with hers before she slugged some down, and wiped her mouth with the back of her hand. "Gee," she said, an impish grin wrinkling her face, "I was gonna ask you to show me around, but I see we can do the whole tour from right here. You know, a box of baking soda in the corner would kill the ... uh ... "

"Odor. You can say it. You should have smelled it before the cleaning lady did her thing." Vic allowed a bit of faked threat into his voice. "But, hey, don't be ranking on my new place. Any apartment where you can take a shit and watch TV at the same time ain't all bad."

Roxanne let her tongue graze her upper lip. "But, I can't quite see the bedroom from here."

"Ah, that happens to be our next stop on the tour." Vic guided her using her elbow. As soon as they cleared the door, Roxanne swigged her beer, put the bottle on the dresser, and began to unbutton her blouse. "Hey, that's my job." Vic lifted her and gently placed her on the bed. He lay next to her, kissed her, and slid his hand through the opening in the buttons she'd made.

"Ooo, sex on a bed. This'll be new," she whispered, seductively.

Vic unfastened another button, lifted the material, and shook his head. "No, that's the same old breast."

Roxanne slapped him. She pointed her finger reprovingly. "Never say 'old' to a gal in her forties. And anyway, you don't have any complaints, do you?" She raised her shoulder to lift her breast toward him.

Vic cupped her in his hand, and squeezed. "None at all," he breathed, lowering his head to mouth the soft flesh he held.

She moaned. "What I meant was I might get out of this without carpet burns, for a change."

"Blanket burns can be just as painful," Vic joked, opening the clasp at the waistband of her slacks.

"Have at it, big boy." She pinched his jaw in her fingers. "Any burns under third degree are fine with me."

An hour or so later, they were lying in a tangle of sheets. The two minute warning had been given in the Bear's game which, in their haste, the two lovers failed to switch off. The apartment was illuminated solely by the TV, its bluish glow flickering in through the bedroom door to outline Roxanne's features as she lay on her back. "In a real bed was nice," Vic murmured. Roxanne grinned and wrinkled her nose. "So, what did you tell him when you left?"

"That I was going to my sister's."

"No chance he'll call there?"

"No-o-o. No way. He doesn't get along with Marla, or Bob." She rolled over and brushed Vic's arm with her finger. "He'd never call." She hesitated. "And Marla would cover for me if he did."

"Your sister knows where you are? She knows about me?"

"Not specifically ... " She raised that carefully penciled eyebrow again.

Vic flushed with a warm rush of excitement. It sounded like she'd told her sister something, anyway. He tried to push away the good feeling that thought gave him, not wanting to raise false hopes. The little Catholic girl isn't leaving Tom, Vic told himself, again. "As long as you're covered," Vic said.

"On the contrary," she countered, playfully kicking the sheet off her legs. She licked his nipple and blew on it. "O-o-o! Think I might be doing some good here."

"Forget it," he said, rolling onto his stomach. "You collected all there is for today, Roxxie. I ain't Superman."

"Aw, come on, lover. What good is a young stud if he can't perform?" She started to tickle him.

"You screwed up, baby! Your young stud is pushing thirty-four! Twice is the best this guy can do, in one afternoon." He grabbed her wrists, and she relaxed against his grasp. They kissed. "Now, later this evening— that would be a different story."

"I can't stay that long." She sighed. "But I'll keep you anyway, I guess."

"I'd like that. Say, what's in the box you brought?"

"Pots and pans. Some utensils and a couple of settings of plates and silver. Old stuff we don't use anymore. Thought it might come in handy."

"You're the best, Rox," Vic said, giving her a hug.

"Hey, man! The Welcome Wagon lady delivers."

~ * ~

Vic typically arrived at work by six-thirty. He liked an hour in the nearly vacant and quiet building to ready his supplies, finalize his plans and relax and enjoy banter with teacher friends before the first bell rang. But on the morning of his return to school for the first time in over a month, his

177

excitement, both positive and negative, awakened him at four. Realizing he was done with sleep, he rolled out of bed and ran in a pretty good little snowstorm, showered, dressed and cleared the doors of Alexis High School at six.

Snowstorm aside, Vic experienced a blizzard of emotions when he walked into Alexis High that Monday morning. This was his first day after six weeks of recovery, and it triggered a host of sensations. Vic realized he forgot how the school smelled—a commingled blend of pungent institutional floor wax, the semi-sweet musk of book bindings and the aroma emanating from the cafeteria. Vic decided it was pizza that day, usually a safe bet. His shoes squeaked against the shiny floor and nearby, a door, heavy solid wood with three panes of translucent glass, slammed. Nobody at Alexis, it seemed, ever closed a door gently. And the light. Color-killing vanilla light flooded from the ceiling fixtures, diffusing in a way that minimized shadow. The recollection of the cold light leaching through the clouds when Vic was in his coma was inescapable.

His emotions ran the gamut. He loved teaching, but found it becoming more and more difficult. Parents, once reliable allies, had become "my kid's right" adversaries, or namby-pamby wimps with "we've tried everything but we can't control him/her" alibis. And of course, Vic's life outside of teaching was rich with his painting and golf, something many of the other teachers didn't seem to have going for them. He was up to his elbows in the creative process all day, helping his students, and he couldn't wait to get home and get to work on his own painting. Between that and golf, there never seemed to be enough off-hours to pursue all his interests. The choice between the activities he loved, or living a school day dictated by class change bells, was no contest. Consequently, Vic entered Alexis that morning feeling bi-polar about the whole experience.

"Hey there, Vic!" the head janitor called from the lobby staircase. "Great to see you back!"

Custodians can be an art teacher's best friend, and Vic worked hard to cultivate a good relationship with all the custodians. "Howdy, Jack! It's great to be back, although I wondered if you might shut us down this morning, with all the snow."

Jack's face wrinkled into a smirk. "Shit. Your first day back and you're talkin' snow day. But you look great there, young fella. You feeling okay?"

"Yeah, terrific, thanks. Luckily, the shot was to the noggin." He knuckled his head several times. "Too hard to be damaged," he joked.

He couldn't say the same for his classroom. When he flipped on the lights, it was obvious a lot had gone on there, little of it educational. He spent half an hour erasing drawings and juvenile epithets from the blackboard, inventorying and arranging his art supplies, and bulldozing an avalanche of paper and other junk from his desktop. Ted Duffy, the machine shop teacher, walked in as the last of it hit the bottom of the wastebasket. Duffy's room was their usual meeting place, and Vic couldn't remember the last time Ted had ventured across the hall.

"Dammit, Vic, you look good! How're you feeling?"

"Tip top, my man, other than the fact I'm back at dear old Alexis. You know how it goes, time to yourself is great, there's never enough."

Duffy winked. "Ain't that the truth? But you're back none too soon. Towards the end there, I think the kids were kind of eating your sub alive."

"They were going to have to line up behind you, Duff," George Flanner, who taught wood shop, said as he walked in. "You were after her like a fly on shit."

Duffy didn't miss a beat. "Those chubbies *are* tasty ... and grateful."

Both Duffy and Flanner were hired straight out of industry to teach their shop classes. Though they were beyond reproach when students were nearby, they tended to be too crude for some of the teachers at Alexis. Vic enjoyed their rough humor. Both shop teachers were skillful tradesmen, and Vic respected their abilities and their knack for connecting with students who would, no doubt, follow their footsteps into the world of skilled industrial labor. Vic liked to seed the off-color before-school banter. "A large woman?"

"Long as they can sit on his face without covering his feet, they're not too big for Duff," Flanner joked.

"You were jealous," Duffy said, cuffing Flanner on the arm. "Coffee's on in my office." He tipped his head in that direction, and Vic and George followed him out.

The machine shop was rich with the odor of grease and that coppery, electro-magnetic smell aging electric motors leach into the air. The lathes, saws, and milling machines the school district provided were World War II vintage, and though they were quality pieces, they were pushing the limits of their useful life expectancy. Half of the time, according to Duffy, his students' assignments were to use one machine to make replacement parts for another. "Copies of copies," Duffy often complained. "Each one gets a little worse." The cement block walls of the huge room were painted industrial green. The ceiling, very off-white with yellow-orange abstract watercolors, products of bygone roof leaks, loomed sixteen feet above. Large armored cables dropped like thick silvery ropes to supply current to the equipment. Windows ran the length of one wall. When daylight finally arrived, those windows would show the vestiges of years of the smoke, oil, and grime the shop's machines launched airborne.

The three men assumed their usual positions in Duffy's office—Ted, a lanky Mr. Greenjeans look-a-like, sitting at his machine tool-cluttered desk, while Vic and George leaned where they could find space against a counter supporting more heavy tools and mechanical parts. George was an imposing man who coached the Alexis wrestling team. He looked like a heavyweight, and little of what his six foot frame carried was fat. The three of them drank coffee while Vic recounted his adventures, sidestepping the episodes during his coma. Eventually, the issue of his newfound golf prowess surfaced. Word had spread.

"Yeah, been shooting pretty well, lately. I don't know. You get shit on, then you get reimbursed for your trouble. Opposite and equal, I guess. That's the best explanation I can come up with." The memory of how Reefer debunked that theory crossed his mind.

"According to Sal, you're shooting under par," Duffy said.

Vic shrugged. "You know golf, Duff. Good one day, bad the next."

"Don't spend too much time on the course," Flanner joked. "Duff's been talking about servicing your wife ever since we heard you got whacked."

Jokes like that one were normal fare among the three friends, so the looks on Duffy's and Flanner's faces showed surprise when Vic didn't chuckle and toss a witty comeback at them. He was busy ticking off the points of his story, making certain he'd hit on only the particulars he decided to allow. "I, ah ... kind of ran away from home," Vic said. "I'm not living with Angie anymore. I have my own place now."

"Aw, shit," Flanner said, the whites of his eyes showing all the way around his irises. "I'm sorry. I had no damned idea."

"Not a problem. How would you've known? It was a tough move, but it's for the better, I think."

"I never gave a thought to you and Angie having problems," Duffy said.

"That's because I did all I could to hide it. I mean, no one wants people to think they aren't happily married. I didn't, at least. I'm kind of prideful, and I hid the truth and pretended things were great. Maybe I hoped doing that would make them that way. I finally decided to face the facts. She's a wonderful woman. The two of us aren't wonderful together."

"And you're doing all right?" Duffy asked.

"I'm in an apartment, a little furnished place in Maumee." Vic tried for more mirth than he actually felt. "Kind of reminds me of my dorm room in college, except I don't have to go down the hall to take a shit."

"Wow," Flanner said. "Gotta be a huge change from a house with a pool."

Vic shrugged. "Paradise can be Hell when you're sharing it with the wrong person."

The warning bell interrupted. Vic and Flanner said goodbye to Duffy, who was still grappling with his surprise, and the two of them started for their classrooms.

"Jesus, Vic. I can't believe it. Let me know if there's anything I can do—anything you need," Flanner said when they reached the door to Vic's classroom.

"I appreciate that, George," Vic replied, patting his friend on the shoulder. "For now, I'm doing good." He walked into his classroom as the final bell rang.

Aashell White, a six-foot seven black kid everyone called Ace, stood and began to clap. The others followed suit, their applause echoing off the yellow concrete block walls. Ace stepped forward as the clapping ebbed. His smooth-shaved head looked like it was Turtle-waxed, bathed in florescent lights that hummed incessantly. "Say, Mr. Vic-ry," Ace said, in his characteristic rhythmic cadence, "we glad ta see you, man."

Vic reached way up to slap Ace's hand in what was truly a high five. "Well, gang, I have to say I'm equally glad to be back here with you. For a while there, I wasn't sure we'd ever cross paths again."

Sonia Eddinger, a quiet girl who often sucked on a licorice-thick rope of her Goth-black hair, and wore a fringed suede jacket and cowboy boots every day, stood holding a box of donuts. The class chattered happily while a couple cheerleaders, who Vic couldn't remember ever acknowledging Sonia in the past, helped her pass them out. Vic spent the rest of the hour recounting the events surrounding his accident and answering his students' questions. Once again, he didn't delve into the nether-world of his coma, or the upheaval in his personal life, but he related as much as he felt proper regarding what had gone on in the previous six weeks.

His purpose wasn't to place the focus on himself, but to emphasize the fact that a decision made in a split second could forever change the course of a person's life. The fact Vic decided to putt the ball, instead of reacting to Tom Bayer's warning shouts, very nearly cost him his. What if he never regained consciousness? Worse by far, what if he'd regained consciousness and found himself with a damaged brain? And, of course, he could have been killed. Any of those scenarios could have resulted from his decision to hit the ball instead of dropping the putter, using his arms to cover his head, and crouching to make himself a smaller target. Sensible action might have saved him from injury. This was what Vic wanted his students to take away from what he related about his experience. With many of them beginning to drive cars, and with the easy availability of drugs, legal and otherwise, Vic believed it was important to spend time recounting the effects of what he'd done, and hadn't done. Although his subject was art, Vic tried not to miss opportunities to offer lessons in other aspects of life. As first period came to a close, Vic expressed his regrets the class had degenerated into a circus, and promised he would get it back on track.

He repeated his performance four more times that day. By the 2:10 bell, his raspy throat hurt from talking, and he was emotionally spent. He gathered his things, and was about to leave, when an announcement came over the P.A., asking him to come to the office. He probably should have seen it coming, but he was surprised by a number of administrators and teacher friends, balloons, and a cake. Vic was genuinely touched, and found himself tearing as he explained head injuries brought emotions close to the surface. A few people asked general questions, how long he'd been in the hospital—that kind of thing. For the most part, it was a welcome back party. After a day of teaching, everyone was as tired as he, so the gathering was over in less than an hour.

As Vic stopped to button his coat, before stepping out into the remnants of the snowstorm, Rona Barrington, an English teacher with whom he'd coordinated some cross-discipline projects from time to time, walked up and clasped his arm in both her hands. Buck-toothed, with thinning hair, Rona was not an attractive woman, but her heart was a good as her features were unfortunate. She tilted her head close, as though she was about to deliver a national security secret. "I'm so sorry to hear about your separation," she whispered. Vic was shocked, and it obviously showed. She patted his arm. "Don't worry, I won't spread it."

"How did you find out?"

She glanced toward the ceiling tiles. "It's around." She began to pull on her gloves. "I heard it somewhere, but like I said ... "

Vic smiled. "No, it's okay. Not a big secret. I'm surprised the people I told were so quick to pass it on."

"Anyhow," Rona said, stepping through the door Vic held for her, "if you ever need a home-cooked meal, and a shoulder ... " Her Voice trailed off, and she finished with a wink that qualified as a full-fledged flirt.

Vic thanked her, but his mind was occupied. He couldn't decide what surprised him more, a thinly-veiled come on from a lonely middle-age spinster, or the fact his buddies obviously spread the word about he and Angie. By the time he made it home that Monday afternoon, he decided he wasn't upset with them, and fell asleep on the couch with Muldoon curled up on his stomach.

The next day, Vic arrived home from school to find the phone had a dial tone. He called time and temperature to test the equipment. Forty-one degrees at eleven after three. He opened a beer and contemplated the call he knew he had to make while his stomach coiled like a boa constrictor.

Vic's parents' marriage broke up because The Old Man, in addition to being a workaholic moody drunk, played around on Vic's mother. Now Vic left *his* wife because of another woman. Or maybe for another woman? He wondered which of those was closer to the truth, and wasn't certain. Regardless, he was going to do his best to keep that tasty tidbit from his mother. He wondered if she would see through him, especially with all the doubts clouding his psyche. She loved him, to be sure. But at the same time, she had high expectations of him. If he was to keep her on his side and not allow her to be hurt with the revelation he left Angie due to some other relationship, he had to be sharp. He had to be there with logical answers to the questions she would ask. Except when he convinced her he didn't care about the trucking company, he'd never been much good at lying, especially to her. What he had to pull off now was a hell of a lot tougher, and he had to get it right. He drained his beer and got another, all the while organizing a set of facts he could present and answers he could give. The phone rang four times. Vic was eager to hang up, and started to, but his mother answered while the receiver was in midair.

"Oh, Allan! I'm so glad you called! How are you feeling?"

"Fine, Mom. You?"

"Simply great, Allan. I've had such a wonderful day."

Vic watched dust motes float in the shafts of sunlight that streamed through the window while he listened to her recount her day: an early morning jog on McCorkle Avenue, lunch with a couple of the girls at a great restaurant serving tofu sandwiches that tasted like turkey, and a ride through the park on her bicycle. All the while, Vic wavered between wanting to break into her soliloquy, and wishing it would never end.

He finally decided this was something he had to do immediately. "Mom," he said, cutting in, "I left Angie. I moved out." He held his breath and waited for her to break the silence on the line.

"Oh, Allan!" His name became a gasp. Her West Virginia twang vanished. "I never had any inkling. Everything seemed fine between you at the hospital. Once you woke up, you both seemed so happy. You always seemed so in love."

"I know. I know. I tried to hide it. I was embarrassed."

"Embarrassed?"

"Sure. Everybody thought we had the perfect marriage. I *wanted* everybody to think that. But she's changed so much, Mom. She's not the girl I married."

"Nobody's the same after ten years, Allan. You're not the same, either."

"But I kept trying to make her happy, Mom. That's what I'm trying to say. I never stopped doing what she needed, what she wanted. Angie stopped a long time ago."

"So, where are you now?"

"In an apartment. I moved out last Friday."

"Last Friday? My God. And what are you going to do?"

"I, ah ... geeze. I don't know, exactly. I just moved. I haven't had time to think."

"And you're going for counseling with her, aren't you? My friend Tootie Perkins did that with her husband. She found a great counselor up there in Toledo."

Vic was silent while he decided what to say next. Going for counseling made perfect sense if both partners wanted to resolve their problems, but Angie wouldn't admit there were any, and Vic's decision to leave was final. He wasn't going back to her, and he had to come up with a good reason for nixing the counseling idea. "No, Mom. I'm too angry".

"Angry? But did you ever tell Angie there was a problem?"

"Sure, plenty of times. Not more than a week ago, we argued and I said we had a lot to work on. But she wouldn't admit it, because then she'd have had to do something about it. I've worked as hard as I can to make her happy. The house she wanted, the pool she wanted, nights out with her friends. I figured if I did what she wanted, she'd eventually make me happy. But she hasn't."

His mother's voice morphed into an instructive tone. "You can't expect her to figure out what makes you happy. You have to tell her what she needs to do."

"Everybody knows what makes their husband or wife happy, Ma. It's a matter of whether they care enough to do it."

"Oh, Allan. I'm so, oh, I'm just so upset, about all of this. What can I do?"

"Nothing, Mom. I didn't call because I need anything. I wanted you to know. I'm sorry this is what I had to tell you. I'm sorry about everything."

"I can't understand any of this. Should I come up there?"

"No, Mom. Angie isn't even in town. She went to Chicago for the week."

"Then will you come down?"

"For Thanksgiving? No, Mom. I'm whipped."

"Are you okay?"

"Yeah, it's not about my injury. Tired. Run down. But my head's fine. Maybe for Christmas?"

"Yes, Christmas. You'll come down. And you'll stay in touch? Keep me posted? And please, consider the counseling, dear." Her drawl returned.

Vic promised to think about the counseling and hung up. Muldoon jumped onto his lap and yowled. Vic stoked the cat's sleek coat. "Everything will be all right, Mully," Vic said.

~ * ~

It kept trying to snow on Thanksgiving Day, but an icy drizzle was the best it could manage. The gloom matched Vic's mood. Even though his new situation was of his own creation, he allowed himself the luxury of a good mope. His experience was that trying to escape the blues seemed to worsen them. He learned long ago the best remedy for a bout of melancholy was not to fight it. Wallow in it. Get right down and root around at the bottom of it.

After a lackluster run, he showered and lay on the couch, trying to remember as many of the preceding thirty-two Thanksgivings as he could. He couldn't remember many specifically, but he knew beyond any doubt this was the first one he'd ever spent alone. Alone. Roxanne was with Tom at his family's Thanksgiving celebration. She told Vic she had fun with Tom's two sisters, and Vic imagined her amidst what sounded like a large extended family. While mental snapshots of her filled an album in his head, he listened to Leonard Cohen's sad poetic chronicles of love and humanity gone bad, set to music that wept in minor keys. When that didn't induce suicide, he was reasonably certain he'd survive. He forced himself to paint for a few hours, and capped the afternoon watching the Bears lose to Dallas.

Later, he drove to a Denny's and ordered an open face turkey sandwich. It was served with soggy dressing, and mashed potatoes that reminded him of the white paste he used to eat in first grade. A generous light brown moat of low-viscosity gravy surrounded it all. Vic shared company with two others in the restaurant. An over-the-road trucker, whom Vic decided qualified as a pilgrim, sat at the counter and pounded down his meal in less than five minutes while his rig idled outside. The other, a girl who didn't look much older than his students, could have been of American Indian descent. The perfect addition to this holiday's guest list. Her dark completion and darker hair made Reefer flash through Vic's mind, but this girl was as hard and coarse-looking as Reefer was relaxed and open. The heavy makeup slathered on and above her eyelids, the caked mascara, and half-inch long lashes hid her eyes almost like Reefer's sunglasses concealed hers. She wore fishnet stockings, stiletto-heeled shoes, and a short tight satin-like dress. After Vic finished eating, he happened to glance her way as she lingered in a booth over her coffee with a cigarette. She raised a sickle-shaped eyebrow and winked. Vic gave her his best shot at a fatherly smile and left by himself.

When Vic pulled into the parking lot at his apartment building, someone stood by the entry door. It was dark, by then, and he couldn't see who it was at first. As he approached, he realized it was Olivia, the woman who cleaned his apartment. *What the heck is she doing,* he wondered, walking up to her. "Hey, Olivia. Are you locked out?"

She hadn't noticed him coming, and quickly tucked her arm behind her. She looked startled, at first, but her expression changed to that of a kid caught stealing a pack of gum. She held out the hand she'd hidden, displaying a half-smoked cigarette.

"You can smoke in your apartment, can't you? The jerk who had my place sure did."

She shook her head. "It's not that, ah … I'm sorry, I can't recall your name."

"Allan Vickery. Call me Vic."

She smiled. "Vic. Anyway, I'm trying to quit this filthy habit." She rolled the cigarette in between her thumb and index finger until the ash fell onto the wet sidewalk. She ran her shoe over it, leaving a soggy charcoal smudge. "So I told myself, no more smoking in the apartment. It's worked pretty well. I only smoked a couple, yesterday." She held up the dead butt. "This was my third one today."

Vic glanced at his watch. "You're doing pretty well. It's already 6:30. Did you have your turkey dinner, yet?"

She pulled her coat closed. "Yes, I just got back from my sister's. Decided to have one before I went inside. How about yourself?"

Vic grinned. "Back from Denny's." He made a face. "It wasn't great, but I don't have any pots to scrub." He stuck his key in the lock, then turned back to her. "Hey, you did a great job on the apartment. I don't feel like I have to disinfect my shoes after I walk across the carpet, anymore."

"Thank you. You're the first one who's ever said so."

Vic held the door open and she stepped into the hallway. "Well, for sure, the apartment really looks super. Glad I ran into you and had the chance to say something." He pointed at the lifeless cigarette she still held in her hand. "And good luck kicking that. Cold turkey worked best for me." The fact that it was Thanksgiving flashed through his mind. "It was tough, but better than the cold turkey at Denny's." They chuckled and said their goodbyes.

That evening after Tom passed out, Roxanne called to say she'd be over the next day. That picked up Vic's spirits, but the hours dragged. After some fitful sleep, he was up at five o'clock, cleaning the apartment in anticipation of her arrival. He filled the rest of his wait working at his easel and watching MTV.

When Roxanne arrived, just before noon, they melted cheese over some nacho chips in the oven broiler, drank margaritas Roxanne brought along in a vacuum bottle, talked and made love. The hours together whisked by, and when she left, Vic's spirits fell like a skydiver, the way they used to on Bittersweet. His ripcord was her promise to return as soon as she could, maybe even the next day, if the weather was good enough for Tom to play golf. Vic was convinced she would tire of the charade with Tom and eventually leave him and move in. Sometimes he actually believed he didn't care if Angie, his mother, or anyone else found out about them. No matter who was hurt, he yearned to be with Roxanne. This was one of those days. He was lonely, and wanted Roxanne for his own. The weather warmed somewhat on the long weekend, but never attained golfable status. Tom wasn't bowling yet, so Vic and Roxanne stole some conversation on the phone several times, but that was the best they could manage. The hours sat in his apartment like unwelcome guests who were slow to leave.

Sunday afternoon, he trundled Muldoon back to Bittersweet. The house harbored ghosts of memories and emotions as plentiful and persistent as cobwebs in the attic, and his stomach tightened. He jotted a short note, explaining Muldoon had been with him during the preceding week. He almost tore it up to write another saying he was keeping him. He loved Muldoon, but the agreement with Angie was he would remain with her, for the time being, at least. "I may be a cheating bastard, but I'm no thief," he said aloud, stroking the cat's sleek back. Ames hadn't gotten back to him about allowing pets, and he made a mental note to ask him.

His hand still hovered above the paper. He didn't want to add his phone number, but there were any number of reasons Angie might need to call. However, giving her his number felt like giving up some of his new self. His new life. He wavered, then finally lowered it and scribbled the seven digits.

He rubbed Muldoon behind the ears, "Hey, Mully, Angie'll be home soon." A great sadness swept over him, and he wished he could explain to Muldoon why he was leaving. He'd shed more tears since the golf ball hit him than he had in the past ten years, unhappy as many of them were. Old Doc Pembrooke was right when he said a head injury could make people more susceptible to emotion, Vic thought, as he stroked the cat's coat. "I love you, Mully," he said, blinking his wet eyes hard and fast. Tears splashed on the Formica countertop.

Back at the apartment, Vic emptied the car of more booty he'd liberated from the Bittersweet attic, an old bean-bag chair and some large throw pillows. He piled them in a corner across from the TV, then contemplated the soft heap for a moment. On a whim, he fashioned a hollow in the bean-bag, pulled out his sand wedge, and dropped several balls on the carpet. Setting up for a pitch shot, he brought the club through, clipping the ball with a pleasing click that sent it arching toward its target. The club left a telltale scuff in the shag which reminded him of the ones he and Bascolm made on the carpet in the clubhouse at Loon's Lair. The memory warmed him. He pitched and putted into the evening by the flickering glow of the TV until the phone interrupted. He was so certain of who it was, he almost didn't pick it up.

"I called to let you know I'm back," Angie said, a chilly undercurrent in her voice.

"Oh, good. How was the traffic?"

"Not bad."

Manufacturing small talk was difficult. "Car run all right?"

"Dad bought me new tires."

"What?"

"I told him about the flat and he bought me a new set."

"Angie, there was nothing wrong with those tires. I told you it was only the valve."

Angie's tone went sub-zero. "He wanted me to have them, now that I'm on my own."

Silence returned. Vic couldn't think of one thing he could ask or say that wouldn't bring a response he didn't want to hear.

She spoke first. "How was your Thanksgiving?"

"Quiet. Ate a turkey sandwich at Denny's"

"You're not coming back, are you?"

He hesitated. He thought about Roxanne. His choice was made. "No."

Another dose of silence.

"I can't believe you fell out of love with me. Mother says there has to be something else going on, and I believe her. It doesn't happen like that."

The mention of Angie's mother made Vic bristle. "What your mother doesn't know about relationships, ours or anyone else's, could fill a book. I think it's been happening for a long time, with both of us. It's a slow process."

"What do you mean, 'with both of us'? Don't put words in my mouth! I still love you."

"You think you do, but you love the situation, not me. You love the way things were. The life you had." He could hear Angie's muffled crying, and he wanted off the line. Even now, her crying inflicted pain, something she knew well. He'd given in to her tears many times, surrendering his needs in the process. Not tonight. "I'm glad you're back okay. I have to go."

"Wait!" Her tone turned cold as dry ice. "Tomorrow, I'm going to talk to Nathan. I've decided not to drag this out. If you're not coming back, then he'll help me. He's not a divorce lawyer, but he'll do this for me … and he'll do a good job."

"Dissolution, Angie. Dissolution keeps us in control. No adversarial crap. We agree to a settlement, file, and it's done."

"I'm talking to Nathan."

"You don't even know what my offer is yet."

"Offer?"

Vic inhaled. "Everything in the house is yours: furniture, sheets, towels, dishes—everything. You get the Honda. I get my clothes, my car, my golf clubs, and art stuff. If you want to keep the house, you make the payments and stay as long as you like. When you do decide to sell it, I get a third at that time. Otherwise, if you want to sell it right away, you live there while it's on the market. I pay half of the mortgage and expenses. I'll keep the snow shoveled and the grass cut. When it sells, we split fifty-fifty."

He was on automatic. He rehearsed this speech many times in his head. "You make about a hundred a month less than I do," he continued. "I'll split the difference with you and pay you fifty a month for the next two years." Waiting for her reaction, he endured another dose of silence. "Anything I forgot?"

Her voice melted to a puddle. "What about Dooner?"

"He'll probably be better off with you, especially if you keep the house. It costs us about four hundred a year for food and vet bills. I'll give you two hundred, and cover half of anything out of the ordinary."

"I don't want the house ... not if I'm alone."

"Then we'll sell it."

"I can't believe this. You used to love this house. You used to love me. You can just walk away? Leave everything behind?"

"It's less painful than the last five years have been." He winced, wishing he hadn't said it. "Talk to Fairchild tomorrow. Tell him what my offer is. If he's truly looking out for your interests, he'll tell you to take the deal. Have him write it up and I'll sign. I've got to go."

Vic put the receiver on the hook gently, as if that might make what he told her less hurtful. He watched the light from the TV reflect on the golf balls scattered on the carpet. After years of hating the fact Angie controlled their marriage, he was amazed at how little pleasure he derived by taking the reins from her.

Chapter Seven

The school days between Thanksgiving and Christmas whistled past like tee shots. Vic worked hard at giving the kids what they'd missed during his absence, and the majority responded as he hoped. It felt good to be back in the classroom, doing something he was good at, and felt good about doing. He marveled at how others could work in professions that polluted the environment, or made life more complicated for others, and could go home and get a blissful night's rest. Of course, working with hormonal teens was difficult. Vic was always friendly, but never tried to be a friend to his students. After all, he witnessed how they treated their friends every day. But it always seemed when he was at his wit's end, something happened to give him a boost, and validate what he hoped he was doing. Sometimes, it came in the form of students saying they recommended his class to friends; other times, former students stopped by to let him know how their lives were going. Little occurrences of that nature kept him from throwing in the chalk.

In the meantime, winter dropped its frigid white coat on Toledo and made golf impossible. Vic and Roxanne made the adjustment. He gave her a key to his apartment, and she was often waiting for him when he came home from school. Still, weeknights and weekends were hell without her. Vic certainly didn't entertain thoughts of marriage, not in the foreseeable future, but if she left Tom and moved in, he would have her twenty-four hours a day. He tried not to foster hopes, but he always believed that, given enough time, Roxanne would choose him over her husband. Some of that,

Vic admitted to himself, was rooted in ego. All the same, he knew he treated her better than Tom did. Vic kept hoping her feelings for him would overrun her religious misgivings. After all, he said to Roxanne in one of the imaginary conversations he allowed himself on lonely nights, you're committing heavyweight Catholic sin every time you're with me.

Then, one afternoon after school, Roxanne hit Vic with a blind-side curve. She met him at the door to his apartment with a margarita, and the smell of the nachos she'd made swirled around them as they kissed at the threshold. "Wow," Vic said when they broke their kiss, "hell of a welcome home. Can I leave and come back again?"

"Do that, your nachos will get cold," she said, vamping it up with a look that promised more than melted cheese.

Vic used his foot to push the door closed, then guided her to the sofa. He lifted the margarita from her hand, sipped it, and gave her a gentle shove. "Screw the nachos," he said, as she flopped onto the threadbare cushions.

"Oh, really?" She reclined against the armrest. "See something else you'd rather screw?"

They were new enough as lovers so that sex was always an adventure. Vic liked to believe it would always be that way. Roxanne was inventive. "I want to be everything for you," she told him one afternoon. "Everything you need or want. I'll be your little virgin, or fuck you like a whore." She punctuated her promise with a slow deliberate wink. "Your choice." That afternoon, he was in a romantic mood, and they made leisurely love on the sofa while MTV played softly in the background. As they lay in each other's arms afterward, Vic's consciousness bobbed along somewhere between the warmth of Roxanne's body and the comfortable and familiar sounds of Nina Blackwood's raspy-giggly voice and the music videos she introduced.

"Oh, I love this song." Vic walked over to turn up the volume. He sang along as he returned to the sofa. "It's gonna be a cool night, just let me hold you in the firelight ... "

"Now all we need is some firelight."

195

He waved toward the door. "Hey, if it don't feel right, you can go." He watched her closely to see how she would react. He strictly forbade himself from asking what her plans were, or even if she had any, but he wasn't above baiting her to see if she'd strike. She quickly stood and wrapped her arms around him. He heard her snuffle, pulled away, and sure enough, her eyes were tearing. "What?"

She locked him in her arms, and pasted her hot wet cheek against his. "That's the problem. Even though it does feel right with you, I *will* have to go." Vic said nothing, only returning her embrace and rubbing his fingers up and down the little regular bumps where her skin stretched across her spine. She pulled back and looked into his eyes. "Maybe after the holidays," she whispered. "A new year and a new life."

"I love you, Roxxie." He paused. "So much that I won't ever mention what you just said, or ever try to hold you to it." She looked like she felt she needed to say something, but he laid his finger against her lips and shook his head to end the conversation he wanted so desperately to continue. Huge holes are excavated one small shovel-full at a time. He felt like they'd done enough digging for one day, and was afraid to go deeper without shoring up what was already complete. "Let's eat some cold nachos."

Roxanne liked to be home in time so that, on the off-chance Tom came straight from work, she'd be there. Vic didn't bother to put on a coat when he walked arm-in-arm with her to her car. The street his apartment faced, which dead-ended against more apartment buildings, was only used by residents, so they didn't worry about being seen together. Roxanne reached in to start the engine, then turned and held Vic close. "You gotta be freezing." She opened her parka and wrapped it around him, as best she could.

Vic snuggled against her, sliding his hands up to hold her breasts. "I'm getting warmer every second. You better get the hell out of here before I decide to drag you back in for another round."

She pulled back and looked into his eyes. "I wish, but I have to go." She tossed her head, then finger-combed her hair back into place. "I'll call

196

when I can. Maybe I can make it over day-after-tomorrow." She pushed on the end of his nose with her index finger. "Be patient." She got into her car and backed out. They traded waves and the duel exhausts on her Pontiac blew vapor against the chilly pavement.

Ordinarily, her leaving left Vic feeling deflated as a week-old balloon. Not that day. "She is going to leave Tom and live with me," he said aloud, just as Ames, the apartment manager, pulled up in his pickup. He shut off the engine and was out of the cab like it was on fire.

"That your gal I passed?" Ames asked, tilting his head toward the road. Vic weighed the possibilities, and nodded after deciding there was no way the admission could cause them trouble. After all, Vic reasoned, Ames had no idea who she was. Ames winked and leered. "She must be something special, leaving you with a smile like that."

Vic grinned, but he didn't say anything, trying to avoid getting roped into a conversation. When he returned to his apartment, he opened a beer to celebrate the apparent crack in Roxanne's wall of determination not to leave Tom. The holidays would pass quickly, then Roxanne might actually move in with him. It would be good if that didn't happen before the dissolution was inked, he decided. Angie might get pissed off, which could throw a wrench into the works. But early in the year, at least. Maybe February or March. Vic pulled on his beer, and basked in the warm belief it all would work out the way he wanted it to. He consciously avoided thoughts of what his mother would say.

There were other things to toast, as well. In addition to painting as well or better as he ever had, Vic had what he'd always believed was the unattainable: a solid golf game. So, when he wasn't smushing acrylic emulsions around on a canvas, he putted on the linoleum, or popped short chips and pitches into the beanbag chair, trying to emulate the moves Bascolm taught him at Loon's Lair. These two diversions filled the hours while he waited for the call that could come any time Tom Bayer fell asleep or stepped out. Vic became a voluntary hostage to the phone, but in the hours he spent waiting for it to ring, his inventory of paintings increased and his prowess with a putter and short iron increased exponentially. The wall behind the beanbag chair took a hit occasionally, but not often. Vic was getting to where he could put the ball where he wanted to. If Bascolm could only see me, Vic often thought. He had two of the three things most people desire, success in his professional and in his leisure lives. After what Roxanne said that day, Vic allowed himself to think the third part, having her as a full-time companion, might be close to reality. That would seal the deal on happiness in his personal life. He was willing to wait, something he was growing used to, anyway. "Be patient," she'd said. Was there another choice?

On the Bittersweet front, Vic believed he was solidly in the driver's seat. Fairchild advised Angie that Vic's offer was generous and worth taking. He signed the dissolution papers the Tuesday of Christmas week; Fairchild filed them and obtained a final hearing date in early February. When Vic arrived home from signing the papers, his mother called to make certain he would leave the next day to spend Christmas with her in Charleston. The temperatures had been mild, and his mother's friend, Hobart, played golf almost every day. Hobart joined a new country club, and he said he'd like to take Vic out for a round or two. Vic's reluctance to be away from Roxanne was offset by his desire to get out on the course. He was dying to see if he still had his game.

When Vic came home Wednesday, Roxanne met him at the door wearing only a big red ribbon. After an hour of ardent gift exchange, she began to dress so he could leave for West Virginia.

"So, you never really told me. How'd the paper signing go yesterday?" she asked as she slipped into her blouse. "Angie made it through okay?"

"Oh, Angie wasn't even there when I went in. I haven't seen her since I went over to fix a leak in the kitchen sink last week. I think Fairchild made sure she was out on an errand or something," Vic explained. "And Fairchild, he was really nice. Went over everything to make certain I understood, and everything was written the way we'd agreed." Vic handed Roxanne her purse. "Man, when he walked me out to the lobby, he had his hand on my shoulder like we were old buddies. It was actually a little strange."

"In what way?" Roxanne wanted to know.

"Hard to put my finger on. It was more of a feeling, nothing overt. Almost like he felt sorry for me or something." Vic shook his head. "I mean, it isn't going to be a picnic paying my half on the house and the cost of this place, too, until the house sells." He shrugged. "But worst case, I'll get a salary step next year, and I'll find a summer job when school's out. My uncle has a business. I've driven truck for him, before." He pulled her into his arms. "One way or the other, I'll make it work." They kissed, and she started for the door.

"I hate that you're going to be so far away, buddy, but I'm glad you're going to see your mom." She talked over her shoulder.

"I'm going to miss you, too, Rox." He wrapped her in his arms again and nuzzled her neck from behind. "But I'll be home Monday and we'll have the rest of the week together."

As the sun set, Vic's RX7 roared under the overpass where River Road crossed the Ohio Turnpike. Many times, during early morning jogs, he'd looked down upon the toll road and fantasized this very scenario, heading southbound with the speedometer needle on the happy side of seventy and his golf clubs behind the seats. As the skies darkened, the dash lights seemed to intensify. Driving was one of his favorite things, and now he was headed to Charleston to see his mother and play golf. Great golf, he hoped. His golf clubs rattled as the little car thundered over the tar strips covering the expansion joints in the concrete. He tuned up an FM rock station and settled into the drive.

~ * ~

Charleston was spectacular at Christmas. The city's downtown was aglow with twinkling lights. With red and green spotlights trained on the golden dome of the West Virginia State Capital building, it looked like an outsized opalescent tree ornament. Three hundred miles of latitude made more difference in temperature than Vic would have guessed. On their way back from dinner, when he drove his mother along the Kanawah River, there were several boaters plying the waterway in the mild, mid-forty degree darkness. They even spotted a pontoon boat with a lighted Christmas tree on the forward deck.

In spite of the holiday aura, the tension between Vic and his mother was palpable. She touched on the subject of the impending dissolution a couple of times, and Vic's tack was to change the subject. Eventually, an unspoken, if strained, truce evolved. That night, he opened the window of his room a few inches and snuggled down under a quilted comforter. Memories of past Christmas Eves drifted through his mind like colorful specters. He fell asleep, cradling the recollection of a yellow and gray American Flyer locomotive he awakened to find, many Christmases ago, pulling an array of freight cars around the tree.

The next afternoon, Hobart Early arrived for Christmas dinner. Other than what he'd heard from his mother, all Vic knew about him was what he'd been able to garner during those fuzzy days after he awakened from the coma, when the signals were coming in as though the tuner in his brain was a blip off frequency. He spent much of the holiday afternoon gauging the man about whom his mother had always spoken with so much fondness. Vic asked a number of questions, which Early seemed shy about answering, at least at first. Mr. Early was a man of contradictions, making him a hard one to get a read on. As it turned out, his lack of formal education and strong West Virginia twang belied his intellect. Looking for business opportunities after his separation from the army in 1945, he happened across tool and implement rental, a new and relatively unknown enterprise, in those days. He was lucky enough to stumble across the idea, and smart enough to embrace it. His efforts and business savvy paid such handsome dividends, he was now semi-retired and in the process of selling his chain of twenty-some rental stores to a consortium of young lions who were paying him millions.

"But enough about me," Hobart said, placing his fork on his plate. "Barbara tells me you've become quite a golfer, Vic." He used one of the thick linen napkins to pat his lips, then pushed his eyelids into a squint. "I can call ya Vic?"

"Absolutely. Everyone does, except Ma," he said, tilting his head in her direction. "To answer your question directly, I only played three or four rounds before the weather turned."

"But they was good ones?"

"Yes, I have to say they were about the best I've ever shot. But I haven't played for over a month."

"And you feel like the coma had somethin' to do with it?" Hobart asked, side-glancing at Vic's mother. "I hope I'm not out of line. It's real intcresting."

Vic assured him asking was fine, and gave him the same version he'd given his mother and his friends, dreams he'd had about playing good golf, and remembering the moves after he came to. He included nothing about the after-conscious world or Loon's Lair, but he did recount the theory he'd dreamed up, when his mind reconnected with his body, the hook-ups were stronger than before. Vic was fairly certain Hobart never heard of The Mamas and The Papas, so he left out the bit about Cass Elliot's magic pipe, even though he loved the way he'd come up with that for the guys, something he still considered to be nothing short of a stroke of genius.

"That *is* amazing. I always wanted to have a good game, but I sure wouldn't want to have to go through what you did to get one." He patted Vic on the arm, and the gesture seemed genuine enough. "Some a' my friends talked me into joining a new club here called Cherry Hill. Glad I listened. Great track. It'd be my pleasure to take you up there for a round. I hope ya brought your clubs."

Vic grinned. "Ma told me you might offer. Yes, sir, I'd love a game."

"Hobie, please. Just call me Hobie," he said, smiling and bobbing his head, making his loose jowls bob and sway. "Supposed to be warm tomorrow. I'll get us a tee time around noon."

~ * ~

Vic zipped up his slacks and looked for a flush handle, but there was none. When he stepped away from the urinal, water cascaded into the green porcelain fixture. Must be some type of electric eye device, he decided, eyeing a dark red lens mounted above the urinal's plumbing. He'd never seen that, before. Everything about the locker room at Cherry Hill was opulent and fascinating. The colors of the wallpaper, carpet and the ceramic tile counter top were various shades of green. What wasn't money-green was oak, terra cotta tile, or gold-colored metal. The shelves bordering the mirrors above the sinks were stocked with shaving cream, disposable razors, and after-shave lotions. As soon as Vic finished washing up, a steward dressed in a green jacket with black trousers stepped forward to offer him a fluffy towel, and bowed slightly at the waist. Vic tipped the man a wink and a dollar.

Hobart called over to Vic as he walked into the pro shop. "Ya good with balls? What kind do you play?"

"Titleist Balatas, sir. I think I have enough."

Hobart turned and looked Vic in the eye. "I really wish ya could ease up and call me Hobie, Vic. Ain't much for formalities. Most only ones call me 'sir' are my competitors."

"I'm sorry, Hobie. 'Sir,' to me, is a show of respect."

"Shit, Vic, don' want no respect. Let's just be friends." Hobart gave him a sleeve of new Titleists. "Here. You're my guest. Take these." He discouraged Vic's protest with a wave of his unusually large, rough hand. "I took the liberty of getting up a little game with a couple of my friends. Hope ya don't mind."

"Not a bit, Hobie. What are we playing?"

"Low ball. We all four play the hole, each team cards their best score. You and I are playin' them even. Nobody gets no strokes." Hobart whispered like he offered a national security secret. "Quarter a hole. Don't worry, I'll cover you."

Vic smiled, thinking his mother must have laid it on thick regarding his financial straits if Hobart thought Vic couldn't afford pocket change.

Hobart's friends were waiting on the first tee. Bob Shymer was a big, smarmy guy who had the demeanor of a used car salesman crossed with a televangelist. He swung like a hacker, but he proved to be able to get the ball straight down the fairway and into the hole. His partner, Trent VanVorhis, was the evening news anchor on Charleston's most-watched television station. With that job and those initials, the man could have only one nickname. He swung a club with the grace and finesse of a professional, but the results were most often less than spectacular. His tee shot on number one wasn't a good one. "Nuts!" he hissed, through clenched teeth.

"No problem, TV," Bob Shymer said. "That's why we play eighteen holes."

Vic was at the back of the tee, rehearsing his swing and getting reconnected with Bascolm's catechism. Hobart gestured toward the tee box. "No pressure," he said.

Vic didn't feel any. With all his indoor practice, Vic forged a lot of confidence in his short game. Bascolm told Vic time and again, even if he had trouble with his woods and irons, a sound short game would pull him through. He plunged his tee into the turf and placed one of the shiny new Titleists Hobart gave him on it.

Number one was a par four that bent left, perfect for Vic's draw. He'd selected his five wood for the opening tee shot, a forgiving club that would leave him with a six or seven iron shot to the green. With unwavering confidence, he caught the ball solidly and it rolled to a stop on the edge of the fairway, about a hundred and fifty yards from the green.

"Nice poke," Hobie said, beaming. He executed a cut with his three wood, knocking it straight down the fairway one hundred and eighty yards or so. He chuckled as he started for their cart. "I'll take ones like that all day long."

"You betcha!" Vic replied. "Like they say, the woods are full of long hitters—all of them looking for lost golf balls." He chuckled. "I'm gonna walk a little, if that's all right." Hobart gave him a wave.

Vic ambled along the narrow path through the rough leading to the fairway. The deciduous trees stood bare, and although pines were plentiful, he couldn't smell them. The quality of the light coming through the cloudbanks made him think of Loon's Lair, and of Bass. Vic was certain Bascolm was out there somewhere, playing golf with Donald and Jason. He wondered if they ever thought of him. He remembered what Bass said about not playing for money. Vic doubted even Bass would quarrel with twenty-five cents a hole.

None of them made the putting surface with their second shots. TV's ball was close, off the front of the green, Hobart was a good fifty yards short, and Shymer was in a bunker. Vic's ball hit the putting surface, but rolled to rest in the long rough on the back of the green. Shymer needed two shots to escape the bunker. His second one landed twenty feet short of the hole, and skittered back down the green's smooth front slope, leaving him looking at a thirty-five footer for bogey. TV chipped his ball with too much conviction, zipping it across the green where it jumped into the long grass, not far from where Vic's ball rested.

Hobart gestured toward where Vic's Titleist was nested. "Trickier than fartin ' around a turd."

"Yep. Have to hit it right, get it up quick and land it soft." Vic pointed to a spot halfway to the cup. "About here."

"Do it and we won us a hole," Hobart said.

Vic made several practice stokes, and found one that felt right. He recreated the short swing and the ball jumped high, landed close to the spot he'd picked, and stopped inches from the cup. Hobart pulled the pin and Vic tapped in, using the toe of his sand wedge.

The others putted out, and Vic and Hobart walked to their cart. "Great par, partner," Hobart said. "We're two-hundred fifty bucks richer!"

"Two-hundred fifty bucks? But you said we were playing for ... "

"Quarters." Hobart belly-laughed. "Quarter of a grand a' hole."

Vic felt like he'd gotten a threatening letter from the IRS. "Shit," was all he managed to say.

~ * ~

When they arrived at the next tee, Vic was so occupied with thoughts of the money riding on each hole, there was no room left for swing thoughts. Teaching required two weeks to net two-hundred fifty dollars, and now they were trading that much on golf holes that ended in fewer than fifteen minutes. Big money rode on something as capricious as his golf swing, and that made him very nervous. When he shanked a shot on the second hole, Shymer and TV managed to win. The match was even. Then, on the third hole, Hobart came through to equal TV's par, so the two teams remained tied after three.

"Feeling some heat?" Hobart asked, as they walked from the cart to the fourth tee. Vic pursed his lips, making his cheeks bulge as he blew out a big breath of air in reply. Hobart gently grasped Vic by the arm, stopped and turned to face him. "Lookie here, Vic. Don't trouble yourself 'bout the money. I told you I'm standing good for it. Play your game." He let go of Vic's arm and patted his shoulder. "Do that, and we won't have to worry about no money. You got an ass-kickin' swing, son. Let it free."

Vic practiced his swing at the back of the tee and watched his club head snap across the grass blades. Close your hips, he repeated to himself. Pull the rope.

Number four at Cherry Hill was a long par five. After TV and Shymer hit off, Vic, to his relief and Hobart's delight, piped one straight down the fairway. His second shot landed short of the green. When he pitched close and made the putt for birdie, Vic was confident his game was back and his head was where it should be.

During the rest of the round, Vic's only nemesis was the course itself. There was no substitute for experience on such a demanding track, and although Hobart did his best to guide him, Vic lost a couple strokes because it was his first trip around the course. Several hidden hazards and some misjudged yardage exacted their toll. Regardless, TV and Shymer wound up the victims of a sound trouncing, so Vic and Hobart headed to the club's grill for a victory dinner.

Like the rest of the clubhouse at Cherry Hill, the men's grill had the look and feel of a room steeped in years of history and tradition. Eying the rich colors and textures of the wood, tile, stone and fabric, Vic found it hard to believe that place was a few years old. It even had a pleasant musty odor that implied years of gatherings and camaraderie—of stories related, of excuses made and of jokes told.

The waiter walked up with a fresh drink for Vic. "Another 'un for me, then no more drinks, no matter how I beg, young fella," Hobart joked, before turning to Vic. "You played one hell of a game of golf today, Vic. One over par your first time playing Cherry Hill. Damn! Was a pleasure to watch."

In his wildest imagination, Vic never dared to envision receiving that kind of praise for his golf game. He could feel his face redden. "Thanks, Hobie, for the compliment, *and* for dinner."

Hobart waved that off and rocked to the left, extracting a wallet from his hip pocket. He laid seven one-hundred dollar bills and a fifty on the green and white checked linen table cloth. "We wound up six holes to the good. That's your half. For all the help I was, I should give ya all of it."

"*We*," Vic said. "Without your help, I wouldn't have had any idea where to hit it."

Hobart put his elbows on the table and leaned forward to whisper, "But you do now?"

"Sure, I think I have the course mapped pretty well."

"Your ma says you're fixin' to leave Monday. Could you stay one day extry?"

Vic shrugged. "Maybe. Why?"

"There's a guy I'd like to see you play. Shymer'll set the match, but Monday would be the soonest."

Vic's mind spun. He missed Roxanne and wanted to get home, but Hobart's proposition had all of Vic's attention. "Money game?" he asked.

"Big money," Hobart said, looking Vic straight in the eye. Vic formed the idea Hobart was testing him. "He don't put a tee in the ground 'less the stakes are huge."

"Who's *he*?"

"The club champ, Sam Blackstock. Owns an explosives plant over in a little town west of here, called Nitro. Manufactures dynamite. Everybody calls him 'Boomer.' He's about the best player around, at this club anyhow. But I believe you can beat him." He popped a French fry into his mouth and chewed it, his lips making wet smacking sounds. He swallowed. "I'd purely love to watch ya take his money."

"How much money we talking?"

"You don't wanna know. Don't worry, I'm puttin' up the money for our side. You keep your head in your game."

A strange feeling came over Vic. He had the sense a huge key was turning, moving the tumblers in some great cosmic lock. And while locks can open or close, free or imprison, no matter how Vic looked at it, he couldn't envision Hobart's offer as the threat of incarceration. On the contrary, it seemed more like a "get out of jail free" card, a ticket out of the financial lockup he'd put himself in with a dissolution on a teacher's salary. His rent, on top of his half of the mortgage and the other expenses he incurred living on his own, made his finances even tighter than he estimated they would be. That made the urge to attach his destiny to Hobart and his proposition irresistible, even if it did fly in the face of Bascolm's philosophy regarding the ethics of playing golf for money and delayed his seeing Roxanne by a day. She was only five hours away. He could play, and still make it home Monday night. "Can I get in one more practice round tomorrow?" Vic asked.

Hobart's smile reduced his eyes to slits. "Shit, boy! We'll play all damned day if you like."

~ * ~

Vic poured another cup of coffee for his mother, and warmed up his own. They were still in their running clothes, and the dusky smell of their sweat mingled with the aroma of Maxwell House.

"You're in better shape than when you and Angie were here last summer."

Angie's name fell like a tray of china. "I don't like the way we left things, Mom," Vic said, like a man carefully picking up sharp pieces. "I've been avoiding it, but there's more needs to be said."

"I'm sorry I mentioned her. I don't want to discuss any of it, Allan," his mother said, shaking her head. "I plain don't understand you," she added, turning sideways in her chair. Vic thought for a moment she would get up and walk away.

He reached across the table to touch her hand. "I know. I know you're upset with me. I'm upset with myself," Vic said. She turned toward him and Vic looked into her eyes. "When I called and first told you I left her, I put it all on Angie. That was wrong. Look, I made mistakes too. It's hard to admit, but it's true. She and I both made mistakes. There are so many things I wish I'd done differently. I wish I would have confronted her earlier on, made her understand things were bad. I wish I'd given her an ultimatum. I wish I'd let her know things had to change or I was out the door, but I did the best I knew how at the time."

"And don't you believe Angie did, too? Did the best she could?"

"I ... ah ... gosh, I don't know. Sometimes I wonder what she was thinking. But maybe you're right there, too. Maybe my thinking she was selfish was another of the mistakes I made." Vic experienced one of those odd moments when something he said merely to grease the conversation suddenly seemed possible. Maybe he had misread Angie and her intentions. Maybe he'd been incorrect in assuming Angie was purposely selfish and controlling. The more time passed, the harder it was for him to recall all the details and facts that led him to where he now was. The tendency in humans to forget the bad and remember the good, that revisionist inclination clouded Vic's memory of what brought him to this point. However, he'd made his decisions based on what seemed correct when he made them, and he chose to trust those decisions. He'd picked his path, and he wasn't about to turn back.

"And you can't give her one more chance?"

"I told you, Mom. I let it go on for too long. Stored it up, and let it turn into anger." That, he knew for a fact, was true.

"But why did you store it up? That's what has me bothered. You have a temper like ... You expected her to sense you were unhappy?"

Vic ignored everything except the mid-sentence u-turn his mother made to avoid comparing him to The Old Man. Vic couldn't hide the sting, and his reaction pulled her out of her seat. She hurried around the table and draped her arms over his shoulders from behind. She nuzzled against the side of his face and whispered, "I didn't mean that."

Vic thought of the other comparisons she could make if she knew about Roxanne, and the sting grew to a burn. Why does a basically good person, who knows what is right, find himself incapable of ceasing to do wrong, he asked himself as he reached up and rubbed her cheek. "It's okay. In a lot of ways, I am like him." She started to shake her head, but Vic stood up and put his hands on her shoulders, looking again into her reddening eyes. "I look a lot like him. And I do have his temper. But ... look, Ma. I don't know what went on between you and ... " Vic couldn't refer to The Old Man as his father. "Tom," he finally said. "I don't know and it's none of my business anyway. All I can say is I'll never believe Angie didn't know there were problems. I'm not going to get explicit here, but when a married couple goes weeks without ... affection, well, there's no way a normal person isn't going to see that there's a problem. Not unless they don't want to. And that's what I believe. She was happy running things the way she wanted, and didn't care about my needs. So, yes, *now* I wish I could have found some way to change things. But I didn't. I didn't even know how. And I didn't think I should have to, with someone who supposedly loves me." Vic drained his coffee. "Of course I wish things would have turned out different."

"If wishes were horses ... " his mother intoned, turning to look out the window above the kitchen sink.

"Beggars would ride. You taught me that when I was a kid." He chuckled. "Thing is, if wishes were horses, *I'd* be a damned rancher."

His mother dabbed at her watery eyes with a tissue, then trained her attention on his face. "And there's no one else?"

Until that moment, the biggest lie Vic ever told his mother was he didn't want the trucking company when she wanted to sell it. The stakes were so much higher now. He didn't know if he could do it. He wasn't sure if it would be too difficult to convince her there was no one like Roxanne lurking in the shadows. He knew it was a no win, regardless. If Vic could deceive his mother, then he *was* very much like The Old Man, though she wouldn't know it. If he couldn't pull it off, she would *know* he resembled The Old Man in still another way, besides his looks and temper. Vic didn't have the time to decide which of these two untenable choices would make him hate himself more. He looked her dead in the eye and said, "No, Mom. This is about Angie and me. Nobody else."

Vic could see his mother processing what he'd said, her face working through consternation, then softening into something approaching peace. Finally, her expression came close to, but never quite managed, a smile. "Aren't you meeting Hobart around eleven?"

Vic looked at his watch and stood up. "Yeah, I better clean up and get going." He bent to kiss her cheek. "You don't mind me spending all this time out on the course?"

"Heavens! Go and have fun."

Vic headed upstairs to shower and dress, all the while trying to suppress his guilt over the lie he'd told. So perfectly.

~ * ~

Vic's conscience was relentless. All the way to the golf course, he veered between believing he deserved to feel guilty over the lies he'd told his mother, and trying desperately to justify them. Either way, he had to cleanse his mind of anything that might interfere with his ability to win the match on Monday. As Vic guided his coupe up the serpentine incline to Cherry Hill, the flat, buttery, late December sunlight that slashed through the pines lining the drive began to raise his spirits. When Vic pulled into the parking lot across from the pro shop, Hobart was waiting to introduce him to yet another of his friends. Merle West owned a company that manufactured machine tools he marketed to coal mining operations throughout the Appalachians. He looked like one of those movie extras who stand behind the star, nodding and maybe grunting in agreement with something a major character said. Merle's face was as bulbous as his body, and it appeared to take a good five feet of belt leather to encircle the fruits of his prosperity. His game was about on par with Hobart's, so the only betting was the "closest-to-the-pin-for-a-beer" type of thing. Vic's game was spot on and by the end of eighteen holes, Hobart and Merle owed him a six-pack or two. After a quick stop in the locker room for them to change out of their golf shoes, they shepherded Vic to a booth in the back of the grill and ordered drinks.

"You shot one hell of a round, Vic," Merle said. A diamond the size of a dime in his pinky ring caught the light as he put down his scotch and water. "One under on the front, three under on the back."

"My putting came together on the back."

"You got a real game, son," Merle said. "I'm anxious to see you put it to ol' Boomer."

Vic tried to sound less sure of himself than he felt. Modesty never hurt anyone. "I just hope I don't let you down." He leaned forward. "Want a hot tip?" Hobart and Merle canted in over the table, both of them turning their heads slightly so as not to miss a word. "Golf's a fickle game. Don't bet the farm." There was a moment of silence before the older men realized they'd been suckered, then all three of them laughed hard.

By the time the ice had hit bottom in their glasses, they were trading good-natured barbs and joking like old army buddies. Vic realized he held a genuine fondness for Hobart. His friends seemed like terrific people, as well. In addition, Vic relished his stature as the golfer they believed could unseat Blackstock as the local top gun. He swirled the cubes in his glass, and basked in the warm tingle of Southern Comfort and bright prospects.

~ * ~

"So, what exactly is going on here?" Barbara Vickery asked, her languid expression belying the truth of where she was headed. She and Vic were relaxing in her living room after his round.

Vic had heard this tone before. "Nothing, Mom. The weather's great, so I'm sticking around an extra day to play some golf with Hobie and his friends."

"He mentioned something about the club champion, but you can't be the club champ if you don't belong. Is this some kind of gambling deal?" She sipped the martini he'd talked her into, but her eyes were unwavering.

Vic's mind raced before he settled on a perfect explanation. A chill tickled his spine as the thought occurred he was becoming way too good at fabrication. "You remember the blizzard we had a few years ago in Toledo? Back in '78?" he began. Her eyebrows almost collided, but she nodded. "Remember those sweatshirts they were selling afterwards, 'I survived the blizzard of '78 and all I got was this shirt?' So okay, I survived a shot to the head, a coma, and all I got for my trouble was a good golf game. It's winter in Toledo and I'm going through a dissolution. Nothing going for me back home. I can sit in my apartment and watch MTV, or I can get out and do something I'm good at, for *free*. Hobie's nice enough to invite me to play here. I'd be nuts not to take him up on it. All I have to do is hang around an extra day ... that, and take my gorgeous mom out for dinner tonight. Where we going, by the way?"

She was too savvy an interrogator to fall for his ruse. "I haven't given it a thought. But are you gambling?"

"Mom, I can't afford to gamble. I'm doing okay, but I *am* on a budget. I have half a house payment on top of my rent, plus alimony that'll start in March. Keeps me from having any dough to throw around."

"Allan, I've known a gambler or two in my life, and very damned few could *afford* it."

Vic put down his drink and held her hand in both of his. "Mom, I'm not going to say there won't be some money on our game. I don't know for sure, one way or the other. But I am telling you that *I* don't have any money on it." He squeezed her hand for emphasis. "None! What Hobie does is up to him. I don't ask and I don't want to know. I'm going to play a match against a good golfer. If I beat him, I get bragging rights. If I don't, I'll still have fun playing."

A glint in her eye signaled the inquisition was drawing to a close, for the present, anyway. "If I know Hobart Early, you lose him much of his money, your days of free golf at Cherry Hill are numbered."

Vic gave her a kiss on the cheek and came away from the interrogation feeling mostly good about it. Yes, he'd lied to her again because he did stand to win money. But it was also the case that he didn't stand to lose any, so he wasn't really gambling, and that's what she'd asked him. Besides, Vic didn't view the match as gambling, anyway. He put his skill against another player's. It was a contest, not a gamble.

The Monday after Christmas was forecast to be partly cloudy and close to fifty degrees in Charleston. Vic woke up early and, burdened with a handful of quarters, went for a run. He found a pay phone several blocks from his mother's house and fed it like a slot machine. Five bucks bought almost an hour of conversation with Roxanne. Shivering in the gusty chill, Vic savored every moment.

"Kick that guy's ass today!" Roxanne said, as they were saying goodbye.

"Were you a cheerleader in high school?"

"No, but I had a pretty good set of pom-poms."

"You still do," Vic replied. "Can't wait to get home and make them shake. I'll be home late tonight. See you Tuesday."

~ * ~

Vic's nerves had his stomach on a rolling boil when he met Hobart at Cherry Hill later that morning. "What kind of guy is Blackstock, Hobie?" he asked, as they walked into the locker room.

Hobart cocked his head. "I knew you'd ask. Been wondering what to tell you," he said after the silence told him they were alone. "He's one a them guys … bigger'n life. He's an asshole most of the time, but he can be downright charming, too. One thing's sure, he don't like to lose." Hobart poked Vic's shoulder. "He ain't above cheatin'."

"No shit? Cheat how?"

"Once he ripped a big old fart in the middle of a fella's back swing. From the sound of it, he mighta shit his pants. But the guy duffed it, and Boomer won the hole and the match."

"God, that's amazing!"

"Sam Blackstock is amazing. Hell of it is, he don't need to cheat. He hits it long. He'll use that to intimidate you, try to get ya to over-swing to stay with him. He's real stuck on himself, likes to wear expensive clothes and jewelry. He's a piece of work."

"It sounds like he'll give me plenty to use, if I need to," Vic said, noticing his statement put a confused look on Hobart's face. "Look, I'm a teacher, Hobe. A teacher learns how to work on people's heads, play mental games. How do you think I keep a roomful of insane teenagers in line all by my lonesome? I always play it straight up at first, but if a kid gets out of line and starts giving me trouble, I figure out his weaknesses and work on them." He raised an eyebrow. "I'm pretty good at it."

"You got a good head on your shoulders, boy. 'Tween that and your golf game, I'd say old Boomer is gonna have his hands full." He gave Vic a nudge. "And unless I miss my guess, we'll have our hands full, too, of loot!"

"Oh, yeah. That reminds me. The situation with Mom is ... delicate. Her son is a *teacher*, not a gambler. I told her you might have a little money on the game, but I'm playing for the fun and competition." He gave Hobart a wink.

Hobart raised his right hand. "I understand, son. Your momma'll never hear no different from me."

At ten minutes past their agreed tee time, Sam Blackstock had yet to show. They'd already allowed one group to go off ahead of them. Vic stood with Hobart on the first tee, warming up his swing and wondering exactly how Bascolm would view Vic's playing for money. Would Bascolm actually be disappointed in Vic for using what he taught him to win money? That was possible, but Vic decided he was more inclined to think Bascolm would see it more like watching someone misuse a tool. Amused exasperation, perhaps. Knowing Bascolm as he had come to, Vic tended to believe the latter. He preferred to see it that way, for certain.

He looked up at the sky. It wasn't the day they'd predicted. With the overcast, it didn't feel like it would hit forty degrees, much less the fifty the weatherman promised. With the breeze, it was downright nippy. Vic believed that was to his benefit because in Toledo, he frequently played in similar conditions. Additionally, running cranked his metabolism to where he didn't have trouble keeping warm. A light turtleneck and a sweater were all he needed. Blackstock would undoubtedly be wearing heavier clothing. Even an extra sweater or jacket could change a player's swing path. Vic hoped it might.

"You doin' okay?" Hobart asked, in a raspy whisper.

"Nervous. Had the shits back in the clubhouse, but I think that's over with."

"Good. Just don't go to fartin' during Sam's back swing."

Vic lip-farted on his next practice swing, then he walked over to his caddie and handed the boy his driver.

The kid gave Vic a surprised look. "Three wood then, sir?" he asked.

"Not sure yet, Lenny." His caddie was a tall, thin teenager with light reddish-brown hair, a nose profiled like a ski jump and according to Hobart, as much knowledge of the course as anyone. "Depends on what Blackstock does."

"He'll hit driver," Lenny said. "I've looped for him lots of times."

"I meant it depends on *how* he hits it."

"Oh, he'll bang it good, draw it around the dogleg. Leave himself a sand wedge in, about eighty or ninety yards."

"So, your money's on him?" Vic asked, baiting the boy.

"No sir, Mr. Vickery. You're my player. I just know his game."

Vic gave the kid a pat on the shoulder. "Good. Anything you think might help will be appreciated," he added, rubbing his thumb on the tips of his fingers to indicate money. Lenny's eyes widened and he smirked.

"Here comes Eric Killburn, Blackstock's observer," Hobart said, looking toward a man approaching the tee. Killburn's gait was rangy and loose. As he neared the tee, Vic saw the man had a face that looked Cro-Magnon, with a protruding upper jaw, a wide flat nose, and strong cheek bones, which emphasized the hollow below them. Faces like his adorned the walls at post offices all over the country.

"Boomer will be right out," the caveman announced, cinching his long, oilskin duster around his thin frame. "He busted a shoelace. Where's your player, Hobart?" he asked, looking straight at Vic.

Hobart swept his arm in Vic's direction. "Eric, I'd like you to meet Allan Vickery."

Vic reached out to shake Caveman's hand. "They call me Vic."

Killburn folded his arms and looked toward the clubhouse. "Hope you brought your best game, Al," he muttered. "Here comes Boomer."

Blackstock strolled languidly in their direction, the wind fraying his wavy, long, chestnut-colored hair. He pushed it back and shoved a hat with a wide flat brim down on his head. Blackstock had the swagger of a swashbuckling pirate. The closer he came, the more Vic was struck by the man's good looks. Tanned and ruggedly handsome, he exuded the theatrical self-assured quality of a movie star. The first sun of the day broke through as Blackstock stepped onto the tee, illuminating the landscape behind him. Stage-lighting, Vic thought.

Blackstock made an offhanded wave at no one in particular. "Sorry I'm late. My locker door was jammed." He looked at Vic. "I've not had the pleasure. You must be Al Vickery." The antithesis of his friend, Blackstock extended his hand politely.

"They call me Vic," he said, wondering which story was correct, the broken shoe lace or the jammed locker?

"You gonna whip my ass today, Mr. Vic?"

"No, sir, probably not. But then, you never know."

"We'll find out, won't we?" Blackstock replied, grinning. "Hobart! Strokes or holes?" he shouted against the breeze. His eyes never left Vic.

"Holes, Boomer. That's the agreement," Hobart said.

"Just checking," Blackstock said. "No savings," he added, laughing alone at his own joke. He extended his arm toward his caddie, like a surgeon awaiting a scalpel. The young man pulled out Blackstock's driver, yanked off the head cover, and snapped the club into his player's outstretched hand. "This is one of those new metal woods, Mr. Vic. You ever seen one?"

"Yeah, but I'm a dinosaur," Vic replied. "Prefer persimmon. Real wood was good enough for Hogan, Hagen, and Snead."

"Yeah, but persimmon was cutting edge back then, Mr. Vic. Those boys would be playing metal woods today," he said, twirling the club like a baton. "I have the tee?"

"Hobe says that's the agreement," Vic deadpanned. "Do it."

Blackstock strode to the box and teed his ball. He swung several times, his club whooping through the air, then stepped into his address. He broke his routine long enough to press his expensive looking leather hat down against the wind, then began his swing. It was as quick as any Vic had ever seen. In an instant, he drew his club back and followed through. The metal wood rang like a bell and the ball screamed out over the fairway, bending left around the dogleg, as Lenny said it would.

He bent to pick his tee from the grass. "That should be out there two seventy-five or so. Think you can hit yours past me, Mr. Vic?"

"Maybe." Vic leaned casually against the stone tee marker. "But I know I'm not going to try. Six iron," he said to Lenny, holding his arm in the caddie's direction.

"Six iron!" Blackstock nearly squealed. "This hole is playin' over 360 yards today, into the wind!"

"Yeah, gosh, golf is a complicated game, Mr. Blackstock. Sometimes I get crossed up and play my second shot first." Vic visualized Bascolm's swing in his mind's eye, before he triggered his own. The shiny Titleist jumped into the gloomy skies and landed in the fairway, just over one hundred-fifty yards away. He handed his club to Lenny, and looked into Caveman's beady simian eyes as he passed by. "Hope I know what I'm doing," he chuckled. Then he turned to Blackstock and shrugged. "I must be nuts, eh?"

Hobart looked like he'd seen a ghost, so Vic fired him a wink. Confidence coursed through him like lust. "This'll be fun, Hobe," Vic said. "Make sure you get to Blackstock's ball when he does. Don't want him taking any paradise lies."

As he walked off the tee, the only thing Vic feared was overconfidence. General George Custer, Adolph Hitler, Sonny Liston … none of them believed they could be beaten, but each of them was. Vic felt invincible. It was all he could do not to run up to Blackstock and shout, "You're my lunch, man! You're sandwich meat!" But an inner voice that sounded a little like Bascolm's spoke convincing sense, saying stay in the game. Take your time. Think each shot through. When they arrived at his ball, Vic saw he was the beneficiary of some good fortune. It had rolled through a divot, up onto the edge of the surrounding turf. It might as well have been sitting on a tee.

"Two hundred ten yards, sir," Lenny said, setting Vic's bag down. "Wind is left to right. The balls are cold and the air's heavy. You might want to go one club stronger. The pin's at the front left, bunker protecting it."

Vic processed the information. In ordinary conditions, he'd hit an easy five wood. But Lenny was right, the cold, heavy atmosphere and wind would affect the flight of the ball. He tossed a few blades of grass into the air, watching for the effect the chilly breeze would have on them. Should I hit an easy three wood, or lean on my five, he wondered.

Caveman used his pocketed hands to secure his heavy duster tight around his torso. "I'm gettin' frostbite, here," he barked.

Vic locked onto Killburn with the most baleful glare he owned. Caveman didn't waver, and they stared at each other several seconds before Vic leered, maintaining the high-voltage with his eyes. Vic, his voice a low rumble, spoke slowly and directly to Killburn. "You fuck with me, man, it's gonna work to Mr. Blackstock's disadvantage. See, I got a hellacious goddamn temper, and the madder I get, the better I play. You don't believe me, you watch this, asshole," he said, yanking his five wood from the bag. "This shot's for you, Eric."

Vic decided short was better than long, so he put nothing extra on his swing. As he anticipated, the wind fought his draw. The ball flew straight, landing a few yards short of the putting surface, on the green's apron.

Hobart grinned big. "Nice shot, Vic."

"We owe it all to our friend, Eric." Vic puckered and made an effusive kissing sound. "So, keep on dogging my ass, okay, Eric?"

"Now, now, Vic," Blackstock said, in a calm-your-dog kind of voice. "Eric really didn't mean anything, other than it's colder out here than a nun's kiss." Then Blackstock flinched like he'd belched at a formal dinner. "No offense meant. You aren't Catholic, are you?"

"No, but I French-kissed a nun once," Vic said, with a snarl he intended to serve notice to Blackstock the ice could get thin again quickly. "Let's just play golf."

Blackstock's conciliatory demeanor changed to chagrin when he discovered his tee shot netted only two hundred forty yards. His eight iron to the green showed every sign of wanting to go into the front bunker, but by some quirk of fate, it bounced into the rough above it. Both Blackstock and Vic pitched close and made their putts, each man recording a par on the first hole. As he walked to the second tee, Vic believed he had demonstrated he had no reason to fear Blackstock's long game. Proving distance off the tee wouldn't win the match neutralized one of the champ's main weapons.

Blackstock still had honors on the five hundred yard second hole, and his desire to rocket one apparently overrode his concentration. His body was too far in front of his arms, and he blocked the shot into a grove of pines on the right. He glowered, while his caddie and Killburn offered optimistic spins on his situation. Vic was delighted. Not only would Blackstock's mistake most likely cost him a stroke, but Vic saw an opportunity to do some more work on his opponent's head.

"Timing was off, Boomer," Vic said, as he set his ball on a tee. "You've been swinging to a two-and-a-half count. That last one was more like one and a half."

Blackstock sneered. "Do I have to pay for this lesson?"

Vic affected polite concern. "You'll pay if you don't listen. Look, I'm a student of the swing, and brother, you got a beauty. But it goes to a two-and-a-half count." Vic swung several times to loosen up, then stepped into his address, and waggled his club head. "Now, mine goes to a four-beat. One," he began, initiating his back swing, "two," he continued, as his arms reached shoulder level, "three," he said, winding to a stop with the shaft of his club parallel to the ground, and "FOUR!" he grunted, sweeping through his release. He caught the ball sweet and it started low, skirting the right boundary of the fairway. It gained altitude before drawing back toward the middle and dropped onto the short grass. He shot Blackstock a big friendly grin. "That concludes my presentation."

Blackstock's tee shot apparently went out of bounds, because none of them could find it in the five minutes the rules allow. He stalked back to the tee, and hit a nice second drive, but couldn't make up the stroke he'd lost. He conceded the hole when Vic's third shot rolled to within a few yards of the pin.

Vic was now sitting on a one-up lead. Boomer seemed to take it in stride, but Vic could see the muscles working like moles beneath Caveman's cheeks, and his jaws didn't get much rest after that. Blackstock tried to find the rhythm Vic suggested he lost, slowing his swing way down and hitting shots fat, sending clumps of turf flying and cutting distance from his ball's flight. Then he tried speeding it up, which made for better contact, but he rained balls everywhere, except onto the fairway. Blackstock lost two of the next five holes, and was fortunate not to lose more. Vic admired the man's game and his persistence. A player with less of either would have collapsed. Vic figured Blackstock had to be worried, but his demeanor said he was dead set on winning the match. Meanwhile, Vic maintained a jovial patter he was certain drove his opponent crazy.

"That's a real cool cowboy hat," Vic enthused as he and Blackstock walked onto the eighth green. "Do you have a cow?"

"Nope," Blackstock snarled, "but you apparently have plenty of bull."

"Oh, I bet you say that to all your friends," Vic said, chuckling, before he railed in a ten-footer for birdie. Blackstock missed his birdie putt, picked up his ball, and stomped off toward the next tee without a word.

When Vic and Hobart crossed a footbridge to the ninth tee, it was the first opportunity they'd had to speak privately. "Old Boomer can't seem to get back to his two and a half count," Hobart said.

"I made all that shit up," Vic whispered. "I have no idea what his tempo is."

"Jesus Christ, Vic. You are somethin'. No wonder he hasn't tried to cheat or pull none of his tricks. You got him so sideways, he can't spare no time to try nothing."

"Yeah, well, don't get too excited, Hobe. He's doing the survivor shuffle to finish this nine. There's still a lot of match left." He paused. "New nine, new state of mind. That's what I always tell myself." He gestured toward Blackstock. "He's one hell of a player. I'd have loved to go at him straight up. I feel bad about working on his head."

"The head game's all part of it, Vic. It's you or him. Believe me, boy, he'll do the same if he gets a chance. Shit, already did, having Killburn work on ya. Boy, you turned that around on 'em."

Vic grunted in agreement. He watched as Blackstock pulled a windbreaker out of his bag. "You cold, Sam? I might have an extra sweater with me."

"Just hit off," Blackstock snarled.

"Or you can wear the one I have on. I'm plenty warm."

He turned to his caddie. "Lenny?"

"One eighty-six, downwind."

Vic pretended to ponder his next move, but he knew what he would to do from the minute they walked onto the tee. "Five iron," he said, and crushed his tee shot, which found the green. Blackstock's shot landed in the heavy rough, with a tree directly between his ball and the cup.

"I'm in my pocket," Blackstock grumbled, stooping to pick up his ball. "You're five up. See you on number ten in fifteen minutes." Vacant of his former presence and grace, he trudged away, with Caveman engaged in some manner of emphatic discourse. Blackstock didn't appear to be paying much attention to his pal's soliloquy.

Vic looked at Hobart and shrugged. "I'm holing out. I could birdie here for a thirty-four." When Vic missed his putt, Hobart hurried inside for coffee. Vic chose to wait on the tenth tee, hoping to reinforce the idea in Blackstock's mind that the cold didn't affect him.

"You gonna be okay, not too cold?" Hobart asked, when he returned from the clubhouse. He dug his hands deeper into his coat pockets as he stepped onto the tee. It clouded up, but the wind had died.

Vic wrinkled his nose and imitated Hobart's drawl. "I'm fine. Us 'nautheners' are used to this."

"You really play better mad?" Hobart asked.

"Nah. Made that up, too. Figured it would keep Caveman off my back."

"Caveman?"

"Shit, yes. Doesn't Killburn look like he should be out clubbing dinosaurs instead of wandering around a golf course?" Hobart chuckled. The fifteen minutes Blackstock mentioned when he conceded on number nine came and went. It was closing in on half an hour.

"Sure ya're not catchin' a chill?" Hobie asked, again.

"I'll be fine, if that fucker ever gets out here so we can start playing! Jesus, Hobe, how long can this shithead keep us waiting? Isn't there such a thing as a delay of match penalty?"

As Vic's question diffused to silence of the afternoon's gloom, the Blackstock party reemerged from the clubhouse. Having regained his former demeanor, Blackstock strode audaciously onto the tee. Wary of his resurrection, Vic started right in on him.

"Good to see you, Sam. Thought you might have loaded up your clubs and moseyed on home."

"Not a chance of that, Mr. Vic. You make your putt on nine?"

"No sir! Lipped out for a thirty-five. Thought sure I'd sink it, but what the hell?"

Blackstock pulled his driver from his bag. "Yeah, well, my heart bleeds. So tee your ball and let's get it on."

Blackstock came out strong and won the next three holes, putting him within two of making the match even. His tempo returned. Vic figured it was because he'd stopped worrying about it. At any rate, Blackstock was building some serious momentum. Vic was nervous and desperate to derail him. Vic struck the ball well, but Blackstock was playing like a pro, and Vic was losing confidence he would prevail. He needed something to take Blackstock out of his game. When it came to him, Vic was certain the idea was brilliant. Something familiar that would move right into Blackstock's mind and displace his swing thoughts. They called the man Boomer because of the way he hit the ball, and because he manufactured explosives. The two were tightly meshed parts of the man, and Vic looked for that kind of fit. He decided it was worth a try. "Hey, Sam," Vic said, as they walked to the thirteenth tee. "How much would a stick of dynamite cost me?"

"Huh?" Blackstock replied, doing a take as though he manufactured bubble gum rather than explosives.

"Dynamite. How much for a stick?"

"I honestly don't know," he answered, shaking his head. "We only wholesale it out. Why?"

"I was hoping you'd sell me some. You know, a dozen sticks or so."

Blackstock teed his ball. "What the hell you gonna do with dynamite?" He flashed a furtive grin at Caveman.

"Oh, you never know when it might come in handy. Now, does it come with the wick already in it?"

"Fuse, Mr. Vic. It's called a fuse." He chuckled. "The fuse is sold separately." Blackstock had his driver in his hands, and he made practice swings.

"So, could you sell me a couple dozen? And some *fuse*?"

"No, man, I couldn't," Blackstock said, impatience surfacing in his smooth pool of calm confidence. "We only have a wholesale license. You have to buy it retail." He stepped into his address.

"You mean like a hardware store, maybe a farm supply? Something like that?"

Blackstock turned to look at Vic. "Yes! You can buy it at a goddamn farm store, for Christ's sake. Any other questions?"

"Yeah, what do you guess it would cost for a stick? A couple bucks? Like, twenty, maybe thirty bucks for a dozen?"

"Something like that," Blackstock said, before shanking his ball out of bounds, his second off-course sojourn of the day.

Four holes after that, Blackstock was still three holes down. They were on the number sixteen green, and the champ had to sink a long putt, *and* win the last two holes to force the match into sudden death, the best he could hope for. Vic didn't believe that would happen. He stood next to Hobart, appraising his adversary from across the green. Blackstock, Caveman, and the caddie looked like a team of grim surveyors as they read his putt.

"I don't think he stands a chance in hell of making this," Hobart whispered.

Vic scoffed. "Hasn't one-putted since thirteen, and this one ain't no gimme. Ten feet downhill, right to left."

"Think I'm a dead man, Mr. Vic?" Blackstock called over, breaking the silence. "Think I won't make this?"

Vic went deadpan. "You're certainly due."

Blackstock picked up on the implication. "None of the other putts matter, Mr. Vic. And I *am* draining this son of a bitch. You watch."

With that, Blackstock eyed his line one last time, executed several practice strokes, then brought the putter head through.

Vic flashed back to his fateful putt at the Chili Open. Did Blackstock have the same gut feeling about the destiny of his putt as Vic had then, or was he riding some bravado? Vic held his breath as the ball rolled across the slope, losing speed at just the proper rate to let it drift toward the cup. The little white sphere became Vic's universe. He saw nothing else. His toes curled in his running shoes, nails digging at the insoles, as the ball rolled slowly to the lip of the cup where it ... stopped. Much of its mass was in the air above the opening, but it planted itself and wouldn't take the plunge.

Blackstock stepped over to shake hands, but he never made eye contact with Vic. "Nice game." Then, over his shoulder to Hobart, "The money's in my locker. I plan to leave right away, so I'd appreciate it if you'd come get it, pronto."

Vic and Hobart stood in silence until Blackstock's group disappeared into the Clubhouse, then the two of them began to whoop and dance like miners at a gold strike. Vic's caddy dropped the flagstick in the empty cup, and before he could stoop to pick up Blackstock's orphaned ball, Vic threw his arm over the boy's shoulder and the two celebrants became a trio.

Chapter Eight

Hobart went into the locker room to collect Blackstock's money, leaving Vic to wait in the hallway. If Blackstock had a locker-full of money, it meant Hobart did, too. After all, he had to cover the bet in case Vic didn't win. He had no idea how much cash was involved, but Hobart made it sound like the figure was considerable, and he hadn't shown himself to deal in hyperbole. Vic shook his head. This was foreign territory for an art teacher whose idea of a big night out featured a ten dollar steak.

In minutes, Hobart came through the locker room's door, gave Vic a wide-eyed look that reminded him of Rodney Dangerfield, and the two of them headed for the men's grill to celebrate. Vic expected to enjoy a drink and a quick bite, collect a share of the winnings, and head straight for home. It turned out very differently.

The first jolt came in the form of the blue plastic cash envelope Hobart pushed across the table. It was heavy and thick. "What'd Blackstock do, pay off in singles?"

Hobart smiled, put his finger to his lips to indicate the need for privacy, and wagged his head.

"Twenties," he whispered.

Vic's eyes bulged wide when he opened the zipper and found five neat packages, each with a paper band indicating it girded fifty bills. He'd never seen so much cash before. There were so many bills, the five packages actually felt heavy. He dropped the bag and looked at Hobart. His whisper escaped like steam, and his face ripped into an open grin. "Jesus Christ! That's, that's five thousand dollars. Holy shit. How do you want to split this?"

Once again, Hobart wagged his grizzled old head. "It's split. That's your half." He patted the pocket of his sport coat. "I got mine. Best part is, he's already talkin' about a rematch in the spring, and we ain't going to play him for no measly ten grand next time! Stakes is goin' straight up!"

Vic was speechless. Then, a second shock came in the form of a proposition.

Hobart hunched forward, his forearms against the table linen. "Listen, Vic. Me and the boys, TV, Bob, and Merle, we come across somethin' called 'syndicate golf.'"

Vic's eyelids butterflied. "Syndicate?" he echoed.

"No, it ain't what you think. Got nothing to do with mobsters, least ways, not that I know of. See, some boys get together and find 'em a good player. Not PGA tour good. Somebody like you, shoots around par. A good scratch player. Anyways, that syndicate lines up matches with other syndicates' players. Way they do that, there's an outfit back east, in Philadelphia, runs the whole shebang. They got rules set up about how the matches go. They print a weekly sheet, rates the players, tells which one played who, and which of 'em won."

Vic couldn't take his eyes off Hobart's. The older man was intent on his own hands, the tips of the fingers on his right hand tapping the fingertips of his left. Hobart looked up and raised an eyebrow.

"Go on," Vic said.

Hobart shrugged. "Well, me and the boys want in on the action. We was lookin' to ask Blackstock to be our player, but, when your momma told me about your game, we decided to give *you* a look." Hobart reached across the table and grasped Vic's wrist. "The boys and I'd like you to be our man."

A kaleidoscope of thoughts exploded in Vic's mind when Hobart made his offer. Vic saw it as an incredible opportunity. He wanted to accept, but he had a few reservations. Those two opposing responses became twisted all around each other, causing attempts at speech to tumble out in unintelligible lumps. Vic gave up, and only smiled as the waiter appeared with their orders. "You think I'm good enough?" he asked, after the waiter retreated.

Hobart grinned. "Doan know. But you beat Blackstock shitless, and he's the only other one we was lookin' at." Then Hobart's grin expanded, displaying a small gold mine of dental work. "Besides, the boys and I like you. Blackstock's an asshole, speakin' plain."

Vic winked in agreement. "So, when would all this start?"

"Right away. You're hot. Your game is good. I'd say there's no time like the present."

"But, it's December."

"There's always the Carolinas. Georgia. Merle's company owns a plane. His pilot can fly up to Toledo and take you to wherever the match is. Hell, Florida is just five or six hours from there in Merle's ... Apache ... Comanche, some damned in'jun name. Quick little shit. Cruises at over two hundred." His face became serious. "You ain't afraid of flying?"

"Only been in a private plane once. Mom's brother used to fly. I got to go up with him on my twelfth birthday."

"How'd it go?"

"Puked all over my shoes."

"Hope you waited 'til after you landed."

"All over the carpet in the backseat of The Old Man's car."

They laughed. "But you'd be okay now?" Hobart asked.

"Probably. Good pilot?"

"Oh, shit yes! Foss Bannigan. Hell of a pilot! Flew in World War II and Korea. I've been up with him lots of times."

Vic was still struggling to understand it all. "So how would all this work? I can't miss school."

"You won't. The syndicate will do the leg work. We'll pick opponents and set everything up. After you get off school on Friday, get yourself out to the airport. Foss'll be there to fly you to wherever the match is."

"At night?"

"Sure. He's instrument rated. Anyway, we'll get a car at the airport when we land and find nice rooms somewhere."

"We ... you and me?"

"It'll be me or TV. Neither Merle nor Bob like to travel all that much. Ya need someone to handle the details. You're the player. I want your mind clear of anything but your golf game. Anyway, we got to have a spotter, make sure the other player don't go kicking his ball around, takin' no golf shoe relief from trees, or whatnot. Saturday, you'll have a tee time so you can play a round or two, get familiar with the course. Saturday night, the host syndicate's gotta pick up the tab for a dinner at the club, or some nice restaurant. Sunday, you play the round, and we're back on the plane, and headed home."

Vic fell silent, marveling at how life could wander off in such unexpected directions. When he thought he had a fair read on where things were going, the fates forced a metamorphosis he never could have predicted. From the moment he was hit by Tom Bayer's golf ball, the events in his life had taken totally unexpected compass headings. He managed a couple of bites of his sandwich, but savored the rich possibilities Hobart offered over the food.

"There's another thing that might be a problem, Hobe," Vic said, after several seconds of thought.

"Fire away."

"I don't know quite how to broach this. Have you considered our business dealings might interfere with your friendship with Mom? Or vice versa? I mean, if I'm your employee, which I would be as your player, couldn't your relationship with Ma complicate things if you have to make ... ah, some kind of business decision?"

Hobart nodded. "I appreciate your concern, young man. I mean that. It's real considerate of you. But it won't be no trouble." Hobart sipped his Old Fashioned. "For one thing, you were right. Barbara, ah, your momma, we're friends. She made it plain from the start that's all it would ever be. We enjoy each other's company. Take in a theater show now and again. Go to dinner. It'll never be no more than that. Second, like we agreed, far as she knows you're a teacher, not a high stakes player. She ain't never going to know about our arrangement, 'less you tell her." He winked to seal his covenant.

"Third," Hobart drummed three fingers on the table, "I got no doubts about your game and abilities, but we know going in, you ain't gonna win every match. Shit, we'd be millionaires, but we'd have to spend it all on security to keep the others from stealing you away. So, either you *or* the four of us decide to get out of the golfing business for whatever reason, well, I know we're all men enough to respect the other side's point of view. Right?" He extended his hand and Vic grasped it to seal the bargain, but Hobart had more to add. "You may have shaken on it too soon, Vic. We ain't talked money yet."

Vic held up the cash envelope. "I'm not much worried. I had no idea my cut on today's match would be," he'd throttled back to a whisper, "five thousand bucks. And you *knew* I didn't know. You could have given me a thousand, kept the rest, and I'd have been happy and none the wiser."

Hobart slapped his forehead. "Damn! How'd I get so stupid?"

"It's not about stupidity. It's about integrity. I trust you. You earned that."

Hobart drained his drink. "The boys and I decided you get one third after expenses. Expenses come off the top: cost of the plane, rooms, food, and whatnot. Then the four of us split the remaining two thirds. You get the rest. Sound fair?"

"More than fair! Better than a fifth."

"Hey, you're the engine. You do the big work. We just along for the ride." He sucked on his eyetooth. "Play good golf, and we'll do fine. We ain't out to make no killing. The boys and I, we all got nice incomes. We lookin' to have some fun, and if some money comes out of it, good for us. And I know as a teacher, you could use a little extra."

"A little. Shit, Hobie." Vic pointed to the money bag. "That's about a quarter of my yearly salary, right there! More, if you figure it's tax free."

"Now, there's something we might want to have a little sit-down about." Hobart rocked forward and rested his elbows on the table. "I mean, it's none a' my business, and you're welcome to tell me so, but I might be able to offer some advice. Maybe even some help." He leaned even closer and his voice became a lower whisper. "I've gone a round or two with them revenuers."

Vic pushed his plate to the side. "I'd appreciate any advice you have."

"Make sure your soon-to-be 'ex' don't find out nothing about this," Hobart started in, tapping Vic's money envelope, "or the seven-fifty we took off TV and Shymer. My advice is to put it all in a deposit box somewhere, and leak it off a little at a time. You know, walkin' around money. Don't go buyin' nothin' big. Least ways, not 'til after your divorce is final."

"On February fourth."

"Yeah, the fourth. At the hearin,' the judge'll ask you if there's been any change in your financial status. He'll be referring to your *regular* work. Ah, you're still only teachin', right?" Vic winked. "Any future money ya win playing the syndicates, I could pay you through my company, Earlybird Enterprises. I'll put you on as a consultant, take out the withholding and make the money legal. You don't wanna get caught hidin' money from them revenue boys."

"Yeah, that would be perfect, Hobe."

Hobart stuck a toothpick in the corner of his mouth. "'Course, that consultin' job won't start payin' right off. You'll be probationary, until I see how you work out. Your first check will get cut, oh ... let's say a day or two *after* February fourth."

Vic raised his glass and Hobart tapped his against it. "You're the boss." Vic winked. "Literally."

They finished their drinks, and Vic looked at his watch. He was anxious to get back to Roxanne. His universe had shifted and there was only one other person he could share the new coordinates with. Even though chances for a conversation that night were slim, Vic was still anxious to be back within a few miles of her. Tom Bayer might be bowling, or passed out. Roxanne might call. Vic couldn't wait to hear her voice.

"I better get a move on," he said to Hobart, who drained his glass and dropped it on the table.

When they walked to Vic's car, he unlocked the door, then turned to shake Hobart's hand.

"Drive safe, son," Hobart said, grasping Vic's shoulder and pulling him into a fatherly embrace. He patted Vic's shoulder several times and stepped back. A look that might have read of embarrassment crossed Hobart's face.

"You too, Hobe," Vic replied, sandwiching the older man's hand between both of his. "I came down here not knowing what to think about you. Now I feel like I've known you for years." He tipped his head forward. "And I'd be saying that even if Blackstock kicked my ass. Syndicate or not, any day I spend with you is a good one."

Hobart's face tightened as though he fought to control his emotions. "You better fire that little sporty car up and git," he said. "You got some road time to do. I'll call ya when I know something."

Vic had to make a quick stop at his mother's house to pick up his suitcase and say goodbye. On the way there, he vacillated between marveling at the new turn his life had taken, and chiding himself for worrying she would find the moneybag. It was stuffed under the passenger seat, and though there was no chance a fifty-something year-old woman would poke around under there, Vic went to the length of wrapping it in his golf towel. That reminded him of the days when he'd hidden girlie magazines between his mattress and box springs, which was worth another good chuckle. He knew his mother would try to get him to stay the night, and he spent the last few miles coming up with the best logic he could invent for leaving right away. He wanted to spend as much time as possible with Roxanne the next day.

"I don't understand your big hurry," his mother said, while she gave him a final hug. Vic's bags were stowed in the Mazda, and its engine loped at idle near where they stood, on her front walk. "It'll be almost midnight by the time you finally get home. Why not stay the night and get an early start."

Vic pulled from her embrace, but rested his hands lightly on her upper arms while he started the alibi he rehearsed. "Oh, you know how it is, Mom. I want to relax for the rest of my vacation. I have a painting I want to finish, and I want to spend as many days as I can sitting around in my underwear drinking beer. Besides, some of the guys are going out for lunch and bowling tomorrow."

"Bowling?" she said, shaking her head. "I didn't know you bowled."

He shrugged. "I don't. But they can't beat me on the golf course anymore, so it seems only fair to let them whip me on the lanes." He kissed her. "Thanks for a wonderful Christmas. I love you."

"Be careful." She wiped at her eyes as he climbed into his car. "And call me."

Vic rolled on the gas as he left Charleston. I-77 was one of his favorite roads. The Appalachian Mountains tumbled along, dark silhouettes against the star-filled December sky. His high beams picked out rich purple-browns and half-hearted greens that gave way to rock facades, some bristling with glowing icy shards where lazy cataracts froze while trying to cheat the chill. For all the pleasure pushing his little sports car through the mountain passes gave him, he had difficulty maintaining his concentration as he drove.

Golf. Vic was a player. His fondest wish was reality. He had a game that was damned good, and what he lacked in game, he made up for in smarts. He beat Blackstock, who was in all probability a superior player, because he outplayed and outsmarted the man. Blackstock and his caveman chum tried to work on Vic's head, but he successfully turned their efforts around on them. Convinced their mind-games would only work against them, Blackstock gave up his mental ploys and tried to flat outplay Vic. He might have done it, too, had he not succumbed to Vic's theatrical swings between angry outbursts and happy patter. He thought again about the exchange over the dynamite. "Does it come with the wick already in it?" he said aloud. Vic couldn't remember when he'd had more fun. Money aside, taking Blackstock down was one of the great accomplishments of his life, and he spent many miles savoring it.

Then there was Hobart. What an incredible man he turned out to be. The whole episode reminded Vic of how it often went at Alexis, when a student would walk through the door on the first day of class, looking or acting like a jerk. Vic would take one look at him or her, roll his eyes and wonder what he'd done to deserve the kid. More often than not, Vic was pleasantly surprised when the student he initially viewed with contempt turned out to be diligent, delightful to be around, or both. Those snap decisions were often faulty, and such was the case with Hobart. Vic had reservations about the man when his mother first described him, and nothing Vic saw in Hobart at the hospital did anything to change his opinion. But after the Christmas weekend in Charleston, and the time they spent together on the golf course, Vic felt as though he had truly met someone he was lucky to be able to call a friend. Vic often heard it said a round of golf exposed character flaws a man could hide in other situations. Hobart showed himself to be kind, gentle, and honest. In a matter of days, Vic came to feel closer to Hobart than friends he knew for years. Even without the syndicate golf and the promise of money on top of what he'd already won, Hobart was a man Vic liked to spend time with. He felt knowing Hobart enriched his life as much as it did his bank account.

Inevitably, Vic thought of Bascolm. "I wouldn't play for money," he once said. His reasons were as simple and pure as his unstudied eloquence. He believed trading his skill for money somehow cheapened the game. Now Vic did exactly that—trading the skill Bascolm helped him develop into the cash lying on the floor of the Mazda. Vic crossed the trestle bridge that carried the interstate over the Ohio River and tried to busy his mind with the lights on the outskirts of Marietta, Ohio. The attempt didn't take. He had to think it through.

Vic told Bascolm he could give up painting for golf, but it turned out to be painting that helped justify playing syndicate golf. After all, selling paintings was something all painters did. The greats, Rembrandt, Whistler, and Renoir, one of Vic's personal favorites; all of them traded their skill with a paintbrush for money. Vic sold a number of paintings, himself. Fair to say, Vic decided, if there was nothing wrong with selling your art, then why was it wrong to trade your skill with a golf club for money? It was like making money with a paintbrush, or with the ability to teach. Maybe it would be wrong for Bascolm to cash in on his game, because he believed it was wrong. Vic did a search of his soul. Although he'd done things since his coma that tarnished the image he once had of himself, making money from his newly acquired prowess with a golf club wasn't one of them. Logic told him using his skill on the course to make money passed his smell test, and that was all that mattered.

Another thought came to him, about how fortunate he was to have met both Bascolm and Hobart. Bascolm taught him to hit a golf ball better than most players could, and Hobart offered a way to parley that skill into financial security, or the promise of it. Two men came out of nowhere and guided Vic toward a new destiny. Bascolm, of course, was gone now, but Hobart was tangible. He was a friend who would soon call to tell Vic where he would play his first match. He wondered what he'd done to be so lucky.

He checked his speedometer, brought his car back down to seventy and slid his right foot against the carpet on the transmission tunnel to keep his speed from creeping. Poor man's cruise control, Vic always called it, but he was by no means poor anymore. And he knew beyond a doubt he didn't want to try to explain to a trooper why a teacher from Toledo had a moneybag packed with cash in his car. He reached behind the passenger seat of his car, and freed it from the golf towel. The feel of the plastic zippered envelope was comforting. He gripped it hard. The money felt solid, a sound fifty-seven hundred and fifty dollars. He couldn't wait to get home, spread the bills out, look at them and show them to Roxanne. "This is only the beginning," he said aloud. Then instead of putting it back behind the seat, he put the envelope on his lap. All the rest of the way to Toledo, he relished the money and the fact he'd put the issue of winning it into a perspective he was comfortable with.

~ * ~

Vic wanted badly to call Roxanne as soon as he was back in his apartment, but he didn't know if Tom was awake, and too many "wrong numbers" could raise his suspicions. Roxanne did call a few minutes after eleven, but only long enough to whisper she'd be at Vic's apartment the following morning around ten. "Cool. We'll have lunch," Vic said, also in a whisper, which made him shake his head in wonder as he hung up. Later, he made a trip to an all-night Kroger's. Vic liked grocery shopping late at night. Angie had insisted they go on Sunday afternoon, when it seemed like everyone in Toledo was there. "All elbows and assholes," he remembered complaining once. Angie only clicked her tongue and handed him the car keys. Late at night, the store was empty. Sometimes there were more stock clerks than customers. Rock music pulsed through the sound system, usually at a higher volume than the elevator tunes they played during the day. No lines at the register, either. And Vic basked in that magical feeling he used to get when he was a kid, and his mother let him stay up to watch *Shock Theater* on Saturday night. He was awake and most of the world was asleep. Additionally, going to the store after midnight eliminated the chance of missing a call from Roxanne. As he pushed the shopping cart to his car, he endured a deep breath of late December air and looked at his watch. She'd be at his place in nine hours.

Vic was able to kill six of the hours by sleeping; another two, he spent making a pot of spaghetti sauce from scratch, and setting the table with candles and a small vase of flowers for their post-Christmas, pre-New Year's, celebration. The final hour crawled like a caterpillar, but Vic knew it would be worth the wait when Roxanne came through the door.

When she finally arrived, they talked for a while and shared a beer before leaving a trail of clothing behind on their way to his bedroom, where they adjourned for some here's-how-much-I've-missed-you lovemaking.

The sex, as always, was spectacular, but Vic really savored the closeness he felt with the lady he'd spent nearly every minute, except for the ones on the golf course, thinking about. They languished for nearly an hour afterwards, talking, joking and cuddling. "I'll be right back," Vic finally said, but Roxanne followed him into the kitchen. "You going to put something on?" he asked, when he noticed her following him. He wanted to get the pasta into the water he'd kept near boiling on the stove.

"Why?" she asked, walking over to worm her way into his arms. "Afraid of cooties?"

"Not even a little bit," he said. He poured two glasses of Merlot, and they stood, entwined against the counter, until the noodles were done. As Vic ladled sauce on the pasta, Roxanne poured more wine. The Italian feast filled the little apartment with the spicy smells of tomato sauce, Italian sausage, and garlic bread.

"God, Buddy! Your spaghetti looks great! You have any Parmesan?"

"In the fridge," Vic replied. He put the plates on the table and they sat down. He had pulled the curtains to thwart any prying eyes, and to create an artificial midday darkness. Roxanne's eyes glistened in the warm candlelight. She used a napkin to blot her lips after her first bite. "This is the best."

"Thanks, *dawlin'*. That's how we say it down Charleston way."

Roxanne smiled, stuck out her tongue and silence enveloped them as they began eating. Vic wrestled with the urge to show her the money, or tell her how much he won, but decided to stay with his plan to wait. He twirled more spaghetti onto his fork.

"I'm so glad you're back, buddy. I really missed you. What with the holiday, we probably wouldn't have been together much anyway, but knowing you were so far from me was the pits."

"I'm back now and we have lots of time left. Coming over tomorrow?"

"Sure, but not for as long. Have to put in a *little* time around the house."

"I'll take what you can spare." They continued to eat and share small talk. Roxanne accidentally splashed some tomato sauce onto her collar bone. "I have it," Vic said, licking it off before she could reach for her napkin.

"Say! You're quick." She giggled and gave him a little shove. "And speaking of quick, I'm going to have to get going as soon as I finish this."

"Aw, no time for dessert?"

"That's right ... I saw the Reddi-Whip in the fridge. What did you buy to put it on?"

Vic grinned. "Nothing."

"You're so bad!" Roxanne put her arm around his neck. "Dessert sounds wonderful, but let's save it for tomorrow. Then it won't be like sloppy seconds." She kissed him and stood, one hand holding her napkin in place while she grasped her wine glass in the other. The candle's flame flickered from the movement, and her skin gleamed in the saffron glow. "Know what, buddy? This is the first time I've ever eaten dinner wearing nothing but a napkin."

"It's incredibly becoming, but I suppose you'll want to dress for the drive home." He followed her into the bedroom, where she put her wine on the dresser, next to the cash envelope. "You can't leave until you have a look inside that."

"Your winnings?" she asked, sitting on the bed and unzipping it. When the bundles of twenties and the loose $750 fell onto her thighs, the amount didn't appear to register at first. She riffled through one of the packets for a second, then dropped it, almost as if it gave her an electrical shock. The money fell onto her lap, and she jumped up and spun, brushing it onto the bed as though the bills were on fire. "Jesus Christ," she shouted, turning her wild eyes on him. "What the hell's goin' on?"

"Hobe and I won fifteen hundred bucks from two of his friends, and the match I played against Blackstock was for ten grand." He raised his shoulders, and let them drop. "Hobie gave me half."

"Holy shit! This is crazy. I don't freakin' believe it."

"I didn't rob a bank."

"*That's* comforting. But I can't believe there're people with ten thousand bucks to bet on golf."

"Of course there are, and I'm going to be playing for a syndicate of four of them."

"Syndicate?" she yelped.

Vic quieted her, and sat her down. He explained everything Hobart told him, how the games were set up and played. She listened, never responding in any way. When he finished, tears moistened her lower lashes. Vic was dumbfounded. "What?" he asked, widening his eyes as though he required extra effort to force the word out.

"I'm afraid this will be the end of us."

"Why?"

"I'll only be playing on weekends. We usually only see each other during the week, anyway."

"Now." She wiped at her eyes. "But in a couple months, Tom will be golfing all weekend. Besides, what if I decide to move out?"

"If you move out, then you can go to the matches with me. It'll be great."

"And what am I going do while you're playing?"

"You could shop. Yeah, go out and hit the stores. There'll be plenty of money. Or, even lay out and bake by the motel's pool."

"I'm not shopping on your money."

"But, Rox, it wouldn't be *my* money if we're living together."

A curious look worked its way onto her face. "You're assuming quite a bit."

Roxanne's words hit him like a backhand across the face. Anger and embarrassment drag-raced through Vic's mind. He didn't wait to see which would take the checkered flag. "Where else would you go?"

"My sister's. Marla told me she and Bob would put me up anytime, until I get my bearings and decide what I'm gonna do."

Vic walked to the dresser. He took a pull of her wine, looked at her reflection in the mirror and thought about how he used a mirror to get truer views of his paintings. Now it seemed he was able to do the same with

Roxanne. "I guess you're right, I did assume too much. I feel kind of stupid."

She walked up behind him. "Vic, I could never live here. It's so cramped and small. And the manager, that Ames guy, gives me the creepy crawlies, always watching me from his window when I get out of my car. I think he's some kind of perv. And there's nothing to do here, either. At home, I have the yard and the garden. And Mofus, I could never leave Mofus." The fleeting image of Muldoon stung Vic. "And I'm not gonna fly around in some damned little airplane, either. I'd be afraid, even in a big plane. Besides, I hate golf. Golf is one of the things that came between Tom and me."

Vic turned, his anger suddenly surging toward its redline. "Oh, that makes a lot of fucking sense. When you finally decide Tom bores you and you need a little action on the side, you find yourself a, what?" He spread his arms to the side, then let them drop, slapping his upper legs. "A fucking golfer! Christ, I was playing golf when Tom whacked me on the head. So, what the hell were you thinking when you started coming on to me?"

Tears slid through her lashes and dashed down her cheek. "I don't know," she said in a very small voice. She began to shake her head. "Honestly, I don't. I was attracted to you. I didn't think about you being a golfer. Besides, I didn't know I'd wind up caring about you so much."

"So much, all right, but not enough to give up the comforts of your house, and your garden, and your *dog*, for *this* shitty little place! All that *stuff* makes it worth putting up with your goddamned husband." Vic began pacing. He caught his own reflection out of the corner of his eye every time he passed the mirror. "And what about all that shit a week or so ago?" He wheeled to face her. "That song, if it don't feel right, you can go. Remember? What about that? You said it did feel right, and ... " Vic fell silent when he remembered what he promised then, he would never throw what she'd said back at her. He promised. Now she looked like a crumpled child, and that almost killed his anger, but it clawed its way back like a zombie. "Maybe you should get dressed and go back *home* to Bittersweet," he finally said.

"Wait, Vic —"

"Wait what?" he yelled. "That's all I do is wait. Wait for your phone calls. Wait to see if you can slip away to come over here. When you do come over, I wait to see how long you'll be able to stay." He tried to keep himself from going on, but his anger was firmly in control.

"Yeah, and waiting to see if you'd finally decide to leave Tom." He stepped so close to her, their foreheads were nearly touching. "So now I find out I've been waiting for nothing, because you'll never leave your house and your dog and your yard."

"I told you when you moved out I'd never leave Tom," she hissed. Her demeanor had changed. Now she was angry, and showing some fire.

"Yeah, that's what you said." He waved his finger in her face. "But when I said I was moving out and you said you wouldn't leave Tom, I thought it was because you cared about his feelings, or maybe your marriage vows. Or even for the great mystical powers of the goddamned Catholic Church. *Something* noble, anyway. Now I find all you're staying with him for is stuff!" He picked up her clothes and tossed them on the bed. "You can keep your fucking stuff! I escaped with the most valuable thing I could take when I moved out. *Me!* Now I want to be alone." He sneered. "My natural state. I was alone when I lived with Angie, and I'm still alone. Different address, same fucking situation." He started for the bedroom door, but stopped and turned when he reached the threshold. "But don't believe for one minute I regret anything, because I love my new life and this shitty little place. I do! And like I said before, you showed me there was more to life than living in that house with Angie. Thanks, I'll always owe you for that one. Now get your shit and go."

Vic walked into the kitchen and began clearing the table. He needed something to do because otherwise, he knew he'd go back in the bedroom and tear into her again. He felt betrayed. He felt despondent. He felt foolish. He'd allowed himself to make assumptions, and now he paid the price. He knew there was plenty of fault to go around. *One of Us Cannot Be Wrong*, he thought. His favorite Leonard Cohen song.

Roxanne stormed through the kitchen. "Fuck you," she muttered, but she didn't look at him.

Vic experienced a weird moment when he thought he would explode again, but the fuse didn't catch. Instead, he stopped her as she opened the door.

"Thanks for the offer," he said. "But you can do better. There's a Jeep worker on Bittersweet who has a real nice house with a yard and a dog." She slammed the door on her way out, and the waft of air reminded him he was still naked.

He left the rest of the mess in the kitchen, dressed, and laid on his couch to embark on a full tilt mope. Lighting by the MTV-fueled Zenith, and refreshments by Budweiser. He had no idea who'd manufactured the beat-up sofa he lay on, but he appreciated their sponsorship as well. His body reclined in comfort, while his emotions chewed through his insides like ravenous rats.

The television flickered, creating and dissolving shadows by turns. The Cars were singing and mugging their way through *You're All I've Got Tonight*. Their front man, Ric Ocasek, swayed stiffly, a little Ray Orbison-like. Vic watched the images flow across the screen, and confronted the new reality of his relationship with Roxanne. Today, she'd made it clear she had second thoughts about leaving Tom, and her house. And in no uncertain terms, she made it plain she wouldn't be moving into Vic's apartment, even if she did leave Tom. The affair could continue, but that was all it would be. He was, as she often called him, her buddy. A buddy of the soul, and of the flesh, but no more than that. He'd cheated and lied to foster a relationship that would never develop beyond a dalliance.

He cheated on Angie, and lied to her *and* his mother in maintaining there was no "other woman." A fleeting image of The Old Man flickered in his mind, but he pushed it away. What he couldn't dispose of was the fact he'd even lied to Roxanne, asserting the main reason he was leaving Angie was because he couldn't stand lying to her anymore. That much was true, but he also hoped his move would coax Roxanne to follow his lead, something he'd repeatedly denied.

He glanced back at the TV. Ocasek and the boys were finishing up, the crescendo dissolving into synthesized chords. Vic swallowed some beer. I'm all I have tonight, he thought.

That prompted him to confront what amounted to the biggest lie of them all, the one he'd told himself. He wanted to believe he loved Roxanne. It felt like love, as he'd understood it, good as a massage when he was with her, and bad as a beating when he wasn't. But there was every possibility he'd been deceiving himself, too. Maybe he needed to believe it was love so leaving Angie felt less evil and made him feel less like The Old Man. After all, that made it love rather than mere lust. Love? Vic wasn't positive anymore, but lying on the couch in the light of the flickering music videos, he wanted to believe there was more between them than sex alone. He wanted to believe he wasn't merely playing around, like The Old Man. The phone rang. He usually couldn't pick up fast enough, but it was bound to be Roxanne or Angie. He wasn't anxious to speak to either of them. Three rings. Four.

"Hey there, Vic. It's Hobie."

"Oh, Hobie. Great to hear your voice. How are you?"

"I'm fine, but ya don't sound so good, son."

"Nah, I'm fine. Just a bit of a cold." He cleared his throat. "What's shaking?"

"We got ya a match for the weekend of January ninth. Should be a good one."

"Great! Where's it at?"

"Close outside Atlanta. Private club name of Red Ridge. Player named Elwin Garwood. It's a bit of a ways, but like I told you, we wanna pick guys we think you can beat pretty easy while you're learning the ropes. Course set-up should be to your liking, too. We checked it with some of Merle West's people down that way. Should play real good to your draw."

"Sounds perfect. What do I do?"

"What time can you be out to the airport there in Toledo?"

Vic did some fast calculations. "3:30 with no sweat. 3:00 if I crowd it."

"Nah. Take your time. 3:30's good. Foss and I'll be at Falcon Air Flight Service at 3:30. Ya'll got rains?"

"Rains?"

"Yeah. A rain suit. These matches go, rain or shine. Pick up a rain suit of some kind. Be at Falcon with all your gear and I'll see you then."

They said their goodbyes. Vic dropped the receiver on the hook, picked up his beer and sucked the rest down. When Roxanne revealed she didn't want to move in with him, Vic was embarrassed. He always assumed she would leave Tom to be with him. Embarrassment gave way to hurt, and of course, anger. Her disclosure caused his plans and dreams to crash, leaving him trapped in pain. Hobart's phone call extricated him from his emotional wreckage. "Atlanta," he said, aloud. It sounded exotic and exciting, especially in a cheap apartment that smelled of mildew mingled with stale beer.

At that point, an idea surfaced with the magnitude of a breaching whale. Vic spent weeks sitting alone in his apartment, waiting for Roxanne to call to tell him when she could next come over, or to sneak some conversation. Vic even ran errands based on Tom Bayer's schedule so Vic would be there to answer if she called. Now she was out of the picture, for the time being at least. He was nearly divorced with nothing to do, and no one to answer to. Besides, he was still smarting from the blowup. His little apartment was no place to celebrate an upcoming golf match. He went into his room and put on some Levis and a nice-looking sweater, combed his hair, and was out the door inside of five minutes.

The Bombay Bicycle Club was only a few miles from his apartment. The bar and restaurant was well-known as a popular hangout for singles in their twenties and thirties. Vic's heart was beating excitedly as he walked inside.

"I should have done this a long time ago," he mumbled as he sauntered across to the bar. The lighting was subdued, and bathed everything and everyone in a warm orange glow that deepened the contrasting shadows. Vintage 40s and 50s bicycles adorned the walls and hung from the high ceiling, so many that they outnumbered the patrons. Vic glanced at his watch as he sat down. Early on a Tuesday evening; more people would be rolling in, he figured. The last time he sat at a bar was with Bascolm at Gaylord's. "Or did I?" he whispered.

"Excuse me, sir?" the bartender said. "I didn't catch that. What will it be?"

"How's your Southern Comfort Manhattan?" Vic asked.

"Only the right amount of dry vermouth to take off some of the sweet," he said. "You'll like it fine." The barman hit him with a confident smile.

Vic nodded and the man set off to mix one. Steve Miller sang about magic. *Abracadabra* was never one of Vic's favorites; it was overplayed on MTV, in his opinion, and he didn't care for the video. Regardless, the night held a palpable magical quality. Legerdemain was the high-brow term. Yes, that was the mood of his first night out in weeks. Months, even. The song was perfect. The bartender placed his drink on a cocktail napkin. Vic sipped. It tasted perfect, and he let the tender know with a wink and a tip of his head.

Vic sipped his drink and tried to take it all in, without coming off as a tourist. Couples and singles were sitting at the bar, in the booths tucked against the walls, and at the regiment of tables that surrounded the dance floor. It was empty save for two women dancing to Hall and Oats', *I Can't Go for That*; a nice change from Miller. The women were both quite attractive, and Vic decided he could go for either of them.

"Hey, Teddy," a woman who strode toward the bar called out. Christ, Vic thought, she has to be over six feet tall. "Another Long Island," she said, "then cut me off."

"I could never cut you off," the barman said. "Not much good at saying no to pretty ladies." He picked up a tall carafe.

She side-glanced at Vic as if to include him. "You're one silver-tongued devil."

"The only silver I got," he quipped, pouring a generous shot of vodka. "None in my pockets."

Vic looked the woman over while she and the bartender continued to talk. She was as tall as he first guessed, but she did a lot with her elevation. Her taut thighs fit snugly in the dark pin-striped slacks she wore, but the material flared at her knees, allowing sharp creases to guide the rest of the material down to her ankles. She probably added two or three inches to her height with the shiny black heels she sported. Her face wasn't pretty, at least not in the classic sense. Expressive and handsome was how Vic would have described it, surrounded by blonde curls that darkened at her scalp and were held in check by a grey bandana. Silver hoop earrings that had to be three inches in diameter dangled above the collar of her crisp white shirt. He liked to watch her talk. She was one of those people who used their whole face to speak a word, and every wink, smile, or facial tic happened at light-speed.

"So," Vic said, when she sat next to him to watch the barman make her drink, "what's a Long Island?"

She tilted her chin up and let her dark irises fall to the corners of her eyes. "A new drink, fresh from Babylon." She said that final word syllable by syllable, the way one of those televangelist ministers would. "Babylon, New York," she added, with a dramatic flourish. "I brought the original recipe back and gave it to Teddy, here." She stopped to watch the man place it in front of her, then grabbed hold of Teddy's wrist. "Would you be a dear and get ... " She paused, turning to look at Vic full-on. "I don't know your name," she said.

"Vic."

"Vic," she said, nodding as if she approved. "Okay, Teddy, get Vic a straw so he can see what he thinks of it." She pushed the carafe toward Vic, the bartender produced a cocktail straw and the woman offered it to Vic. "No backwashing, now," she said, raising an eyebrow. "We only just met."

Vic smiled at her. She liked to come on strong, but sparring with her was a lot of fun. She had enough Roxanne in her, he felt right at home trading verbal swings. "You haven't told me your name, either."

Christopher T. Werkman

"Thought you'd never ask," she whispered. "Kym," she said, jumping back into her big voice. "Kym with a 'y.'" She pressed the straw toward him. "Here. Take a pull and see what you think."

The drink came on much like Kym did. It had the bite of a strong mixture of liquors, but an underlying sweetness made you want a second taste. "Wow, that's great. What's in it?"

Kym gave her head a barely perceptible shake, and the tip of her tongue made a quick sweep of her glossed lips. "You name it, it's there. Gin. Tequila. White rum. Vodka. Triple sec, some bitters and a splash of Coke for color." She leaned close, and Vic could smell her perfume; the expensive kind that smelled good, but had no relationship to any source Vic could name. "They're seductive, but you have to be careful with them," she added. Vic had the feeling she could have been describing herself. "And, what brings you to Bombay tonight, Vic?"

"Oh, a little celebration." He wanted to sound mysterious. He thought about the fact that much of his life was a mystery, and he enjoyed the fact. He suddenly felt very powerful, which was not at all like him. He enjoyed that, as well.

"A celebration? And all alone?" She drove a knowing look straight into his eyes. "You left the little woman home?"

Vic didn't flinch. "As a matter of fact, I imagine that's exactly where she is."

Kym had the look of someone who suspected mice in the pantry, and found a hole gnawed in a bag of chips. "Oh, really?"

Vic finished his Manhattan, pointed at Kym's Long Island and gave the barman an affirmative nod. Vic turned back to Kym. "We're separated. Dissolution on the way, in February."

Kym let go with a hearty laugh, but the din in the club increased with the population, so Vic was probably the only one to notice. "Every married guy here is separated from his wife, Vic. The wife's at home, and he's cruising the Bombay. If I had a nickel for every time some married guy told me that, the money would keep me in Long Islands for a year."

"Yeah, you figured me out. I'm a lying sleaze." *I only wish that was totally untrue,* he thought.

She patted his arm. "Oh, I didn't mean that. We'll find out if I ask you for your phone number. That's my test. Married guys suddenly only remember their work phone." She sipped her drink, then changed conversational gears. "So what is it we're celebrating, here?"

"A golf match."

"No way," she said. "It's freezing out there. You played golf today?"

"No, I'm celebrating a match I'm playing after the holidays, in Atlanta."

"A match?" Kym's brow furrowed, and her eyes were alight with interest. "You play on the tour?"

Vic shook his head. "No, I'm not a pro. I play arranged matches."

"For money? You win money?"

"If I'm good enough." He chummed her along, giving her only enough of an answer to make her want more. He imagined Dirty Harry, gathering more info than he gave out.

She leaned in close and he noticed a dusting of glitter on her cheeks. "And are you good enough?" she breathed.

Her double entendre was obvious, but Vic chose to play dumb. Eastwood would have. "I was the last time out, but you're only as good as your next time."

"Isn't that the truth. And that's how you make your living?"

Vic chuckled. "No. I'm a teacher."

Kym's eyes ballooned. "A teacher! A teacher who gambles. Now I've heard it all."

He gave her Eastwood's squinty stare. "It's not really gambling. Gambling is betting on someone else. I'm banking on my own skill. Not gambling, in my book. And what do you do?"

It turned out Kym was a caseworker for the county social services, which Vic found every bit as surprising as his teaching was to her. Their conversation settled into a gentle patter, highlighting and discussing the good and the bad of their respective occupations. Kym, Vic decided, was much more thoughtful and sensitive than she liked to advertise. She genuinely cared about the people she serviced. They sipped their Long Islands and chatted for close to an hour, when two young men walked up to them. Kym jumped off her stool and embraced them, giving each a brief kiss and running her hand through the shorter man's hair as they began to talk.

"Vic, I'd like you to meet a couple friends of mine, Bobby and Michael," she said, after their initial hellos were complete.

Vic stood and shook their hands. Neither gave Vic the big squeeze, but both could have. They obviously weren't strangers to the gym. Both wore loose dress shirts, but the material couldn't hide the contours of their muscular bodies. Vic always marveled at guys whose necks pyramided down to rolled-roast sized shoulders, and these two fit that category. The taller one named Michael wore his brown hair long, and he combed it back with huge hands at least four or five times a minute. Bobby, square-jawed and animated, locked onto Kym, but Michael seemed to be looking at Vic much of the time, to the point Vic began to wonder if the guy thought he recognized him from somewhere. "You play any sports?" Michael finally asked, when the conversation between Kym and Bobby ebbed for a second.

"He's a golfer," Kym blurted.

"Think some weight training might lower my score?" Vic said, to keep the money aspect of the matches from coming up. He wasn't sure why that suddenly mattered to him.

"Couldn't hurt," Bobby said. "Truth is, the golfers I see on TV look more like they specialize in twelve ounce curls." He mimicked lifting a beer to his lips.

Bobby talked to Kym a bit longer before announcing he and Michael should be on their way. Vic shook their hands and watched them as they walked toward the door, each swinging their muscular arms like they were ornaments. When he looked back at Kym, she had a questioning expression.

"What?" Vic asked.

"Now you know how a gal feels out here on the single scene," she said. Her expression was now a sly one. "Or do you?"

Vic wagged his head. "I don't have the slightest idea what you're talking about."

"I thought you noticed," she said. "Michael was really giving you the once over."

"I thought maybe he was trying to place me from somewhere," Vic said. The way she leered at him suddenly made her point. "Wait a minute. Do you mean what I think you do?"

"Don't feel bad. I dated Bobby for almost a month before I figured it out." She sipped her drink. "And I think women sense sexual orientation much better than men."

"So, they're a couple?"

Kym scrunched her face and shrugged. "Not a couple, really. They share an apartment. Bobby feels the need to date women. He says he's bi. Michael, he doesn't do women at all. They get it on together sometimes, but they both see whoever they want."

"And you went out with Bobby and never knew?"

"Oh, I eventually figured it out. At first I didn't want to believe it. Then I took him on as a cause, sort of. My ego kicked in and I figured I could straighten him out, no pun. It was hopeless."

"And you aren't worried about that new disease? The one they don't have a name for yet?" Vic asked. Stories were cropping up in the news. He even saw some actor on the Tonight Show complaining he was newly divorced, finally loose on the dating scene, and now had to worry about the disease. There was no known cure, people were dying and the doctors didn't seem to know much about it.

"Ah, that's just out on the coast. And it's more druggies than gays, from what I hear. Besides, what are the chances? There's only like, maybe a thousand cases in the country."

Vic wasn't out to convince her, but sirens went off in his head. He drank the last of his Long Island. "Yeah, you're probably right." The noise and the cigarette smoke were getting to him. He looked at his watch. He'd spent a long time nursing his drink and talking to Kym. "Wow, I still have some grading to do." He stood and gave her hand a formal shake. "I really enjoyed meeting you."

"Hey, wait a minute," Kym said. She held out a pen she pulled from her purse. "You haven't … "

Vic jotted his number on a napkin, then handed it to her.

She lifted an eyebrow. "Maybe I'll call," she said.

"You call, maybe I'll answer."

On his drive home, and for the rest of the evening, Vic's mood was much different from the excitement he experienced when he embarked on his big night out. Kym was attractive and seemed like she would be fun to get to know, at first. A little over the top, but under the artifice, she had a lot of good qualities. However, the fact she'd been involved with a bi-sexual man, in the new uncharted world of a terminal disease, threw a bucket of cold water on any desire Vic had to pursue a dating relationship with her. As he drifted toward sleep, Vic decided sex with a woman with a known sexual history was what he wanted. The blow-up with Roxanne would most probably blow over before long. He could wait. Waiting was what he did. He'd become better at it than he ever thought he would. Certainly better than he ever wished to be.

But the blow-up had an effect Vic never anticipated. The next morning, he awakened feeling emotionally numb. He didn't call Roxanne. All his friends were busy celebrating the holidays with their families, so he whiled away the remainder of Christmas vacation practicing his short game, painting, and watching MTV. He sometimes wished he'd stayed in Charleston. At least he could play golf, in West Virginia.

New Year's Eve proved to be lonely and depressing. As the night dragged on, he poured Southern Comfort and watched the music videos. They were soothing. Some were amusing. But he didn't pay close attention. A woman who resembled Roxanne in some way would appear onscreen, and Vic's mind would drift away to manufacture some lurid fantasy of the sweaty sex he and Roxanne were so good at. Kym's image materialized a couple times, then faded. Later, his thoughts even wandered back to Angie. He found himself wondering what she was doing while 1981 was busy becoming 1982. He hadn't talked to her since the last time something at the house needed fixing, a week or so earlier.

Around midnight, some guys spilled out of an apartment rented by a young man who wore Carhartt work duds and drove a pickup with a cement mixer in its bed. Most of the time, the guy was quiet enough, but he and some friends were celebrating. Yee-ha! Another year of mixing concrete, Vic thought, peeking out through the curtains when the noise erupted. Two of the revelers were tussling near his Mazda. Vic decided to go out and warn them to stay clear of his car as the big ball dropped in Times Square. Several of the men began firing shotguns into the air. The decision not to confront drunks brandishing firearms was an easy call. Later, in bed, with the radio murmuring softly, Vic reminisced about past holidays, and sleep was slow to come. This was not a happy New Year's, but Vic convinced himself the next one would be. He found comfort in that belief, and slumber in that comfort.

~ * ~

School resumed on Monday, and when Vic made it home that afternoon, he was happy to see Roxanne sitting in her car outside his apartment. He knew he wouldn't be the first to break their wall of non-communication, but he expected she'd call, not come over. "I came to check on you," she said when he walked up to her driver's side window. "You okay?" She always maintained the set of his mouth telegraphed more about his feelings than his eyes did. He noticed her looking at his lips, and wondered what her conclusion was.

"Yeah," he said. "I'm good."

"You didn't call."

"Neither did you."

"Touché!" She laughed. It was a sound Vic missed. Longed for. "Can a girl get a beer here?"

He pulled her car door open. "*You* can. You have a key. You could be inside drinking one now."

"I thought you might want your key back." He looked into her eyes and shook his head. They started for the apartment. Once inside, they didn't even kiss, only stood and held each other, heads pressed together. Roxanne snuffled. "I didn't say it right. I didn't mean I wouldn't leave Bittersweet to be with you." She pulled away to look Vic in the eye. "I meant I couldn't move in here, is all. Not this apartment."

He shucked his coat and helped her with hers. "You think I'm going to spend the rest of my life here?" He walked to the refrigerator and grabbed beers for them both. "The only reason I'm here is because of the location. Close enough to do the chores until the house is sold," he said, leading her into the living room. They sat on the couch. He usually turned on MTV the instant he walked into the room, but the TV stayed dark. "I'm a Toledo guy, born and raised. All my life, I wanted to live on the river. Bittersweet was a block away, but not good enough. I want to wake up in the morning, walk to the window of my bedroom, and look out to see what the river's doing. Winter, spring, summer, fall. Every season and every kind of weather, I want the river flowing outside my window." He sipped his beer. "I've been looking at the real estate ads. There are a couple nice places, really beautiful places. One's a hundred and a half, the other is closer to two."

Roxanne's eyes bulged. "Two-hundred thousand. Are you shitting me? On a teacher's salary?"

Vic held up a finger. "Ah, a teacher's salary, plus what I can make playing the syndicates." He held her hand. "I already have a bit under six grand from my weekend in Charleston. More on top of that when we sell the house. Shit, that's almost enough for the down on a hundred-fifty grand house, right there." He blew a puff of air through his nose. "Look, I'm not talking in a month." He fired off an impish grin. "But maybe in a year. Gonna have to see how this golf thing plays out. I'm not going to jump too soon, but now I have a goal, a river house." He pressed his finger against the tip of her nose. "Play your cards right, I might get one big enough for there to be some room for a friend. If she's a close enough friend, of course."

Roxanne faced him on the sofa, her legs tucked under her. She rolled up onto her knees, and kissed him. "Just for the record, good as all that sounds, I personally think you're nuts." She added a wink for punctuation.

"Hey, since you brought them up," Vic said, squeezing her breasts.

She rubbed his crotch. "Oh, they need attention, do they?"

"Yeah," he said, rising and taking her hand, "but only if you're a close enough friend."

They decided she was. Later, Vic found his attention focused on a spot of late afternoon sun spearing through a small opening in the bedroom curtains. It struck Roxanne's glistening thigh like the white-hot point of a laser beam. Detached. Vic was amazed at how distant he felt while they were having sex, almost like an actor in a porno film. The pleasure they'd shared was excruciatingly good, but on an emotional level, he experienced very little. He lay with Roxanne for a long time, wondering why everything felt so different. Was he afraid to let his emotions free? Things were smoothed over after their talk, but the argument, the first cross words they'd ever exchanged, hurt him and made wonder what the state of their relationship actually was. He thought he understood how the two of them fit together, but now he wasn't so sure. She had her own vision of what the future would be, and after the blow-up, he was less certain he understood what that future was. Apparently, until he had a better handle on it, his reflex was to keep emotions on a tight rein. Or, maybe his lack of emotion was due to the tremendous changes in direction his life took in the last several months. Regardless of the cause, the upshot proved to be an ability to zero in on the physical sensations he and Roxanne traded, and the results were nothing short of phenomenal.

"Are you still alive?" Roxanne murmured, her voice low and husky.

"I think so," Vic mumbled. His mind glided. He closed his eyes and imagined he was a pilot, cruising above the terrain of their bodies, watching the nerve pathways fade and cool from the red-hot glow their sex had fired. He radioed in. "I'm flying to Atlanta after school Friday."

"Atlanta? Georgia?"

"Um-hmm. Playing a guy named Elwin Garwood. Supposed to be an easy mark. Hobie wants me to start against easier players before I take on any heavy hitters."

"How much is this one for?"

"Don't know. Hobie doesn't want money on my mind, but I don't think it's for much. Garwood's not a big dog."

"And for that, you're flying all the way to Atlanta? Seems crazy to me. Is the pilot any good?"

"Supposed to be the best. I'll know better once I've flown with him."

There was another long silence. Roxanne stroked his chest with her fingertips and he opened his eyes.

"I'll worry about you," she said.

"No need." He was surprised at the chill even he detected in his voice.

~ * ~

That evening, Vic noticed the cool in his voice again when the phone rang, and Kym was on the line. "Oh, hi, Kym. How you doing?" Vic said. He wondered if she might call, but he wouldn't have been surprised if she didn't. He guessed he was caught more off-guard because she did.

"Great. Thought I'd call and see what you were up to."

"Actually, I'm on my way out the door. Is this the part of the married test where I get graded?"

"How did you guess?" She chuckled. "Is your wife there? Could you put her on the line?"

"No. She's still back at the house." He paused. "But I have to tell you, I'm on my way to pick up a woman I've been seeing for a while." I wish I was going to pick up Roxanne, he thought. "We had a disagreement the night I ran into you at the Bombay, but we've patched things up."

The air went dead. Apparently she was surprised. "Oh, yeah, I understand. The ups and downs." More silence. "I enjoyed meeting you, Vic. Tell you what, I'll give you my work phone, and if things change with your lady, give me a call sometime. I think you're a neat guy."

Vic thanked her for the compliment, assured her he felt the same way about her, and wrote down her number. After they said goodbye, he wrote her name above the digits, looked at the letters for a few seconds, and tossed the paper into the trash. Then he walked into his living room and practiced chipping balls into the bean bag chair. An hour or so later, he'd poured some Southern Comfort over some ice when the phone rang. He glanced at his watch. Almost ten. Maybe Tom passed out, he thought, smiling as he walked to the phone.

"It's Angie, Vic. I hope it's not too late."

"Nope, I'm still up. What's the matter?" He sipped his drink and wondered if she could hear the ice cubes in the glass. Then he wondered why he cared.

"Nothing's the matter, really. But Jenna Banks, the realtor, called earlier. She has a couple who want to look at the house Friday. She's real high on them. They're looking for a house in the south end, and they really like ours from the outside."

"That's great. Should be no problem. I wasn't planning on being there, or anything."

"That's not what I called about." She paused, and Vic wondered if this was a "let's think this whole thing over before it's too late," call. "What I was hoping was that you could come over some afternoon after school and fix a couple things. I'm going to make sure the place is all spic and span, but there are a few things that need to be looked at."

"Oh?" was the best response he could come up with. She'd mentioned several things before, and he'd taken care of them when he was over cutting the grass, but the final cutting was over a month ago. "What needs doing?"

"I made a list. It's short. I wrote them down so I wouldn't forget to mention them all. Little things." She paused. "The faucet in our, uh, the upstairs bathroom is dripping again. And that damned furnace; every time the circulation pump comes on, which is pretty frequently, this time of year, it makes a rattle. I think you said it was a cover, or something."

"Yeah. The heat shield. It must be loose."

"Uh-huh. Anyway, that type of thing. Shouldn't take more than an hour, I wouldn't think. I want the place to come off as well as possible. Oh, the front door lock could use a squirt of oil, too." Another pause. "Anytime between now and Friday is fine."

The next day, he left school and drove to the house. All day, he dreaded the thought of it. He was anxious to see Muldoon, but other than that, he'd have been happy to never make the turn off River Road again. On the other hand, Roxanne would probably see his car and call, or he would call her.

He pressed the garage door opener as he pulled into the drive, and spent a few minutes in the garage before he went inside the house, straightening and arranging. He still had tools there, but he wasn't interested in taking them to his storage unit after he left the house that day. He merely neatened his workbench area, all the time remembering how he enjoyed working out there when he and Angie were a happy young couple. He had to blink back tears. He built the workbench himself, with the anticipation he would use it for many years into the future. He marveled at how short that future proved to be.

As soon as he walked into the kitchen, the phone rang. He picked up with one hand while he scratched Muldoon's head with the other.

"What a pleasant surprise to see you drive in. So, what's up?" Roxanne asked.

"They're showing the house Friday. Angie called last night with some things she wants me to fix before the people see it."

"An asshole-do list."

"A what?" Vic asked.

"Opposite of a honey-do. Man, you're slower than usual. Long day with the kiddies?"

257

Vic chuckled. "Naw, not that. There's any number of places I'd rather be, than here. This place puts a lot of stuff I don't want jingling around in my mind." Muldoon jumped down, and Vic started going through the stack of bills Angie left on the counter as he talked. "Bittersweet would be a blip below Hell on my list of recreational destinations." He shuffled through bills for gas, electricity and the phone. "Oh, shit! Real nice."

"What now?" She sounded alarmed.

"You know how you have to dig through the Sunday paper's ads to find the comics? Somehow, a letter from Doug and Carol Traymoor, a couple we've known since college, wrote Angie a nice letter of commiseration. I had to go through this stack of bills so I could write my checks for the utilities, and she knew it. The letter happened to find its way into the pile." He paused to read. "We're so-o-o-o sorry to hear Vic left you." Sarcasm dripped from every syllable. "If there's anything Doug or I can do … Call us, dear, and we'll get together. Real fucking nice."

"But that's only understandable—" Roxanne started.

"Oh, yeah," he cut in. "It's nice of them to offer their sympathy to Angie and I, except mine must have gotten lost in the mail." He paused. "Shit, yes. This thing is dated three weeks ago, and it happens to show up in these current bills? Fuck her!" His eyes felt like someone sprinkled salt dust in them, for the second time since he'd arrived. He sniffed. "Look, I gotta get shit done around here so I can get the hell out of this place. I'll call when I get home."

He dropped the receiver on the hook, and a new reality hit him. He usually referred to his place as "the apartment." That was the first time he could remember calling it home.

Chapter Nine

"Nervous as a mouse at a cat show," was one of Hobart's down-home expressions, and it accurately described how Vic felt as he paced in the lounge at Hawk Air. Trepidation was luggage he didn't want to acknowledge, but it felt like a cat might be chasing a couple of mice running loose in his stomach as he tried to look stoic, and keep from fidgeting.

"We're monitoring the tower frequency," the woman behind Hawk Air's counter told him. "They're a few miles out. Should be touching down in a minute or two." She was about Vic's age, and his first impression was she'd found the perfect place to work. Her prominent nose and receding chin gave her a vaguely bird-like appearance. She had an unruly mane of woolly dark hair that reminded him of Gilda Radner's Roseanne Rosannadanna, from *Saturday Night Live*. However, Vic remembered how unreliable first impressions could be. After all, her body was spectacular; athletic and curvy. She looked directly into his eyes when she spoke to him, and he liked that. Vic nodded an acknowledgement, and hoped his nervousness didn't show. He walked to the windows that offered a panoramic view of the east-west runway. Hawklady walked over and stood next to him as an off-white plane, with blue striping on the fuselage, nosed-down toward the runway. "Is that my ride?" he asked.

"That should be the one," she replied, firing off a smile Vic could practically feel on his skin. The plane's tail sank and the sleek, angular little

259

ship settled onto its rear landing gear as it flashed past the windows where they were standing. "Comanche Twin," she said, as it dropped gently onto its nose wheel and began to slow. "Great bird. You fly much?"

"No. Only once when I was a kid. Some kind of Piper. Tri-Pacer, I think."

Hawklady laughed. Her voice was warm and alluring, like that of a woman out to level the playing field at the Beauty Bowl. "You have a treat in store. Piper makes them both, but the difference between a Tri and a Comanche is like between a buckboard and a Cadillac. Going far?"

"Atlanta," Vic said, trying to sound like Georgia was two doors down, and he traveled there all the time.

She gestured toward his clubs with a pitch of her head that had no apparent effect on her gravity-defying hair. "To play golf?"

Vic raised his eyebrows. "Can't play here."

Hobart was out of the plane before the propellers could judder to a complete stop. He broke into his big homely grin as soon as he spotted Vic coming out the office door. They shook hands in the brisk chill and walked back into the building. "Good flight up?" Vic asked.

"Bea-yutiful. Can't wait for you to get up there and see the view. We'll still have a little sunlight left. Foss is gonna top off the tanks. We'll be back in the air inside a half hour." Vic was afraid his former facade of calm began to show cracks. "You ain't gonna be scared?" Hobart asked.

"I told him he's in for a luxury ride," Hawklady cut in, smiling as she extended her hand to Hobart. "I'm Treese Cosgrove. Will you be taking care of the charges?"

"Hobart Early," he replied, giving her hand a couple strong southland pumps. "Pleased to make your acquaintance. How we gonna handle the money, ma'am? You want me to pay now? "

She shook her head. "Landing charges are waived since you're fueling with us. I'll let you know your total when the fueler finishes, but I can bill it, if you'll give me your business card."

Hobart pulled a card out of his wallet and handed it to her. He leaned forward and whispered, "You ain't worried I print up fakes?"

Treese rolled her expressive eyes toward the plane parked on the tarmac outside. "I have your tail number," she said, flashing him a wink. "You wouldn't be hard to track down," she added with another wink, before returning to her counter.

Hobart obviously enjoyed their repartee. "She passed that test," he said to Vic. "She knows her way around. Wait just a moment and we'll get your stuff loaded, and I'll introduce you to Foss."

Hobart went to use the restroom, so rather than wait, Vic picked up his suitcase and clubs and walked outside. Foss Bannigan's tanned face was generously upholstered with smile lines, and his silver-gray hair set off his aquamarine eyes. He moved like an athlete, with the smooth fluidity of a good running back, even though Vic was certain he was at least Hobart's age. The pilot's full smile showcased a perfect set of teeth.

"Hobie speaks highly of you," Foss said in his rumbly voice. "Says you're a hell of a golfer."

"I have my days," Vic replied, shrugging off the compliment. "Sounds like the three of us are a good match, though, because he says you're one hell of a pilot, and Hobie's a hell of a guy."

"Damn. I crash this girl tonight and you know where the three of us are headed." Foss said. The pilot picked up on Vic's lack of genuine mirth. "Don't worry, son. I been driving these birds since I was twelve. That's no lie. Come on, we'll check the oil while the fueler finishes up."

"Foss is an interesting name," Vic said as he followed the pilot to the plane. "You mind me asking, what's it short for?"

"Not a bit," Foss said. "Foster, my mother's maiden name. Foster Barrington Bannigan," he added, chuckling. "Barrington was my grandmother's maiden name. Old family tradition." He leaned against the plane's left engine cowling. "If my Louise and I had had a boy, he'd have been Talmadge Foster Bannigan," he continued, grinning. "Hated the thought of saddling a kid with a handle like that." He opened an inspection hatch on the left engine. "One of the reasons we never had children." He pulled the dipstick and held it for Vic to see. "Doing good. These motors are supposed to consume some oil, so I keep an eye on it." He slid the stick back into the tube and closed the hatch. "Topped it off before I left Charleston, but anytime you land, checking the oil is a good idea. Let's go check its sister."

Vic stuck his hands deep in his coat pockets as they walked around to the engine on the other wing. "Then you do a walk-around?"

"Nah. Do that before you take off at the beginning of the trip. Everything was working when I set it down. Nothing's going to change while it sits for half an hour." He checked the level on the dipstick, slid it into the engine, and closed up. Vic didn't know much about airplanes, other than what he learned from building and flying models as a kid, but the more he talked with the steady and articulate pilot, the better he felt about putting his fate in Foss's hands.

Hobart came out of the office, and the three of them climbed into the plane. Hobart moved to the rear-most row of seats, and Vic slid into the one next to Foss. The ship's doors closed with a solid ca-chunk, unlike the tinny Tri-Pacer Vic remembered. When Foss hit the starter on the left engine, it turned with a high-pitched squeal, giving way to a roar as it tried for life and found it. The instrument panel rattled until the big engine caught its rhythm, then the vibrations evened out and the entire plane throbbed pleasingly. He began the same process with the one on the right wing.

"You don't start both at once?" Vic asked.

"Takes a lot of juice to turn up one of these motors. Left engine's the primary on this bird. Runs the generator. Juices up the batteries so we have plenty of spark to start the other." Foss didn't seem to mind his questions, and Vic was a sponge for information on anything mechanical. Especially if his life depended on it. Foss put his headset on and adjusted the mic. "Toledo Ground Control," he said, "this is Piper Comanche one-five-five-four-niner. Ready to taxi, VFR southbound." He side-glanced at Vic, lowered his headphones, clamped them around his neck, and flipped a toggle on the dash. "Now you'll be able to hear," he said.

"Piper one-five-five-four-niner, this is Toledo Ground. Cleared to runway two-five via taxiway Charlie."

Foss released the brakes, added a touch of throttle and they began to roll. Treese Cosgrove gave them a wave through Hawk Air's window and Vic waved back. Hobart reached over the second row of seats to tap Vic's shoulder. "I think she's got an eye for ya, boy."

"I wouldn't kick her out of bed." Vic thought that sounded incredibly crass, and wanted to moderate it. "I like women with unusual looks, and her body is amazing."

Hobart shrugged. "Like my ol' granddaddy used to say, ya never look at the mantelpiece when you're pokin' the fire." They laughed, and Vic felt even more at home with Hobart. They could trade in sophomoric humor, like with his golf buddies from school.

Watching the wing bounce as the plane rolled along the taxiway was unnerving, even though Vic knew that, like a tree limb, the strength of it was in its ability to flex. The sun was still a half hour or so from setting, but its rays were stained yellow-orange by the atmosphere, making the eggshell-colored wing glow an iridescent salmon color. Foss was busy flipping toggles on the panel. "Checking the magnetos," he said when he noticed Vic watching him. "Each motor has two totally separate ignitions systems. Called redundancy. Two of everything; that's important on this plane, except for the pilot," he joked. Vic scoffed, but Foss was busy power-testing the engines and missed it. He eased the throttles up and back, watched the gauges, and appeared satisfied with what he saw.

When they reached the eastern end of the taxiway, Foss turned the plane toward the runway and brought it to a stop. "Toledo Tower, this is Piper one-five-five-four-niner. Ready for takeoff," he said into the microphone.

"Piper one-five-five-four-niner," came the reply. "Taxi into position on runway two-five and hold, sir." Vic's nervous stomach felt like it was taxiing around his liver as Foss released the brakes and rolled out onto the runway.

Foss wore an impish grin. "This is as much fun as I can have with my clothes on, even after all these years."

"Piper one-five-five-four-niner, cleared for takeoff on runway two-five." Vic held his breath as Foss pushed the throttles forward. The propellers chewed at the air, and the plane began to roll. In seconds, Vic felt himself being pushed into the seat. He watched the air speed indicator needle sweep past seventy, then Foss drew back on the yoke. Vic looked out his window and watched the wing lift. The rest of the plane went with it.

The take-off and flight reminded Vic of standing at the edge of a swimming pool on a hot day. Anticipating the cold shock to the system was the worst part of it, and after taking the plunge, the soothing water soon wiped away the initial nervousness. A few minutes of watching Foss work the controls eased Vic's concerns. The overriding sensation Vic experienced was of a gently swaying hammock. There was no sensation of speed once they lifted off, although the air speed indicator showed the little plane was doing nearly two hundred miles-an-hour. And Hobart was right, the view from ninety-five hundred feet was spectacular. As the sun slipped under the horizon, the sky looked like a James Turner watercolor, exploding with vibrant oranges and yellows accented by purple-blue clouds. There was a period when the sun still shined on the plane while the ground two miles below was in darkness, with only streetlights to delineate the grid of human pathways below.

Vic reveled in his feeling of isolation. The plane might as well have been nine thousand miles from Earth, from Toledo, and from his apartment. Roxanne and other significant things in Vic's life were invisible, hidden in the darkness below, but golf was with him; an invisible passenger. His clubs were stowed in the compartment behind the cabin, and his body and mind were hooked up and ready to pull off a winning match at Red Ridge Country Club.

Vic reclined his seat, tilting his head for a good view of the dark world below. The steady thrum of the engines became an irresistible lullaby and between that and the gentle sway of the plane, he slipped into sleep. At first, his slumber was shallow, and several times he started back to consciousness. The time between these short naps, he spent watching Foss, sealed away in his headphones and working the controls. Then, the drone and the gentle vibrations seduced him for a longer trick in the dark alley of his subconscious. He dreamed in surreal and confusing images. Differing aspects of his life interfused and were extruded into a crisp, clear, visual scenario. He was playing golf at Loon's Lair with Bascolm, Jason and Donald. Vic hit a tremendous drive well past the others' tee shots. He walked toward his ball, drinking in the course, thrilled to be playing golf with his good friends again. Then, while Donald set up for his second shot, Vic noticed movement in the woods. What was it? A glimpse of something. There, he saw it again. It turned out to be a woman holding a harness of a Seeing Eye dog. Reefer? Just as he was going to call out to her, he awakened, the images dissolving into the mists demarcating the gulf between dreams and consciousness. At first, he remembered a few scant details, but when he tried to retrieve more, the ones he'd clung to disappeared into an indecipherable fog, the way he told Dr. Pembrooke his memories of the coma had.

Foss bumped Vic's knee with his. "You awake?"

"Yeah. What time is it?" Vic levered himself to a sitting position.

"Almost eight-thirty. We'll be on the ground in a few minutes." Foss reached up and turned on the speaker. "Sleep much?"

"Yeah. Some. The seat's real comfortable," Vic replied, looking back to see what Hobart was up to.

"Hobe won't wake up until we touch down. Planes put him straight to sleep, too," Foss said. "Atlanta approach control, this is Piper one-five-five-four-niner," Foss said into the mic. "Level at nine thousand five hundred feet. Squawking one-four-seven-six. Landing Covington."

"Covington," Vic repeated. "We aren't landing in Atlanta?"

"Too much traffic. Sometimes they keep you stacked for an hour or more before you can land. And expensive. Way too much hassle, and too far from the golf course. Covington's close down the road from Conyers, where the course is." He tipped his head toward Vic's side window. "That's Atlanta." Vic could see the lights of the city, shimmering in the distance like jewelry on the velvety black landscape. "Covington traffic, Piper one-five-five-four-niner is on final for runway two-eight."

Vic's previous nervousness returned. He waited for the tower at Covington to acknowledge, but the radio remained silent. "Aren't they going to answer?" Vic asked.

"Nobody's there."

"You're joking," Vic said, waiting for the punch line.

"Nah, these little airports aren't twenty-four hour operations. They go home at five or six. I let anybody flying in the area know we're on our approach so they can stay clear." Foss handed Vic the mic. "Push the squawk button five times," Foss instructed. Vic did as he was told, and two bright strands of landing lights that bordered the runway came on. "Wow, did I do that?"

"Yup. Like opening a garage door. Remote control." Foss took the mic and slid it onto its hook on the panel. "We'll make a pilot out of you yet," he added, as he pushed the yoke forward to bring the plane down.

Then Vic settled in to watch Foss work. *Performance art,* he thought to himself. The runway lights stretched out before them, pinpoints of light in the distance. Foss talked himself through his various tasks in soft whispers. "Gear down," he breathed. Vic heard a thump as the wheels dropped into position and the plane slowed noticeably. "Flaps full." Vic sensed the plane riding a huge wave of air, and Foss worked the yoke to keep it balanced as he surfed the small ship toward the runway. What were previously pinpoints of light were suddenly two strands stretching far enough into the distance to accommodate the plane. As the lights began to zoom past the side windows, Foss cut the throttles and pulled back on the yoke. "Flair." The word hissed from his lips as the plane tilted tail-down.

When the tires chirped up to speed against the concrete, Hobart snorted, and came to life. "We there already?" he mumbled, sitting up to stretch.

Vic, like a kid stepping off of a scary rollercoaster, rode a crest of relief and bravado. "Nah, Hobe. We crashed. We're all going straight to Hell."

~ * ~

Vic and Hobie were seated in anticipation of the Saturday night meal, at a linen-cloaked table with sterling silver place settings near the back of the main dining room at Red Ridge Country Club.

"That's the guy, Hobie?" Vic asked. "That's Elwin?"

"Think so. Looks to be. He's a big 'un, eh?"

"Big?" Vic held his water glass in front of his mouth to cover his smirk. "You ever watch *Saturday Night Live*?" Hobart answered with a blank stare. "It's a comedy show on TV. They do a skit with these people called the 'Wide Ends.' It's a whole family of people with great big asses! Man, this guy must be a first cousin," he whispered as they stood to meet Garwood and his syndicate representative.

"Mr. Early, Mr. Vickery, Ah'm Lestah Navah," the older man said, his voice rich with a strong, syrupy drawl. They all shook hands. Navarre was a short, rotund man who looked to be in his sixties, with untrimmed salt and pepper chin whiskers. "This's our player, Mr. Elwin Garwood."

Garwood, who looked to be in his twenties, appeared quite normal from neck to waist, but his buttocks and legs were incredibly outsized. In addition, his head was so long and narrow it reminded Vic of Mr. Peanut. Elwin's dark hair was shocking in its contrast with his skin, the color of a carp's belly. The topper was crusty white accumulations of something in the corners of his mouth. He was the funniest-looking man Vic had ever seen. Garwood gave Vic and Hobart each a limp handshake, but avoided making eye contact. His lips looked like fat, wrinkled earth worms. They moved, but nothing audible came out.

"Yah practice went well?" Navarre asked.

"Yes, real well. Nice course," Vic lied. Flat and uninteresting, the course played easy and was downright boring. Many of the public courses in Toledo would have presented more challenge and more fun. Vic couldn't imagine anyone wanting to pay an initiation and the monthly dues to play a course like Red Ridge. At the same time, it was an excellent layout for a money game because there were lots of holes that offered good, low-risk gambles for birdie. Unless Elwin was a much better player than it appeared he could be, Vic was sure he would reign victorious.

"Play twice?"

"The back, I did. That's where it gets tricky." Again, Vic invented convenient truth. The back nine narrowed down a little, but there wasn't a tricky hole on the course. "But, yes, I could have. You made us a real good tee time, thank you. I like to hit it and go, so I had plenty of afternoon light left."

"Good, good!" Navarre enthused, sounding happier than Vic would have predicted, which struck him as a bit strange. He shrugged it off. Everything about Red Ridge and the Navarre syndicate was a bubble or two from center, it seemed. The food, however, proved to be excellent. Vic couldn't remember eating prime rib that tasted any better. While he drank Southern Comfort, Elwin slurped Seven-Up through a flex-straw. The white cakes of only-God-knew-what in the corners of his mouth never dissolved.

Lester and Elwin weren't great conversationalists, in fact, Elwin never spoke more than an occasional mumbled yes or no. That made it very easy for Vic and Hobart to excuse themselves as soon as they finished rich cups of coffee at the close of the meal. "See you on the tee at nine tomorrow morning," Vic said to Elwin, who answered with a noisy sucking sound as his straw drew air when the Seven-Up bottomed in his glass. Vic and Hobart joked about Elwin all the way to their car.

"Feelin' good, boy?" Hobart asked.

"Abso-damned-lutely," Vic replied, using Bascolm's favorite phrase. Vic relaxed against the headrest, vacantly watching the street lights go by. He was delighted Hobart drove the big Oldsmobile sedan. Olds' current advertising slogan went through his mind, "... they'd never believe it, if my friends could see me now." Vic truly wished some of his friends could be there to witness this episode of his new life, but no one could know he played golf for money until after the dissolution. And though he'd squared the idea of playing money games in his own mind, he was happy Bascolm wasn't there to witness it.

"Room all right?" Hobart asked.

"Hell yes, Hobe. I'm easy to please. Got a shower, a bed and cable TV. What more could I want?" He chuckled. "I'm a little drunk. Back home, I buy grocery store Southern Comfort, only 42 proof. This stuff tonight ... " He let his voice trail off, shaking his head.

"You'll be okay for tomorrow?" Hobart asked, sounding as though a bit of alarm surfaced in his voice.

"No problem, Hobe. I'll get right to sleep. Be ready to kick Elwin's big ass in the morning."

Vic didn't get right to sleep. Something about the motel room charged his imagination. So many people had stayed in the room. Awash in the sheets, and bathed in the flickering glow of MTV, he wondered who else slept there. Anybody famous? Probably not. Beautiful women? Sure. He wondered what the most beautiful woman who slept in the bed looked like. Was she with someone? Did they have sex? How many women achieved orgasm in this very bed, and what was the kinkiest sex act performed? Lascivious images swirled in Vic's head. *If Roxanne was here, we wouldn't take a back seat to anyone in that category.* Then he decided it was probably better that he was alone. "No women before a fight—weakens the legs," he once heard a boxing trainer say. Vic used the remote to tune away from the libidinous girls in the music videos, found a station doing the news, and drifted off watching a high pressure ridge move up from the Gulf of Mexico.

The next day turned out to be exceptional. In the presence of some pale, hazy sun, the temperature that morning stood at fifty degrees, with a scant breeze. It was a fantastic January day.

On the flip side, Elwin Garwood proved to be the slowest human Vic ever had the misfortune to share a course with. His walking gait was ponderously slow, which Vic attributed to the sheer bulk of his buttocks and legs. Elwin placed each footfall with what appeared to be obsessive care, and his stride never exceeded what could have been charitably labeled "baby steps." After watching him lumber from the pro shop to the first tee, Vic looked at Hobart and rolled his eyes.

"Say, Lester, we got no problem with taking carts, if you'd rather," Vic offered.

"Oh no, Mr. Vickery," Elwin replied, hooking more than a few words together for the first time since they'd met. "I enjoy taking my exercise out here on the course." His grin made the unidentifiable snow-white deposits, still attached to the corners of his mouth, gleam in the sun. Elwin teed his ball, and with a swing employing no part of his body below his shiny white belt, managed to knock his ball two hundred yards straight down the fairway.

"Christ!" Hobart whispered, blinking at Vic in disbelief. "If he put a little a' that ass into it, he'd hit the ball to the other side of tomorrow." Vic grinned, teed up, and piped his drive fifty yards past Elwin's. The match was on.

At first, the dilatory pace of play didn't affect Vic's game, and he easily won the early holes. As the match wore on, however, Elwin's mannerisms began to take their toll. The man never made a clean swing. He'd address the ball, begin his backswing and repeatedly return to the address position. Over and over, Elwin moved the club head away from the ball, only to pause and return it to his starting position. There was no pattern to it. Sometimes he false-started as many as ten times, but the number always varied. On the green, Vic found himself shifting his weight to begin a step toward his ball, only to discover that, no, Elwin had returned his putter to address and was still building his courage, or whatever he did. This, on top of his old-lady walking pace finally began to drive Vic to the edge. Frustration coursed though his system like a blood-borne virus.

"Jesus *H.* Christ," Vic whispered to Hobart on their way to the seventh tee.

"We've been almost two hours playing six goddamn holes. We've let three groups play through. This is bullshit! My fucking clothes are going out of style."

"I know. I know, son. But you gotta maintain. You can't let him get to ya because *that's* his game. He can't beat you straight up and he knows it. He's tryin' to get your goat."

"My goat died of old age."

"Simmer down," Hobart cooed in his soothing drawl. "I'll call Foss at the turn, and we'll be in the air thirty minutes after you sink your winning putt."

"If Foss hasn't retired by then," Vic replied.

"Shouldn't take no eighteen holes to beat this guy, way you're playin'. Keep your head in the game," he added.

Vic thought his spinal fluid would boil when he miss-hit his tee shot on seven. Elwin dawdled past him with a creepy, open-mouthed half-grin on his face. He planted his peg, set his scruffy, discolored ball on it and rapped it down the fairway. In two more shots, he was three feet from the pin, while Vic was pitching from a good sixty feet. When his ball hit the pin on the fly and ricocheted twenty feet into the greenside rough, Vic told Elwin his putt was good, and picked up.

Hobart looked worried. "Son, I know you're not gonna let him get to you," he said, walking to the eighth tee. "Take it easy now, and don't beat yourself up. You're still six holes to the good. Win four more and you got the match."

Vic put his arm around Hobart's shoulders. "How much is riding on this match, Hobe?"

"Remember, we figured it was better if you didn't know."

"It's okay. Not a biggie, right?" Vic asked, ushering Hobart to the tee-side bench.

"Nah. Three grand. We'll be lucky to make expenses."

"Hey! If this match takes six hours, that's still five hundred per, right?" Vic settled himself and relaxed next to Hobart. "That's worth it." He waved his caddie over. "Do you have a watch?" he asked the boy.

"Not on me," the youngster answered.

Vic unfastened his and gave it to the boy. "After Mr. Garwood makes a shot, wait five minutes before you hand me a club, no matter what anyone says to you. Got it? Five minutes, no sooner. That's good for an extra twenty-five bucks on top of your regular loop money. Comprende?" The boy nodded, grinning. "So let's relax, Hobie. This may be the slowest goddamned round ever played here at grand old Red Ridge."

The dynamic of the match changed immediately. Rather than trying to speed the round to a normal pace, Vic was now in the driver's seat, playing as slowly as he possibly could. Joking. Telling Hobart stories from school, from his childhood, and even telling Elwin stories he made up as he went along. The result was exactly as he'd hoped. He won the eighth and ninth holes, and hit his best tee-shot of the day on ten. Garwood was, of course, farthest from the green and the first to hit his second shot.

"Hey, Hobe," Vic asked as Garwood toddled up to his ball, "did I ever tell you I'm thinking about writing a book?"

Hobart's eyebrows collided amongst the furrows that appeared on his forehead. "You a writer, too, son?" he asked.

"Naw ... well, yeah, I have a feeling I could be. I still love to paint, but I'm looking for another creative outlet," Vic began, resting his hands on his hips. "I have this idea about a guy who goes into a coma, see, and the coma turns out to be really life-altering."

"A coma? Like yours?"

"Not exactly. See, mine was the big sleep. Had some dreams, but I don't really remember them anymore," Vic explained, wondering how far he would take this. "But this guy in my book, he always wanted to be a great pianist. His father deserted the family, and his mother didn't have enough money to pay for lessons, much less a piano."

"Mr. Vickery," Garwood interrupted, "it's your turn to play."

"Oh, gosh, Elwin, did you hit already?" Vic asked, turning toward his opponent and doing his best to look both surprised and interested. "How'd you do?"

"Missed the green."

"Aw, shucks. You'll have that," he said, fanning his arms out from his sides like a minister giving benediction, trying to sound compassionate. Vic turned back to Hobart. "So where was I?" he said, rubbing his chin as though deep in the process of recollection. "Oh yeah, the kid who wants to play the piano. So, anyway, he drops out of high school and gets a job with a moving company. And one day, they're moving this rich couple out of their Manhattan apartment, and he gets knocked on the head by the piano they're lowering from a third-story window."

"Mr. Vickery," Lester Navarre cut in. "It's time for ya'll to hit."

Vic glared at Navarre. "Hey, I'm telling a story here. Back off," Vic warned, trying to sound angry. "I'll start from the beginning if you want to hear it, too," he offered, "otherwise, I'd appreciate the same courtesy I've been giving you. Golf's a game of etiquette, you know." Navarre's eyes widened and he blinked them several times, before he glanced at his watch. "Come on," Vic said to his caddie, leading the small group slowly to where his ball rested in the middle of the fairway. "So anyhow, when the kid goes into the coma, he winds up in a world that reminds him of real life, but it's different, a little strange. No sun. Constant overcast. And he meets a bunch of people who are in comas, too. One of 'em turns out to be a great piano player. Somebody like ... ah, gosh, I don't know ... "

"Jerry Lee?" Hobart offered. "Jerry Lee Lewis is about the best player I ever heard."

"Yeah, like Jerry Lee, Hobie. Old Jerry Lee," Vic repeated. He held his arm out to his caddie as the group neared his ball. "Seven iron," Vic said to the boy. Then to Hobart, "And the guy he meets, the piano player, he teaches the kid everything he knows. And man ... "

"There's a foursome playing up on us," Garwood whined. He sounded like a child with his kite caught in a tree.

Vic shot a look back down the fairway. "I'll be darned," he exclaimed, shaking his head. "Oh, what the heck, let's let them play through, like we did those other groups. I mean, we're in no hurry here." He turned and motioned for them to hit their shots.

Navarre looked like he wanted to protest, but it was too late. One of the members of the following group stepped into his address. Vic led the others to the fairway's edge, twirling his seven iron like a baton. "So where was I, Hobe?" he asked, giving his friend a furtive wink.

~ * ~

Taffeta. Vic looked down at the lacy fabric of early evening clouds beneath the Comanche, and that word came to mind. His mother sewed a lot when Vic was younger, and he heard her talk about that fabric often. Taffeta. He didn't know what it looked like, but the word sounded the way the clouds below appeared; soft and gauzy.

Foss was busy, his head swiveling like a kid's on his first roller coaster ride. Of course, Foss wasn't on any *ride*. He was "driving this bird," as he was fond of saying.

Hobart tapped Vic on the shoulder, and motioned for him to come on back. Vic nudged Foss and let him know he was moving. "What's up?" he asked, wiggling between the seats and dropping into the one next to Hobart.

"Wanna show you how the money works."

"Yeah, I never saw Navarre fork over. I was gonna ask you about that."

"Ain't how it's done. When we set the match, both us and Navarre's syndicate wired three grand to the Philadelphia offices. They hold the money and release it to the winning outfit after both syndicates confirm who won. That way, don't nobody have to worry about unscrupulous bastards who might try a rip-off. Makes the whole transaction a whole lot cleaner. And safer. No cash. No shotgun stocks stickin' out of golf bags."

Vic's eyes widened, and Hobart grinned. "Yeah, used to there was players whose fourteenth club was a Remington semi-auto. Anyway, the governing body nicks both syndicates for two and a half percent, covers their trouble, profit and publishin' costs for the weekly sheet. So we'll get a check for fifty-seven hundred." Hobart had a pocket calculator out and punched numbers like a CPA. "So that, minus the three our side put up is twenty-seven. The cost a' this rig—fuel, maintenance and Foss' salary—is about a hundred an hour. Times ten hours is a grand. Leaves seventeen. Our motel, meals and car was another two-fifty, leaves fourteen-fifty. Your cut is a third, comes to four hundred seventy-eight and change," he concluded, tapping on the window of the calculator. "That's rough. I'll figure it to the penny later," he said, patting Vic's arm. "Wish it could be more. That son of a bitch worked ya for it."

"Almost five hundred bucks is a lot of money for a weekend's ... play," Vic replied. "I almost said work. The real victory was on ten, when old Garwood asked if I could speed it up."

"Ya beat him, son. Beat him at golf and at his own game, too. You enjoyin' this?"

"You bet!"

"Wanna do it again next weekend?"

"Damned betcha!" Vic said. "But not with Elwin."

Vic stood in the cold damp Toledo darkness and bore witness to the Doppler effect as the Comanche hurtled past on the runway, the engines wailing as Foss and Hobart lifted off into the overcast. The plane banked south and Vic bounced the strap of his golf bag a little higher on his shoulder, picked up his suitcase, and started for his car. The guy who'd fueled the plane was coiling the hose on a hook near the pump, and Vic gave him a wave.

"How was the golf, Mr. Vickery?" a feminine voice inquired as he loaded his clubs into the Mazda.

Vic looked over his shoulder and saw Hawklady walking his way, her heels clicking on the blacktop. His mind whirled as he tried to retrieve her name.

"Hi there. Golf was great, so was the weather," he replied, returning her smile. It was too dark for him to see his watch, but he knew it had to be almost eight o'clock. "The people at Hawk must be slave drivers, got you working so late. On Sunday, no less, Teresa?"

"Treese," she said, waving off his attempt at apology. "Treese Cosgrove. Yeah, the boss is a witch. Long days every day." She giggled. "So, you enjoy the trip?"

"Yeah, I really did. I was a little nervous."

"I knew you were," she said.

"I hoped it didn't show."

"It's only natural if you're not used to flying. I'd be nervous walking onto a golf course."

The more Vic talked to Treese, the more her personality grew on him. She had a self-assured air that was engaging, and she looked him straight in the eye in a way that seemed challenging, yet charming. First impressions, Vic thought, remembering how he decided she resembled a hawk. Tonight, she had her bale of dark hair tied back loosely and Vic liked the effect. Sure, in profile, her receding chin emphasized her nose, but unusual looks on a woman always appealed to him more than Barbie Doll perfection. "Do you fly a lot?" he asked.

She nodded. "Fly, instruct, light maintenance. You name it. Hey, I could teach you to fly."

"That'd be cool. My uncle was a pilot. He gave me my first plane ride, in the Tri-Pacer."

"Was? He doesn't fly anymore?"

"Crashed." Vic arched his eyebrows with the memory.

"Ooo. I'm so sorry to hear that." She patted his shoulder. "You'll have to tell me about it. I'd love to talk some more right now, but I haven't eaten all day and I'm famished." She pulled her leather coat closed against the chill.

"Me, too. You know, I was going to stop at Loma Linda's for some Mexican on the way into town. Join me?" The offer was out before he had time to realize he'd made it.

"Oh, Mr. Vickery! I'd love to and I'm so glad you asked, but I'm taking a little time off, and I have lots of loose ends to pull together. Promise you'll ask again?"

"I will, if you'll call me Vic. All my friends do."

"You got it. Definite rain check for dinner, Vic. And a flying lesson, too."

Vic grinned, but he was busy trying to figure out what caused him to ask Treese out. It was like when Doc Pembrooke tapped his knee with a little rubber hammer. Vic twitched out an invitation on reflex. But reflexes follow a stimulus. What was the stimulus? He closed the Mazda's back hatch. It seemed he barely knew what to expect from himself anymore. That was unsettling. Unsettling wasn't comfortable.

All the way home, he asked himself questions, and they made for an uncomfortable ride. What was the state of things with Roxanne? How much longer could he live as he was, a veritable recluse, waiting for a phone call from a woman he couldn't acknowledge he knew, beyond her being his former neighbor? He and Angie used to go out on weekends with friends, but that was the trouble. All their friends socialized as couples, and Vic was no longer a member of that club. Not only that, friends take sides when there is a divorce. It seemed anytime Vic stopped to repair or maintain something at the house, there were always letters or notes from people who were friends to both Angie and Vic, but who now put their support toward Angie alone. Like Doug and Carol. Angie made sure there was always a display of mail affirming his pool of friends was diminished. Regardless, what Vic longed for was to go out to a restaurant with someone, or to be able to call Ron, or Sal, or one of his remaining friends and say, "Hey, let's take the girls out to a movie, and grab a bite afterwards." He wasn't certain he could face another night of MTV and chipping balls into the beanbag chair. At the same time, the night at the Bombay proved what a minefield the dating scene could be, when Kym revealed her dating history. And what if she hadn't? Vic wondered if he over-reacted. What really were the chances of her having something he didn't want to catch? He heard a doctor on TV say when you have sex with someone, you're having sex with everyone in their past. He was talking about the new disease, but that threat aside, there was still syphilis, gonorrhea and the usual host of others. As long as he was only sexual with Roxanne, he didn't have to worry about them. But what about Treese?

As he pulled into his parking space at the apartment building, he marveled at the ironic turns his life had taken. When he was married, he and Angie had an active social life, and little or no intimate relationship. Now, after leaving her, he had no social life, and a rich intimate relationship with someone who couldn't be seen with him in public. He used to play lousy golf with his friends, and now he had a game that was so good, he made thousands with it. But he couldn't let anyone know.

When he got out of his car, Queen was on the radio, but Mick Jagger's voice brayed in Vic's head, "You can't always get what you want." He chuckled, thinking he'd like to have a little sit-down with Mick and offer an addendum: Sometimes you *can* get what you want, but then you have to live with it.

Olivia was outside, smoking a cigarette when Vic walked up to the entry door. He smiled. "How many today?"

She gave him a look like she'd been caught stealing candy, her lips pulling downward into a grimace. "This is the sixth." She reached to hide her eyes. "I'm weak, I guess."

"Don't feel bad about it. Quitting is tough. Took me lots of tries before I managed to kick it." He opened the door. "You might try exercise. Worked for me. I started running, and I knew right away I had to quit one or the other. I'd ponied up thirty bucks for running shoes, and I think a carton of cigarettes was only three or four bucks back then. The choice was a no-brainer." He winked. "Think about it."

She giggled. "I might do that. Thanks for the advice."

The phone was ringing when he let himself into his apartment. He was certain it would be Roxanne.

"Hello, Vic," Angie said.

"Hi. Is something wrong?"

"No. I thought something was wrong with you. I've been trying to reach you all weekend."

"Oh. I had an offer to go out of town and decided to take it. One of those last minute deals. What's up?"

She hesitated. "That couple came through the house last Friday? They made an offer."

"They did? How much?"

"Seventy."

A torrent of thoughts washed through Vic's mind. They were asking seventy-five thousand, an amount Vic thought was very fair for the street and the neighborhood. He hated to sell short, but he was anxious to be rid of the place. Spring would mean grass-cutting, along with opening the pool and keeping it vacuumed. It was getting so he hated the thought of going there, for any reason. If Angie was there, he felt uncomfortable around her. If she wasn't, he found himself haunted by memories. It seemed like there was always something in need of repair, and the repairs cost him time and money. It looked like the purses from golf matches would clear up his financial situation, but he still wasn't happy about contributing half of a house payment on top of his rent, not to mention money he laid out at the hardware store.

"What do you think?" he asked.

"I've worked it through. If we accept, we'll clear at least six thousand a piece. Is that enough for you?" Before he could answer, she went on. "I mean, I'll be honest, the sooner I'm out of this house, the better. Just ... I don't like it here." She paused, then started again before he could respond. "Vic, I'm moving as soon as everything's cleared up here."

That hit Vic like a head-shot. "Moving? Where to?"

Angie's voice changed a bit, like she was carefully editing what she said. "Not sure, yet. I've never been happy in Toledo. You knew that."

"What do you mean, I knew that?" Her accusation stung. "You never let on."

"I tried to hide it. You were hired at Alexis so we lived here. But before we met, I'd always believed I'd go back home once I graduated."

"I knew you'd planned to go back, but you never said anything about not liking it here. Much less hating it. You never told me."

"I guess I tried to downplay it."

His tone became accusatory. "So, apparently I wasn't the only one who tried to hide the fact that I was unhappy."

Angie ignored that and pressed on. "Anyway, I know Toledo is not where I want to stay."

"I guess I understand," Vic said, deciding not to push his point, but still upset he never was aware of Angie's dislike of Toledo. Was she good at hiding it, or was I insensitive to her feelings? "So, you want to take the offer, then?"

"We could counter and maybe get a little more, but I'm not sure it'd be worth it. I'd say yes. Let's take it."

Vic barely remembered saying goodbye and hanging up. He sat for a long while, stunned by what Angie said. Never happy in Toledo. Vic sifted though his memories. Had he been that numb to her feelings? Could he live with someone for eleven years and never pick up on the fact she was unhappy about where they lived? Sure, at times she talked fondly about Chicago and her parents. But thinking back, he could remember distinct cases where she said she hated the crowds and the traffic back there. You could drive anywhere in Toledo in fifteen minutes, and she always said she liked that. Additionally, Angie never mentioned it, but it seemed to Vic she got along with her mother a lot better when there was some distance between them. She had always been "daddy's girl," and got along fabulously with her father, but conflicts with her mother were normal when she lived at home, and their relationship, as far as Vic could tell, was closer when they saw each other half-a-dozen times a year.

Regardless of any of that, the thing that bothered Vic the most was she never told him she didn't like living in Toledo. She tried to hold him responsible for not spelling out the fact he was unhappy because of the state of their relationship, but then she withheld the fact she hated Toledo until now. In Vic's mind, it was a heck of a lot easier to know there were problems in a relationship with sporadic intimacy than it was to figure out she wished she were living somewhere else. Inevitably, the question rose like a monster: how much had her unhappiness led to the breakdown of their relationship? And, had she been up front with him about missing Chicago, would he have been willing to move there? Vic liked Toledo, and he liked teaching at Alexis. Teaching jobs were a scant commodity, and he would have had to teach at an inner-city school, because getting a job in one of Chicago's suburbs would be next to impossible.

Before he even began to dig for answers, Roxanne called. Her latest shtick was to pretend she phoned her sister, Marla. She could be sitting right next to Tom, and he was none the wiser. In fact, sitting with him in sight was a requisite so he wouldn't accidently pick up the phone.

"How are you, Sis?"

"Great," Vic answered, her call vaporizing thoughts of Angie's announcement. "Great trip. Just walked in the door."

"And how did you do at the bingo game?"

"I won. Oh, baby! You should have seen the guy I played! You know the 'Wide Ends' on *Saturday Night, Live*? This guy, Garwood, he could be John Belushi's brother! His ass was as big as a golf cart."

"No kidding?"

"Oh, God! I thought I'd die! I'll tell you all about it next time I see you. Oh, and it looks like we sold the house!"

"Wow! Lots of news. And that's why I called. Tom bowls tomorrow night. Thought I'd invite myself over for dinner, if you don't think Bob will care."

"Oh, I think I can safely say Bob will never even know you're here."

Chapter Ten

Once more, time seemed to accelerate. Days at school whooped by; amazing, in light of the fact syndicate golf had all but wiped out Vic's enthusiasm for teaching. Also surprising was the rapport he was able to maintain with his new semester's students. He worried they would pick up on his disinterest and become troublesome, but that wasn't the case. His art classes had gained a reputation at Alexis High, and Vic was apparently the beneficiary of his laurels. Each morning, he awakened dreading the day ahead, but when the last bell rang, he'd wonder why the school day seemed so insurmountable eight hours earlier. And when Friday rolled around, he'd wonder where the week went. The ease with which time slid by did little to fire his interest, however, and he saw teaching as nothing more than something that prevented him from devoting more time to his game.

The next Friday, he and Hobart flew into Dalton, Georgia, about seventy-five miles north of Atlanta. The game was with a good son of the South named Jonas Walker Brown. The flight down was terrific. Foss even let Vic take the controls for a while.

The course, a very traditional track named Royce Meadows Golf Club, was challenging and fun to play. It was tight, with lots of water, and it rewarded a control game, usually Vic's strong suit. He and Hobart played thirty-six practice holes on Saturday, under cloudy but temperate skies, and Vic's game was the weakest it had been since he'd begun playing for the syndicate. When he stepped up to the ball, he never felt his usual confidence, and couldn't find his swing. "Hope to God I can pull this one out for you, buddy," Vic said, as they loaded their clubs into the rental car.

"Remember, son. You lose this match, ain't nobody going to go into cardiac arrest or nothin'. Do what you can and don't worry none."

Dinner that night was in the elegant, candle-lit dining room of the clubhouse at Royce Meadows. Jonas and the two representatives from his syndicate were friendly, entertaining and hospitable.

Jonas was only five feet seven or eight, and couldn't have weighed more than a hundred and fifty pounds. His reddish brown hair was a close match to the color of his heavy spatter of freckles. He was about Vic's age, but the southern exposure levied its toll, and generously wrinkled his skin. That, coupled with a neatly trimmed mustache that grayed at the corners of his mouth, would've led anyone to guess he was ten years older. A skilled storyteller, Jonas regaled the group with a number of well-told jokes and golf-related anecdotes. Vic couldn't remember the last time he felt so at home with virtual strangers.

Vic laid his napkin next to the plate that previously held a large piece of peach pie, "Say, Jonas, where's the bathroom?"

"Ah, hell," Jonas replied, his eyes reflecting the yellow candle flame, "ya'll are here with a bunch of shit-kickin' southern boys." He fired off his infectious smile and tossed his head in the direction of the door to the terrace. "Go on outside, there. Third flower pot on the left."

Vic smiled back. "You'd love that, I bet. Probably have Boss Hogg out there, waiting to run me in for indecency, if I do. We'd have to forfeit, and you'd win the match."

Jonas obviously enjoyed this kind of repartee. "If that's got you worried, it's down that hallway, last door on the left." Vic nodded and pushed his chair back to leave.

"Before you go, though," Jonas said, "I heard a little story the other day. Fits up good, here." Vic settled back into his chair, coaxing Jonas on with a grin. "Seems a Georgia boy and a Yank wind up in the same john together, both usin' the urinals. So, the Georgia boy finishes first, zips up and scats for the door." Jonas leaned forward on his elbows, his voice dropping like he offered privileged stock tips. "So the Yank, over his shoulder, he says, 'Hey, up north, we're taught to wash up after we urinate.' And the southern boy, he says, 'Oh yeah? Down here we're taught not to piss on our hands.'" Vic shook his head and joined Jonas and the others in a quiet chuckle, then he pushed his chair back again to go. "Hey, Vic," Jonas called as Vic cleared the portal to the hallway. "Soap's to the right of the sink."

"Thanks anyway, Jonas," Vic replied with a wink. "Like with all small arms, accuracy's related to length of the barrel. I won't need to wash."

When Vic returned, the evening was on the ebb, so Jonas invited Vic to leave Hobie with the others and join him in the bar for an "eye closer." The bartender knew the call as soon as Jonas held up two fingers, and placed a pair of glistening flutes on the polished dark wood bar. He filled each with Frangelico, thick liqueur that smelled sweeter than Southern Comfort.

"Hope you ain't diabetic," Jonas said. "Green Jesus, I love this stuff."

The Frangelico tasted smooth and sweet, with a slight aftertaste of hazelnut. It was delicious in small quantities, but Vic wouldn't have asked the barman to leave the bottle. "Tastes good. Thanks."

Jonas' watery dark eyes gleamed. "It's to make up for takin' your money tomorrow."

"You might do 'er, too. Not at the top of my game, I'm sorry to say. But, you win, this drink'll suffice."

~ * ~

Vic's salvation, as it was when he'd played Blackstock, turned out to be the weather. A front moved in overnight, and the Sunday greeting them was in Vic's favor. It was bright and sunny, with clouds that looked like puffy white explosions, but the temperature stayed in the high thirties and a brisk wind cut at them like ice shards. Vic was comfortable enough in a turtleneck, a lined sweater and a knit hat. Jonas, however, was bundled up with several sweaters, and a quilted winter coat.

"You going to be able to make a swing with all that on?" Vic asked, as they readied to tee off on number one.

Jonas chuckled. "Don't know. We get these cold snaps now and again, but when we do, I usually tee my ass into a lounge chair by a fireplace."

Regardless of the chilly conditions, the man from Georgia shucked his outer coat when he hit the ball, and managed to humble Vic on the first seven holes. The only thing that prevented Vic from sinking in the wake of Jonas' juggernaut was his abiding belief the cold would eventually help him win out. When Vic saw Jonas trying hard to hide a shiver on the ninth tee, he believed the tide would swing his way. It did. Jonas never won another hole that day, though he did manage to play Vic even on number twelve. But the temperature and Vic's short game, which was as solid as Lake Erie ice, subdued the tough little southerner.

When Vic won number seventeen, it left Jonas down two holes with one to play. Jonas tugged off his glove and extended his hand. "Nice match, snow bird."

Vic clasped Jonas' hand in both of his. "I don't take any pleasure in winning this way. Come here a minute." Vic walked to his bag, unzipped a pocket and pulled out a small bottle of Frangelico he'd purchased after he and Hobart left for the hotel the previous night. "Hope this will suffice."

Jonas' face wrinkled into a smile. "You're a pretty class act for a Yank. Thanks. This'll hold me 'til I get to play you again, sometime when it's warmer."

"It'd be a pleasure, my friend, long as the match isn't for money."

~ * ~

Vic was down on his game and on himself. Hobart apparently noticed, and asked him to ride in the back with him on the flight north.

After Foss leveled the plane off, Hobart pulled out a silver flask and two matching shot-sized tumblers. "Thirsty?"

"What do you have?" Vic asked, without enthusiasm.

"Wild Turkey. Give it a try?" Vic wasn't much for straight whiskey, but he held onto a tumbler and watched as Hobie poured. "Here's to you, son," Hobart said, making a toast. "Two for two, now. Three for three if you figure in the match with Blackstock." Vic acquiesced, sipping at the powerful liquor. "Wanna talk?" Hobart asked.

"I dunno. It's ... I played like shit today. I didn't beat Jonas, the weather did." Vic looked out the window. "If the temperature had been like Saturday's, he'd have kicked my ass. He *did* kick my ass the first seven holes. Cold weather saved my bacon with Blackstock, too."

Hobart's chuckle rumbled. "Are you a better golfer than Jack Nicklaus, you think?" Vic gave him a look, curious to see where he was headed. "Well?" Hobart pressed.

"Hell no, Hobe. Nobody's as good as Nicklaus."

"Oh, I don' know 'bout that. Ol' Jack, he don't win every tournament, does he? Think you gonna win every time, Vic? Think you're going to out-golf ol' Jackie?" Vic tried hard not to smile, but it didn't work. Hobart poured more whiskey. "Old Jackie, I bet he beats himself up pretty good, too, but I bet he saves it for when he loses. Why don't you do the same an' enjoy the fact you're over two large richer after the round today."

"Two thousand dollars?"

"Yep. Match was for eight. After expenses, your cut will be a little over twenty-one hundred. I'll bank it with the rest, 'til a week or so into next month."

"More 'consultant's fees?' Hey, if I ever get audited and they ask, what the hell am I consulting with you about, anyway?"

Hobart's eyes scrunched into a squint, something he did when he was thoughtful. He grinned. "Golf, of course. You're my personal golf instructor." He shook his head. "Nah ... even better, tell 'em you're helping me find a good course to invest in. Tell them that's why we fly all over. Worse case, they'll think we're queer, and you're my young gay boy." Hobart brayed his hearty donkey-like laugh.

Vic blew Hobart a kiss. "Just so the gals in Toledo don't find out."

~ * ~

"Must be nice, flying outta here to play golf every weekend. You got it made, man," the fueler said, as Vic passed by on the tarmac at Hawk Air. At first, Vic thought the skinny kid in coveralls might be dogging him, but decided he was actually envious. "It's a living," Vic deadpanned.

"No shit? You on the tour?"

"Nah. Small money games. Make enough to cover expenses if I play well." He looked out at the parking lot. "Treese must not be back yet. I don't see her car."

"Treese?"

"Treese Cosgrove. The gal who works in the office."

The guy gave Vic a look that told him he was way outside the loop. "Ms. Cosgrove *owns* this outfit, man. Has since her father died a year and a half ago. She's been around a little the last few days, but she's layin' low. Face is still bandaged up."

"Bandaged up? She had an accident on her vacation?"

The kid started to smirk, then drew up short. "That's what she told you, she was going on vacation?"

The boy's expression became a smirk that worked its way under Vic's skin. "Said she was taking some time off, so that's what I figured."

The fueler put his hands up defensively. "Hey, Ms. Cosgrove signs my paychecks. She told you she was on vacation, you didn't hear nothin' different from me." He turned to walk into Hawk's hanger, leaving Vic to wonder what really happened.

~ * ~

Once more, winter thundered into Toledo the last week of January, dropping eight inches of snow Monday night. As soon as Vic set foot outside Tuesday morning to run, he knew there was no chance school would be open that day. He slogged through the drifts for five miles, showered when he made it back to his apartment and made coffee.

Roxanne called soon after the official announcement on TV. "Hey, buddy! Heartbroken this morning, are we?"

"Not hardly."

"So, what's on tap?"

"Nothing. That's the beauty of a snow day, unstructured time. Woke up thinking I would go to work and found out I was mistaken. I'll probably practice my short game. Maybe work on the painting of the woman on my easel."

"O-o-o ... that'd be different."

"Yeah, I've been pretty unfaithful to her. She deserves better. I really should finish her off."

"God! I love it when you talk dirty. I wish you could finish me off today."

"The pleasure would be ours. Why not get your pretty self over here later and I'll see what I can do."

"Oh, I *know* what you can do, but you know what I *can't* do. Driving in this stuff is way too scary for me, buddy. Besides, my sister's coming over for lunch. She has four-wheel drive."

Vic was disappointed, but it wasn't the crushing melancholy he'd have experienced even a month ago. His emotions had been end zone to end zone recently, ranging from the cool distance he experienced after the big blowup over her not wanting to live in the apartment, to intense feelings that eventually leaked back in. Lately, their relationship evolved again, and though neither of them ever discussed or acknowledged it, the affair had developed into a structure of solid friendship, coupled with high voltage sex. Vic never confronted the question of which was mortar and which was brick. He didn't really care. In his mind, Roxanne was more of a place than a person. She was where he felt acceptance, comfort and happiness. When he thought of her, she materialized in the abstract, as the feelings she engendered when they were together. He assumed it was like that for her, but he never asked. Besides, he figured his sentiments would probably change again soon, anyway.

That day, he painted for the first time in weeks, never stopping until the unfinished image of the woman on his canvas was complete. In the past, he often had trouble knowing when a painting was done, starting and stopping many times over. More than once, a painting came down off the wall, to be stripped of its frame and reworked, or tickled. On that snowy day in the dying hours of January, Vic applied one last stroke, a highlight on the woman's right breast, and decided it was finished.

And so was he. He recalled his final conversation with Bascolm, after the dinner at June Mancy's restaurant. Vic told his friend he could see himself giving up art for golf. Now, that was exactly what he would do. The years he'd spent learning his craft and using his talent to pursue the dream of becoming a successful painter were difficult to let go of. Yet, painting lost much of its meaning to him, along with Angie, teaching, and much of the rest of his former life. A vast shadow of sadness swept over him as he accepted the fact that, like many other components of his past, painting was no longer important. He'd often joked he was one of the few teachers at Alexis who practiced what he taught; not many science teachers went home and dissected frogs, or went out collecting specimens to support a hypothesis they were testing. Vic taught art by day and went home to paint and print photos at night. Having to look at the unused brushes and gnarled tubes of paint each day only emphasized his hypocrisy. After all, he was no longer a practicing artist who was also a teacher.

The hope this might be a temporary hiatus eased his regrets. *I'll get back to it,* he assured himself as he carefully packed his equipment and supplies in a box. He dismounted the lights from his easel, readying that, too, for a trip to the storage locker. The strange thing was, looking at the painting itself didn't bother him, the way looking at the Bittersweet house, or his classroom where he'd excelled as a teacher, did. The painting he completed was a monument to what he'd been able to accomplish over the years. He saw it as a milestone, affirming how far he'd come. He slid the canvas of the woman into a frame, and hung it in his living room, across from the couch. Then, he opened a beer, sat looking at the painting and wondered if he would ever do another.

~ * ~

"Hey, lady. What's happening?" Vic said to Roxanne, when she called the next morning.

"Nothing at Alexis, that's for sure. Can you believe it? Two days in a row."

"Been a while since that's happened, but it *is* bad out. I hauled some stuff over to my storage unit earlier and man, the car was all over the road when it wasn't trying to hang up on snow drifts. And that wind, colder than a witch's tit."

She giggled. "And how would you know how cold that is?"

"Oh, I've known a few."

"Present company excluded?"

"You're no witch, and no part of you is cold."

"I'm getting warmer every second."

"That brings me to the fact that I still have some tools and stuff at the house. I want to get them over to the storage unit."

"Did you find out about the closing yet?"

"Yeah. The realtor called yesterday. Angie scheduled the closing for the morning of our dissolution hearing."

"You're kidding. Get rid of the house in the morning and the wife in the afternoon?"

"Yep. See how easy it is to erase eleven years? Anyway, the new people don't get possession for thirty days after the closing, but since I have another snow day, I figure I might as well get the last of my stuff out of there." He paused. "Angie will be at work, so if you feel like going for a little walk ... "

"Ooo, like through the neighbor's backyard, maybe?"

"It's up to you. I mean, there's gonna be dangerous drifts and sub-zero wind chills."

"What about Angie. You're sure she won't show up?"

"Yeah, no way. Middle of the week. She's never home before five or so. Of course, you might want to stay all snuggly in your warm little house."

"And miss my last chance to screw you blind on Bittersweet? Like hell!"

~ * ~

Vic rode his usual high as he left Bittersweet for home. The last of his possessions were packed around him in the small cabin of his sports car. Mid-morning on a Wednesday, there was practically no chance Angie would come home from work, so he and Roxanne spent a good two hours talking, necking, and capped the visit with some hot lovemaking on the sofa in the den. Time with her left him lofted on a huge swell of satisfaction and happiness. But the fall from euphoria began as he neared his apartment, the emotional equivalent of hitting a tree at eighty miles an hour. The exhilaration smashed by the reality of the crash; the pain of it far-and-away surpassing the former pleasure. When would he see her again? Not Thursday, without a doubt. That was the one day of the week Tom usually came home right after work. And he'd most likely stay home, in anticipation of a night with the boys on Friday.

Vic got out of his car, grabbed an armload of clothes and trudged through the drifted snow. He wondered how he would open the door to the apartment building without dropping anything. As Vic approached the door, Ames emerged, his face glowing like a fat, round ember.

"Hey there, Vic. I'm just in time, I guess." He swung the door wide and stepped out of the way. "You got more to haul? I'd be happy to help," he roared, with the enthusiasm of a Boy Scout working for a merit badge. "Only cost you a beer for the labor." He smirked, but it appeared to take more effort than Vic would have imagined. He'd apparently already had enough beer to challenge his facial control.

"Nah, thanks anyway, Gilly," Vic replied, forcing the name the manager preferred. Vic didn't like him, and would rather have called him "Mr. Ames," but Gilly wouldn't hear of that. "I have it under control, thanks." Vic stepped through the door.

"Here," Ames said, putting on an unlikely burst of speed to pass Vic on the stairs down to the apartment. "Let me at least help you with your door."

Vic felt trapped. How was he going to get rid of this guy without causing bad feelings? He didn't want to listen to Ames recount his latest sexual conquests, the main topic of conversation when he wasn't crowing about how many medals he won in his last indoor archery competition. Still, Ames gave Vic the same feeling he sensed with certain dogs, that if the animal wasn't licking your hand, it could as easily be tearing it off. So, Vic stood with the clothes pressed against the hallway wall while he fished out his key, and cursed himself for taking a bigger load than he could easily carry without help. As Ames took the key from Vic and opened the door, the phone began to ring. "Shit, Gilly." Vic tried for a facial expression that would convey sincere disappointment. "I guess we'll have to do the beer some other time. That's an important call I've been expecting. See you, and thanks." He kneed the door closed. He had absolutely no idea who was on the phone, but he was delighted whoever it was decided to call.

"Hello, Vic? It's Treese."

President Reagan's voice would have surprised Vic less. "Treese?" It was the best he could manage.

"Yes. I hope this isn't a bad time?"

"Oh, no." He regained himself, but he couldn't figure how she came up with his number, much less, why she called. "I've been moving some stuff." He realized that probably made no sense, but elected against trying to explain. "How did you get my number?"

Treese giggled, and it sounded like the nervous kind. "Oh, now I feel bad. I shouldn't have bothered you."

"No, no. You're not bothering me at all." Vic fished a beer out of the refrigerator, and clam shelled the phone between his shoulder and his head while he twisted off the cap. "I'm surprised, is all. But pleasantly."

"If you're sure. See, Mr. Early called this afternoon. He wanted to clarify something on the bill from last weekend, and I asked him for your number. He said he didn't think you'd mind if he gave it to me."

"No, not at all. You say Hobie called you? Is there some kind of problem?"

"Not really. I transposed some numbers when I sent the bill for the fuel-up last weekend. Actually, I didn't bill enough, and he called to make sure we made it right. Mr. Early is really quite a guy. Most people would have been happy to overlook a mistake made in their favor. Anyway, I asked him for your number because I thought you might like to schedule that flying lesson we talked about, remember?" The line went quiet. "I've been a little under the weather, but I'm fine now, so I thought I'd let you know we could get it set up."

"Yeah, your fueler said something about your face being bandaged. You're okay? You weren't in an accident?"

"Nothing like that. It wasn't a big deal. Okay, sort of a big deal. I'll tell you about it later." She sounded purposely vague.

Vic's mind percolated. He looked around his apartment, his little one-bedroom prison. He felt confined there much of the time, but he knew he was his own jailor. He could free himself. The Bombay escape didn't work, but enough time passed he wasn't against another attempt. "I wasn't kidding about wanting to try a little flying. Foss, our pilot, actually let me take the yoke for almost an hour on our way to Georgia." He chuckled. "That was scary. But cool. Thing is, as I remember, there was more than a flying lesson involved in our little discussion. How about we have dinner Friday night? We can talk it all over."

"Friday," she repeated, as though she was checking a calendar. "Sure, Vic, Friday would be great."

He got directions to her house, confirmed when he would pick her up and dropped the receiver on the hook. "Wha-hoo," he yelled, as loud as he could. Then, in a normal voice, "I am going *out*. With a woman." He pumped his fist like a gambler who busted the jackpot. He was not going to spend another Friday night waiting for Roxanne to call. Or not call. He was not going to drink Southern Comfort and watch MTV all evening until he fell asleep on the couch. He was going back out into the world with other men and women who talked and danced and enjoyed good meals with friends. He couldn't believe how excited he was to be going to a restaurant. How long had it been? The last time was Thanksgiving at Denny's. Before that? With Angie, the night before the Chili Open. Lots of fast food stops, and the country club dinners before matches, but they didn't count. They were when he was alone, or with Hobart or his mother. This was a date. And Trecsc didn't know it, but she was going to the fanciest steakhouse in Toledo. She would be fun to spend an evening with. She was nice. It wasn't going anywhere; not romantically, anyhow. Roxanne was who Vic would have rather asked; but if she could sit on Bittersweet and pretend to be Tom's faithful wife, Vic could take a lady to a restaurant and at least pretend to be single and free.

Thursday was uneventful. The snow situation on the roads improved, so school was back in session, which helped time pass. Friday dragged, regardless. All Vic could think about was his night on the town. "Have a date tonight," he allowed, as casually as he could, during the morning meeting in Duff's office. That was the other thing about the affair with Roxanne, Vic wasn't someone who wanted his friends to know he was seeing a married woman. The guys joked about that kind of thing, but the reality would put him in a light he wasn't anxious to step into.

"The boy's getting laid tonight," Duffy said to Flanner. They both raised their eyebrows and leered.

"Nah, it's not like that. Only taking a young lady to dinner," Vic said.

"That's why he isn't getting laid," Flanner bawled. "He's taking a *lady*."

That evening, he puttered with a golf ball on a rack he'd mounted in the living room of his apartment, killing time until he would leave to pick up Treese. Suddenly, Roxanne burst through the door. "Jesus, you scared the shit out of me," he said. "What are you doing here?"

"Tom called and said he'd be late. Stopped for a brew-ski after work, and his buddies talked him into bowling. I thought I'd surprise you." She dropped her coat and keys on the chair, walked over and gave him a kiss. "Told him I was going shopping, so I could come have a Friday night visit with my bestest buddy." She stepped over and looked at the rack. "So, what's this?"

Vic was reeling, and he was delighted to have something to talk about while he decided on a course of action. "A ball rack I bought yesterday," he began. "I buy a logo ball everywhere I play a match." He lifted one off the rack and handed it to her.

"Royce Meadows Golf Club," she read aloud. She rolled the ball in her fingers until the inscription he'd applied with magic marker appeared. "Jonas W. Brown, 1-17-82, $2,180. Cool." She put that ball back, and picked up the one from Red Ridge. She giggled. "Elwin. Wish I could have seen that guy! Now, this is the ball you beat him with?"

"No, I buy these in the pro shop for display. They've never been hit."

"H-m-m. Maxfli," she read aloud, before returning the pristine ball to its spot. Then she picked up the Top Flite that was inscribed, "Tom Bayer."

"Except that one," Vic said. He forced a chuckle. "That one has two hits on it that I know of, the one Tom put on it, and the one it put on me."

"So why is it here with the others?"

"Because if it weren't for that one, there wouldn't be any others. Like I said when you and Tom stopped over that Sunday, that's my magic ball." The irony made him smile. "Good fortune masquerades on unexpected faces."

"Is that original?"

"Nah, I think I stole that from a fortune cookie."

"You're quick, lover." She grasped his hand and rubbed his index finger across her lips, flicking her tongue against its tip. "So what's a gal gotta do to get a beer in this joint?"

"I ... ah, was going to leave in a few minutes."

Roxanne's eyes widened in surprise. "Leave?" The word came out as more of an accusation than a question.

Vic's mind revved like a propeller. "Yeah, this woman who runs Hawk Air, the place where Foss and Hobie pick me up, we're talking about her giving me flying lessons."

"A woman's gonna teach you to fly?"

"Yeah, she might. She's a licensed instructor."

"She teaches flying? At night?" Roxanne appeared to be straining to control a gang of emotions, and anger was evidently the ringleader.

"No, we're kicking it around, right now." Vic was pretty sure none of this was getting off the runway.

"So, you just kind of invited her out to talk about flying airplanes. Like, maybe over dinner?"

He arched his eyebrows in resignation as the voice in his head began to scream, *May Day!* Roxanne's demeanor softened and she stepped toward him, looked into his eyes, and stroked his cheek with the hand holding the magic ball. "I'm sorry, buddy." She tried to execute a smile, but she looked more like a thirsty vampire. "I'm sorry I didn't get here earlier, so you could *fuck ME before you went out to dinner with your new little girlfriend,*" she yowled. The hand that stroked became a club that whacked the side of his head. Tom's golf ball inflicted less damage than the first time around, but Vic's anger ignited like aviation fuel. There was a millisecond when he teetered on the brink of swinging back, but it never spiked beyond an impulse.

As the pain abated, Vic rubbed the side of his head and strafed Roxanne with his eyes. "I didn't deserve that." He fought to keep his voice from rising in volume.

"Like *hell* you didn't. When did you ask her out?"

There was no reason whatsoever for him to answer, but the words were out before he realized he'd spoken. "Wednesday afternoon," he said, realizing as he spoke that he'd committed a huge mistake.

"You son of a bitch!" she shrieked. "Invite me down for a little suck and fuck in the morning, then phone another chick in the afternoon for a night on the town." For an instant, she looked as though she might take another swing, but Vic piped a look into her eyes that stopped her. Instead, she threw the magic Top Flite in the general direction of the TV. It missed the set, ricocheted out of the corner, and rolled down the hall toward the bedroom.

Vic began in a near whisper. "You are a *crazy* woman. I wanted to ask you. Would have in a heartbeat. You're the only one I *want* to go out with. You're all I want. The one I moved out to be with. Thing is, I didn't bother to invite you out, because I was nearly certain you'd be busy tonight ... *PLAYING HOUSE WITH YOUR FUCKING HUSBAND!*" Those last six words came out as loudly as Vic could shout them. Angry as she was, Roxanne flinched.

"I never asked you to leave her."

"Don't even start with that happy horseshit! The point is, you want it all. You want your house and your yard and your dog and your lifestyle. And your marriage. You want me to sit here alone—no life—to watch TV and be at your beck and call. To wait patiently for the next time you decide to give old Tommy the slip, so you can come over for a *GOOD* jump." Vic sweated like he'd run five miles. "I'm nothing but a fucking amusement park to you. A cheap trip to Cedar Point. And a much shorter drive."

They stood chin to chin, staring at each other through the palpable vitriol of their exchange. Vic was finished. He didn't have any more to say, but he was ready to wait her out. She retreated to the chair, put on her coat, and picked up her keys. She slid the one to his apartment off the ring and let it drop to the floor. "You're gonna miss me when I'm gone," she said.

"Miss you? Won't be nothin' new, lady. I've had a lot of practice, every *fuckin'* day."

Roxanne whirled, flung open the door and stomped out. Vic was on his way to slam it closed, but a calm washed over him like a cool wave as he neared the open door. Then he saw Olivia, standing in the hallway with her shoulders hunched, looking like a bank customer caught in the middle of a robbery. Vic winced and gently pushed the door shut.

~ * ~

The packed snow crunched beneath the tires as Vic brought his little sports coupe to a halt in Treese's driveway. All the way to her house, the row with Roxanne was all Vic could think about. The two emotions tangled in his psyche were sorrow and anger. This date with Treese was merely an excuse to enjoy an evening outside the walls of his little apartment. That's all he ever intended it to be. That's all he wanted. Then, when Roxanne showed up unannounced and unexpected, he felt badly about the way he'd handled the whole thing. Why didn't he merely sit her down and explain? Could he have explained an evening with another woman? Would she have understood? As he thought about it, he wasn't so sure. Failing that, why didn't he think to tell Roxanne he was going out with the boys, to play poker or something?

The anger sprung from her reaction. He nearly lost it when she hit him. It wasn't that she hurt him, not physically anyway. It was the shock. The way she jumped to all the conclusions she did, without giving him a chance to explain. Then, there was the fact she felt it was okay to hit him. That it was perfectly fine for her to stay with Tom and live a normal suburban life, but she wanted Vic to herself. For all he knew, she still had sex with Tom. She always claimed they didn't, but rather than press her about it, he chose to believe her. The only time it even crossed his mind was when he heard something about the new sexually transmitted disease. Was Tom having sex with Roxanne, and with someone else, too? Improbable, but possible. That was also something Vic tried not to think about.

By the time he pulled into Treese's driveway, he had calmed down and vowed he would enjoy himself. He double-checked the address. He had the right one, on a street lined with big, friendly-looking brick homes, spacious lawns, and stately old-growth trees. A number of the city's up-and-comers lived in the Old Orchard area, which surrounded Toledo University's bell tower.

Vic climbed out and walked up onto the lighted porch and pressed the doorbell. When Treese answered, he experienced one of those panicky instants, positive he was at the wrong address. The bridge of her nose sloped where it previously bulged, and her chin was much more prominent. As she later explained, a surgeon had reconfigured her nose and inserted an appliance through a small incision under her chin, to strengthen the contour of her jaw line. She treated herself to a make-over at one of Toledo's premier hairdressers, and that, along with the surgery, transformed her into a classic dark-haired beauty. "Holy crap," Vic exclaimed, quickly editing from the word "shit." "You look fantastic."

"That's nice of you to say, Vic. It was time for a change."

"Change? Is that ever an understatement. You are absolutely gorgeous, Treese." Then he put on an exaggerated frown, his lower lip reaching for his nose. "Problem is, now you're not going to want to be seen with a guy like me."

She playfully slapped his shoulder. "Hey, you accepted a date with me not knowing I had my face fixed, so you're exactly the kind of guy I want to see. Besides, you're not so bad looking, yourself. I'm excited about tonight."

"You and me both." He grasped her arm after she locked her door. "Now let's go get some dinner and talk about flying." As he closed the passenger-side door and walked around to his, he thought about Roxanne again. He wondered if it was over with her. He had no way of knowing, and he wasn't even certain whether or not he wanted to see her again. But he did marvel at how often his life seemed to run this way, with good fortune shining down on the darkness of adversity. As poorly as the evening started off, the date with Treese showed every sign of being a lot of fun.

He did all he could to make certain it was. He diligently employed impeccable manners, and made sure he didn't talk too much by asking Treese plenty of questions. Her answers were interesting, and convinced him she was someone he would enjoy getting to know. He thoroughly enjoyed the evening, and the witty conversation they shared.

When the talk turned to aviation, Vic told her pursuing a pilot's license was something he would love to do, but it would have to be on hold for a while. "I have to get out of the little place I'm in, and I need to save a down payment."

"Sure," she said, "I understand. No problem. I'll still take you up for a fly-around, but the truth is, I can't take on another student right now, anyway. Maybe in a few months?"

That sounded like perfect timing to Vic. In a couple months, he'd have a lot more of his life sorted out. By then, he would know if buying a river house was a viable possibility, based on how the syndicate play went. If the money came in as he hoped, he would be able to siphon off a thousand or so to pay for lessons. Learning to fly his own plane could eventually be a great asset in playing the syndicates. Foss, after all, couldn't fly forever.

The food was sumptuous, and Vic enjoyed being out in the world. It was a world he'd missed since he moved out, back in November. He and Treese talked over coffee, then drove back to her house, the headlight beams illuminating the snowy outlines on the skeletal trees and the carefully sculpted shrubbery on her street. "I really enjoyed dinner," Vic said, as he pulled into her driveway. He switched off the headlights, but let the engine idle for heat.

"I had a wonderful time, too. I'm glad I decided to call you. I'd planned to wait another week."

"I can't imagine why. Your face really looks terrific."

"Thank you." She smiled through a moment of silence. "Would you like to come in?"

He opened his door. "Absolutely."

On his way to open her door, Vic wondered where this was going. She asked him in. In some circles, that was tantamount to an invitation for some necking, if not all-out sex. Treese didn't seem like a woman who would drop her clothes on the first date, and the truth was, Vic hoped she wasn't. Things were rotten with Roxanne, but he didn't want to compromise the possibility of a long-term relationship with Treese for some short-term pleasure. Sex could complicate even an established relationship. Still, the excitement over all the possibilities, and his desire to find out how things would go, put him in mental and physical hyper-drive. That was one of the aspects of a date he'd forgotten about: mixing yourself with another human and seeing what kind of blend resulted. He held her at the elbow on the way up her slippery sidewalk, and found himself doing comparisons. She was taller than Roxanne. Where Roxanne was lean and angular, Treese was fleshy and round, with larger breasts and wider hips. Her penchant for aerobics and weight-training, however, kept her firmly feminine.

Once they were inside, she hung his coat in a closet that smelled of cedar. "So, what would you like to drink? Coffee? A nightcap?"

"I'm with you. What are you having?"

"I can't handle any more coffee this late at night." She giggled. "You know what I'd really like? Some Southern Comfort."

"You're kidding." Vic couldn't hide his surprise.

"I know," she said, laughing. "Tastes like cough syrup. Go ahead and make fun, but I like it."

"No, you don't understand. I drink a glass or two almost every night. I love the stuff." She gave Vic an incredulous look. "Honest," he added as reinforcement.

Treese poured the drinks and guided him to the sofa. He enjoyed watching her stoop to put a Janis Joplin tape in the deck, and her body did wonderful little sways as she walked over to join him. "We like the same music, too," Vic said, trying to choke off fantasies of a naked romp on the sofa. "What a loss. I can't imagine what a singer she'd be today, if she'd lived." Treese nodded. "Do you like Albert Brooks movies? I haven't seen *Modern Romance* yet. Would you like to go?"

She met his invitation with a look that surprised him. "I hope you're going to understand." She cleared her throat nervously. "Like I told you, I was always the ugly duckling. Olive Oyl, they called me in school, and, worse yet, The Beak. I never even was invited to the prom my senior year of high school." She sipped her drink. "I promised myself, when I had my face done, I'd date around for a while, kind of make up for lost time, you know?"

"I've toyed with the idea myself, now that my dissolution is almost final."

"So, you understand? I know it sounds strange. I do want to go out with you. I don't want to get heavily involved with any one person for a while."

Confusion predominated in Vic's mind. Some irritation was in the mix, but he pushed that away. "Let me see if I follow. You like me, so you won't go out with me?"

"Not right away. I'd love to go out with you again, maybe in a couple weeks. I don't want to get into a steady dating situation yet. Especially not with a guy I really like a lot."

"Would it help if you knew I'm actually a complete jerk disguised as an okay guy?" He touched her forearm. "I mean, I undressed you with my eyes while you put in the tape, and I have a collection of over 3,000 dirty limericks I can recite from memory. Wanna hear the first hundred?"

Her laugh was throaty, not exactly like Roxanne's, but close. "I'm not convinced."

Vic finished his drink. "You're lucky you didn't excuse yourself to go to the bathroom. I was gonna steal some silverware after I peeked at you through the keyhole." He stood to leave. "But I had a nice time, anyway. I'll call you in a couple weeks."

She followed him to the door. "I hope you will. I really do."

Acting purposely formal, he turned and shook her hand. "I'll see you sooner than that, though. The plan is to play in Tennessee next week, if the weather straightens itself around."

"Yeah, what's the deal with that? How can a teacher afford to fly all over to play golf?" Treese asked. "I mean, I hope I'm not being nosy."

He gently touched the tip of her re-sculpted nose. "That would be impossible, my dear. But the more correct question is, how could a teacher *not* afford to fly all over to play golf? I'll explain it all sometime, but not now. Gotta keep a secret or two. Make myself more intriguing than my competition," he added, before stepping out into the cold.

Once more, the polarities reversed. Roxanne dropped the key to his apartment on the floor before stomping out. Then, he had a great time with Treese, and she seemed like someone with whom he shared a lot of common interests, but she held him at arm's length so she could play the field. He understood, on an intellectual level. The reason the whole thing burned was because the evening was so enjoyable, but she didn't want to go out again for a couple weeks. Waiting that long to have another good time seemed an insurmountable task.

What it all came down to, he was without a woman. How long had it been since he hadn't had someone in his life? At first, he figured it might have been the summer before Angie and he married, while she was in Chicago, only to recall he'd spent that time with Reefer. And before Angie? That would have been Colleen, the Angora-sweatered, freckled redhead who lasted into the first few months of college. She'd gone off to Kent State, and the sheer distance between Kent and Bowling Green stretched the bonds of that relationship beyond the breaking point. Vic fished up images of other girls who had preceded Colleen, as well as the ones who'd populated short term relationships between the major ones. Yes, from the time he'd first kissed a little girl, a pretty thing with dark hair and remarkably white skin, in the playhouse at nursery school, Vic always had something going with a woman. He swung from one to the next like a gymnast on the rings, until tonight. When he reached out for Treese, he grasped only cold, dark January air.

And what if it had turned out differently with her? What if she'd accepted his invitation for a movie date? Would he have started seeing Treese and ended it all with Roxanne? The more Vic pondered, the less certain he was. For one thing, it could already be over with Roxanne. The last time they had a blow-up, they reunited and, although their relationship changed, it continued on. That didn't mean it would happen this time, and he was resolute in that he wouldn't be the first to cave in and call. But, if she did want to pick things back up, where would that leave him? She seemed to be digging in her heels regarding Tom. She wasn't leaving him. Would Vic trade the possibility of a relationship with a woman who was actually available for the clandestine affair with Roxanne?

And what the hell was a normal relationship? He hadn't had one with Angie for years. He didn't have one with Roxanne. Could he even sustain a coupling based on equality and give and take? At that point, emotions entered the picture and further muddied his stream of thought. He didn't know if he loved Roxanne, but he cared deeply for her. Treese was someone for whom he might grow to feel the same way, but he had no way of knowing for sure. The simple fact he had no idea what course of action he should take made him crazy. Crazy or not, the main thing was he had no woman, and the rest of the weekend dragged. He called a couple of his friends from Alexis, but they were involved in family activities. He almost drove over to the storage lock-up to get his painting equipment, but instead decided to use the time to catch up on things he'd been neglecting. He called his mother. He got current with his grading, and gave the apartment a needed cleaning. It felt good to reestablish a weave in areas of his existence he'd allowed to unravel. Good, but not good enough to raise his spirits any appreciable amount.

Horny. Back to jerking off. He wondered how long it'd been since he'd masturbated, then he remembered he'd only stopped when he began seeing Roxanne. Sex with Roxanne was such a staple in his life, and now he'd moved from feast to famine. Someone used to regular feedings feels hunger as much in their mind as with their body. Maybe more.

Hobie called on Wednesday to say the game for that weekend was on in Tennessee. Although winter's grip remained firm on Toledo, the weather in the bosom of the Smoky Mountains had returned to its moderate norm. He would play a man named Jimmie Wingo at a club called Waycross, near Tennessee's eastern border.

Shortly after he hung up with Hobart, the phone rang again. "Hi, Vic, it's me," Angie said.

Vic immediately noticed her tone of voice was different than usual. Maybe it was merely a change of inflection. Whatever, he was certain something was up. "Oh. Hi, Ange," he said, in a guarded way, using the voice he reserved for calls if he suspected a telemarketer on the other end. "How are you?"

"Fine. Tying up some loose ends, you know." Her pattern of speech was very peculiar. Vic wondered if she was drunk. "Staying busy."

Vic decided not to ask if there was a problem. He wanted to play along until she tipped her hand and gave him some clue as to where this call was headed.

"Yeah, I'll bet you are. When are you leaving for Chicago, anyway? Right after the ... " He couldn't find the phrase he wanted to blunt the words, dissolution hearing. "The court deal?" he finally said.

"Actually, that's why I'm calling." Her voice dropped in volume as the sentence progressed. Vic barely heard the word "calling." Then she rose out of her whisper. "There's been a change. In plans, I mean."

"Oh?"

"I'm actually leaving town tomorrow. *Before* the dissolution hearing. And the closing."

"Tomorrow?" Vic tried hard to control his surprise, but he was certain his voice telegraphed it. "Is everything okay with your folks? Nothing wrong?" Vic always worried about Angie's father. He huffed down two packs of Camels a day and seemed to thrive on the chaos of the commodities markets. Vic always worried the same pressure that seemed to rev him up would push his heart past its redline.

"The truth is, my plans have changed."

"You already told me that." A bit of impatience surfaced in his voice, against his will. "What's shaking?"

"I'm not going to Chicago. Nate and his brother decided to go in together," she allowed, as though she were revealing a great secret.

"Nate? Nate who?"

"Nathan."

"Your boss?" In the ten years she'd worked for him, Angie never referred to her boss as anything other Nathan, and Vic's mind fogged over when he tried to place who "Nate" was.

"Yes. Nate and his brother. See, his brother, Jonathan, graduated law school a couple years ago and opened a firm in Evergreen, Colorado. He's been doing real well. Picked up lots of Denver business. He has so much work, he needs help, and Nate's buying in as a partner." Angie sounded instructive now. A teacher's voice, not like the one she began the call with.

"Evergreen?" That was the best Vic could manage.

"Yeah, outside Denver. About fifteen miles west. Up in the foothills. I'll have to get used to the elevation. It's higher than Denver, even."

There was a long pause as Vic tried to process what Angie told him. Facts he couldn't find categories for were slamming around in his head, and he couldn't grasp any of them well enough to start putting them in order. Silence was all he heard through the receiver's earpiece, but it was noisy in his head. He closed his eyes to cut out visual input, at least.

"So, you're moving to Colorado, too? What about Chicago? I thought you missed your folks. The city. Your friends." None of this made sense to him. "You're going to Colorado? To be his secretary?"

Angie met this batch of questions with a steely silence. Seconds went by. Then she coughed. It sounded like the voluntary kind. "Look, Vic,

I'm not discussing my personal life with you. We're dissolving our marriage." Vic heard her take a breath. "So it's really none of your business. I wanted you to hear it from me. About the change. In plans." Vic's legs bent at the knees, something he hadn't instructed them to do. He felt like he'd been punched. In semi-slow motion, he lowered himself to the floor, bottoming out awkwardly with his legs askew. Angie went on. "What *is* your business is that Starr Haigen is my lawyer now. She has power of attorney, so she'll be handling everything for me at the closing and the hearing. She'll do the signing."

"Starr who?"

"Starr Haigen. She's the new owner of Nate's firm. She's buying him out. She's been so successful in Detroit, she wants to branch out into Toledo. You'll like her. She's into cars. Drives a Porsche."

"But you and Nathan?" Vic's question trailed off to barely a breath on the last syllable.

Angie sounded exasperated. "Look, all I'm going to say is nothing, *nothing, ever went on between Nate and I when you and I were together.* Nate and I have been close friends for a long time, but that's all it was." Her voice was flat now, like a cop asking for a license and proof of insurance.

"You never let on—"

Her voice clubbed him to silence, like a night stick. "There was *nothing* to 'let on' about. That's all I'm going to say about it. Ever again." More dead air on the phone. "The other thing I need to tell you, Muldoon is yours. I know you wanted to keep him. You can come over later tomorrow to get him. He was always more your cat than mine, anyhow."

"Muldoon?" Vic worked on reflex. Her words were like islands, and his mind swam to the most familiar one.

"Yes. You *will* come and get him tomorrow? He'll be here by himself. Make sure you do," she instructed.

"Will you leave an address? Someplace I can reach you if I need to?"

"I doubt you'll have that need, but yes, I'll mail you my address once we get out there and decide where we'll be. Jonathan needs Nate right away, and there are licensing issues that have to be cleared up before he can practice in Colorado, so we're going now and we don't know exactly where we'll land yet. When we do, I'll let you know." Another pause. "Meantime, anything really important happens, you can always call my parents. They'll know how to reach me."

Vic felt like he'd been dropped, mid-semester, into a calculus class. None of what he heard made sense. He had nowhere to put this huge helping of information. His mind refused to digest it.

"Look, I have to go." Her voice was as cool as slate. "I told Starr you could take anything you want from the house. She's going to contract with someone to auction the rest. We'll split the proceeds. Anything else?"

What Angie said seemed vaguely familiar. It sounded like some of what he told her the night he moved out, or when he made his dissolution offer. He wasn't sure which, but the words created a wave of déjà vu.

"Angie—"

Again, she cut him off. "I mean, anything else about the house and its contents." She waited. "Anything?" she asked again.

"No," Vic said, in a very small voice.

"Okay. I have to go. I'll send an address."

Vic waited for her to say goodbye, but all he heard was the click as she hung up. He sat for several minutes with the receiver still pressed to his ear, waiting for the dial tone to begin. Then, when it occurred to him that the line would still be open if she picked up, he let the receiver tumble onto its cradle.

He sat on the floor, staring at the phone. Finally, he eased himself down onto his back. The kitchen ceiling was stained in a number of places, something he'd never noticed until then. One, directly over the stove, looked like a mustard-colored map of Africa, but what would be the east coast vaguely resembled the profile of a human face. A human face with a smallish, sloping nose. A nose like Angie's. Or Treese's new one.

Vic rolled onto his stomach, pillowing his head on his forearm. He looked at the phone. Angie's words still played in his head. "My plans have changed." "I'm not discussing my personal life with you." "Nothing,

nothing, ever went on between Nate and I when you and I were together."
He closed his eyes again.

What he couldn't figure out was why Angie's pronouncement
bothered him so much. *What the fuck,* he thought. *I left her. The hell do I
care if she takes off with Nathaniel-goddamned-Fairchild? Nate.*

But Vic did care. The emotion surged to his brain's cortex. Nate, the
pencil-necked little weasel. Little Nate. Barely taller than Angie. Skinny.
Moved like a spider. Wore thick glasses. *Round*-lens, gold-framed
spectacles. And tailored, double-breasted suits. And wide, red "power ties."
Angie could say what she wanted to, but there was no way Vic could make
himself believe her "friendship" with her boss, with "Nate," hadn't
influenced her in their marriage. Even if she wasn't sleeping with him, Vic
now believed he knew the reason she hadn't been sleeping with *him.* "Nate"
had been a boulder in the stream of their relationship. "Nate!" Vic shouted
into the empty apartment. It didn't echo, but the volume made his voice
resonate in a way it never had before, even during the blowup with
Roxanne. "Nate!" he yelled again, trying for more volume. All his voice did
was go up a few notes higher. It came out sounding like a screech.

Vic left her, but he left her because she'd changed. And now, NOW
he believed he knew why. It was that little legal lizard, Nate, all the time.
Angie said they never got it on, but even if that was the truth, she still had a
thing for him. For that little motherfucker. "Motherfucker!" Vic howled.

Roxanne was right. She asked him if he thought Angie might be
cheating when they were at The Old Man's grave. He'd laughed it off, but
she had it right. He was so goddamned stupid. "Stupid!" he shouted, but not
as loud as before. Regardless, the burn in his throat told him that was
enough.

Vic sprang from the floor as though it was skillet-hot and grabbed
his Southern Comfort. He spun the top off with such speed the plastic cap
flew out of his fingers and soared like a Frisbee. He gulped a big slug. His
body felt like a battlefield, and the warming gush of liquor did nothing to
change that. His brain shot colors at his eyes. Even when he closed them, it
looked like fireworks. The sweet smell of the Southern Comfort soured in

his nose like buttermilk. He nearly retched. His legs began to ache in that creepy twitchy way, like they did sometimes in bed, when he felt like a marionette controlled by a puppeteer with Parkinson's. A subtle ache that was only relieved when he flexed his legs. And flexing didn't feel all that good. He began to walk in circles, from the kitchen straight to the dining nook, right into the living room, across the living room, and right again, back into the kitchen. He walked around the wall separating the rooms. Five times. Ten. He couldn't stand still, but walking wasn't enough. He finally ran out the door, slamming it behind him. He didn't lock it. No keys anyway. No wallet. All he wore was a sweatshirt and some flannel lounging pants that looked like pajama bottoms. And his running shoes.

He sprinted down the hallway and out of the apartment building. When he reached the street, he lit out for the Trail, the big, divided four-lane that connected to downtown Toledo, nearly six miles away. Traffic was light at that time of night, so he never broke stride, and crossed the west-bound lanes. The median was two lanes wide, and some grass showed through in patches where the snow melted. He looked up past the streetlights and into the cloudless sky. There was no moon, but a number of bright stars and planets showed in the crystalline blue-black firmament. "Take me," he whispered, but it apparently wasn't his time.

He sprinted like a halfback. When he couldn't maintain that pace any longer, he slowed to a jog. Soon, he felt a resurgence of energy and kicked the pace up again. He alternated, fast and slow, but he never stopped. When he ran past the country club golf course, he looked over to where he knew Bittersweet was. He wasn't certain if he could see the street in particular, but he knew the general direction. From a quarter mile away in the dark, he couldn't tell which lights were from houses on Bittersweet, but Roxanne's was over there. Two doors down was where he'd lived with Angie. The house where Muldoon would be waiting. Tomorrow. Vic would have to return to the Bittersweet house one more time to get Muldoon. Then, never again. "I told Starr you could take anything you want from the house," he could hear Angie saying. Nothing, Starr. I want nothing from that place. Dump it all.

Vic ran for a bit over forty-five minutes before he arrived where the Trail dumped him off onto Erie Street, as it did the suburbanites who used it to get to work each day. He couldn't believe he ran all that way, and he remembered little of the run, other than when he'd passed Bittersweet. He didn't recall passing the zoo, or crossing several major intersections. Now, although he had no idea what mental mechanism caused him to come into downtown Toledo, he knew exactly where he would go.

It was four more blocks to Adams Street, where he turned west, and two more to the corner of Adams and Michigan. Vic crossed the empty intersection diagonally, and jogged up to the office building where Angie worked for Nathaniel Fairchild. The signage on the big glass window out front was changed. In gilt gold lettering, the window now read "Haigen and Associates, Attorneys at Law." Big letters. Swoopy and stylish. He looked closely and could barely make out the ghostly silhouette of Fairchild's name.

Vic leaned against the window, his forehead the only part of him touching the glass. The pane was cold. It felt good. Six miles of sweat pasted his head against the cold smooth surface. If it was metal, I'd be frozen to it, he thought, which made him chuckle. What would Starr Haigen think, finding a man stuck to the front of her new office building? He rested against the window for a long time. A few cars passed, but nobody stopped, or even slowed, as far as he could tell; probably assuming he was drunk or a derelict, or both. He suddenly realized he was cooling out fast. His sweatshirt, wet with sweat, clung to his body like a frigid second skin. He pulled his head free of the window and stood, looking at the strange image he'd stamped on the glass. Down the street, the sign in front of First Federal Bank and Trust flashed the time, twenty past eleven. Then came the temperature: twenty-six degrees. He was tired, and it was cold. He'd run hard, and he wasn't certain he could jog the six miles back to Maumee. He was afraid he'd get hypothermic if he walked. Thirsty, too. He looked at the snow piled over the curbs. It was a dishwater-dirty, grayish-white, with meltings from the street splashed on it. He wasn't that thirsty, he decided.

A cab pulled up and stopped at the light. Vic hurried over to it and tapped on the passenger window. The driver rolled it down a few inches and peered at Vic with jittery, suspicious eyes that jerked, instead of sweeping smoothly. The guy was young, with a bony face and a day or two of patchy razor stubble. Vic could smell the vague history of marijuana loose in the car. No matter, he decided. Cabs weren't big business in Toledo, a town where most people relied on their cars. It could be a while before another one came by. "You go as far as Maumee?" Vic asked through the narrow gap the cabbie allowed between the window and the door frame. The driver smiled, revealing empty real estate where several of his teeth used to reside. "Shit, mister. I go as far as L.A., you got the money."

"I got the money," Vic said. "It's at my apartment, where you're going to take me. Be an extra five dollars in it for you, you trust me to go in and get it." He gave the driver a wink. "I won't stiff you." The driver paused, seeming to size Vic up. He finally reached to unlock the door, so Vic eased his exhausted body in and gave the cabbie his address. Vic let his head loll against the headrest, shut his eyes and shivered all the way home.

Chapter Eleven

The next day, he had to drag himself out of bed and be a teacher, again. Mondays were never easy, and this one felt like boot camp. His emotional state was fairly solid, which surprised him, but he'd beat up the muscles in his legs pretty good on his run the night before. Once underway, however, the day went smoothly. The kids were involved in their projects, and Vic always enjoyed offering them tips and chatting with them. His teaching seemed to take an amazingly tiny amount of maintenance, almost as though his classes were on automatic. Vic was supposed to be the pilot, but he felt like he was merely along for the ride. Regardless, the day at school helped keep his mind off the things he didn't want to think about.

After school, he made the trip he'd dreaded all day, to fetch Muldoon. An unexpected calm swept over him when he pulled into the driveway on Bittersweet and stopped in front of the gleaming white garage door. He pulled the remote off his visor, pressed the button, and put it in his pocket when he climbed out of the car. He glanced toward the Bayer's house without turning his head in that direction. There wasn't much on the block that Roxanne missed, so she was probably watching, he figured. Vic didn't want to reward her with an overt look in her direction.

Muldoon met him at the door, meowing loudly and rubbing against Vic's pant leg. "Hey, Mully," Vic said, picking the cat up and cradling him in his arms. "Ready to blow this pop-stand?" Vic carried Muldoon into the kitchen. There was a note on the counter by the sink, written in Angie's precise script, every letter formed exactly like the ones Vic remembered

313

above the blackboards of his elementary school classrooms. "Take anything you want," it reminded him. "Starr will set up a sale for what's left."

Vic felt his lips pull tightly against his teeth. He petted Muldoon, who usually didn't like being held all that much; but the cat purred softly and pushed his head into each stroke. Vic blew a puff of air though his nose. "All I ever *really* wanted is going to Colorado, Mully," he said. "You want to do a final walk-through?" Muldoon rubbed against Vic's cheek and meowed. The cat seemed compliant. Although Vic didn't want to look around, as with the overpowering urge to gape at a dead body, his curiosity to see what Angie left with, and what she left behind, overrode his desire to get the hell out of there.

He put Muldoon down and walked into the dining room, where the nick-knacks that had populated the tables and shelves throughout the house sat, spread neatly on the table. The ashtray her father used, when her parents visited, was there. Several Hummel figurines. Vic didn't even know where many of the objects came from. Wedding gifts? There was a fondue set, which was definitely in that category. Had they ever used it? Vic couldn't remember. He suddenly realized he couldn't tell what she'd taken because everything was out of place. If objects were still where they'd been in the house, he might have been able to make a better accounting. With it out of any context, he didn't know what was missing. If anything. He shrugged.

Walking through the hallway to the living room, he noticed the difference in the timbre of the sound his footsteps made on the floor. With the walls denuded of his paintings, and the curtains folded and placed in neat stacks on the sofa and chairs, the house had a hollowness to it. A tomb was the obvious comparison, but as Vic thought about it, it was more like a mausoleum, housing separate tombs that held memories of differing parts of the life he once shared with Angie. The recollections floated through his mind like ghosts. He looked at the carpet in front of the living room window, where they always set up their Christmas tree. It still bore a vague stain of pine-sap laden water, from the first Christmas they had Muldoon and he managed to topple the tree. He recalled how, early in their marriage, he and Angie used to make love by the tree, the room bathed only in the soft glow of the blue lights she favored.

In the den, Vic looked at the lifeless TV and recalled the morning Angie woke up, at some ungodly hour, to watch Princess Di and Prince Charles get married. Then he climbed the stairs, and wandered into their bedroom. The pink Posturepedic mattress, bare of bedclothes, glowered at him in the gray light of the cloudy afternoon. He glanced toward the open closets. Only a single wire hanger lay hung inside. He stepped into his studio and was flooded with memories of the hours he'd spent there, painting and printing photographs. His memory drifted over some of the ideas he'd come up with, and over the successes and failures he'd synthesized in the darkroom and at the easel. Now this space, where he spent so many of his hours, was only an attic once again. No one would ever know the beauty he'd been able to create amidst these rafters and walls. Vic felt a huge sadness building, like the pressure when he used to scuba dive deep into a quarry or a lake. The difference was the pressure was from the inside, not from without. And unlike the water pressure, it was impossible for him to equalize against it.

There was one more place he had to go before he left. He forced himself out of the studio and the bedroom, into the hallway, and down to Angie's workroom. The door stood open, and when he looked inside, as he guessed, the dollhouse she built and every vestige of her equipment were gone. Instead, sitting on the floor was a crate, nearly three feet square and about as tall. Professionally constructed, it looked sturdy as a safe. Vic nudged it, but it didn't budge. Written on the top was a shipping address: Storage-4-U, on a street in Evergreen, Colorado. There was a millisecond when he fought the almost-overpowering urge to smash it. He had no idea why. He admired the house, and the craftsmanship she'd employed to build it. The house had nothing to do with the downfall of their relationship. Did he want to hurt her? Was that the seat of his motivation? Regardless, he merely ran his hand across the top of the crate, then turned and walked out.

On his way to the garage, he noticed more of their belongings, plates and cookware, stacked on the counter in the utility room like a display at K-Mart. A tear finally found its way into the corner of his eye. Someone he didn't know would price the things he and Angie used to own, and sell them to people he would never meet. Faceless individuals would buy the remnants of his life with her, take them home, and use them in their own way, for their own purposes, and never give a thought to what they once meant to a young, happy couple with dreams for a future that eventually imploded.

Vic picked up Muldoon and walked into the garage. He tried hard not to look around, but much was still there to taunt him. Their bicycles. The lawnmower. The workbench, where his tools no longer hung on pegboard above it. Angie's gardening tools. Vic gave it a fast once-over, then carried Muldoon out to his car. He went back inside and retrieved the litter pan, food, and a small bag of cat toys. When those were stowed in the car, he walked back into the garage. He noticed the garbage cans, and wondered if any needed to be taken out. Pick-up was the next day, but they may be empty, he thought. In the first one he opened, still encased in its gold frame, but with shards of broken glass scattered across it, was their wedding photograph. The breath caught in his throat. He lifted the photo, and turned it over to let the loose glass tinkle onto the rest of what was in the can. When he turned it back over, the picture was still spider-webbed by jagged pieces of glass, like a kaleidoscope that lost it symmetrically. Vic looked at Angie's smiling face, wondering if he wanted to take the picture with him. He was certain he'd never see her again. Did he want to have her picture? Was it worth the pain of having to look at the two of them on that day, when he remembered thinking he would be happy until he died? Worth the pain to have a visual record of how a woman he married and shared love with looked on an August day in 1971?

He heard Muldoon yowl, and glanced toward his car. Muldoon hated cars, and Vic was prolonging the cat's anguish. He put the photo back in the can, face down, and gently replaced the lid. "Fuck it, let Starr haul the trash," he snarled. He yanked the remote out of his pocket, pressed the button, and walked out under the garage door as it closed its yawn. When it was inches from being shut, Vic threw the remote under the lip as hard as he could. He heard it skitter across the smooth concrete floor, and it sounded like it broke when it hit the back wall, an instant before the rubber gasket on the bottom of the door seated against the cement.

~ * ~

Having Muldoon in the apartment was comforting. Even though he didn't like being held, the cat was an inveterate lap dweller, and loved to snuggle. He laid on Vic's lap at night while he watched TV; and as soon as Vic pulled up the bed covers, Muldoon jumped up to find his spot on the blanket where it covered the crook of Vic's bent knee. At the same time, Muldoon constantly conjured memories Vic wanted to do without. Angie was the one who found Muldoon cowering in the bushes next to the garage, and brought him into the house. Vic didn't really want a cat at the time, but the blue-eyed, fluffy ball of black fur, along with Angie's pleadings, soon melted his heart. As Angie often said, Muldoon became more Vic's cat than hers. Still, the sight of Muldoon ripped the scab off memories of Angie, the Bittersweet house and of a time in his life, now irretrievably gone.

After school Friday, Vic made sure Muldoon had plenty of fresh food, water, and litter before making the familiar drive to Hawk Air at Toledo Express. His heart wasn't in it, but being on the course and competing would channel his mind away from the canyon of sadness he had yet to escape. Besides, Vic had no idea what the penalty for the syndicate would be if he pulled out. There was no way he wanted to cause trouble for Hobart and the others. Of that much he was certain.

As he unloaded his clubs and suitcase from the car, a late-model, yellow Corvette swept through the gate and rumbled to a stop at the curb. At idle, it sounded like a heavy metal drum solo. A man who looked like he stepped out of *Gentleman's Quarterly* got out and hurried inside, leaving the car to continue its concert. By the time Vic locked his Mazda and started for Hawk's office, the dashing young guy reappeared with Treese on his arm.

"Oh, hello, Vic," she gushed. "Tennessee, right?"

"Tennessee, yep," Vic affirmed, smiling as though he meant it.

"The radar scan's clean. Have a great time." *GQ*-man held the door of his rumbling coupe for her.

Vic waved in acknowledgment of her benediction, but before he could make it into the building, he had to listen to the sound of the 'Vette rocketing away on the service road. He and Treese had only gone out once, and he had no right to feel jealous and melancholy. That's what he told himself. Like with Roxanne, living with her husband. Vic tried hard to never let that become an issue. Of course, what could he have said? Regardless, the big blow-up of a week ago made Roxanne nothing but curious history. In a week, he'd ask Treese out again, and he was confident he could eventually win her over. Regardless, he was glad when the door at Hawk Air closed on the distant sound of the Corvette's exhaust.

In a few minutes, the little Comanche swept down out of the sky. Foss taxied it onto Hawk's tarmac. After the engines spun down, the door opened and Trent VanVorhis, the TV newsman, stepped out onto the wing. Vic expected Hobart, and was surprised he wasn't informed that a different syndicate man would be making this trip. I'm a good employee, he thought. I'll roll with this.

"Jesus, Vic! It's cold here," VanVorhis said.

Vic waved at Foss, before turning his attention to the news anchor. "Hey, it's winter in these parts. Great to see you, TV, but I gotta say I'm a little surprised. I expected Hobie. He's okay, isn't he?"

"Yes, he's fine. Woke up with a bit of a head cold this morning and, what with the congestion, he didn't think it'd be smart to be at altitude. I told him to give it a rest since I had a few days off. Anxious to see you in action, anyway. You been winning us a heap of money."

Vic opened the outside hatch behind the passenger compartment and began stowing his bags. "Yeah, Lady Luck's been a good girl lately."

"Luck?" VanVorhis screeched. "You're a golfing son of a bitch, boy."

Foss walked up and shook Vic's hand. "Say, young fella, how you doing? I'll close up the storage here, and we'll be ready to climb on out."

"No fuel?" Vic asked.

"Nah, we got plenty for the hop to Tennessee."

Less than three hours later, the plane's tires chirped up to speed against the concrete at a small, private airstrip outside Maryville, Tennessee. VanVorhis and Vic caught a taxi to Avis, then went looking for a motel in a rented Ford Pinto, the least expensive car Trent could lease. He was very different from Hobart. For example, Hobart always drove. VanVorhis didn't like to. And Hobart's attitude was, we're here, let's spend a few dollars and enjoy ourselves. With VanVorhis, the unfolding scenario was, let's have a good time, but I'll enjoy myself more with every buck we can save. "Red Roof okay with you?" he asked. "Less money."

"Yeah, I'm not partial," Vic replied. He spotted one up ahead on the left, and signaled to change lanes. A Camaro coming up behind them changed at the same time, almost punching the Pinto in the rear end.

"Fucker!" Vic snarled, before a break in traffic allowed him to turn into the lot.

"What?"

"Ah, that asshole back there almost banged us." He decided to put a little heat on VanVorhis for insisting on a cheap rental, to see how he would react. "You know the word on these Pintos, don't you?"

"Exploding gas tanks," the newsman said, laughing, apparently taking no offense.

For a joke, Vic once bought a girl in one of his classes a bag of marshmallows after her father bought her a used Pinto. "Put these in the glove box," he told her the next day. "As long as you're prepared for the worst, it never happens." *Wish we had some,* he thought, as he parked and climbed out.

He followed VanVorhis into the motel office where a very large homely woman, with yellow plastic curlers in her rust-red hair, and what

319

looked to be a man's pair of black-framed glasses, grunted as they walked up. Vic felt her appraising stare, and suddenly formed the idea she thought he and VanVorhis were gay. That never crossed his mind when Vic was with Hobart, probably because of the difference in their ages. But VanVorhis was only in his forties, and Vic felt both uncomfortable and foolish for feeling that way. Why did he care what this desk clerk thought? Regardless, he purposely stood farther from VanVorhis than he would normally have.

"We'd like a room," VanVorhis said.

"Sixteen ninety-five," she growled, "plus tax," she added, still scanning them like an undercover officer.

"Okay," VanVorhis said, pulling his wallet from his slacks. "We'll take one on the top level." He turned to Vic and whispered from behind his hand, "Don't like to hear people through the ceiling."

"Wait a minute," Vic said, "you mean two rooms on the top level." He felt his face reddening to a blush, certain the clerk assumed the two of them were there for a little "afternoon delight." Her stony seen-it-all eyes said so.

"Gee, Vic. Why waste money on two rooms?" VanVorhis whined. "The syndicate—"

"I'll pay for my own, then," Vic cut in. "I don't share rooms with anyone I wouldn't share my toothbrush with, and she isn't here," he added, turning to smile at the clerk. Her disinterested gaze never wavered, and neither did Vic's discomfort. On top of that, he couldn't imagine why an anchorman, who likely made six figures, was such a tight-ass about money, a propensity that never surfaced during the round they'd played at Cherry Hill.

"Two rooms, then," VanVorhis said, shrugging. He handed the clerk his credit card. "Put them both on this," he added.

The phone in Vic's room rang soon after he had his clothes unpacked. It was VanVorhis, saying their tee time for the practice on Saturday wasn't until noon. "Noon? The fuckers," Vic muttered. "The course will be crowded as hell. It'll take forever to play eighteen."

"Yeah," VanVorhis conceded. "Anyway, there's a free continental breakfast in the lobby tomorrow. Meet me?"

"No thanks, TV. I don't eat breakfast. I'm going for a run, instead. But I'll be at the car with my clubs at eleven." Had it been Hobart, Vic would have been delighted to go with him to have some bacon and eggs, but VanVorhis was wearing thin, and Vic decided the more distance he could keep between himself and the tight-fisted anchorman, the more bearable this trip would be.

The next morning, VanVorhis insisted Vic drive. Again. The little Pinto stood out like a garbage truck as he negotiated the red brick drive to the parking lot at Waycross. The club, draped across the Smokey's foothills like a three-hundred acre blanket, exuded the look and feel of old money.

When Vic and VanVorhis arrived in the pro shop, they found someone hadn't done his job, and there was confusion over why two non-members were there to play the course. VanVorhis proffered the name of the syndicate's contact man and, after the twenty minutes needed to track him down, the pro gracelessly "allowed" them access. They specified, and paid for, two "A" caddies, but it was obvious, after a hole or two, that the youngsters on their bags were inexperienced second-stringers. That, or the A caddies at Waycross didn't know the course any better than they knew the surface of the moon.

The course was fun and challenging, but the round went badly. Vic worked hard at keeping thoughts of Angie and "Nate," in addition to the rest of his evaporating love life, at bay. Perhaps because of that, he couldn't seem to find his tempo. He didn't hit the ball cleanly, and sculled a number of shots. VanVorhis spouted fountains of advice, none of it useful. It was obvious the newsman was worried about the money he stood to lose. Eventually, Vic started hitting the ball well, but his putting never rose above miserable. On the thirteenth hole, he missed a straight two-foot putt. As far as he was concerned, that put the cap on a round. Partnered with TV, he wasn't enjoying it anyway. Not only that, golf didn't slam the door on his off-course life the way it usually did. Vic picked up his ball. "Let's get out of here."

"What about the last five holes? You don't even want to give them a look?" VanVorhis asked, in his clean, accent-free newscaster's voice.

"The way I'm playin', it isn't going to matter. He'll have me beat before we get this far." Vic enjoyed the obvious discomfort that statement applied to VanVorhis.

~ * ~

Jitters. Jimmie Wingo had them, and Vic couldn't help but worry about their communicability. When he first sat down across from Wingo in the chandeliered glow of the private dining room at Waycross, Wingo appeared to be a very ordinary guy of forty or so. Closer examination of his twitchy blue-gray eyes, however, revealed the distinct possibility his skull was a clubhouse for some downright weird goings-on. For one thing, Wingo never stopped moving. If he wasn't tapping his foot on the floor or drumming his fingers on the table, he rapped his fork against his plate or on the stem of his water glass. He was a case study in facial tics, and he pulled at his necktie like Rodney Dangerfield and tugged at his sleeves like Johnny Carson. He cracked his knuckles and clicked a ball point pen he periodically pulled from his breast pocket. He never wrote anything, merely pulled it out and clicked away in some insane Morse code. And he stuttered.

"S-s-so, h-how long ya been playing the syndicates, Allanvick-ry," Wingo asked, a laconic sneer creeping across his face. Since they'd first been introduced, he'd spoken Vic's name as though it was a single word.

"You can call me Vic. Not much more than a month."

"Just a m-month? P-practically a v-virgin," Wingo said, his teeth opening wide enough to allow him to rap his pen between his uppers and lowers like the clangor on an old-fashioned alarm clock. The sound reminded Vic of a threatening rattle snake.

Vic smiled. "Yep, saved my cherry for you."

"Aw, I b-bet you tell that to all the boys."

"Yes, sir."

The waitress was a thin, pretty girl, with long wavy hair. She seemed shy, and, as she placed Wingo's plate on the table, she appeared to be trying hard not to make any missteps.

"K-keep a c-close eye on me, darlin', cause if this steak ain't done to p-perfection, I'll be sendin' it b-back." The girl's eyes widened in the face of his threat, and Wingo used his fork to point at the shiny black nametag she wore above her left breast. "Annette? Annette, is it?" She nodded. "That's c-cute. What ya c-call your other one?" He laughed explosively. No one else at the table joined in, and his syndicate man lowered his head and stared at his food.

As the terrorized young waitress retreated, Wingo set about carving his New York strip into small, identical-size cubes. He stacked them into a wall that bisected his plate, segregating his asparagus from his twice baked potato.

"Architectural or landscape design?" Vic deadpanned. As repulsive as Wingo was, Vic couldn't resist baiting him.

Wingo used his fork to play his plate like a snare drum, and leveled a mirthful leer at Vic. "You're g-good, Allanvickery. But how good are you gonna be t-tomorrah? You g-gonna kick my ass?"

"Don't know. Going to try."

The fork started brushing the plate double-time, and Wingo's sneer broadened. "Then you're fucked," he said, in more of a hiss, than a whisper. "If you d-don't *know* you're gonna beat me, then you w-won't. I'll pound the f-fuckin' game up your virgin poop chute."

Vic pushed his face into a tight smile, and resisted the urge to come back with something snappy. Instead, he rested his arms on the linen brocade tablecloth and vowed to himself that he would not lose. No matter what.

~ * ~

His poor practice round earlier that afternoon at Waycross was all Vic could think about when he went to bed. Lying awake late into the night, he fired perfect drives into the dark skies of his imagination and hoped that would help. He viewed and reviewed the swing thoughts Bascolm had given him. Bascolm. Thinking of him forced him to contemplate that which he always tried to avoid—what Bass would think about him playing high stakes golf. That, Vic's dislike for VanVorhis, the trio of women revolving in differing orbits around his life and the poor practice round converged to leave him sleepless.

Suddenly, he decided the only way he would get any sleep at all was if he rifled a good shot. It was a little after two in the morning, but Vic knew he needed to stripe one and put his restless mind at ease. He was certain one well-struck drive would close the book on the bad practice round, and smooth away the rest of his mental morass. He rolled out of bed and put on some sweats and his running shoes.

The motel was like an outpost in a wasteland of parking lots and roads. With nothing but concrete and blacktop around, he had to come up with a way to tee a ball. Puzzled, he walked to the bathroom and flipped on the light. The answer was in a dispenser next to the sink. He grabbed a paper drinking cup, then picked up a ball and his driver.

He walked toward the highway in the cool, damp, early-morning air, bathed in the glow of the street lamps which were the product of some brand of new technology or another. Sodium vapor, maybe? Quartz-iodine? He didn't know, but whatever the elemental cocktail was, it gave off an eerie Dreamsicle-orange light. There was little traffic on the four-lane fronting the motel at that hour of the morning. A car sped by as he walked down the driveway ramp, but when he reached the road, there was nothing approaching in either direction.

The highway sloped into a valley, where it became a bridge that spanned a yawning hollow. Vic "teed" his ball on the upside-down paper cup, executed a few practice swings to loosen up, and looked toward the bridge to pick his target. The total width of the highway's four lanes appeared to be no more than forty or fifty yards, narrower than even the most unforgiving of fairways. After a last look at the concrete median before beginning his swing, he followed through. The paper cup popped like a champagne cork, which startled him, but it didn't affect his swing. The ball climbed like a tracer round as it shot out over the right side traffic lanes, disappearing above the streetlight's aura. Vic held his breath. Seconds later, the ball reappeared, dropped onto the median, and bounced out of sight. A perfect draw. He raised his club toward the dark heavens and watched the ball bounce along. "Wingo, you son-of-a-bitch, your scrawny ass is mine."

Vic started for his room, the shaft of his driver tight against his straight right arm, the head tapping his shoulder blade as he walked. A short distance from the outside staircase leading to his second floor room, Vic noticed some movement and a reflection in the shadows near some vending machines. At first, it looked like two men were buying a snack, but a second look told him something else was going on. He stopped, and realized one of the men was looking back at him.

"Hey, Hoss," the guy called over to Vic in a raspy whisper. "Spare a quarter?"

Both of them turned and began to walk toward Vic. Everything in him said to sprint for the stairs, but it was like he was in one of those nightmares where his feet wouldn't move. He discovered he *could* shake his head, however.

"Nope. Sorry. Out for a walk. Didn't bring any money." He wondered if he sounded as conversational as he intended.

"How 'bout in your room, then," the other one said. They stopped next to the rear of a parked station wagon, about twenty feet away. They were young and rough-looking, wearing jeans, hooded sweatshirts, and different versions of the same street-punk sneer. In the glow of those orange lights, Vic could see their eyes gliding over him appraisingly.

"Sorry. Don't have a room here. Only cutting through," Vic countered.

"Bad idea," the same punk replied ominously. His hand moved and Vic saw what earlier reflected the light: a big, nasty-looking hunting knife. The other tough carried a small crowbar and a cloth bag, which appeared to be full of the change they'd busted from coin boxes.

Vic's heart slammed around in his ribcage like a punching bag. He decided if either of them had a gun, he was screwed anyway. If all they had was the knife and the small breaker-bar, he stood half a chance if he handled the situation correctly. "Look. I don't know what you gentlemen are up to tonight, and, frankly, I don't give a flyin' fuck," Vic began, astounded at how steady his voice was. "I have no money. Not even wearing a watch," he added, raising his bare forearm. "Now leave me the fuck alone, go back to whatever you were doing and we'll all forget we met here."

The one with the knife went vacant of expression, as though processing input and appearing menacing at the same time were beyond his capabilities. When the sneer returned, Vic knew it was time to reinforce his ultimatum. Gripping his driver tightly, he swung with all his might. The club made a low whooping sound as the head flashed past their faces. From their expressions, it was obvious neither of them noticed the club until that moment.

"That pig sticker is scary, brother, but this motherfucker is over forty inches long, and before you can touch me, I'll bash your skull open." He ripped one more cut with the driver. "Ball's in your court."

If the ball was ever really in the young thugs' court, it didn't stay there long. Had they immediately turned to walk away, as Vic hoped, the incident would have been over. They didn't. Moneybagman stepped away from his partner. Knifeman moved no closer, but sidestepped so the nearby car was no longer an obstruction. Vic's pulse pounded in his ears, while he tried to keep an eye on both men at the same time. He realized he couldn't afford to be in the position of reacting against two men, and had to take the offensive. The voice in his head began to scream, "*NOW.*"

Vic lunged at Knifeman, swinging the driver with all his might. The punk lurched under the club's swath, and Vic's brain went into hyper-drive. Everything shifted into what seemed like slow-motion. He felt a concussion, a dull vibration that registered as a rattle in his hands from the club's grip. The club hit something, but what? Engaged in a weird little do-si-do with Knifeman as each whirled for a second charge, Vic didn't have time to risk a glance. But he could tell the club wasn't broken when he felt the weight of its head building inertia as he swung at his attacker on a new, lower path. Vic dodged the blade as the club caught Knifeman on the side of his head. The blow sent the young tough sprawling, and his knife dropped to the blacktop. When Vic spun around, Moneybagman lay in a heap, spitting out teeth that looked like bloody Chicklets. Now he knew what he struck when his first swing missed Knifeman. Coins were scattered all over the pavement, glistening in the orange glow of the street lights. Vic kicked the knife under a parked car, and gathered himself. Although both thugs were still down, Knifeman began to stir. Vic felt a surge of rage ramp through him like high voltage. If luck had spun differently, these two would have killed him. Now he could finish them off. The urge to smash their skulls was overpowering, and his eyes burned holes in the back of Knifeman's head where he planned to hammer him. Still disbelieving what he was about to do, and feeling almost as though someone else had control of his body, Vic lifted the club skyward.

"What the hell's goin' on out there?" a silhouette in the doorway of the motel office shouted.

The sound of another voice reestablished Vic's sense of reality and blunted his desire for vengeance; or it may have been that there was someone watching him. He lowered the club. "Couple of guys fighting. Call the cops," Vic yelled back.

"Already did. Stay right there," the silhouette instructed, before disappearing inside.

"Yeah, right," Vic muttered. He bolted up the stairs to his room. His pulse coursed audibly through the arteries in his neck when he slammed the door. He looked at the frazzled man in the mirror across the room. Something was wrong with the reflected image. In seconds, Vic finally recognized what it was.

"Aw, shit," he said aloud. The shaft of his driver sported a noticeable bend an inch above the hosel, where it disappeared into the head. The licks he'd put on the young toughs saved his life, but they were the last swings he'd make with that club until he had it re-shafted. He turned off the lamp, tossed the club on the floor and headed for the bathroom.

Vic sipped Southern Comfort in the hot shower's spray and replayed the events in the parking lot. The image of the knife kept coming back, the pumpkin-colored light reflecting off its blade—so bright, so sharp, so close. That, and the scary question which would not stop repeating in his head: what would he have done if the motel manager hadn't intervened? Would he have actually killed those guys? He was poised to. His club was in the air, and he was in a rage. Would he have come to his senses? A chilling thought surfaced. Maybe he could be a killer. He sipped his drink. It was watery, diluted from the shower spray. He poured it down the drain and wondered what had diluted him. He didn't know if he would have brought the club down on Knife-man's head or not, and there was no way he ever would, but he decided to believe he would have walked away.

Vic stepped out of the shower, toweled off and turned out the light in the bathroom before opening the door to the room. The man from the motel office may have told the police someone else was involved. If there was no light in his room, there was no chance he'd be implicated. Those thugs could have been the mayor's sons, for all he knew. Whose story would the cops believe? Time spent explaining, time answering questions. Time. Vic looked at his watch. A few minutes after three o'clock. His wake-up call was coming at 7:00.

Red lights flashed across the ceiling of his room. Vic peeked out through the gap in the curtains and saw two police cars, one sheriff's cruiser and an ambulance. *Probably a year's worth of excitement in Maryville,* Vic figured.

He slipped under the covers and watched the flashes from the police cars' overheads shoot across the ceiling. He snuggled down and enjoyed a feeling of insulation from the police, from their investigation, and from the two hoodlums who started the episode. Nobody but the thugs even knew he was involved, and they had no idea who Vic was. He told them he was only cutting through and didn't have a room there, so even if they convinced the police of his existence, there was no way they could locate him.

Still, Vic was as isolated from the rest of the world as he was from the action outside his motel window. He survived the most horrifying experience of his life, and there was no one he could tell about it. He was without a woman in his life. None of his friends even knew he was playing the syndicates because the dissolution wasn't final and he couldn't risk word of his winnings getting around. He disliked Trent, and was down to speaking with him as little as possible. And even if Hobart was there, Vic doubted he'd tell him. Hobart was almost a father-figure, and there are things you don't tell your father. And definitely not to your mother. Alone. He was alone with a story he died to share, but there wasn't a soul on the planet he could talk about it with.

He watched the lights until they began to blur and he became drowsy. He drifted off, and a dream formed in which he was in a dim alleyway. There was a figure in the shadows, a dark silhouette. When a figure stepped into a shaft of dirty orange light, it turned out to be Jimmy Wingo clutching a huge knife, his eyes twitching above a crazed smile.

~ * ~

Vic insisted VanVorhis drive to Waycross the next morning. "Goddamn," VanVorhis said, as he edged out onto the highway. "I can't believe you slept through the whole thing. It was amazing." It turned out he was on the scene as soon as the police arrived at the motel the night before, like a young reporter readying himself to pitch a story to the desk anchor.

Vic let his head loll against the seatback. "So what happened?"

"There are still a lot of unanswered questions. The two perpetrators, seventeen and twenty-year old brothers who escaped from an Arkansas prison two weeks ago, killed the older boy's girlfriend and some guy she was with."

Vic closed his eyes. This was like listening to the six o'clock news.

"Then they killed another man in Smackover, Arkansas, and stole his Ford pick-up. It was found in the parking lot of the K-Mart adjacent to our motel. After that, things get foggy. The police theorize that they were out of money and breaking into vending machines. Apparently, some kind of altercation broke out between them; a squabble over the money, maybe. According to the night clerk, Mitchell Barber, he went out to break up the dispute and they attacked him. He used a baseball bat to subdue them."

Vic's eyes butterflied. "That's what he said? He hit them with a baseball bat?"

"Yes. Why?"

"I don't know. Seems weird, that he just happened to have a ball bat lying around." He shrugged, closed his eyes again, and relaxed against the headrest to rejoin the "*News at Six.*"

"Anyway, that's about it. Oh! Except that it turns out young Mr. Barber is in line for a pretty sizeable reward."

"Yeah?"

"Apparently, Arkansas is offering twenty-five hundred apiece for the two brothers' capture."

Vic rocked his head toward the window and looked at the dim reflection of his face on the glass. "Ain't that the shits? Some guys have all the luck."

~ * ~

Luck may have saved Vic's bacon earlier that morning, and he couldn't help but wonder if he had any left for his match with Wingo.

330

"You ready for a g-good old-fashioned ass-k-k-kickin', Allanvick-ry?" Wingo asked as Vic reached to shake Wingo's extended hand on the first tee.

"I sure am. You shoulda worn some darker pants that wouldn't show my shoeprints."

Wingo laughed insanely, then all signs of mirth vanished like smoke. "You're a c-card, but the scorecard's g-gonna wipe that s-smile off your face, we get done here. H-hit the fuckin' ball," he added in a sinister growl.

Vic fed VanVorhis an unlikely story about how his bag toppled against a table to account for his bent driver. The newsman bought the story and insisted Vic use his graphite-shafted metal driver. Blackstock was right when he sang the praises of new technology. It proved to be a very forgiving club, allowing Vic to stripe his opening tee shot, and most of the rest, as well. He had become quite accomplished at putting thoughts of the rest of his increasingly messy life on hold when he made a shot. It was the times in between, walking to his next shot or standing on the green, waiting to putt, when intruding thoughts of Angie and Nathaniel, Roxanne and Tom, and Treese and 'Vetteman, not to mention his near-murderer status, wormed their way in. How much effect the weight of his personal life had on his game wasn't clear, but he did enjoy a number of long periods when his only thoughts were on the game, and how to turn it around. Regardless, his play around the greens started out weak and atrophied as the round wore on. Too many poor escapes from too many bunkers, and chip shots that either didn't clear the rough, or came out hot, added poison to his game. Additionally, three of his putts lipped out on the front nine, by which time Wingo was up two holes, and strutting like Jimmy Swaggart in mid-sermon.

"Come on, pal, you can pull this out. We got some big money riding on this match." That was VanVorhis's best effort at inspiration in the snack bar between nines. Vic couldn't bring himself to tell one of the syndicate owners to fuck off, but he came close.

Wingo pranced around the tenth tee like he'd been appointed master of ceremonies. "There's the m-man!" he shouted as Vic approached. "The aspiring syndicate p-player hailing from Toledo, Allanvick-ry," Wingo announced, holding his club as though the head was a microphone. He lowered his arm, letting the shaft slide through his hand until the ersatz mic hit the turf with a thud. "You ready to meet your m-maker now, young man?" Wingo asked, his eyes twitching mirthfully.

Vic opened up with hearty laughter.

"What's so f-funny?" Wingo asked.

"The idea of a fucker like *you* introducing me to God."

The confounding reality was it looked more and more like Wingo would introduce him to another new acquaintance. Not to God, but to defeat. After a shanked pitch shot, Vic lost number ten to go three down. Wingo's glee was apparent, but Vic did manage to play him even on the next four holes. It wasn't that Wingo had a great game, Vic couldn't get the ball in the hole as he normally did. It would be painful and humiliating to lose to an inferior player, especially one who was such an insolent jerk, but Vic began to prepare himself for that very eventuality. Helen Keller could have read the writing on the wall by the time they walked onto the fifteenth tee.

"This is it, b-big boy," Wingo said, the irises of his eyes ricocheting wildly back and forth. "C-crunch time. I win this hole and the m-match is mine." He punctuated his statement with a good, solid drive that left him in the middle of the fairway.

Vic placed his ball on a peg, ripped a couple practice swings to make certain his swing was tracking, and began his backswing. A guttural croak exploded from behind him as he began his follow-through. Vic's miss-hit ball jumped crazily off the tee, and he whirled toward Wingo, surprised and angry. But Wingo staggered like a spastic marionette, obviously embarked on some type of seizure. Dropping his driver, Vic stepped tentatively, then froze. Wingo's feet desperately tried to keep up with his torso, but his knees locked, allowing his body to tumble forward. IIe cracked his head good on the tee-side ball washer as he dropped. His syndicate man and his caddie were all over him in seconds as he continued to twitch and jerk in the grass. Vic's mind flashed back to Mrs. Mancy's restaurant, and to the convulsions he experienced when he came back from his coma. The major difference was, blood oozed from the scythe-shaped gash the washer left in Wingo's scalp.

Half an hour later, Wingo was stabilized and being loaded into an ambulance. Vic, drained emotionally and physically, thought about the ambulance that picked him up on the fourth green at Heather Hills. "Do you think he'll be all right?" he asked one of the several Waycross members who'd responded when the caddie ran frantically into the pro shop.

"Yeah, no doubt," the man said. "Jimmy's had at least one other epileptic seizure I know of." He clapped Vic on the shoulder. "Don't feel bad. You had nothing to do with it. They'll get that cut on his head stitched up and he'll be back out playing next week," the man said, his tone quietly assuring.

VanVorhis elbowed him in the side. "We won. We won, goddamn it," he hissed, in a coarse whisper.

"Huh?" Vic grunted.

"Wingo … he can't finish the match. We win by default. Says so right in the contract. 'If either player cannot, or does not, play the match to completion, for any reason, his opponent will be named the winner.'" He gave Vic another poke in the side. "We cleaned them out for seventy-five hundred big ones."

Vic didn't share in VanVorhis's delight. There was little doubt in Vic's mind that Wingo would have won. For Vic's syndicate to demand he be declared the winner because Wingo had a seizure during the match might fit the letter of the contract, but it wasn't fair. Not only that, VanVorhis was practically dancing a jig over another man's mishap! What an asshole, Vic thought.

On the flight to Toledo, VanVorhis was up front with Foss, while Vic lounged in the third row of seats, Hobart's usual haunt. When he wasn't sleeping, he pretended to be. After they crossed the Ohio River, VanVorhis climbed back and kneeled on a seat in the second row, gripping the seat back like a kid looking out the back of a station wagon. "Can I talk to you for a minute?" he asked.

"It's a small plane."

"Look, Vic, I know you're upset, and I'm sorry things turned out the way they did. Honest. Even though it looked like Wingo might win, I wish the two of you could have finished out the match. But you couldn't. It didn't work out that way. There's nothing you or I could have done differently. That's the way it is." Vic looked out at the feathery clouds, denying the man any eye contact. "I know you don't like to see it this way, but this is a business. Yes, it's a game, a game of honor and tradition. You play it that way. But you're playing for big money, money that I, and Hobie, Bob, and Merle all ponied up. You can't blame us for wanting to see a return on our investment."

Vic fired VanVorhis a baleful stare. "When Hobie first asked me to play, he said the main object was to have some fun, and if I made money for the syndicate, that was icing on the cake." VanVorhis started to say something, but Vic pointed his finger like a handgun and cut him off. "That's what he said, goddamn it! Hobie and I *had* that conversation. Now, all of a sudden, it's this cutthroat big business bullshit. Listen, that doesn't play with me. Maybe you ought to start lookin' for another player. I'd wager Blackstock's available."

"Oh, now, Vic!" VanVorhis looked like a man who'd been told he has cancer. "Please. You're blowing what I said out of all proportion."

Vic held up his arm to silence him. "No, I'm trying to put what was said to me back into the proportion I was led to believe existed. Look, we're gonna land soon. Tell Hobie to call me," he said, figuring that would really push the man's buttons. The expression on the newsman's face said it did.

"Look, there's no reason to involve the others. We can settle this right now. The two—"

"Have Hobie call," Vic ordered, breaking in. He sat up straight and buckled his seat belt.

"We're gonna be landing."

Vic watched VanVorhis climb back up front with Foss. It felt good to flex a little muscle, especially if it put the squeeze on such a jerk. Soon, Foss lined up on the runway at Toledo Express and began to descend. Vic chuckled to himself. Trent VanVorhis was up front with Foss, but Vic believed *he* was the one in control.

~ * ~

When the phone rang Monday evening, Vic expected it to be Hobart.

"Can you talk?"

It was Roxanne. A wave of excitement and surprise hit Vic so hard, he sat down.

"Sure." Inexplicably, he found himself whispering. "How are you?"

"Rotten. I miss you, buddy. I've been so lonely. I hate life without you."

In the ensuing minutes, Vic confirmed that dates with Treese were on hold, and that he, too, was miserable without Roxanne. He also filled her in regarding the previous weekend's match with Wingo. But he decided against telling her about the confrontation with the two thugs, or about the call from Angie, over the phone. "I have more I want to tell you, but it's too complicated to go into now," Vic said. "I'll wait 'til the next time we're together."

"Tomorrow," Roxanne said. "As soon as you get home from school."

Hobart called shortly after Vic hung up with Roxanne. The conversation consisted of an hour of complaints, of contrition, and of reconciliation. "I'm really sorry I wasn't there with you, boy," Hobart finally said.

"I'm sorry, too. I know the travel is tough, especially if you're not feeling well. But no more trips with VanVorhis, Hobe. I can't stand the guy. Bob, Merle, or you. Keep VanVorhis away from me." As an afterthought, Vic added a "please" to soften the directive.

"I think we'll be able to work around him. Guess we'll have to. You're our player. We want you happy." Hobart paused again. "Speakin' of which, your court date is this week?"

"Yep. Thursday."

"How ya doin' with it?"

Vic's first reflex was to cover like a Mohamed Ali, but Hobart was like Vic's ring-man, so he lowered his defenses. "Don't exactly know, Hobe. Think I'm all right. Guess I'll find out Thursday." Vic exhaled. "Angie's not gonna be there. She, ah, she has a job offer out of state and left already." That was as close to the truth as he could make himself go, even with Hobart.

"She don't need to be there?" Hobart asked.

"No. Her attorney will handle everything." After a pause, Vic said, "Angie's gone."

Hobart didn't say anything right away. The silence bothered Vic, but he couldn't think of any way to fill it. He sat, wondering if Hobart sensed there was more Vic didn't tell him. Over the past weeks, the older man proved he knew Vic like the back of his age-spotted hand. "Ah-huh. So, I thought since all this is happenin', might be wise to take a week off from golf."

"No way, Hobe," Vic blurted. "Look, it's not easy, getting divorced, and all. But when I'm playing golf, it helps keep my mind off the things I don't want to think about. Not the perfect solution, but better than sitting around stewing in it. So if you can get a match, do it. Anything in the works?"

"Sort of. The syndicate I'm talkin' with says this weekend or next. Either is good."

"Book it, Hobe. This weekend."

"Okay. It'll be in Myrtle Beach, South Carolina. Club called Pine Lakes. Player's name is Bo McJunkins. He's good."

"So am I," Vic said. "Book the match. I'll see you out at the airport Friday. Usual time, unless I hear different."

~ * ~

When Vic arrived home from school the next day, Roxanne sat in her car, waiting. Of course, she no longer had her key to his place, so waiting was all she really could do. But beyond that, the vibes Vic felt were entirely different as he approached and she climbed out of her car. She gripped his hand in both of hers, almost as though she was shaking it. She didn't kiss him, but she smiled warmly and her eyes looked teary. "We have a lot to talk about," she said, pulling him along to the apartment building.

Vic chuckled. "You don't know the half of it."

"So catch me up," Roxanne said after she settled on the sofa next to Vic, with a cold beer in her hand. "I've been dying to hear the rest. Now, the guy from your syndicate turned out to be a total asshole, but the weirdo you played down there had a seizure, and you won your match, right? Lots of money?"

Vic nodded. "About two grand, probably a little more. But now, the bad part." Roxanne shifted so she could look directly into Vic's face, her eyebrow raised in expectation. "A couple guys tried to rip me off in the parking lot of the motel the night before the match," he began. "My swing was shit when I practiced Saturday, and I couldn't sleep that night, worrying about the match." He combed his fingers through his hair. "So I went outside with my driver to hit a shot, you know, to prove to myself I still had it. I rifled one, but on the way back to the room, these two punks, turned out to be brothers, stopped me. Wanted money, but I didn't have any."

Her eyes were wide. "Big guys?"

"Not really, but the one had a knife that looked like goddamned Excalibur, and the other had a small crow bar. I tried to talk 'em into leaving me alone, but when that didn't work, I nailed them both with my diver. I mean, it was me or them. They weren't gonna say, 'Oh, okay, sorry we bothered you.' No way. The guy with the knife tried to stick me with the son-of-a-bitch. Caught the other one in the face when I missed the guy with the knife on the first swing, but I busted Knife-man with the second one."

She rubbed his arm. "Jesus, buddy."

"But that's not all of it, Rox," He rolled his head back and trained his gaze on the ceiling. "I damned near killed them." He snapped his head down and looked at her eyes. Her eyelids no longer eclipsed any part of her irises. "No shit, I was about to crush their skulls. If the motel clerk hadn't come to the office door and yelled when he did, I might very well be a killer right now. Christ, in one sense, I guess I am one, 'cause that's exactly what I wanted to do. What I was going to do, I think." His breath escaped slowly in a long sigh. "I know something new about myself now, and I don't like what I learned. Those guys, they were killers. Knocked off a couple people in Arkansas. Of course, I didn't know that then, but they weren't the only murderers out in the parking lot that night."

Roxanne squeezed his hand. "But you don't know that for sure. You can't assume you'd have gone through with it." She touched his chin lightly. "I don't think you would have."

Vic shrugged, then went on. "Maybe not, but there's one more thing I have to tell you." His mouth drew into a frown. "Not about the match or anything."

"What?" she asked.

Vic pushed himself up off the sofa and walked over to look out the window. He barely whispered. "Angie's gone."

"She's what?" Roxanne asked. She jumped up off the sofa so quickly, it looked like a gymnastics move.

"She left for Colorado Monday."

"Colorado?" Roxanne parroted, her voice pirouetting into yet a higher range. "But you said she was going home to Chicago."

Vic turned to face her. "That's what I assumed, but you were right."

"Right about what?"

He blew a puff of air through his nose. "Remember when we went to The Old Man's grave? You asked if I thought she was having an affair."

"And?"

"Angie left for Colorado with her boss, Fairchild."

338

"I don't frickin' believe it." She rushed over and looked into his eyes. "Her goddamn boss?"

"She called Sunday night. Said Fairchild's joining up with his brother in a law firm he started outside Denver. I asked if she was going to be his secretary, and she became real evasive. All she'd say was they were friends for a long time, but nothing ever went on between them while she and I were married."

"Do you believe that?"

Vic pulled his hands from her grasp, walked back to the sofa, and sat slumped on the edge. "I don't know."

Roxanne turned to face him. "And it matters, doesn't it?"

"I guess that's what pisses me off, that it matters to me at all. I mean, *I'm* the one who left her. But I left her because she'd changed. She wasn't the Angie I fell in love with." Roxanne sat next to Vic, and he put his hand on Roxanne's shoulder and gave it a squeeze. "I mean, neither of us would be here right now if Angie and Tom were the people we met and fell in love with, right? Then I find out Angie was *friends* with her boss " He moved his hand from her shoulder to her back, and pulled her close. Roxanne pressed her cheek against his chest. He wondered how his heart sounded to her, if she listened to it. "The hell of it is, I'll never know one way or the other."

Roxanne tipped her head back and looked up at him. "Easy for me to say, but at this point, it doesn't really matter much, does it?"

"Guess not."

"But, one thing that does matter is what I found out. The last week has been hell, buddy. I was wrong. I can't expect you to sit here and do nothing when I'm not around." She reached to kiss him, catching his chin instead of his lips. "If you want to take somebody out, go to a movie or out to dinner, that's fine. I can handle it; I just don't want to know. Don't tell me. Okay?"

He gave her a look. "That's gonna be difficult, isn't it? I mean, if you call and—"

"Tell me you're tired or something," she cut in. "I'll never question it." Then she looked into his eyes, and stoked his cheek. "But no sex, right?

I mean, especially with all that stuff that's going around now. You and I, we're going to stay exclusive, okay?"

Vic cocked his head. He was involved with and perhaps in love with a woman who lived with her husband, wouldn't or couldn't commit to leaving him, but didn't want Vic having sex with any other women. Given the new dangers lurking on the sexual frontier, he understood her logic, but the idea he shared her made the heat of jealousy flare. He usually dowsed such thoughts, or smothered them as best he could, but not this time. "You said 'we.' So, you *do* mean both of us are exclusive?"

She didn't miss a beat, and her voice was even and controlled. "I told you before. Tom and I live in the same house, that's all. He crashes on the couch about half way through his seventh or eighth beer if he's even home, and if he wakes up and comes to bed, it's only to sleep." She wrapped her arms around Vic's chest and squeezed as though the floor had fallen from beneath the sofa. "You're the only man who touches me."

Vic brushed his lips across her forehead. Not a kiss, but in his mind, some higher form of affection. "Then that's the way it is. Going out for a show or dinner with someone will break the monotony of sitting here in the apartment, but no other woman will touch me, either." He felt comfortable making that statement. And he swore to himself he would tell Roxanne if Treese or any other woman changed the way he felt. The fact he'd cheated on Angie still gave him mental nausea. He would not cheat on Roxanne.

They sat back down, and spent another hour hashing and rehashing their experiences during the preceding week. Finally, Roxanne looked at her watch. "I really need to get going," she said, getting up and leading Vic into the kitchen. She put her empty on the counter by the sink, then wrapped her arms around him. "I like that we didn't get it on today," she said. "I mean, I wanted to, but I'm glad we only spent the time talking. You know?"

Vic winked. "I can't say I wouldn't have loved to ravish you. Thought about it all day, to be honest. But I agree. Talking was more important, this time."

Roxanne picked up her coat and gave him a seductive wink. "And there'll always be the next time," she said. "Only thing is, I'm not sure it will be before Thursday." Vic shrugged. "You've got a big day, your closing on the house and the dissolution. I hope it all goes okay."

Actually, it's just the dissolution, now. The title company had me stop over and sign off early, since Angie did before she left town. So that part's over.

Roxanne walked over, wrapped her arms around him, and talked over his shoulder. "You going to be all right? I can't even imagine what it will be like."

"Stop in Thursday and I'll tell you," he said, nearly whispering.

She stepped back and kissed him. "I will. Count on it. And I'll be thinking about you all day."

"The hearing's at one o'clock. Downtown at the courthouse." He swiped his lower lip with his tongue. "I should be home by two, two-thirty at the latest."

Vic watched her walk to her car. At that moment, he really thought he'd pinned it down. He believed he loved her. But, he reminded himself, he'd felt that way before, followed by times when he didn't know for sure. In his heart, he had to admit there were times he thought he hated her, too, for her willingness to leave him and her reluctance to leave Tom. As she drove away, he pulled another beer from the refrigerator and let everything turn in his mind. He sat in the glow of MTV, vacantly listening to the music and wondering why he was always so confused about something as elemental as his own feelings.

What was clear, the situation was a strange and very artificial one. He was involved with a married woman who lived with her husband. Any thought of having normal feelings in a scenario like that one was, at best, impossible. He had, he decided, little hope of knowing how he really felt about Roxanne until he could date her openly. Until they could be a normal couple, going out together to find out the truth of what they felt. He knew it would be some time before he would be able to begin to learn what was in his heart. But, he decided, spending time with her clothed was a start. That day was the first they'd ever been together without having sex since back in November. Vic thought for a long time and decided he agreed with Roxanne. Vic didn't know how he felt about her, for certain, but spending their time talking that day felt right.

~ * ~

Vic sat in the Lucas County court house, bathed in the half-hearted light that managed to clear the windows under the dome, some fifty feet above him. Listening to footfalls echo amongst the pillars and arches, he was surprised there weren't more people passing by. *Perhaps it was busiest in the morning,* he decided. Regardless, the place had that smell; the commingled scents of reams of old paper, floor wax, and polished wood. The doors closed the way they did at Alexis; they always seemed to slam. He glanced at his watch and simultaneously heard staccato footsteps he knew, in that unexplainably instinctive way, would be those of Starr Haigen. He looked toward the staircase, and a tall, very beautiful blonde bounced off the top step and turned in his direction.

"You must be Mr. Vickery," she said, thrusting her hand forward, even though she was still a good twenty feet away.

Her voice wasn't particularly loud, but each word seemed to explode from her lips. As easy as she was on the eye, he would tire of listening to her very quickly, he decided. She closed the gap between them in four or five long, rapid strides, then took his hand and gave it a vigorous shake. "Sorry. I expected to be here sooner. Thank you for coming early."

"Not a problem." He tried to gauge a grip pressure that would match hers, without being too firm. "Pleasure to meet you." He looked into her eyes. They had a ferocity that made him think back to the thugs he'd confronted in the motel parking lot, in Tennessee. The eyeliner she wore punctuated her light, nearly colorless irises. If pressed, Vic would have said they favored gray.

She pulled her lips into a tight smile that faded as quickly as it appeared, then released his hand like it was aflame. She put her briefcase on the bench where he had been sitting, opened it, and began flipping through a number of neatly arranged file folders. "You understand, Mr. Vickery," she asked, while she continued looking for whatever it was she wanted, "you are unrepresented in this proceeding?" She flicked her eyes at him, and he nodded. "I am Mrs. Vickery's attorney, as was Mr. Fairchild before me, so I cannot advise you in any way. I will, however," she said, as she appeared to find what she looked for, "try to answer any questions you may have." She stood, and Vic realized she was an inch, if not two, taller than he. She pulled a packet of papers from a file, and handed it to him. "This is your dissolution agreement. The top of the first page is all legal gibberish, but from here down," she said, indicating a paragraph with a long dark red fingernail, "is the actual settlement language. Make sure you check everything over to be certain it is as you and Mrs. Vickery prescribed.

"When we go before the hearing officer, he will ask you to swear and affirm that your financials are correctly recorded." Her eyes narrowed, in a look Vic read as threatening. "If you do, he will ask the same of me, since I act with power of attorney on Mrs. Vickery's behalf." She pulled on the sleeve of her suit jacket, and Vic noticed that the pinstripes matched exactly where the arms met the body. Pricey. "Then he will ask you if you agree, irrevocably, to the specifications of the agreement, in total. If you say yes, he will ask the same of me. Finally, he will ask if you wish for your marriage to Angeline Louisa Vickery be dissolved. If you answer in the affirmative, he will ask the same of me, in her regard to you." She closed her briefcase, and tucked it under her arm. "At that point, the proceeding will be concluded. The papers will take a week or so to come through. They will be sent to me, and I will forward your copies to you at your home address. Do you understand?" Her manner of speech, which reminded Vic of a machine gun, and her cold demeanor, left him unable to vocalize. "Take a few minutes to look it all over. I'll be back." She turned on the spike heal of her right foot, and strode off to disappear around a corner.

Vic collapsed onto the bench, and tried to read. He wound up merely skimming, paying close attention mainly to the figures. Fifty a month alimony. For two years. Fifty-fifty split of the proceeds from the house and its contents. That was all he needed to see. He laid the document on the bench next to him and sighed. "Fifty a month so she can live with fucking Nathan," he grumbled, aloud. *That should cover a couple nights out on the town,* he thought. At least he was off the hook for the "cat-amony", the money he'd agreed to pay Angie if Muldoon lived with her. He picked up the agreement to double check. Sure enough, the two hundred dollar a year payment was removed, but she'd left in the money he'd agreed to pay her due to the difference in their salaries. The alimony. Now she lived in Evergreen with a lawyer, and as long as she didn't marry him, the money would keep flowing for the next two years. *She and Nathan probably shared a good laugh over that,* Vic thought. The only thing that helped him assuage his anger was the fact that he hid his golf winnings from her. "Hell," he mumbled, "with what I win playing the syndicates, I probably pull down as much as Nathan, anyway."

Rapid clickity-clicks resounding against the stone walls announced Starr Haigen's return. "Have you found everything to be satisfactory?" she asked, when she was still twenty yards away, weaving between a few passers-by. Everything about her presence seemed to indicate there was a long list of things she would rather be doing, and places she would much rather be. Vic nodded. This time, it wasn't due to her overbearing demeanor, but because of his total lack of desire to converse with her. "Follow me, then." It sounded like an order.

Vic reluctantly stood and walked behind her, allowing a good ten feet of distance between them. The whole day was much easier, all of a sudden. As much as he wanted out of his marriage, he dreaded the actual proceeding, and wondered how emotionally difficult it would be. When he found out Angie wouldn't be at the hearing, he wasn't certain if that would make it easier, as he initially believed, or actually more difficult. How would it feel to be dissolving his marriage with a ghost? But, to her credit, Starr Haigen made it extremely simple for him. In less than a total of fifteen minutes, he learned to dislike her, her expensive clothes and her haughty bearing. He wasn't just ending his marriage to Angie, he was ridding himself of Starr Haigen as well. He literally couldn't wait, for *both* divorces.

The referee, on the other hand, seemed genuinely concerned and caring. Did Mr. Vickery understand he was paying fifty dollars a month for two years? Had he carefully read the entire agreement? Did he understand he couldn't come back later and ask that any of it be amended or changed? Vic answered yes to each of the man's queries, and thanked him as soon as he said the dissolution was finalized.

Vic left the courtroom as quickly as he could. When he heard Starr Haigen's footsteps behind him in the hallway, he purposely picked up his pace to maintain his distance from her. He knew she was far enough behind him he didn't feel the need to stop and hold the door for her, so he stepped into the chilly February afternoon gloom and headed for the parking lot. There, in the front row of cars, was a shiny red Porsche 911S, the most powerful road car Porsche made. The vanity plate read, "STARLAW." Then he noticed something that almost made him laugh out loud, but he managed to throttle his mirth in, and merely smile at the rapidly approaching attorney.

He tilted his chin toward the gorgeous machine. "How do you like it?"

She never broke stride or returned his smile. "Very much," she deadpanned. "It's very fast."

"Well," Vic said, pointing to where the rear magnesium wheel sat in a virtual puddle of high-performance tire, "better keep the speed down until you get that tire looked at." He turned and continued walking. "Hope you have AAA," he offered, over his shoulder, chuckling as he remembered the time he let the air out of Angie's tire. This time, however, he was blissfully blameless and thoroughly amused. The flat couldn't have happened to a more deserving human.

Vic glanced at his watch. Roxanne would be at the apartment soon. *With any luck she might be there now.* He breathed deeply as he neared his car. Maybe he saw a married woman, but at least *he* was no longer cheating. For the first time in months, he felt less like The Old Man.

Chapter Twelve

When Bo McJunkins and his entourage of syndicate men walked into the dining room at Pine Lakes Golf Club, the sight of Bo triggered a memory Vic hadn't recalled in years. As a boy, he watched Lloyd Bridges' *Sea Hunt* on TV and was intrigued by underwater adventure. In 1974, he and a friend decided to get their YMCA scuba certifications so they could dive the deep, abandoned stone quarries that surround Toledo.

That same year, Peter Benchley wrote a novel called *Jaws*. Vic read it and the story scared the hell out of him. The image that recurred in his subsequent daydreams and nightmares was a product of Benchley's description of a shark as an unreasoning and unemotional eating machine. No malice. No malevolence. If one was unlucky enough to cross the path of a hungry shark, it would eat you. Nothing personal. Vic and Angie went to see the subsequent movie the night it opened. That next morning, when Vic walked outside to run, chicken bones scavenged from the garbage by stray cats were scattered on the driveway. In the fuzzy illogic of the early morning, the voice in his head yelped, *"Shark!"* As Bo McJunkins walked up to the table, the voice in Vic's head yelped again.

McJunkins resembled a shark. His wide, steeply angled forehead and nose gave his profile a shark-like appearance, and his shaved head made it smooth and shiny. The crowning touch was a pair of swept-back black sunglasses that masked his eyes, giving them the unblinking, dead-eyed look of a foraging shark. He was over six feet of trim, athletic musculature, and he moved the way Vic imagined any great predator would.

Counter to his menacing appearance, McJunkins' voice was a good octave or two higher than Vic expected. When he stood to shake McJunkins' hand, Vic could hardly disguise his shock when the man spoke. "Hey," was his seemingly disinterested reply to Vic's greeting, but was delivered in a reedy voice more suited to an eighty-year-old woman than a twenty-something with a tree trunk for a neck.

According to Hobart, McJunkins was two years out of Florida State, where he'd been a full-ride varsity golfer and captain of the team his junior and senior years. Since graduating with a major in health and physical education, he'd spent much of his time as the recreation director on a cruise ship. He was also a hustler on the public and private links up and down both Florida coasts, as well as on Caribbean courses he could access from the cruise ships. He'd been playing syndicate golf for a year, and carved his way to notability by only losing a few of his early matches, but none since. The reality Vic was left to confront, that Saturday night when he and Hobart returned to the hotel after the pre-match dinner, was that Bo McJunkins would be his most formidable adversary yet. As usual, Vic didn't know the amount, but he was certain the stakes were the highest he'd ever played for. Hobart picked up on his trepidation as they shared a nightcap in the hotel bar. "McJunkins put the fear in ya?"

"Shit, yes," Vic said. "He has that demeanor, that attitude. He's good and he believes it."

"You've beat good players before. Ya'll figure him out."

"If I could get a look at his eyes," Vic mused. "See what the hell's goin' on in there. He's always wearing those fuckin' sunglasses."

"Do your best," Hobart said. "What you can. It's only money. But if ya pull this off, come warmer weather in Charleston, people'll be callin' us to make matches at Cherry Hill."

~ * ~

Even after a night of fitful sleep, and in spite of the mid-winter dormancy of the leaf-bearing trees and azalea bushes, Vic found Pine Lakes Golf Club to be break-your-heart beautiful. He drank in every aspect as Hobart guided the rental car up the red brick drive. The clubhouse was very old South, with brilliant white, fluted columns, and windows replete with black shutters and green awnings. The thought of how Angie would have enjoyed building a miniature of the gorgeous old place tried to boss its way into his mind, but he won the skirmish and routed it away.

"I smell bacon and eggs, Vic," Hobart said as they neared the pro shop. "Interest ya'll in some?" They had almost an hour to kill before their tee time.

"Nah, thanks anyway, Hobe. Stomach's a bit on the jumpy side." Vic tilted his head toward his clubs. "Think I'll take these inside and clean 'em up. You go on ahead."

They agreed to meet on the terrace adjoining the first tee, and Vic carried his clubs into the locker room. Like those at the other clubs he'd played, no expense was spared on the room's décor or the equipment. The walls were painted a warm burnt-orange, which contrasted nicely with the dark oak lockers, each of which had a brass plate for a member's name. The carpet was a collection of browns and tans, and was so sumptuous and soft, Vic couldn't wait to take his shoes and socks off. As much as they'd spent on furnishings, the reality was that locker rooms were alike; no matter the expense, they all bore an undercurrent odor of sweat, liniment, and bad aftershave. The attendant was there in a flash to greet Vic with a smile, and a tilt of his head that served to ask what Vic required.

"Ah, I'm not a member, but can I get a rag to clean off my clubs?" Vic asked. The man held up an open hand to indicate that he should stay where he was, and disappeared through a louvered door. In less than a minute, the attendant, a short, swarthy man, was back with two fluffy, dark brown towels, one dampened and the other dry. Vic palmed him a dollar.

"Thanks so much. And may I use one of these lockers, for my street shoes and gear? I'm a guest of," he had to pause a moment to recall the name, "Mr. Marroan." Vic realized the man must be deaf, because his attention appeared to be riveted on Vic's lips when he spoke. That explained why he never said a word as he guided Vic to the back of the locker room. He pointed at Vic, grinned, then pointed to the final row of lockers. "Thank you again," Vic said, intentionally mouthing the words carefully so the attendant could more easily decipher what he said. It appeared the little man suppressed a grin before he bowed slightly, and turned to leave. Vic felt foolish. *After all,* he thought, *the guy did fine before I figured out he was deaf.*

Vic picked a locker halfway down the last row. There was a key in the lock, so he gave it a twist and pulled the door open. It was nicely equipped with sturdy brass hangers, a cupboard on the upper left for small items, and a mirror on the cupboard door. Vic kicked off his loafers and socks, placed them in the bottom of the locker, and wiggled his toes against the soft pile of the carpet. He set about readying his equipment, pulling his new golf shoes, the ones he bought to replace the old running shoes he used to wear, from their compartment in his golf bag. As he sat down on the leather-upholstered bench and started wiping down his club heads, two men entered the room. Vic couldn't see them, but he guessed they were older. They both spoke in those louder-than-normal voices aging men use as their hearing worsens.

"So, how's the sauna today, Hiram?" one asked. "Nice and hot?"

"Shit, yes," the other man answered. "Good as some steam feels on a chilly morning like this, I couldn't last a half hour."

Vic could hear the sounds of dressing and undressing—the jingle of belt buckles or change and the rustle of material.

"Who all's in there?" the first man asked.

"Mink Marroan is all," Hiram said.

"Aw, Christ on a crutch," the first man said. "If he's in there with his schwanz hangin' out, I'm gonna shower and go home." The man began a theatrical moan. "I mean, I don't need to see that. He never covers up with a towel. Walks around with the damned thing practically slappin' his knees."

"Shit, he's proud of it, Jerry. You would, too, you had a piece like his." Hiram laughed hard. "But if you can wait five or ten minutes, he'll be getting out. He's got that syndicate match today."

"Yeah?" Jerry asked. "Is'zat this weekend? Who's McJunkins playin'?"

"Some sucker from Ohio," Hiram answered. "They gotta pluck birds from way up north, 'cause no one around here is dumb enough to play Bo for money. We followed the guy and his syndicate man on their practice round yesterday."

"How'd he look?" Jerry wanted to know. "I told Mink I wanted five grand's worth of action on Bo's next match."

"Five grand? You bet five grand *against* McJunkins?" Hiram practically squealed.

"Sure. Mink gave me killer odds. That five'll get me twenty, the boy from O-hi wins. Fuck, Bo hasn't lost any of his last ten matches. He's due. I always bet the underdog." Jerry lowered his voice. "So, how'd he look?"

There was a pause. Vic could picture Hiram shrugging, or recollecting. "Not bad. The kid's got some game, from what I could see. Normal height and weight, nothing close to Bo's build. Wears that sissy long hair shit. Not no pony tail or nothing, but long. Looks like any other pasty-faced damned northerner." There was another pause. "You better get that five large ready. I got a feelin' Bo'll rip him to shreds."

Vic glanced at his watch. He'd gotten so involved in his eavesdropping, he'd stopped cleaning his clubs before he was finished. Regardless, it was time to meet Hobart on the terrace. He quickly tied up his golf shoes, keyed the locker closed, and picked up his clubs.

Vic replayed snatches of the discussion he'd overheard, and wished he hadn't, while he walked to the door. Doubts about his chances with McJunkins formed in his mind like specters; wispy but persistent. He attempted to ignore them, instead training his attention down each row of lockers he passed, looking for the two men, Hiram and Jerry. When Vic rounded the front row of lockers, there they were. Two squat old men in various stages of undress stood looking back at him. The one who was dressing after his sauna and shower had to be Hiram. His scrawny white legs looked like they could barely support his bulbous upper body, which was pinched into a tight-fitting golf shirt. Hiram was about to step into his pants, and his shiny bald head shone through some pitifully thin strands of a carefully arranged comb-over as he bent to get the waist of the trousers low enough to risk stepping into them. Jerry held a towel around his ample waist, his almost-womanly breasts corrupted by a Brillo-like mat of gray-white hair.

What the hell, Vic thought to himself. *I may lose today, but there's no glory in crashing with your foot on the brake.* He ramped up his best teeth-revealing smile. "Hey, Jerry," Vic said to the startled old man. "Your lucky day. I'm going to make you twenty grand richer." The two men gaped at each other before Jerry turned back to Vic as though he was about to say something, but his lips merely quavered, and nothing came out. "Oh, and Hiram. Nice hair. *Very* damned manly."

~ * ~

According to the scorecard, Pine Lakes was established in 1927, the same year Vic's mother was born. That arbitrary coincidence, in spite of the conversation he'd overheard in the locker room, made him feel more at home and comfortable as he stood in the cool of a South Carolina late-morning and watched McJunkins, Marroan, and Bo's caddie walk up the path to where Vic and Hobart stood waiting. Vic fought a smug smile, looking at Marroan after what the two members in the locker room said about the size of his penis. Regardless, there wasn't a visible bulge in his expensive-looking slacks.

Marroan wasn't at the dinner the night before, which Vic considered peculiar. He seemed to be the head of McJunkins' syndicate, with his name as the one Vic and Hobart were told to give as a contact. A huge man, taller by a half-foot than McJunkins, he had the semi-flabby look of a guy who'd lifted weights when he was younger, but whose muscle had fallen into flaccid disuse. Vic saw men like that before. They walked like they were still chiseled muscle, the fact their former bulk went to blubber lost on them. Marroan smoked a Pall Mall red—no filter—and was in the middle of telling McJunkins a story as they approached.

"So I take the bitch home, see," Marroan said. "We go in, have some drinks, and she gives me a great blow job." He laughed. "I gave her a nice pearl necklace." The humor washed off his face like loose dirt. "Anyway, I come out, some son-of-a-bitch is in my Town Car, tryin' to steal my sound system." They stepped to the tee-side bench and Marroan looked over at Vic and Hobart. Marroan waved his arm dismissively. "I'm almost done here," he said, then turned back to his player. "So I yell, and the little fuck takes off runnin'. No way I can catch him." He paused to take a deep drag on his cigarette. "But the kid screwed up big-time."

"Yeah?" McJunkins asked.

To Vic, his interest seemed insincere.

"Big-time," Marroan repeated. "I look in my car and the dash is all tore up. The dealer says over a thousand bucks worth. But on the seat, there's the kid's wallet. Musta fell out of his pocket."

"Shit, that's great," McJunkins squeaked, with only a hint of enthusiasm as he pulled his driver out of his bag. "So you turned it in to the police?"

"Police?" Marroan barked. "Why the hell would I do that? The kid would claim someone stole it from him earlier that night." He shook his big head. "Naw, I got some friends are gonna pay the boy a visit. According to his driver's license, the punk turns twenty-one next month." He nudged McJunkins' arm and let loose of a sinister chuckle. "Ya never know, the shithead might find himself at a nice little surprise party."

Vic looked at Hobart and rolled his eyes while Marroan tossed his cigarette in a tee-side flowerbed. Then, the big man turned and walked over to shake their hands.

"Sorry I couldn't be at dinner last night. I'm Mink Marroan. Pleased to meet you both. Are you ready to play, Mr. Vickery?"

Marroan grasped Vic's hand loosely when they shook, which surprised him. He'd have guessed a man's man, the way Marroan liked to portray himself, would try to crunch some knuckles. "Vic, is good, sir. Yes, I'm ready to hit it."

"Good. And Bo won the toss last night?"

Vic nodded. "Yes, he has honors."

McJunkins walked up on the tee, never saying a word to anyone, and hit away. The young man piped his drive straight down the middle of the par five. He may have glanced at Vic after his shot, but his sunglasses made it impossible to tell for sure.

"Nice poke," Vic said, as he strode onto the tee. McJunkins said nothing. Vic had the sense he was self-conscious about his voice.

"Yeah," Marroan said, in his hoarse smoker's rumble. "Great fucking shot!" He turned to Vic. "Hope you can do as well. Don't be nervous, now."

Vic slapped a good one right down the pike, short of McJunkin's tee ball, but straight and safe. With that shot behind him, the fluttering bats in his stomach were reduced to butterflies that merely tickled his nerve endings, keeping him alert and in his game.

Vic stayed right with the youngster, playing him even for the first five holes. McJunkins, however, would have been up several strokes, had his putting been sharper. He missed two makeable short ones.

On number six, a par four, McJunkin's tee shot came to rest in the left rough. "Son of a bitch," he screeched, slamming the head of his driver on the turf.

The shot didn't look bad to Vic, but it was obviously short of McJunkins' expectations. The boy seemed tightly wound, and Vic was curious to see how that affected his game. After dropping his second shot twelve feet from the pin with his five iron, Vic and his caddie joined Hobart to watch the proceedings in the rough.

McJunkins met their arrival with a disinterested glance. "What's my yardage?"

His caddie checked several nearby landmarks and studied his yardage book. "One-thirty-four to the center, Bo. About one-forty to the cup."

McJunkins looked askance. "About?" he barked.

A Chihuahua bark, Vic thought.

"One-forty-one, Bo. Exactly."

Pacing like an artillery officer, McJunkins' attention kept returning to an overhanging branch on one of the majestic old trees bordering the fairway. To Vic, it didn't appear to be an obstacle, but McJunkins couldn't keep his eyes off it. As the man continued to prowl and ruminate, Vic's caddie, Jeff, an industrious and solemn boy, decided to rest his shoulder. Though he lowered Vic's bag carefully to the ground, the clubs rattled softly.

"Tell your fuckin' caddie to keep the noise down," McJunkins squawked.

Vic patted the gawky teen's shoulder. "I think you did it for me."

"Nine iron," McJunkins commanded. His caddie handed him the club and stood back.

"Nice and easy," Marroan advised. McJunkin's head spun in Marroan's direction, but the glasses that hid the young man's eyes blunted the meaning of the look. It didn't appear to be appreciative, however. After a couple practice swings, McJunkins nailed it—right into the overhanging limb he'd been focused on. The ball slammed to the ground only feet from McJunkins, who went ballistic. "Motherfucker!" he squealed, walking over to pick up his ball. "I'm out of the hole," he said over his shoulder, starting for the seventh tee, with Marroan and the caddie scurrying to keep up. "You win this one."

Vic looked at Hobie. "Hell, I'm still gonna putt."

When they reached the green, Vic rolled in the twelve-footer for a bird. He had the honors, and a lot of confidence, as they walked off number six. The kid proved to be a powder keg, and when he exploded, so did his game.

"Think I've got him, Hobe," Vic said.

"Looks like it, if ya can keep him mad."

"I have a trick or two up my sleeve," Vic said, in a lilting falsetto. Hobart laughed, and even Vic's caddie joined in.

"I got somethin' might help, sir," Jeff, Vic's caddie, volunteered.

"What's that?"

"Look, only use this if ya gotta, 'cause if McJunkins or Mink figures out I told ya, this'll be my last loop at Pine Lakes. But, Bo—his real first name is *Rain*bow."

Vic was unable to hide his surprise. "You're shittin' me."

"Nah. For real! Guess his old lady was some kinda 1960s hippie queen, gave him that name." Jeff's voice dropped in volume as they drew nearer the seventh tee. "He hates it. He used to date the sister of one a' the other caddies. When he dumped her, she told her brother and we all found out. Big joke around the caddie shack." Jeff dissolved into laughter with Vic and Hobart.

The next three holes were no laughing matter. McJunkins cooled off and was back into his game. On the par three seventh hole, he put his tee shot two feet from the pin. Vic missed his putt, and conceded his opponent's tap in. That made them even for the match. When McJunkins won the last two holes on the front, Vic was down two, and floundering.

"Them guys is somethin', huh?" Hobart asked as he sipped coffee in the snack bar between nines. Vic had a Coke. "And Marroan, talkin' about orderin' a hit on a kid for messin' up his car, and givin' a woman jewelry for sex." Hobart tilted his head when he noticed Vic smiling. "What?"

"Ah, nothing," Vic said.

"Naw, what's so funny?"

Vic shook his head, and his smile became a wince. "I don't know exactly how to explain this." Vic decided moving away from slang might ease what he was about to tell Hobart. "See, that pearl necklace had nothing to do with jewelry. You really want to know?" Vic hoped Hobart would just let it drop.

Hobart smiled like he was waiting for a joke. "Yeah."

"The woman was, uh, giving Marroan oral sex. When he was about to, uh, climax, he pulled out and ejaculated on her upper chest, I guess you'd say." He wasn't looking at Hobart as he taught the sex-ed. lesson, but he stole a peek when he finished.

"Don't think I'll ever look at a string of pearls the same way again. I guess I really am an old man."

Vic patted Hobart's shoulder. "And a good old man. We better get out there."

Hobart clicked his tongue. "Got a plan?"

"Don't know, exactly, but I better come up with somethin' soon." He put his empty cup down and gave Hobie a look. "I'll figure out some way to mess with his mind. My only option, because I'll never outplay this guy. He's too damn good." Vic pushed his empty glass across the counter top. "Lots ridin' on this match?"

"You really wanna know?"

Vic nodded.

"Twelve large; the least he'd play for."

Vic looked heavenward.

~ * ~

McJunkins won the tenth hole, rolling in a fifteen-footer for a bird. His momentum was building and the bats were back and eating the butterflies in Vic's stomach. Number eleven was another par three. The foursome they were following was still putting, so there was some time to kill. Vic decided to see if he could get under McJunkins' skin.

Vic walked over to where McJunkins sat next to Marroan on the tee-side bench. "You sleep with those shades on?"

"What's it to ya?"

"Didn't mean any offense. Just curious, I guess. Sun's not that bright. You even wore them last night at dinner. Thought they might be prescription, you know, and you forgot your others."

McJunkins bristled. "My eyes're perfect. Gonna keep 'em that way. My old lady, she got eye cancer and went blind." He tapped the sunglass frames with his finger. "Not gonna happen to me. Sun's bad for the eyes."

Eye cancer … 1960s hippie queen.

Vic felt like his mind shut down for a nanosecond, and when it spooled back up, he had to regain his balance and readjust his own eyes. Before the blur completely cleared, he noticed the soft-focus image of McJunkins' face, its shape and bone structure. When the image sharpened, Vic saw his reflection in the dark lenses of McJunkin's lenses, the way he remembered from a dozen years previous, in another pair. Those glasses, the wraparound sunglasses, cemented the bits and pieces together. On one level, Vic didn't believe it could be true. But in his gut, he was suddenly certain it was.

"What's your mother's name?" Vic asked.

"Huh?"

"Your mother, is her name Jillian?"

"What the fuck, man? How the hell'd you know that?"

"She went to BGSU? Graduated in '71?"

McJunkins sprung to his feet. "How the … who the hell *are* you, man?"

Vic knew he'd hit pay dirt, if he could work it right. "I'm an old friend of hers. Jillian Reefe lived across the hall from me in an apartment building on Frazee Avenue my senior year at B.G. We went out, spent a lot of time together the summer after I graduated." He paused, temporarily losing himself in the recollection. "God, what a neat lady! How is she?"

McJunkins' expression never wavered and the single word dropped like a sledge hammer. "Dead." It broke the sunny late-winter air like the concussion of a bomb.

Again, Vic's mind rocked as this news hit him almost as hard as Tom Bayers' Top Flite. He didn't go down, but he came close. "Dead? When?"

"Last fall. Got that new disease." His voice returned to its squeaky pitch. "Don't think they even have a name for it yet. The one they say all the queers are gettin'. But it's not just them. Fuck around enough, you'll get it, too. She did."

Vic reeled. Reefer ... dead. There was so much that didn't compute. Too much to contemplate in mere seconds. Reefer never mentioned a child. Her skin, smooth and unblemished as fine silk, showed no stretch marks. If Bo was in his early twenties, he'd have been ten or so. And how old was she? Vic never asked, but always assumed she was about his age. Could she have been that much older? His mind overloaded with questions, and he stared into Bo's glasses, his expression apparently telegraphing his confusion.

"Look, I never lived with her. She never wanted me. My old man, Sam McJunkins, he was no bargain, but at least he hung around. His mother, my Gram McJunkins, she's the one who raised me. The old lady, Jill is all I ever called her, she wanted very damned little to do with me *or* my life." He paused. "But yeah, she started college when I was eight or nine. Graduated in ... I guess it could have been 1971."

Vic turned and walked to the other side of the tee, blinking against the tears that threatened to overrun his lower eyelids. Reefer, dead. And meanwhile, Vic was locked in a money struggle with the son of the woman with whom he'd had a passionate affair. The affair was many years before, but Reefer was instrumental in awakening him from his coma only months ago, literally opening his eyes. He recalled the sensation of her cool fingertips on his eyelids. He wondered if he could ignore his feelings for a former lover and use what he knew to defeat her son for twelve thousand dollars. It would have comforted him to believe the answer was up for grabs, but the truth was the decision was never contested. "Forgive me, Reefer," he whispered. Then he whirled, taking several steps in Bo's direction. He went with a gamble that was, literally, for all the money. "And so you're Rainbow! Your mother told me all about you." He tried not to sound too gushy.

Bo winced, probably at the sound of his name. "She did?"

"Man, she was so proud of you, talked about you all the time, you and your sister."

"Sister?" Bo McJunkins jumped like he was zapped with a shot of high voltage. "SISTER?" His voice reached new heights.

"That's enough of this," Marroan said, shuffling between the two players in an attempt to intervene.

"Shut the fuck up!" Bo snarled at the big man then he snapped his head back in Vic's direction.

Vic spoke in a low soothing tone of voice. "I guess she never told you. Yeah, she and I had a little girl together. Jillian named her Storm. I always kidded her that the rainbow usually comes *after* the storm." Vic was rolling. He had no idea where all this rich fiction came from, but it seemed an endless stream of the perfect words were there for him to speak. The main question in his mind was whether the story he was crafting would have the desired effect.

"Where is she?" Bo asked.

"Storm? Stormy's dead, too," Vic said, releasing the tears he'd been holding back.

The tears were for Reefer, but now he used them to crush her son's psyche. *I am a real bastard,* he thought, as he swiped at the tears with his sleeve. "Damnedest thing. Started with a skinned knee," he went on, working from the memory of a childhood neighbor who'd experienced that fate. "She was roller skating out in front of the house and fell." He hesitated, wiping at his face again. "In less than a day, it went from a scrape, to an infection, to blood poisoning" He turned his hands up in resignation. "They did all they could."

"Storm ... she lived with my, with Jill?"

"No, she lived with me," Vic replied, rubbing his chin in deep thought, but he was composing, not recollecting. "I don't know how to explain to you, explain how your mother saw things. She loved you, boy. Loved you more than anything, except Storm, of course, after she came along. She never loved herself, I guess. I used to tell her, 'Jillian, you'd be the world's greatest mom. Those kids, their lives would be so much better if you were a part of them,' but she wouldn't believe it." Vic theatrically raised his arms to the heavens. "The most gentle, loving, kindest person I ever knew, but she had no self-esteem. She didn't believe she deserved to be your mom." Vic unzipped a pocket on his golf bag and pulled out a towel. "It killed her not to be a presence in your life, Bo, but she believed you were in good hands with your gram and your dad. I know you have your own feelings about her, and you certainly have your reasons. I only wish you could have gotten to know who she really was before she died."

Hobart cleared his throat. "They's a foursome playin' up on us, we best get a move on."

McJunkins pulled off his glasses for the first time. His irises were a shocking shade of green, made all the more so by the red veins that shot like tiny lightning bolts across the whites of his watery eyes. "You're hitting," Vic said to him, careful to make it sound like a command.

When McJunkins hooked his tee shot into a water hazard, Vic and Hobart shared a look. Hobart raised an eyebrow, but when Vic winked, another tear released and ran down his cheek.

~ * ~

There were few people on earth Vic felt as comfortable with as he did with Hobart. One reason was the man's radar. Hobart was as successful in personal relationships as he was in business because he kept himself keenly attuned to others. So, even though he didn't know the whole story, he well understood the impact news of Jillian Reefe's death had on Vic. Hobart never said a word when Vic won the par three, and the next three holes in a row, to deal Bo defeat on number fourteen. He reached over once and rubbed his big hand between Vic's shoulder blades, but that was the only contact they had until they were off the course. As soon as they returned to the clubhouse, Hobart said he'd get the car and Vic went into the locker room to change. Hiram and Jerry were long gone. Thinking of the big payday he provided for Hiram nearly made Vic smile, but not quite. When he came back outside, Jeff, his caddie, had finished wiping the grass stains and dirt off Vic's clubs.

"That was the most awesome loop I ever made," the caddie said, while Vic fished a bill out of his wallet. "And I ain't saying that to sweeten you up for a good tip, neither," he added.

Vic gave the boy a fifty dollar bill, an amount he was certain was more than the kid usually made in a week of humping bags at Pine Lakes. "If you hadn't told me Bo's real name, I couldn't have pulled it out. You're pretty awesome, yourself." He managed a thin smile. "Thank you."

The young man's eyes literally bulged when he saw the denomination of the bill in his hand. He stuffed it in his pocket, and looked at Vic. "Thanks, sir." Then he cocked his head. "So, you really knew Bo's mom?" His face skewed into the look Vic often saw on his students if he asked something like who Claude Monet was.

"Yeah, Jeff. That much was true. But I'd really consider it a personal favor if what you heard out on the course today didn't become, how did you phrase it … a big joke around the caddie-shack? I think Bo took enough gas out there today. I'd hate to have anything I said haunt him from here on out. Know what I mean?"

"Gotcha," Jeff said. "Oh, and if you play another match here, I'd really like it if you'd ask me to caddie, sir. Jeff *Davies*. I'm usually around."

"Count on it, Mr. Davies."

Hobart pulled up and triggered the remote trunk release, so Vic hoisted his clubs inside, slammed the lid, and ruffled the caddie's hair. "Thanks, again. Be good." Vic climbed into the car.

To his credit, and to Vic's great relief, Hobart never said a word on the way to the hotel, either. Vic rode with his eyes closed, trying to train all his attention on the whine of the automatic transmission as it shifted through its gears. He still wasn't prepared to confront everything he'd learned and done at Pine Lakes, and focusing on the quiet song the transmission sang seemed to do the trick. "I'll get a hold of Foss," Hobart said, when he pulled into the parking lot. "I told him, last night, I didn't think we'd be ready to fly out 'til about four or five." He glanced at his watch. "The match ended early, but I don't see no reason to make a change." He shut the engine off. "That'll give you some time alone. I'll ring ya up about 3:30."

Vic opened the door, but didn't make a move to get out. "When's checkout?"

"I took care of that. Rest easy."

"I know you have a hundred questions—"

"I got no questions you have to answer," Hobart interrupted, something he rarely did. "Tell me anything you want to, son, and don't tell me anything you don't." He reached for Vic's hand and gave it a squeeze. "In your own good time. Now get yourself on up to your room and relax a little. You got that comin'."

There wasn't much in the way of relaxation in Vic's room. He poured a Southern Comfort from the bottle he always carried in his suitcase. A shower sounded good, so after a sip of the liquor, he stripped off his clothes, letting each item drop, wherever he happened to be at that moment. Soothing as a shower might be, the sight of the soft, quilted spread on the bed was too seductive to resist.

He lay on the bed and stared at the ceiling. It was one of those "popcorn" ceilings, with bb-size granules of something-or-other clustered randomly on the off-white surface. They looked like the grains of sand in a bunker, and that's exactly how he felt, as though his soul was in a hazard.

"Think you used enough dynamite there, Butch?" That line, from the movie *Butch Cassidy and the Sundance Kid*, ran through his mind. Robert Redford asked that of Paul Newman after Newman's character blew open a safe in a railroad car. He mistakenly used such a huge charge, it destroyed the entire boxcar. That's exactly what Vic felt like he'd done on the eleventh hole at Pine Lakes. When Bo slapped Vic with the fact that his mother, Jillian Reefe, was dead, Vic was overwhelmed with hurt and anger.

He was hurt by the knowledge she was dead, and angry at the way Bo told him, almost spitting it in his face. In his gut, he was pretty certain just the fact he once knew Bo's mother would throw the kid off his game, but when the boy hit him with her death the way he did, Vic's temper erupted. Instead of merely going for Bo's jugular, Vic went for Bo's aorta, and he used all the surgical steel he could muster. In the movie, the result of Butch's miscalculation was a cloud of money fluttering down around the bandits. That afternoon, Vic could almost feel Bo's psyche raining all over the tenth tee box. The difference, in this case, was that what Vic did was careful calculation, not a mistake. And Vic didn't let up. He kept inventing: Bo's mother loved him; her personal insecurities kept her from being in his life; Bo had a deceased sister he'd never met. It was the equivalent of using a shotgun to kill a deerfly. Despicable. There was no other word for it. What he'd done was despicable. And the words he triggered in anger hit the bull's-eye.

Pin-wheeling around his guilt and shame was the fact that Reefer had apparently died about the same time Vic regained consciousness. She was the one who put her cool fingertips on his eyelids, and pulled them open. Last fall. Bo said she died sometime last fall. Vic came out of his coma on October sixth, and the dream he had about her disappearing into the trees was a few days after that. He remembered hearing a dog barking, and he'd wondered if it was her dog, Ziggy. To Vic, all this pointed to the presence of some kind of an afterlife. On all those Halloween visits, he stood at The Old Man's grave and talked to him, never sure he was out there, on the other end. Now, it seemed clear to him that, even though he may not have heard a word Vic said, The Old Man was somewhere. And so was Reefer. She and Vic crossed paths back in October when their arcs converged, on some other plane of existence.

Again, it came back to guilt. How had Vic repaid Reefer for her gentle kindnesses, both in Bowling Green, all those years ago, and on the way to her afterlife? He beat up on her son. And the beating was mental, which could well leave wounds that might never heal. He made up stories about her insecurities. Vic had no idea what her relationship with Bo was or wasn't, but if there was a word in the world that did *not* describe Jillian Reefe, it was insecure. He would never know the truth about Reefer and Bo, but the truth he couldn't deny was that earlier that day, on a sunlit tee box at Pine Lakes Golf Club, Vic lost complete control of himself. He became someone he never believed he could be, even in his wildest imaginings. A man like the one who almost hammered the skulls of two brothers in a motel parking lot in Tennessee.

Vic refocused on the rough ceiling, and it was the last image his eyes recorded before sleep overtook him. It was a dark, dreamless slumber, something he hadn't had much of, since his dreams were usually vivid and closely tied to his waking life. But his mind finally managed to shy from reality, and he slept like he was dead. Dreamless blackness. When he awakened, he looked at the clock. He'd only been gone for half an hour, but it seemed longer. He sat up, and took a sip of liquor. He put the glass down, cradled his head in his hands, his elbows resting on his knees. "I'm truly sorry, Reefer. That's all I can say. Saying that is all I can do."

The phone began to ring. He looked at his watch. It would be Hobart.

~ * ~

Roxanne was parked outside Vic's apartment when he pulled in after school the next day. They embraced in the gray mid-February chill, especially keen for Vic after the weekend in Myrtle Beach's relative late-winter warmth.

"You look great, buddy," she enthused, as they started for the door. "Enjoyed some sun, I see."

"Yeah, hard not to. But I'm whipped. Didn't touch down at the airport until almost nine." He unlocked the door. "Time I unpacked and settled down, it was late."

"Poor baby," she said. "And did we play some good golf and win lots of money?"

Vic answered silently when he lead her to the kitchen, slid a check from an envelope on the counter and handed it to her. Roxanne's eyes bulged like Jeff's, his caddie at Pine Lakes.

"Seven thousand, four hundred thirty-four dollars and seventy-two cents? You won that much last weekend?"

"No, that's the back pay Hobie's been holding until I was single. That's money from the first four matches," he explained. "But Sunday, I won about three grand, take-home. He'll be mailing it."

Roxanne slapped her forehead. "Three thousand, and seventy-four ... Jesus, buddy! That's over ten thousand dollars. In the last six weeks! Can you keep this up?"

Vic looked deep into her eyes. "That's what I ask myself all the time, Rox. I mean, when I'm playing good, it feels like I'll never hit another bad shot. But when I'm off my game, it feels like I'll never hit another good one." He wrapped his arms around her and rested his head on her shoulder. "Sometimes, the pressure is unbelievable." And some of the things I've done to win are unbelievable, too, he thought. He wondered if he could tell even Roxanne about the mental beat-down he'd administered to Bo.

"That's what I'm here for, to ease some of that pressure," she whispered.

Vic pulled back and looked into her eyes. "I have so much to tell you, some of it you might not want to hear, and some of it you flat out won't believe. How much time do we have?"

"He's got a union meeting tonight. Won't be home until nine or so. I left a note saying I'd be at my sister's. Five or six hours enough?"

~ * ~

Vic and Roxanne were lying in the static waves of the bed sheets, their bodies forming a lopsided "T" with his head resting on her stomach. After a round of feverish lovemaking, he spent over an hour reprising the events of the past weekend. The conclusion of the story was met with silence from his pretty pillow as she processed what he'd told her.

"I just thought of something," Roxanne finally said. "We need to talk about this disease Reefer died from. I mean, are you positive you don't have it?" His head trampolined gently on her stomach as she spoke.

"Ab-so-damned-lutely, and believe me, I've given it lots of thought. Look, the last time I was with her was back in the summer of 1970. From what I've read, they don't think the bug was even around, back then." He paused. "Besides, if she did have it back then, Angie and I would have come down with it by now. I've read a lot about it, and there's no way the incubation period is eleven or twelve years long." He touched her shoulder. "Hey, if I thought there was any way, we wouldn't be lying here naked, right now."

Roxanne chuckled. "If you did have it, buddy, today wouldn't have mattered."

He exhaled a puff of air through his nose. "Very true."

"Okay, but another thing. If this Bo guy was in his early twenties, then Reefer had to be in her late twenties when you knew her. Even if she had him when she was sixteen, she'd have been," she paused to do the math, "twenty-seven in 1970." She gave him a playful slap. "I thought I was your first older woman," she said, a mischievous smile bending the corners of her lips.

"I thought so, too. Swear to God, I honestly thought she was my age, or maybe younger when we were together." He shook his head, rolling it back and forth on her stomach. "I mean she had no stretch marks, nothing that made me think she ever had a baby."

"What about her nipples. Were they pink?"

He scrunched his face. "What?"

"Her nipples, areolas, actually. They usually darken when a woman gets pregnant. After they have the baby, they may lighten some, but they never go back to the way they were." She chuckled. "You wouldn't have known. You and Angie never had kids, and neither did I."

He thought about it. "I can't say I really remember. It's been years. But you're right, I wouldn't have known one way or the other. I never knew about that until now." He sat up and looked into her eyes. "But what do you make of the rest? About her dying when I was coming out of my coma?"

"Jesus, I don't know what to think. Did you find out, did Reefer die the day you dreamt you saw her on the golf course?"

"I couldn't get that pinned down. Last fall, was all he said. That would put it in the ballpark. By the time I finished working his head over, he couldn't have told me his birthday, much less when his mother died. Assuming he even knows."

"And that's how you beat him?"

"Only way I could have. When I was done spinning my yarn, his head was so full of shit, he forgot where he was and which end of the club to hold. He wasn't the hard-ass he pretended to be. He had this huge case built up against his mother, but it was just a seal that held down bunches of emotion he'd never dealt with. The story I made up ripped off the scab."

Roxanne stroked his face. "How did you come up with all that?"

"Oh, I've become pretty good at fabrication." He blew air through his nose in what was intended to pass for mirth. "Not anything I'm proud of." He managed a half-hearted chuckle. "At the rate I'm going, even you won't believe half of what I tell you."

"You couldn't lie to me, buddy. I know you too well."

"That's what Angie thought."

She slugged him playfully. "Hey, you really enjoy beating yourself up, don't you?"

"The Angie thing is history. But what I did to Reefer's kid, using what I knew about her to put a mind-fuck on him, makes me feel like pond scum. And I did it all only for the money."

"But that's the game, isn't it? He'd have done the same to you if he could. He even tried to when he hit you with the fact that Reefer was dead, right?"

Vic rolled onto his stomach and looked into Roxanne's eyes. "Correction. That's *this* game. Syndicate golf. Not pure golf, like I used to play with the guys, or like I played with Bass at Loon's Lair. Not like the pros play. This is golf's equivalent of street fighting. Bash 'em in the head, and win at any cost." He traced small circles on her wrist with his fingertips. "I haven't lost a match because I'm gifted at yanking my opponent's short hairs. Or because I can play in the cold. I beat Wingo on raw luck, his epileptic seizure. Bad luck for him and good luck for me." He brushed his lips against her palm. "Hell, playing straight-up golf in favorable weather conditions, I'm not sure I'd have moneyed in even one of the matches I've played."

"So? Why's that matter? You *did* win. You *can* beat them."

"But I hate it. I feel like a hooker," Vic said, using Bass's analogy. "Like I'm taking something pure, and twisting it to get rich."

Roxanne exploded into that fabulous laugh of hers, taking Vic by surprise.

"What?" he asked. She made him feel better already, as he'd hoped she would.

"My God, a hooker? You're comparing golf and sex?" She freed her hand and gave him a playful shove. "Come on! Golf's pretty neat, but compared to sex?"

For the first time since the match, Vic enjoyed some levity. "What are you talkin' about? There're lots of comparisons. You can do either one by yourself, but they're both more fun with a partner."

"*And* differences," she countered. "In sex, the more strokes, the better. You don't live with Tom Bayer for twenty-five years without hearing 'em all."

"But seriously," Vic said, "do you understand what I'm saying? And there's Bascolm. I'm telling you, the way he looked at me when he said he wouldn't play for money. I think about that a lot. Sometimes I feel like I have it all sorted out, and it's under control. I'm making money with golf, the same way I made money by selling my paintings. Nothing wrong with that, right? And Jack Nicklaus and a lot of other honorable men make money playing golf. Problem is, as good as those arguments are, I feel guilty about what I'm doing with the game of golf."

"So quit. The syndicate can't make you play."

"It sounds so simple when you say it. Problem is, I can't make myself give up the money. I'm weak, I guess, and I hate that in myself. But that check I showed you, that's a third of my year's salary out there on the counter, Rox. More to follow." He paused to think. "I want that house on the river I told you about. I have to keep playing until I have enough cash to buy a big old river house. Then I'll quit. I only wonder what Bass thinks about it. And Reefer, for screwing her kid over."

"That assumes they even know," Roxanne said, placing a cool fingertip on the end of his nose and giving it a gentle push. "And for that matter, how do you know everything from the coma even happened, that the golf with Bascolm and all the rest of it wasn't some kind of hallucination? Coincidence and dreams."

He lifted his head off Roxanne's stomach, crawled up, and cradled her head in his hands.

"Before last weekend, I didn't dwell on it much. To be honest, I didn't really care. The experience, what I believe I learned, was a part of me whether I concocted the whole experience or not." He rolled onto his side and looked at her. "Now, I decided I'm going to find out."

"How?"

"I think I've figured out a way."

~ * ~

A secretary asked Vic to hold, there was a click, and Hobart came on the line. "Yes, Vic. How ya doin,' son?"

"Doin' fine, Hobie. A little embarrassed."

"Embarrassed?"

"For callin' collect. I'm at school and—"

"Shit, boy! I keep tellin' you, we in business together! *Always* call collect. There some kinda problem?"

"No, no, not at all. Callin' to see if you've scared up a match for this weekend?"

Hobart chuckled. "You some kinda machine, boy? After last weekend, I though ya might be ready for some time off."

"To be honest, Hobe, that is what I hoped, unless you found something."

"Nah. Got some feelers out. No solid offers. The syndicate sheet will be coming out. People will be getting it today or tomorrow. Wish it was warmer here in Charleston. You being undefeated, and beating McJunkins, might get us some action on our home course. Why?"

"Actually, I did have something I wanted to do this weekend, if nothing else materializes."

"Let's plan on taking this week off. Do what you gotta." He paused. "You sure ya're okay? I know that McJunkins kid shook you up. Them things about your friend, Miss Jillian."

Hobart's quaint southernism mustered a smile from Vic. "I think my plan will shed some light on all that. Maybe clear up a thing or two."

"So go on ahead an' do what ya got a mind to. I'll get something set up for the following weekend."

Vic had twenty minutes left in his planning period, so he dialed another number. "Hawk Air. May I help you?"

"Treese? This is Allan Vickery."

"Vic! It's so good to hear from you." The tone of her voice made it sound as though she might wiggle right through the receiver. "How are you?"

"Fine ... you?"

"Great. I've been hoping you'd call."

"Oh?" He was surprised at her enthusiasm and tried not to sound like seeing *GQ*-man in his yellow 'Vette at Hawk Air made him skeptical. "Actually, this is more business than anything else. I need to get to Syracuse this weekend. Fly out Friday, come back late Saturday, maybe Sunday. But I'm hoping I can get things wound up in one day."

She giggled. "So, it's a safe bet this isn't for golf?"

"Very safe."

"I have to be honest, it's not going to be cheap. You have the rental on the plane, about four or five hours of air time, and expenses for the pilot." Dead air. Vic imagined her doing calculations. "I'd say you'd be looking at close to eight hundred dollars. And that's if you can get finished Saturday and return that night. Have you looked at commercial?"

"Some business woman you are, trying to steer clients away."

"An informed customer is a happy one." Her voice in its soft and alluring mode. "Commercial would save you a lot of money."

"It's nice of you to clue me in. I didn't check the airlines, but if I can get a Friday afternoon flight out, I don't know how long I'll need to be there, and I don't want to have to sit around in Syracuse, waiting for a pre-booked flight. The money isn't really an issue. Can I fly out around three-thirty Friday afternoon?"

"Sure! And I should tell my pilot one night, possibly two?"

"Two at most. I'm pretty sure I'll get my business taken care of on Saturday. Flying back that night is no problem?"

"Of course not, depending on the weather. The Great Lakes can get crazy this time of year, but there's nothing looming in the long range forecast."

"Terrific," Vic said. "I'll be out there around three Friday afternoon."

~ * ~

Roxanne sounded dubious. "I'm not sure I understand. You're going all the way to Syracuse, based on the dream you had when you were in a coma? I mean, I know you believe you experienced what you remember, but I can't believe you think you'll find any proof out there."

"I already have," Vic said, pinching the receiver between his shoulder and cheek so he could fish a beer out of the refrigerator. "I called the headquarters of the New York State Patrol yesterday. There *was* a trooper named Bascolm Traskett."

Her voice came through the receiver like a thunderclap. "What?"

"I'm not shitting you. The woman I talked to wasn't very forthcoming. I told her I was an old friend of his family who moved away and lost contact. I played it like I thought he was still on the force, like I didn't know anything different. I think she bought it, but she wouldn't answer any questions. Maybe they're not supposed to. It's been sixteen years. She might not have even been around when Bass was stationed there, for all I know. Or maybe she didn't want to spill what she knew to a stranger on the phone."

"I forgot. You *did* say he was from Syracuse. Jesus, that's unbelievable. Then it wasn't a dream. Bascolm really existed. I'll be honest, for a while there, I wondered if you were losing it."

"I might be," he said. "Or maybe I will lose it if all this turns out to be true. I mean, it could still be some huge, weird coincidence. But, it's not like we're talking about some guy named Bob Smith, for Christ's sake. A name like Bascolm Traskett is hard to come up with out of thin air." Vic paused. "Do you realize what it means if the Bascolm Traskett I knew at Loon's Lair is in a coma out in New York somewhere? It gives me chills to think about it."

"So, where do you go when you get there? You have an appointment with someone?"

"No, don't even particularly want them to know I'm coming. But the lady I talked to told me which post Bascolm was stationed at. And get this. The night commander at that post has been there since 1963. Bass had his accident in 1966."

"So he should know."

Vic slugged down the last of his beer and dropped the can in the trash. "You'd think. I plan to walk in there Friday night and find out."

"Friday? How will you get there?"

"Flying. Taking off after school. It's only a couple hours."

"No match this week?"

"Nope. Called Hobe from school today, told him not to make one. He's good with it. He wanted me to take a week off anyway. We're waiting for the new syndicate sheet."

"Is Foss flying you out there?"

"No, someone from Hawk Air. I don't really know any of their pilots."

"You know one." She added a thin chuckle that sounded like a nervous afterthought.

Vic bristled. "Rox, Treese *owns* the outfit. She doesn't puddle jump around on weekends, for Christ's sake. I went out with her once, weeks ago, and I sure as hell ain't taking her on a date to Syracuse." The fact he was explaining himself built more irritation. He fought to demolish it. "Look, you and I, we're a closed loop. I wouldn't—"

"I know that," she broke in. "Honest, I was joking."

"It didn't sound like it." He sighed. "I'm sorry. I guess I'm wound a little tighter than usual. All this is getting to me."

"So, lighten up, buddy. This weekend should answer a lot of questions."

"And maybe ask a lot more. But Treese Cosgrove is *not* flying me to Syracuse. You can take that to the bank. You're welcome to come along. In fact, I only wish you could."

~ * ~

Friday's final bell sounded and Vic's class, lined up at the door in anticipation, exploded into the hall. One girl offered a perfunctory wave, all the rest were damned happy to be on their way. These students hadn't met the former Mr. Vickery, the teacher he once was. Maybe they hadn't heard how good he used to be as they were all too willing to accept what he now offered: mediocrity. Doing what was necessary. Maintaining law and order, but nothing close to the excited and enthusiastic artist and teacher he once was. Better than some, not as good as others. And it made him sad to admit it, but Vic accepted it as truth. The fact he was winning lots of money at syndicate golf Novocained his conscience, and supplied the feeling of self-worth being a better than average teacher and artist once gave him.

"What's shaking this weekend?" Ted Duffy called down the hall as Vic locked his classroom door.

"Business in Syracuse."

"Syracuse, New York? You lucky dog!"

"Lucky? Syracuse?"

"Beats the hell out of Toledo."

Vic shrugged. "Maybe so, but winter is winter, New York or Ohio-style."

The familiar drive to the airport, through the sunless gray February afternoon, didn't take more than half an hour. Gray. That was the tone of the landscape Vic viewed through the windshield, but he could barely contain his excitement over the trip he was about to make. Ever since McJunkins told him Reefer died in October, at about the same time he was with her at the tail end of his coma, his imagination was charged with possibilities and questions. He felt like a modern-day Marco Polo, but the discovery of China paled in the light of what Vic hoped to find, a frontier that could link this world with a spiritual universe. The prospect both excited and frightened him. But he knew he was ready.

"Hello, Vic," Treese called from behind the counter when he walked into Hawk Air. "Be right with you."

It felt strange not to have his golf clubs along. Vic set his one bag down and walked to the window. A fueler was busy attending to a hot-looking plane sporting bright orange and red stripes on its fuselage. The next thing he knew, Treese was at his side.

"Ready to go?" she asked. She wore a black jumpsuit with "Hawk Air" embroidered over the breast pocket, and "Treese" below that.

"Sure. Which plane?"

"We're taking my Navajo." She nodded toward the plane he'd been eying.

"We?"

"Yeah, lots of charters this weekend. Short on pilots, so I'm flying you over." She raised an eyebrow. "You have a problem with a *female* pilot?"

Vic thought of Roxanne, and realized it would take yet another lie to keep this from her. He merely smiled at Treese. "Oh, some might, but not *me*."

By the time they'd leveled off at cruising altitude, Treese had established her abilities as a pilot. Vic was an experienced flier, and it was obvious to him that Treese, like Foss, was at home with her plane, and was on top of the duties required to guide it safely to its destination.

"I'm going to skirt the lakeshore," she explained as they banked to the east. "That will take us through controlled airspace at Cleveland and add a little time. But in an emergency, I'd rather come down over dry land. Find a nice wide road or open field."

Vic looked down at Erie's frozen surface. "But the lake's frozen pretty solid, isn't it?"

"Ah, there's still plenty of open water out there. Plus, this time of year, lots of what looks good and solid wouldn't withstand the forces generated by a landing, even in a normal situation with full power, when you can grease it in. Coming in with a dead engine, splooosh." She opened her fingers upward to imitate splashing water. "And there are other problems a non-pilot doesn't even think about. Ice is flat and white. In those last fifty feet, before you actually set it down, it really helps to have some landmarks; poles or fence posts. Something to give you a sense of scale so you know how close to touchdown you are. Landing without them makes it dicey."

He settled into his seat. "Convinced me. You're the boss."

"So, can I ask what your business is in Syracuse?"

He chuckled. "I was afraid you might."

"Oh, I'm sorry. I don't mean to pry."

"You're not. It's a very long story. Kind of complicated, and actually, pretty damned strange."

"I love a good tale. We're all vectored for Cleveland," Treese said, setting the autopilot and training her expectant brown eyes on him.

Vic was so certain about what he'd find out in Syracuse, based on the call he'd made to the New York Highway Patrol, he wasn't reluctant to tell Treese the whole story. In a sense, it was almost like spilling your life-story to a barber; someone you are friendly with, but enough removed from that any judgment they might pass doesn't matter. He liked Treese, and she liked him, but they weren't dating. He had no reason to believe she would ever be significant in his life, although he'd toyed with the idea a time or two. But as solid as things were with Roxanne, Vic didn't see Treese as a future player in his life. Still, it was exciting to have someone to share his amazing journey with. Now that he was no longer married and his money was his own, he could tell others about how the coma changed his life. He saw this as an opportunity to rehearse, and to see how the story would be accepted. So, Treese spent over an hour listening to it all, from when Vic was hit by Tom Bayer's ball on the fourth green at Heather Hills, right through to Vic's coma experiences at Loon's Lair, and his subsequent strong golf game, which was structured on what he learned from Bascolm Traskett. He didn't even stop before the part about the syndicate golf, something he'd planned to save for when they were dating. That wasn't going to happen, and since it was all above board tax-wise, there was no reason not to explain where he flew off to with Hobart and Foss every weekend.

"Wow, what an incredible story. I can barely get my mind around it, you know, hearing it all at once." She rubbed her forehead. "So, you're going to see if the man you met, Bascolm Traskett, really exists? That will confirm the validity of your coma ... experience?"

Vic looked ahead to the western suburbs of Syracuse. "All of a sudden, it matters. For a long time, it didn't. I kind of pushed it onto the back burner. I have the game I have. How that happened wasn't of burning importance, for a while. But I wound up using some of what I learned in my coma to get one-up on the guy I played in my last match." He pushed a puff of air through the corner of his closed lips. "Something I'm not real proud of, even though that's how syndicate golf works. Regardless, now I need to know if it was all a fortunate pipe-dream, or if what I experienced actually happened."

Treese switched off the auto-pilot, and picked up the mic to contact Syracuse air control. "I hope you find out what you need to. And I have to say, I'm excited about being along on the trip."

~ * ~

"You sure you're all set? Nothing you need?" Vic asked, standing in the hallway outside Treese's hotel room. He winked. "I *am* responsible for the pilot's expenses."

"No, the pilot's tired. She's going to shower, and order some room service, something *very* expensive." Her face became serious and she touched his arm. "Call me when you get back. I'm *dying* to hear what you find out."

"You won't be asleep?"

She shrugged. "Call and wake me."

It was no more than a twenty-minute drive to the patrol post. Vic turned the key and the engine fell silent. He sat for a while in the rented Impala, trying to build the courage to walk inside. Late February was cold in Syracuse, and the big car cooled rapidly. Heaving a sigh, he opened the door.

The inside of the station house was reminiscent of his classroom, with too much fluorescent light, gray-brown floor tile, and tan ceramic brick that climbed the walls to shoulder height before giving way to concrete block painted with shiny pale green enamel paint. The desk was manned by a trooper too young to be the commander. Vic approached him, wearing his friendliest smile. "Good evening, I'm looking for Commander Eulander."

The young patrolman gave Vic what appeared to be an experienced appraisal. "He's taking a break. I'm Sergeant Kincaid. Is there something I can help you with?"

"Actually, I need to speak with Commander Eulander. It's ... something of a personal nature."

Kincaid gave Vic an exasperated look and stood. "Who should I say is here?"

"Allan Vickery. He doesn't know me. I'm here to inquire about a mutual acquaintance."

For the several minutes before Eulander appeared, Vic fought a compelling urge to get back into the Impala and get out of there. But, he wanted the truth, so why would he even consider leaving? He forced himself to stay, sitting in a chair next to a pedestal ashtray nearly overflowing with cigarette butts. He would confront the facts, no matter what they turned out to be. A door across the room opened and a tall, lean man, who looked to be near fifty, entered. His posture was ramrod straight and his demeanor was all official business. He walked up to Vic and extended his hand. "I'm Dexter Eulander," he said.

Vic felt the hair on the back of his neck stand. Dexter. Dex. That was the name of the trooper who helped Bascolm box in the murderer's car, the night of Bascolm's crash. Vic was certain he remembered that name. Like Bascolm's, the other trooper's name was unusual enough to stick. It hit Vic like a thud on the head. He rose from the chair, shook Eulander's hand, and looked him in the eye. "Allan Vickery, sir. I'm sorry to intrude, but I hope you might be able to help me in locating an old friend. I believe he was posted here about twenty years ago. Our family moved to Ohio, and I lost track of him."

Eulander cocked his head and his brow furrowed. "And who would that be?"

"Bascolm Traskett," Vic replied, studying Eulander's face carefully.

The commander's eyelids pinched into a squint, and his eyes bored into Vic's. He tipped his head a few more degrees. "How did you know him?"

"He lived next door, sir, when I was a boy. He was, oh, I don't know, almost like an older brother to me. We used to talk. I used to like to go over and watch him work on his cars and stuff. We moved before I started high school, and I didn't make the effort to keep in touch. Now, I wish I would have. I learned I'd be in the area on business this weekend and called patrol headquarters. A woman there said you might be able to help me out."

The commander stared impassively at Vic for a moment. He chewed gum, something he did between his front teeth. "Why don't we continue this in my office?"

~ * ~

Treese picked up the receiver mid-way through the second ring. "'Lo?" she murmured.

"You *were* asleep. I'm sorry."

"Dozing. Waiting for Carson to come on. What did you find out?"

Vic could sense excitement sweeping the cobwebs of sleep from her head. "I have independent verification of the story Bass told me at Loon's Lair, Treese. This Eulander guy, he was *in* the pursuit with Bass, and saw the whole thing. He saw Bass slide into a bridge abutment. He even gave him CPR while they waited for the ambulance." A chill ran the length of Vic's spine. "This is the most amazing, exciting, and ... scariest night of my life." He picked up his Southern Comfort, but put it back down, untouched. "Do you realize what this means?"

"I think I do."

"Jesus, Treese. This is cosmic. Absolutely cosmic. This connects heaven and earth." Vic paused. "I mean, am I overstating things?"

"No. God! This is like *The Twilight Zone.* So what's next?"

"Tomorrow morning, I'm paying a little visit to a place called Mercywood."

"Mercywood?"

"It's the sanatorium where Bascolm has been for the last sixteen years. Tomorrow, he's going to receive a visitor."

"Wow. That's just too strange."

"But, Treese, it's the only way I can really confirm the whole thing," Vic said. "I mean, I came this far," he added, fearing he sounded overly defensive.

"No. No, I didn't mean you're strange for going. That only makes sense. No, the whole idea of meeting someone in a coma, and finding out they lived when and where they said they did. I get goose flesh every time I think about it." She hesitated. "You okay? I could dress and we could go down to the bar for a drink, if you want to talk."

Vic considered it, but then the voice in his head said, *No date in Syracuse.* "It's already after eleven, Treese. I have to tell you, I'm wrecked. I've been up since five this morning. I ought to get some sleep. Or try to. Tomorrow'll be a big one."

"You're right. Some other time."

"I'm going to Mercywood early, and I should be back by ten or eleven. We'll grab a sandwich, and fly out afterwards. I'll call when I get back."

"Sounds good. Luck tomorrow."

"Thanks. Hope I remembered to pack some."

~ * ~

Mercywood was nestled among some ancient, glacial drumlins on the outskirts of Syracuse. Vic guided his rental through the high, black, wrought iron gates and imagined how beautiful the grounds would be in the summer. Some trees, clustered in plantings bordered by field stone, still clung to papery brown leaves like skeletal misers. He noticed several empty pools with fountains, and each was surrounded with snow-drifted benches that held the promise of shady summertime repose. As the drive wound along its way, an outcropping of huge, spire-like pines speared the sky to announce the orange brick Victorian structure that housed Mercywood Residential Extended Care. Vic parked in a space marked "Guest," pushed open the Chevrolet's heavy door, and stepped into the gray chill.

The surrounding evergreen trees intervened against the wind, and encouraged him to lift his chin from an initial buck-the-cold position. He studied the immaculate old structure, which exuded a quiet majesty that bespoke competence and quality. He looked up to where, paramount to the other gabled peaks and flare-topped chimneys, a wide run of green roof sloped earthward at a severe angle above the front doors. Those doors, along with the window trim and gables, were richly decorated with low relief patterns and sculptural carpentry. A final detail, which almost escaped Vic's notice, was a sculpted owl perched on the sill of one of the third floor windows. He wondered what special meaning it must have had to whoever placed it there.

Next to walking up the steps to Mercywood's front door, standing on the first tee of a money match was nothing. He muffled a belch, the product of the gnawing nervousness in his stomach, then rang the bell. A young woman, wearing what looked like an old-fashioned nurse's uniform, answered the door. "Hello," she said, before her eyes widened in surprise. "Goodness, where is your coat?"

"I wore a car," Vic said, obeying her gesture to step inside.

She didn't react to his attempt at humor, but closed the door on winter, and turned to face him in the warm foyer. A silver pin on her gray and white striped bodice proclaimed her name was Aimee. "Are you here to visit a loved one?" she asked. Her face was plain, but pretty. She wore little make-up, and her long, caramel-colored hair reached to where her white apron was tied at her waist.

"Sort of. An old friend. Someone I knew as a youngster and lost contact with when my parents moved our family to Ohio." It amused Vic that he felt obligated to trot out his whole fabricated story to a young girl who, he was certain, wouldn't care one way or the other.

"And who would your loved one be?"

"Bascolm Traskett."

His name appeared to surprise her. "Mr. Traskett has never had a visitor. Not since I've worked here." Aimee squinted at the ceiling. "Not in the past four years, anyway. Are you aware of his condition?"

"Ah, I believe he's in a coma. Vegetative?"

Aimee grimaced. "When was the last time you saw him?"

"Oh, it's been years. I don't know for sure."

She frowned. "Of course, you're welcome to come up." She gestured toward the stairs and took the lead. "I only want to inform you, he's not, well ... comas are very hard on the body." Vic didn't respond. "He gets the best of care," Aimee continued as they climbed. "Inhalation therapy to keep his lungs clear; that's the main problem for the comatose. Fluid in the lungs. And we reposition him regularly to prevent bedsores."

Vic glanced around at the lush blue carpet and the richly lacquered woodwork. Large paintings adorned the high walls. Vic spotted a nude by Bouguereau, one of his favorite French painters, overlooking the second floor landing. If it was an original, it had to be worth thousands. "Being a patient here must be expensive."

Aimee continued talking as they continued their climb. "Oh, the state pays for everything. He was a Trooper, as I'm sure you know." Vic nodded, even though he was behind her and she couldn't see him. "But, yes, this house once belonged to a secretary of state ... either of New York, or maybe the whole country. I'm not sure which." She giggled, sounding embarrassed. "That was a long time ago. It became Mercywood in the 1940s. You're right, the costs are high, but the care we offer our loved ones is the best."

They crested the final set of stairs, and started down a hallway. "How do you get the patients all the way up here?" he asked.

"Oh, we have an elevator. I'm sorry. I mean, we could have taken it, but I wanted the time to explain a little, you know, about Mr. Traskett's condition."

"Not a problem. Thank you for preparing me."

She held up her arm when they stopped at a partially open door.

"Let me go in and see," she whispered, letting herself in and returning the door to its former position. "Bass," Vic heard her say, in a soft lilt, "you have a friend here today. Isn't that wonderful? An old friend's stopped to visit."

Standing in the dark hallway, Vic's eyes began to water. He swallowed against what felt like paralysis in his throat, snuffled, and wiped his nose with his shirt sleeve. He heard the sound of a rustling sheet inside the room, then Aimee reappeared at the door. She offered him a tissue. Apparently, his eyes told her he needed one. "Mr. Traskett is tremoring a lot today," she said, as Vic accepted the tissue. "I want you to know he isn't always like this. Sometimes he's so peaceful, you'd think he was asleep. Except for his eyes. They almost never close."

She stepped aside and gestured for Vic to enter. He inhaled sharply and walked into the room. The figure in the hospital bed was on its side, facing away from the door and curled into a tight ball. With the sheet pulled up, all Vic could see was the back of a shaved head. "Loved ones in comas assume the fetal position after their physical therapy ends," the nurse explained, heading off one of his questions. "After the first year, they rarely regain consciousness after a year, therapy goes from daily to every other day. After six more weeks of every other day, all physical therapy ceases. We keep their hair cut as short as possible for sanitary reasons." She walked around the bed to face the patient. "Bass," she called, almost singing his name. "He's here, Bass. Your visitor ... oh my God," she exclaimed, shooting Vic a look. "I'm sorry. I never asked your name. I'm so embarrassed."

Vic wrestled his uncooperative facial muscles into a smile. "That's okay. It's Allan. Allan Vickery."

"Allan, Bass. Your friend, Allan Vickery. Isn't that wonderful?" She turned to Vic. "There are lots of theories, but I follow the one that says they can hear us, hear what's going on around them. Haven't been able to check it out. None of our loved ones have come back since I've been here." She paused. "Isn't that right, Bass? We have good little talks, don't we?" She looked back at Vic. "One-sided, maybe, but I would hate it if a patient ever felt neglected. I tell them what day it is, what the weather is like, little personal things." Her cheeks flushed.

"I think your patients are very lucky." Vic's voice sounded shaky, even to him. It felt like an army of ants advanced through his nasal chambers, and he blinked against the resultant tears he felt rimming his eyes.

"Come on around, if you like." She smiled, but it looked like a sad one to Vic. "I think Bass has some color in his cheeks today."

Vic stepped to Aimee's side, turned, and looked at the man. Vic didn't know what he would see, but he was prepared for a surprise, and a surprise it was. Someone riding a roller coaster might break into an expression similar to the one on the man's face, or perhaps a person caught frozen in the millisecond before a hearty laugh. His lips formed an upward "v," suggesting the proximity of a grin. His cheeks were bunched into tight knots of pasty-colored flesh, garnished with roadmaps of thread-thin red veins. His eyes blinked incessantly; sometimes quickly, sometimes slowly, but they never stopped. His hands were clenched in fists under his chin, the way someone would if they were protecting their throat. There were several clear plastic hoses that appeared to be delivering and removing liquids from the man. Vic purposely didn't pay a lot of attention.

"I'll leave you for a while," Aimee said. She began pulling a chair over from a corner of the room. "Make yourself comfortable, Mr. Vickery. And if there's anything at all that you need, I'll be down the hall." Vic grasped the arms of the chair and continued moving it over to the bed. "Stay as long as you like," Aimee added, her footfalls like whispers on the linoleum as she left the room.

Vic stood looking down at the man, trying to decide what he felt. No matter how hard he tried, he couldn't see the person lying there as the Bascolm he'd come to know and play golf with in his coma. That made sense, the more he thought it. He only saw Bascolm in the coma. Logically, even though it turned out the Bascolm Vic saw was, in fact, a state trooper who lived in Syracuse, his image was one Vic invented. There was no way he could have known what the real Bascolm looked like, until now. *Bass never saw the real me, either,* Vic thought. He wondered what he'd looked like to Bascolm. The entire thing was difficult to fathom, especially when it dawned on him that in a mirror, they would each have seen true reflections of themselves, but the image of the other would be each man's own creation. Headache material, for sure.

Vic sat and concentrated on the man's eyes. On a whim, Vic swung his fist toward the man's face, as though he would punch him. Nothing. No reaction whatsoever. The man's eyes were unseeing. Vic experienced great relief in the fact that Bascolm wasn't there. *He was out playing golf with Donald and Jason,* he told himself. *If he'd flinched, that would have meant he was a prisoner in that bony, nearly mummy-like body.* Vic wouldn't have wished that on an enemy, much less a good friend.

Vic began to speak, his voice low enough he was certain the nurse wouldn't hear. "This is a little like when I visit The Old Man, Bass." Vic flashed on the memory of his shoes pressing into the grass at The Old Man's grave, in front of the bronze marker the turf was determined to swallow. "The guy I saw in The Old Man's casket didn't look the way I remembered him, and I don't recognize you, either."

Vic fell silent while he thought about the concepts of afterlife he'd adopted and discarded over the years. Like many people, he'd gone from a boy who believed everything in the Bible, to an adult who questioned it all. "I talk to The Old Man," he whispered, "even though I don't think he can hear me, but I'm not all that sure he'd listen to me, anyway." He rubbed his chin. "You'd listen, but I *know* you can't hear, because I was with you."

Vic stopped talking again while ideas coursed through his mind. He didn't try to control or categorize them, allowing them to flow in free association. "The one thing I keep coming back to is that being with you in the coma showed me there must be other planes of existence out there. I mean, if two people from different parts of the country meet up and connect in a coma, then it's not too big a leap to think the same thing happens with people when they die." He put his elbows on his knees, and clasped his hands together "At least that's the way it washes out for me, Bass. The Old Man, wherever the hell he is, he's with other people."

Vic looked over at the partially open door, and he thought he could catch wisps of someone, probably Aimee, humming somewhere outside the room. He turned back and looked at the man in the bed. "So, I know you can't hear me, but I'm chattering away, anyhow." He stood and chuckled quietly. "Halloween rolls around next fall, I'll be back shooting the shit with, well, *at* The Old Man too, no doubt."

Vic noticed a bit of saliva, poised to become drool, at the corner of the man's mouth. He almost ignored it, but this was his friend's body, even if Bascolm wasn't in it. He saw the box of tissues on a table, snagged one, and blotted the man's lips. They felt rigid, like a mannequin's. Vic dropped the tissue in a waste basket on his way to the door. He wished Bascolm could have bobbed to the surface, if only for a few seconds. That would have put the seal on the new framework of beliefs his trip to Syracuse gave him. At the same time, not knowing for sure was the human condition. You accepted things on faith, or you didn't. There was no way to be sure, even though all evidence pointed to multiple planes of existence. He paused before stepping into the hall. "Thank you, Bass," he whispered. "I'm pretty sure I'll see you again, my friend." He pulled the door open. "The only thing I know for certain is it won't be here, at Mercywood."

The door hinges creaked when Vic stepped out into the hallway, and Aimee, who folded linens at a table not far away, began walking toward him. "Are you ready to leave?" she asked. Vic only nodded, and turned for the staircases.

They never spoke as they descended the flights of stairs. When they reached the foyer, she smiled broadly. "I have to say it, Mr. Vickery, you look so much better."

"I didn't know I looked that bad, before." Vic feigned a worried look he allowed to produce a "gotcha" wink.

"You didn't. You know what I mean, you look a lot more relaxed. Not so tense."

"You're exactly right. I feel much better, thank you."

Aimee cocked her head and looked at him intently from the corners of her eyes. "Did you talk to him?" she asked.

Vic thought it a bit forward of her to ask him that. "Yes, I did. A little." Her question made him feel suddenly self-conscious.

She touched his arm. "I'm sorry, I wasn't trying to pry. I only wondered if a friend would get any response. If Bass moved, or made any sounds, you know, like he recognized you?"

"I understand." He paused. He didn't know what she expected, but he knew what he would tell her. "I'll be honest, I don't think he knew I was there." He paused. "It sounds like you have a different take on it."

She looked up at him. "Not really. I talk to him, like I said, and to all the loved ones in case they can hear. But I talk to my grandmother, too." She giggled softly. "And she's been dead for years."

"I guess we all have a favorite ghost." He cracked the door and a cold slice of wind shot through the opening. "Thank you, Aimee. It was a pleasure meeting you. You've been very kind."

She raised her eyebrows. "Your coat's going to be awfully cold."

She caught Vic off-guard, and his mind spun as he tried to understand what she meant. A tip of her head in the direction of the parking lot reminded him he'd told her he wore a car. "For a few minutes, but it has a great heater, for a coat."

Vic stepped outside into the winter's chill, closing Mercywood's heavy, ornate door behind him. Bascolm's body was inside, and Vic knew he would never return. Still, he rode a huge wave of relief rooted in the conviction his friend from the coma wasn't trapped there. Even more relief sprang from his conclusion that because Bascolm was out there somewhere, playing golf with Jason and Donald, it seemed logical there was some level of existence after life's end. He would find Bascolm again, he believed, and that thought kept him warm until his "coat" reached operating temperature.

~ * ~

Treese hit the kill switch and the Navajo's propeller slowed, then ratcheted to a quivering stop. The silence in the absence of the engine's song was compelling. Vic opened the door so he could climb onto the wing, and jumped to the tarmac. By the time she'd walked around the plane, he had the exterior luggage compartment open, and their bags in his hands.

She took her suitcase from him and glanced at her watch. "Thanks. Pretty good, eh? Mission accomplished, and still some Saturday left."

Vic gave her a thumbs up. They left the plane to the ground crew and began to walk toward their cars. "You sure you don't want to settle up now?"

"It's the weekend, Vic. Don't make me work harder than I have to." She mugged. "I'll finalize your bill on Monday. We'll get square when you come out again, next weekend?"

"I hope. Gotta keep the game in shape."

Treese closed the trunk lid and her smile lifted off. "I hope your offer of a drink sometime is still good."

Vic winced. "Look, Treese, I didn't ask you out again because it seemed like you were seeing the guy with the 'Vette pretty steady."

"And you were angry." Her smile stalled.

"Not angry. Confused? I couldn't figure out what the deal was. I mean, you said you weren't going to get involved with anyone. Going to date around. You turned me down for another date the next weekend, then I see you with him a few times, back to back. I figured you weren't all that interested, despite what you said at your place that night."

"I screwed up, Vic. I told you I wouldn't go on another date right away because I *did* want to date around. But you seemed like you might be the kind of guy I hope to find. I dated Roger anytime because he was fun, but *not* what I had in mind. And, to be honest, no one else has asked."

Vic wagged his head. "I guess it was a mutual misunderstanding. But the point is, I've committed to a relationship with someone, and I'm not dating anymore."

Treese's smile went into a tailspin. "I'm sorry. I'm so angry at myself. I really blew it." She touched his arm gently and started for her car.

On the drive to his apartment, Vic wondered if *he'd* blown it. He didn't call out to her, he let her walk away. Treese was a terrific lady: intelligent, interesting and interested in him. The main thing was that, unlike Roxanne, she was available. He had no idea how long it would be until Roxanne would be single, or if she would ever leave Tom. And he couldn't date Treese. It wouldn't be fair for him to pretend to be available, while still biding time, waiting for a woman he couldn't admit to being involved with. Not only that, the major goal in his life was to buy a river house. He'd told Hobart to line up as many high-dollar matches as he could. He figured he'd need at least $150,000 to get the kind of house he had in mind, and he hoped to amass that amount as quickly as possible. He would be too busy playing golf to date Treese or anybody else, for that matter. His plans were to be gone every weekend, and during the week, he'd have to scramble to keep up with the work needed to get by at school. Dating was time-intensive, and time was something Vic wouldn't have much of.

As it was, his relationship with Roxanne consumed very little time, only the few hours she could embezzle from her Bittersweet life, without bankrupting the facade of domestic solvency. She understood and accepted the fact he would be out of town on weekends. They saw each other two or three times during the work week, enough to maintain their relationship. Their bond remained strong and comfortable. It would sustain him in the near term, and that was all the future Vic could allow himself to envision.

He parked his car, grabbed his suitcase, and let himself into the apartment. He put his bag down, and Muldoon leaped into his arms. "Hey, big guy!" he said, rubbing Muldoon's head and scratching him behind his ears. "Did you party down while I was gone?" Muldoon yowled. Vic looked around at the familiar order of the place. "You straightened up real good, pal. Now, cool out for a little, Mully. Gotta call Roxxie." The phone rang twice. The instant Roxanne answered, an undercurrent in her voice told him something wasn't right. "Is this a wrong number?"

"No. He's not here right now." She paused. "How was the trip?" The words came out like .44 magnum rounds.

"Oh, Jesus, Rox, unbelievable!" The emotions surrounding the visit to the sanatorium resurfaced, and he found himself swimming against the tide of his feelings. "Bass was there. He was. I found him in a place called Mercywood. It was so fucking unreal. A man I met when I was in a coma is in a coma in New York, and all the things he told me are true. I *talked* to a New York State Trooper who was in the pursuit with Bass. He confirmed everything Bass told me." Vic's pronouncement was met with an eerie silence. "What's wrong?"

"I'm not gonna screw you around. I was, but I'll cut to the chase. I called Hawk Air this morning. They told me that Cosgrove woman flew you out to New York, you son of a bitch! You lied to me, goddamn you," she shouted.

"I didn't lie. I told you I didn't think there was any way the owner would be flying clients around on the weekend, and I *didn't*. No one was more surprised than me when I found out, but they had a lot of charters, I guess, and were short on pilots. So what was I supposed to do? Not go? Everything was set up."

"You're right! It *is* real strange the owner would be flying you, unless that was the plan. I bet everything was all set up." Roxanne's voice seethed with anger. "So, did she induct you into the mile high club, or did you wait until you landed?"

"Roxanne! I told you we're a closed loop, and I meant it. *Nothing* went on. We didn't so much as have a meal together, much less a room. I paid for two. I can show you the goddamned receipt. We didn't even go anywhere together, other than the plane trip and the ride to and from the motel. There absolutely was, and *is,* nothing between Treese Cosgrove and me." He hesitated a moment to decide if he'd offer a thought that just surfaced. The light went green. "Not more than an hour ago, she said she'd like to go out with me. I told her I was in a relationship and wasn't dating. And that's the truth."

"It sounds too fishy to me, the whole goddamn thing. You say she's not going, then I poke around and find out she did. Now you want me to believe you?"

"There is that. Who the hell are to you check up on me, anyway? I mean, you're living at home with your fucking husband, and you think it's fine to check up on me? At least now I know how much you trust me."

"All I can say is, I told you I didn't care about you dating, but if you're fucking anyone else, Vic, then you sure as hell ain't fucking me," she shouted. There was a moment of dead air. "Gotta go," she hissed. That was the standard sign-off when Tom pulled in. There was a click, and the line fell silent.

Vic dropped the receiver on the hook and sagged to the kitchen floor. He felt weak. His head was full of too many thoughts. He couldn't focus on any one of them. They swirled in his mind until he actually felt dizzy. He rolled onto his back and stretched his arms toward the ceiling. "Take me!"

~ * ~

There were no calls from Roxanne the rest of the weekend. Out of stubbornness and with some lingering anger in the mix, Vic didn't call her, either. Even though the weather had turned snotty, Tom was normally in and out of the house on weekends. If Roxanne wanted to talk, she would find an opportunity. She didn't.

The drive home from school Monday was gray and wet. Slushy little snowflakes sacrificed themselves against the windshield while Vic worked at keeping the back end of his car from passing the front. When he pulled in to park at the apartment, Roxanne stood under the overhang on the entry stoop. She was outside his driver's door before he could open it, looking down from under the floppy brim of her knit hat.

"Where the hell have you been?" Her face was drawn, and there was no evidence of her impish humor.

"Last Monday of the month. My opportunity to attend a scintillating faculty meeting," he deadpanned, hoisting himself from the car. "But damned nice to see you, too," he said, trying to coax her into some levity.

"I don't have long. I've already been here almost an hour."

"You have? Where's your car?"

"I walked."

"Walked?"

"It's over." She leveled a chilling look at him. "Like it or not."

"Over? Roxanne, I *swear* I told you the truth Saturday."

391

"It doesn't matter. Tom walked in while we were talking. He heard everything."

Vic felt like he stood in an avalanche. "You're shittin' me."

"I wish. I was so busy ripping you, I forgot to watch for his car. I never heard him open the door."

Vic leaned back against his car. Moisture from wet snow soaked into his shirt and pants. He didn't react. "So what's he know?"

"Everything." Her eyes began to tear. "He heard it all. He heard me use your name. I would have kept you out of it, but—"

"You don't have to protect *me*," Vic cut in. "He's the last person on earth I'm afraid of." He stepped forward to touch her arm. "He didn't hurt you, did he?"

"Not like you'd think." She wiped at her eyes. "He tore my heart out. Cried like a baby. Begged *me* to forgive *him*. Begged for another chance."

"Roxanne, you're not staying with him?"

A surprised look crossed her face. "Yes, as a matter of fact, I am. I didn't get married to get divorced."

"Nobody does. But, after the way he's treated you all these years? Left you alone. Ignored you and your needs. Jesus Christ. I treat you the way you deserve, and you choose a drunken jerk over me? Is that what you want? To spend your life with a drunk golf junky who leaves you for the course at the drop of a Titleist?"

The smile Vic tried to coax from her finally arrived, but it was a sardonic one. "Golf junky?" She expertly raised an eyebrow for punctuation. "And where will you be flying off to this weekend?"

"That's different, and you know it. That's only until I get enough to buy my ... our river house."

"*Your* river house," she scoffed. "And that won't end it. Then you'll need furniture. And a boat. You'll play the syndicates a little longer, and a little longer. I know you, and you won't be able to stop. You love them both too much, the excitement of the golf and the money."

"You honestly believe you and Tom stand half a chance?"

She sighed. "Half a chance, maybe." Her impish grin flickered. "But I figure, after all these years, it's worth a shot. He's calling a marriage counselor today on his lunch hour. I promised to go to counseling with him if he promised to go to A.A. I'm going with him."

"A.A.? You're no alcoholic."

"I wish I was that sure. But what the hell? If that's what it takes to get him there."

Vic felt like he and Roxanne were in the eye of a hurricane. It was calm where they stood. A cold, eerie calm. He finally spoke. "You always said you'd make it easy if I decided to go back to Angie. Doing the same for you is the very least I can do." Roxanne began to step toward him. He thought she might kiss him, or give him a hug, and he put his arm up to stop her. "No, we probably shouldn't." He managed to swallow, but the tissue in his throat was taut, and didn't make it easy. "Funny, I remember you saying the same thing to me, back in the days when you had a paper route with one customer." He nodded. "Good luck."

"Thank you," Roxanne whispered. The hiss of a passing car's tires on the wet street almost drowned out her words. "Bye." She turned and began to walk away.

"Bye," he said, unable to tell if she heard him. He remembered the dream, when Reefer couldn't hear him either as she disappeared from the golf course, into the trees. He watched Roxanne recede into the distance while slushy little snowflakes dropped suicidally onto the concrete between them. She finally vanished around the corner, never once looking back.

Vic was immobile. He stood next to his car, unable to believe something as strong, as powerful, and as life-altering as his relationship with Roxanne could end with such a whimper. He felt like he'd been through a six-month-long storm, a storm of massive proportions. Like in a blizzard, or summer thunder and lightning fueled deluge, the danger and lack of control he'd experienced were both exciting and frightening. Now it ended. Overcast gave way to dusk, and the streetlights came on. Vic entertained himself with the idea she would change her mind, reappear from around the corner, to laugh her throaty laugh and admit she couldn't live without him. His hopes for a happier ending insulated him from the temperature for some time. Finally, he realized how cold it was, and went inside.

Chapter Thirteen

"Ya sound low, son," Hobart said, coaxing Vic to smile for the first time in several days.

"Yeah, this week hasn't been the best, Hobe," he admitted, trying not to sound whiny.

"Your business go badly last weekend?"

"Oh, no. *That* turned out real well, but a lady I've been seeing broke it off Monday, and I haven't bounced back yet."

"I'm sorry to hear that, son. We probably ought to figure on taking another week off, I reckon?"

"Nah, not at all. A good game is exactly what the doctor ordered, my friend. What's on the table?"

"Choices, Vic. We could take another match at Myrtle Beach. That'd be for less money. Or, there's a hot shit over in Greensboro, No' Carolina, will take you on. That'd be for more. You make the call, son," Hobart added, after some silence. "Whatever makes you comfortable."

Vic sifted through the facts. He *was* bruised from the break-up with Roxanne, and hadn't played golf since the match with McJunkins, two weeks previous. In addition to that, he hadn't practiced his chipping, pitching and putting as usual.

"This big-shooter in Greensboro, what's his story?"

"Don't know too much. He's 'bout your age. Been playing syndicates for over a year. According to the sheet, his record ain't the best. Played twenty-two matches and only won twelve."

"But he wants the big dollar?"

"Yeah. I don't think we wanna get into exact numbers, but he wants a pretty nickel."

"What's the course like?"

"Called Raven's Roost. I got friends has played it. Your game should be good there. Plays long, 7,300 yards or so, but you gotta place your shots. Your specialty."

"Raven's Roost, eh?" The parallel to Loon's Lair stuck out. "What course in Myrtle? Pine Lakes?"

"No. Another one, called The Tides. Don' know much about it. The guy, a younger fella, maybe twenty-five or so, has only played half-dozen matches more than you. Lost the first three. Been winning since."

Vic plumbed the depths of his gut for a verdict. He liked playing someone closer to his age, as opposed to another fresh-out-of-college-and-looking-to-turn-pro shark like McJunkins. He also liked playing a tight course requiring ball placement, and the name "Raven's Roost" iced the cake. Ultimately though, money made the decision. For Hobart to mention "pretty nickel," Vic figured the purse had to be huge.

"Let's go with Greensboro, Hobe."

"Sounds like a winner. Foss and I'll be along to pick you up Friday."

"Great. See ya then."

"Oh, and Vic? You mind a little personal advice?"

Vic was caught off guard by Hobart's question. They rarely discussed anything outside of golf. "Not at all, Hobe," he replied.

"When I get the blues, don't too often, but when I do, I don't fight 'em. Let them run their course. You're feeling low for a reason. I think it lifts quicker if you just ride it out." He ended with a self-conscious cough.

"We're alike on that, Hobe. Get right down and wallow in it, I always say. And thanks."

~ * ~

As was their custom, they didn't land at Greensboro, shunning the larger, busier airport for a small one twenty miles east, in Burlington, North Carolina. Raven's Roost was several miles east of Greensboro, which made Burlington all the better. They booked rooms in a Hyatt Regency that was a twenty-minute drive from the course, and Vic fell right to sleep that Friday night. North Carolina was far from Toledo, from Roxanne, and from school. It felt warm, comfortable and friendly.

The personnel in the pro shop at Raven's Roost were that and more. "Oh, yes! Mr. Vickery and Mr. Early. We've been looking for you," the man behind the counter enthused. He was an athletic-looking forty-something year old who projected an air of confidence in himself and in the club. "I'm Jacob Lund ... Jake," he said, offering his hand. "Duncan Cunningham told me to accommodate you in any way you desire. You'll be wanting caddies?"

"Yeah," Hobart replied, shaking Jake's hand. "A couple a' boys who know the short way 'round the course."

"Very good, Mr. Early. And you'll be playing eighteen?"

"We may want to do two loops, if that's not a problem," Vic said.

Lund consulted his tee sheet. "Very well. We'll have you going off in about fifteen minutes. The starter will be looking for you. Our Saturday morning groups move fast, so two loops, if that's what you require, shouldn't be a problem." He smiled. "Enjoy our course. Oh, and Mr. Cunningham asked me to tell you your lunch is taken care of. The dining room staff has been notified."

The course, as Hobart promised, was long and tight. Great arcades of trees bordering expanses of three-inch rough combined to punish a player who couldn't keep his ball in the fairway. The real difficulty of the track, as Vic and Hobart were to discover, was its greens. Not only were they huge, but very few of them weren't multi-tiered, and they all undulated like potato chips. Hobart was away on the first hole, with a downhill twenty-foot putt on what appeared to be a gentle slope.

"It looks like it could be slick," Vic warned.

"No worries, son," Hobart said, smiling confidently. "When the greens are quick, I give the ball a push."

Hobart barely tapped the ball on its way, but it began to pick up speed, missed the cup, and rolled all the way off the green and onto the front fringe, parking itself thirty-five feet from the hole. He looked at Vic in disbelief. "Like puttin' down a goddamn windshield," he howled, laughing. Vic joined him, and they joked and practiced more putts, until another group played into sight.

~ * ~

"How's that steak there, young feller?" Duncan Cunningham asked, smacking his lips as he savored the bite he'd forked into his mouth. Although his hair wasn't as gray, he reminded Vic of Colonel Sanders, a salt and pepper version of the finger-lickin' chicken guy.

"Oh, great, Mr. Cunningham! Best I've had in a long time."

"Dunc, is fine. You enjoy the course today?"

Vic and Hobart nodded and grinned in stereo.

"What the hell are the greens here like in the summer?" Vic asked.

Cunningham exchanged looks with his player, Ray Prosser. Prosser was unremarkable in every way; height, weight, and features. He had very dark hair, which he combed straight back. It contrasted with his light skin and even whiter teeth. "That's when they start to get fast," he said, grinning. "They take some getting used to. I'm good on 'em. If I win tomorrow, it'll no doubt be on putts." He swigged his ginger ale. "When I was making my bones in the syndicates, I lost a lot of matches playing on other player's courses. Too many." He gave Cunningham a supplicant look. "Dunc and the rest of the syndicate were terrific about it. Now we're at the point where we can get matches here at the Roost. I plan to pay them back for sticking with me."

"Don't be too confident," Vic said. "We looped the course once to get the lay of it, then we jumped from green to green. Putted each one for five or ten minutes." He paused to slice another bite of meat. "I'm not throwin' in the towel yet. I might give you a run for your money."

"I hope so," Ray replied. "I like to play it straight up, no dumb stuff. Let the best man win, on pure skill."

Vic smiled in agreement and chewed the steak, but he secretly wondered if he would be able to find a chink in Prosser's armor. One he could slide a knife into.

When the meal was finished, they all agreed to break up early and get a good night's sleep. Vic and Hobart shared a nightcap in the bar at their hotel.

Vic rattled the ice in his glass. "I don't mind tellin' you, Hobe, I'm nervous."

"But that's good, son. Nerves'll make you play your best." Hobart indicated Vic's empty glass with a tilt of his chin. "Want another?"

"Nah, thanks. I better turn in, get a good night's sleep."

Of course, Vic didn't sleep. The majority of his room was carpeted, but the dressing and bath areas were smooth, shiny vinyl. He spent a long time putting on the marbleized floor covering, sending Titleists clattering across the unforgiving surface while Vic focused on making his putting stroke a perfect pendulum. The ten-foot ceilings allowed full swings, and, like in the clubhouse at Loon's Lair, the carpet's soft nap served as an excellent telltale to assure him his swing path was on the money. When Vic turned in, his confidence in his game and in his ability to win at Raven's Roost was resurrected.

He was up early on Sunday and ran for half an hour. The pool at the hotel looked inviting, so he let himself in through the unlocked door, ignoring the sign that said it didn't open until 10:00. Kicking off his shoes, Vic did several toe touches before sliding head first into the smooth water. His mind flashed back to Bittersweet, and to the times he swam in the backyard pool after a run. He missed that. It was so easy to let it all slip away, but lately, memories returned to haunt and taunt him with increasing frequency. Something as mundane as a post-run dip could stir unsettling spirits of the past. Vic floated like a harried medium, bobbing along in a séance of recollections he couldn't control.

The phone rang when Vic walked back into his room. Hobart wanted to meet for breakfast. Vic drank coffee while Hobart shoveled down generous helpings of bacon and eggs, offering his normal pep talk between bites.

"You're gonna do real good today, Vic. I can feel it in my bones." The slow southern cadence of Hobart's speech was soothing. Vic savored his coffee and the confident words of his good friend.

Vic asked the caddie he'd used the previous day to loop for him again on Sunday. When they pulled up at Raven's Roost that morning, the young man lifted Vic's clubs from the trunk of the rental, and assured him there was plenty of time to warm up on the driving range. After Vic hit half a bucket of balls, he and Hobart headed for the first tee. Ray Prosser and Duncan Chamberlain were waiting.

"Call it in the air, Vic," Cunningham said as he tossed a gold piece above his head.

"Tails," Vic barked, but the image of a grumpy-looking monarch said Prosser had the tee.

If they'd been out for a friendly game, a round with Prosser would have been a delight. He was funny, courteous, and skillful. Sunday's round was, however, for a "pretty nickel," as Hobart termed it. Vic believed that meant more money than ever before.

From his opening shot, Prosser had difficulty getting from tee to green. He hit into the heavy rough on the first hole, and lost several strokes to bad shot placements and poor ball striking on several succeeding ones. But, hole after hole, Prosser's superior putting negated his mistakes, and left the two competitors tied, each having won a hole and coming up even on the others.

"Ah, shoot!" Prosser mumbled, which apparently was the closest thing in his vocabulary to an expletive. He caught his second shot fat in the sixth fairway and his initial grimace worked its way into a self-deprecating smile as his ball whizzed along the ground for a hundred yards or so. "Sometimes I stand too close to the ball ... *after* I hit it."

Vic didn't acknowledge the old joke because he was deep in thought. His own ball was two-hundred and five yards from the green, which was fronted by a moat-like water hazard that would be delighted to suck down any ball that came up short. "Shit, Hobe, he's eatin' me up on the greens. I gotta make something happen."

"Ya got this shot?" Hobart asked.

"Yeah. Bust a solid five wood. Even if I splash, I'll still be laying three. Chip and a putt, and I have par. He's still *eighty-five* yards out, laying two. I'm going to play it aggressive." Vic lined up on the shot and addressed the ball. He pulled the trigger and they watched the shiny white Titleist sail.

"Be right," Hobart hissed, under his breath.

It was. The ball dimpled the flawless green five feet on the far side of the pin, but wound up rolling another ten before it came to rest. They high-fived. "Yeah, but now I have to putt," Vic joked, handing his club to the caddie.

Prosser put his approach shot fifteen feet below the cup. Vic's first putt scooted ten feet too far. Prosser confidently stroked his par putt in, but Vic's come-backer continued five feet past the cup, even after it caught the lip enough to change direction. Prosser was a hole up. "Tough break." He gave Vic a friendly nudge. "Still two-thirds of the match to go, though." Vic waited until he was out of Prosser's line of sight, then looked at Hobart and splayed his arms in frustration.

Prosser stayed one-up for the next two holes. Then, on the ninth green, something happened that Vic thought he might be able to use to his advantage. When he struck his par putt, the ball did a funny little jump to the right as it came off the face of his putter. The putt still dropped in, and a casual observer might have missed it, but he was certain Prosser hadn't. "Shit!" Vic pretended to fume, retrieving his ball from the cup. "Must have caught a dimple."

"Caught a dimple?" Prosser's expression said he was waiting for some kind of punch line.

Vic rubbed his thumb over the ball. "Yeah, when I putt, I always try to strike the ridge between dimples. I'm real careful about how I replace a ball after marking out. Catch the edge of a dimple with the putter face and it'll twist, like that one did. Can make you miss. I almost did."

Prosser examined his ball closely. "I never heard of that before."

"It's something to think about."

Prosser placed his ball in front of his mark. He adjusted the ball, then readjusted it before picking up his coin. Vic glanced at Hobart and raised an eyebrow. By the time Prosser addressed his putt, he was out of his established routine, and Vic could tell he was freezing up. When he drew his putter back, only to return to address, Vic was certain Prosser's ball would miss the cup.

Cunningham apparently had the same concern. "Step out of it, Ray."

"Nah. I'm okay." Prosser sounded convincing, but his putt rolled wide. They were even again at the turn.

The final nine's fairways tightened up, and Vic's tee shot on number ten leaked slightly right. His tee ball on the eleventh hole bent even more, and so did his second shot. Twelve was a one-hundred eighty-two yard par three, and Vic's shot from the tee was a full-blown slice.

"What the hell am I doing wrong?" Vic whispered to Hobart as Prosser teed up.

"Dunno. Swing looked rock solid."

Prosser striped his tee shot, putting the ball less than ten feet from the pin. When they left that green, his confidence with the putter was resurrected. He made his putt for birdie to put him up a hole on Vic again.

Thirteen's fairway was one of the narrower chutes on the course and Vic knew he had to keep his shot in the short grass. When he searched his memory for a way to cure his slice, he recalled hearing about a player who supposedly found some grease on a golf cart and smeared it on the face of his club. The ball came off with no side spin, allowing him to rope an important shot and win a match. Was it an old shaggy dog story, Vic wondered, or would it work? It seemed logical. Grease would cut the friction between the club face and the ball, so side-spin would be reduced, even with a club head on a faulty swing path. Vic didn't have any grease, so it didn't matter, anyway. Then another thought occurred. He had trouble with dry lips in the summer, and Roxanne bought him some ChapStick to keep in his bag. Would ChapStick do the trick? Vic worked on opponents' heads to psyche them into losing, but he'd never truly cheated. Could he actually do that? Was money that important to him? He wanted to believe it wasn't, but the temptation was nearly overpowering. He had to hit it straight. When they arrived at the tee box, Vic's caddie gave him a questioning look. "Driver," he told the boy. "Oh, and see if there isn't some ChapStick in that upper pocket. My lips feel like the Sahara."

"Driver, son? You sure? This hole's tighter than a virgin bride," Hobart whispered, looking toward the fairway.

"No choice, my friend. I have to get out in front of Prosser, and I'm running out of golf course."

Hobart patted him on the shoulder. "Guess you're right. You'll do good. Relax and put your best swing on it."

While Hobart, Cunningham, and the caddies watched Ray hit off, Vic uncapped the lip balm, the tube poised a fraction of an inch from the face of his recently re-shafted driver. All he had to do was smear it up with the waxy substance. He was certain it would work. Even if his swing was off a few degrees, it wouldn't matter.

His mind suddenly flooded with the memory of Bascolm, and Vic couldn't do it. The image of his smiling friend shouldered its way past the fleeting glimpse his mind presented of the crumpled figure at Mercywood, and Vic could not touch the lip balm to the driver's face. He thought of Bo, and of Reefer, and the horrible way he won the match at Pine Lakes. His conscience already stung from the mind game he'd run earlier on Prosser, when he made a production over hitting the ball on the edge of a dimple. Complete fiction. Complete crap. I may not win this match, he decided, but win or lose, no more crap. No more cheating. If he couldn't win the money fairly, then he'd face the fact the money wasn't his. He wiped some ChapStick on his lips while Prosser's tee shot streaked down the left side of the fairway, bounced to the right, and came to a stop near the center, two-hundred fifteen yards out.

"Five wood?" Vic asked, as they exchanged places on the tee.

"Yeah. Driver's way too scary for me on *this* hole. You're my hero."

Vic tucked the ChapStick in his pocket. "Like I always say, tight fairway? Yank it and crank it."

Vic had no idea if the shot was lucky or the product of a well-executed swing, but the ball came to rest two-hundred seventy-five yards from the tee, camped nicely in the middle of the fairway, with a perfect angle to the green. Prosser, who lead and was able to afford to play it safe, chose to cover the remaining two-hundred-plus yards with a six iron and a pitch, leaving himself an uphill eight-footer. Vic, on the other hand, believed he had to go for the green. He had to use a long iron to make the distance, and since this four-iron made the ball come in low and hot, it hit the putting surface, but rolled onto the rear fringe. Vic chipped and putted in, Ray made his first putt, and they both came away with four strokes. Vic hadn't won the hole, but he walked off the green smiling. He was no longer a cheater. Redemption felt better than he would have ever believed.

Regardless, the game continued as it had. Vic gambled, taking big risks to beat his opponent's ball into the cup, while Prosser played conservatively, hitting more high percentage shots to cover the same yardage. Vic's luck and his skill didn't give out. He executed wondrous shots, but Prosser always managed to make up the difference on the green. He holed putt after astounding putt to undercut any advantage Vic attempted to gain. The result at the end of each hole was always the same, Prosser held the lead by one.

On the sixteenth tee, while Prosser went through his pre-shot routine, Vic realized, in all probability he would lose the match. He stood in the hushed stillness of that tee box at Raven's Roost, and contemplated the demise of his winning streak. The quiet reminded him of the way the end came with Roxanne. Their tumultuous high-intensity affair dissolved in the near-silence of a late-winter snow shower. Vic heard a bird warble somewhere in the distance and the wind whisper through the budding tree branches. His string of undefeated contests was slipping from his grasp amidst the subdued sounds at Raven's Roost. His mind meandered among memories of his past matches: the games with Sam Blackstock, Elwin Garwood, Jimmy Wingo, Jonas Brown, and Bo McJunkins. After all of these wins, his streak was about to end quietly, at the hands of a gentlemanly player by the name of Ray Prosser. There didn't seem to be a thing Vic could do about it.

On the sixteenth and seventeenth holes, Vic played as well as he ever had, but Ray sank amazing putts, and managed to stay one-up. On the eighteenth hole, Vic hit three fine shots tee to green, but, once again, two-putted for par. The last sound he heard as an undefeated syndicate player was the rattle of Ray Prosser's ball, rattling into the eighteenth cup.

~ * ~

While Hobart guided the rental to the airport, Vic let his head loll against the seatback and looked out the window, allowing the clouds mounting in the afternoon sky to smear by in soft focus. Hobart broke into Vic's reverie. "Busy beating yourself up?"

Vic rolled his head toward Hobart, who was silhouetted against the darkening sky. In the gloom of the gathering rain clouds, he noticed Hobart smiling, which made him feel better in spite of himself.

He decided not to deny the obvious. "Yeah. I'm so goddamned sorry, Hobe."

"We knew goin' in you wasn't gonna win them all."

"Still doesn't make it any easier to stomach." Vic noticed the bumper sticker on a blue Porsche. "I'd rather be driving a golf cart," it announced. "I mean, it was so goddamned close. If he'd have flat kicked my ass, I could handle that, but one fucking hole. No matter what I did, I couldn't get it back."

Hobart chuckled. "I bet losing bigger wouldn't have made you feel no better. Fact I know it wouldn't't."

Vic could no longer keep from asking. "How much did we lose today?"

Hobart patted Vic's shoulder. "It don't matter. Really. Let it go. On another day, if he weren't putting like a damned demon, you'd have had his ass. Today, he got yours. No big deal."

"I hope the rest of the syndicate takes your point of view."

"I think I can say it does." Vic gave him a questioning look. "After you had the trouble with TV down in Georgia, I bought him out. Wasn't about to have bad blood amongst the members. VanVorhis was expendable, you aren't." He cleared his throat. "Then Shymer, he had some business reversals. Needed money. So I bought him out, too. Merle, he's pretty much a silent partner. He don't have a lot of interest, to be honest. Don't even call to see how you're doin'. He's happy his plane's in the air every weekend, earnin' him charter money."

Vic smiled. "So the syndicate is you."

Hobart reached over to squeeze the back of Vic's neck. "Us. You and me, son. You're the motor. I just head us to the next gas station." He chuckled and Vic joined in. "So, ya wanna know what I got out of today? We lost some money, no question. But I'm a hacker. Same time, I love the damned game. And I love watching great golf, the kind I'll never play." He put on his turn signal and waited for traffic to clear. "Today, I saw some great golf. From the time you got your ball flight straightened out, there on number thirteen, you was something special. You played some shots I still can't believe. And that Prosser fella, once he was on the green, he was amazing." Hobart turned into the airport, and down the service road leading to the car rental outfit where Foss would be waiting. "So today cost some money, but it was worth it. And, I'll wager it'll set you up to win a lot more matches, so you get that house on the river you been talkin' about."

"I'm sorry, I don't see how losing a match is going to set me up to do anything."

Hobart eased the Crown Victoria into a spot in the Avis lot. "Look at the big picture, son. Somebody beat you, which means it *can* be done. A lot of guys who might have been nervous about it before will be willin' to give you a try now." He brayed his laugh. "Losing the match today was practically a stroke of genius."

"I guess I *am* brilliant. I make positive career moves without even knowing it."

"I ain't shittin' you! See the logic? I think the phone's going to start ringin', and you'll be playing matches at Cherry Hill, soon as it warms up. That ease things for you?"

"A little," Vic said, as Foss pulled Vic's door open wide. He knelt in the opening, and the look in his eyes killed the conversation.

"Let's get this car returned and head for the flight service," Urgency bumped across the surface of Foss' normal tone of voice. "We need to climb out ahead of this storm."

The words pecked at Vic like hail. Weather had never been a concern during any of their previous trips. "Wait a minute, Foss. If it's a problem, we don't *have* to fly home today. I can call in sick for tomorrow."

"Won't be a problem, long as we get airborne within the next half hour. I've been watching the radar and the squall line is still out a ways, but we don't have time to waste. The flight service loaned me a car. The plane's good to go."

Vic looked at Hobart. He nodded. "I'll go turn in the keys, son. Get our bags into Foss's loaner."

Vic put his clubs and the suitcases into the flight service car, then walked to where Foss stood. The western sky was a dark slate blue-grey. Though no actual bolts were visible, the clouds flickered ominously when the lightning flashed inside them.

"It's a pretty good little storm," Foss said. "Still fifteen or twenty miles out."

"But you're sure it's no problem?" Vic tried to hide his uneasiness. "'Cause—"

"Plane's all pre-flighted, and ready to roll," Foss cut in. He paused to look at his watch. "We'll be in the air inside of fifteen minutes. Plan is to head east before we turn north. End-run the bitch." His face exuded confidence.

"All set," Hobart said, walking up quickly, while thunder sounded softly in the distance.

Minutes later, they were in the Comanche, idling a few yards off the runway. The sky had darkened, with a greenish cast creeping into the gunmetal wall of the storm. Several feathery, light-colored clouds floated across the foreboding front. Foss picked up the mic. "NQ1554 niner." His transmission was met with silence.

"Sum'bitches," Hobart groused, from his seat in the back. "Slow as they are, we might as well be flying out of Greensboro."

Foss shrugged and let the mic rest on his leg. "Hey, what do you hear from Shymer, Hobe? He get things turned around?"

"Yeah, I believe so."

The voice of the controller interrupted. "Burlington ground to NQ one-five-five-four-niner. Go."

"Yes, tower. Just to inform, we're still waiting to be cleared."

Once again, there was no immediate response from the tower.

Hobart went on. "To hear Bobby tell it, the bottom's still fallin' out, but he tends to make too much of his troubles. He's a smarty. He got rid of a few people who was, well, let's say they was lookin' out for themselves first. He's a good businessman. He's getting—"

"Tower to one-five-five-four-niner. One moment."

All of a sudden, Vic remembered the transcription of a cockpit voice recorder he once read in *Time* magazine. The second officer on an airliner, flying out of Denver on an overcast day, was trying to decide whether to buy a Toyota or a Honda for his wife. He bantered with the captain and the navigator, both of whom were chiming in with opinions. During an extended exchange between the pilot and co-pilot, the navigator began to break in. "Could be something here." They ignored him. Then, "(Expletive deleted), we might have a problem." That was the way the text in the magazine read, and it captured the captain's attention. "What have you got?" he asked.

"Not sure. We might be too low. We better—" That was where the tape ended, when they encountered a mountain, well below its summit.

Back when he read it, Vic found it fascinating people could be having an ordinary conversation about cars one moment, and be dead the next. Now it gave him chills.

"I'm glad to hear that," Foss said. "I always liked Bob. Was sorry to hear about his reversals."

"Tower to NQ one-five-five-four-niner, over."

"We're *still* here. Go."

"Yes, sorry about the delay. We were holding for another flight, but he's on a go-round. Pull up, sir."

"Acknowledged." Foss released the brakes and taxied into position. He power-tested the engines, scanning the gauges.

"NQ one-five-five-four-niner, now cleared."

Foss opened the throttles. Vic found the familiar sensations soothing. The plane made all the right sounds and vibrations as it gathered speed. He shifted his attention outside his window, watching the painted markings on the concrete snap past the wing. He felt the front of the plane begin to lift.

"Shit!" Foss barked. Vic whipped his head around and saw a flock of geese, bunched like a low cloud, flying across the runway. He braced, putting one hand on the dashboard, and the other against the side of Foss's seat. Foss held the craft steady, feathering the controls to keep it on the ground, at slightly less than takeoff speed. In seconds, it became obvious the flock would clear the runway in plenty of time. Foss heaved an audible sigh, and reopened the throttles. Again, the plane teetered onto its rear wheels. Then more geese, previously hidden from view by some low scrub, struggled into the air, following the first group. "Aw, fuck!" Foss shouted.

Expletive deleted. That was the first thing that went through Vic's mind. If there was a cockpit voice recorder, the transcript printed in the paper would read, "Aw, (expletive deleted)."

Foss jammed the throttles closed. The plane dropped hard and bounced, moments before the first goose hit the starboard wing and exploded like a twenty-pound melon. The next goose hit the windshield, and Vic reflexively threw his arms across his face. A collage of thoughts spun through his mind, like a movie trailer in fast forward. He thought of the robin that skidded across the Mazda's windshield the day of the Chili Open, and of all the games of "Take Me" he'd played over the years. He feared the challenge had been accepted.

He heard several more of the big birds hit various parts of the plane, but snatching a peek, he realized they'd punched through the flock. Foss fought for control, working the brakes and the rudder, taking his hand off the yoke long enough to kill the engines. The plane drifted to the right, and by the time it veered off the runway apron, their speed was down to thirty or forty miles an hour. In a matter of seconds, the plane bumped to a stop on the rough turf bordering the runway. A shroud of silence descended upon them. Foss was the first to cut through it.

His voice was strained, but controlled. "Everybody okay?"

"Yeah, sure," Vic said. "Hobe?" he called out, spinning in his seat. Hobart's eyes were bulging, and a film of sweat coated his skin. "Hobe!"

"Yeah. Sum'bitch ... " he managed to croak. "Sweet Jesus! That was some goddamn ride."

Hobart sounded okay, so Vic relaxed. "Yeah, nice piece of flying, Foss."

Foss was busy flipping switches. "Wish we had been flying. Plane's a hell of a lot easier to control when it's in the air. We probably ought to get out. The safety crews will be here. I want to look this bird over."

Vic opened his door, tried to get out and realized his seat belt was still fastened. After releasing it, he climbed out onto the wing. "Come on, Hobe. Give me your hand," Vic said, reaching back inside. Hobart moved slowly, unsteadily. As he made his way to the door, Vic noticed he was panting. "Take it easy, Hobe! Everything's fine. Everything's cool. Give me your hand."

Hobart's skin was cold as a trout. He gasped. "Can't get my breath, is all. My collar's too tight." Vic looked. Hobart's shirt wasn't even buttoned at the neck.

"We'll get it. Come on out on the wing, here. Everything's gonna be okay."

Hobart no more than cleared the open door before he started to slump. Vic caught him, easing him onto the wing. "Foss!" Vic shouted.

"Keep him up on the wing. Get his pulse!" Foss yelled, ducking under the fuselage. Before Vic could react, Foss was there and working his fingers against Hobart's neck. "You know CPR?"

"Sort of. I dunno—"

"You ventilate. I'll do the compressions. Now!"

As Vic blew in the first lung-full, he noticed the sirens from the emergency vehicles getting closer. Foss did the compressions and, as Vic filled Hobart's lungs with breath, something flashed through his mind. It was an interview with a woman who had clinically died. She said she found herself circling above her body, looking down upon herself. As the paramedics pulled up, Vic looked toward the sky. "Goddamn it, Hobie," he shouted. "Come back!"

The storm came in just as the small swarm of medical people lowered Hobie from the wing and onto a gurney they positioned underneath it. They administered drugs. They hooked up machines. They invoked all of their medical incantations, while the rain pounded down. Vic and Foss stood in the downpour and watched the skilled practitioners work on Hobart Early's body. Lightning flashed as they fired the defibrillator, but even heavenly assistance wasn't enough. When a grim-faced paramedic walked up to them, mascara cascading down her cheeks in the rainy deluge, Vic already knew what she was about to say.

Chapter Fourteen

Vic pushed the buttons and listened to the clicks and beeps that had become all too familiar. The phone on the other end began to ring. He let it go ten times, and looked at his watch. Where the hell is she? He hung up and walked to the motel room window. The thunder and lightning had subsided, but the steady torrent continued. The wind blew the big drops against the panes, fracturing the clarity of the scene outside. Vic stopped struggling to see through the window, instead viewing it as an unfinished abstract painting. Headlights, taillights, and neon signs became an amalgam of color and unspecific form, constantly changing as new raindrops hit the glassy canvas. He sipped Southern Comfort and watched the image mutate and evolve.

Hobart was dead. That was the major inescapable reality. The enormity of his loss was only beginning to sink in. Vic's bond with him surpassed friendship to become that of father and son. Hobart guided Vic with subtle nudges. That was his way; advice and guidance offered, never forced. Vic felt his face twist into a tight grimace.

More pain stemmed from the fact that, when it came right down to it, Vic knew next to nothing about Hobart. Had he ever married? Did he have children, or any other close family? It hurt Vic to acknowledge he had no idea. Their conversations, their entire relationship, revolved around golf. Hobart never volunteered any personal information, and Vic never inquired. He operated on the theory people tell you what they want you to know. Now Hobart's body lay in the county morgue because the only two people

Vic knew to call were his mother, or the last remaining member of the syndicate, Merle West. Neither were answering their phones.

The crushing reality was there was no one else he could call. Foss was out dealing with repairs to the plane. Besides, as with Hobart, Vic didn't really know Foss all that well. Vic and Foss would get together later, and probably eat dinner somewhere, but that didn't attend Vic's immediate pain.

The women in his life were gone; Angie and Roxanne. He didn't know Treese well enough to call and unload his grief on her. His golf buddies didn't even know he spent his weekends playing syndicate golf, and they didn't know Hobart from a load of straw. Besides, the feelings that gripped his heart weren't the kind of emotions he would share with any of the guys, anyway. He didn't operate with male friends on that level.

He was alone. More alone than he remembered being in years. Maybe ever. Nothing he did in the last four months assuaged the loneliness he experienced when he was married to Angie. Every attempt to find love or close friendship failed or slipped away. He was in a motel room, hundreds of miles from home. Alone. He walked over and punched his mother's number again. This time, she picked up on the second ring. "Mom, where have you been?"

"Allan. What's the matter?"

"Oh, Mom ... " Vic paused. He'd been so focused on reaching her, he hadn't considered what he would say when he did. Vacant of any other ideas, he plunged straight ahead. "Hobie had a heart attack this afternoon."

"You're with Hobart? He had a heart attack?"

"Mom, he didn't make it. He died."

"Oh my God! Allan ... " Silence, except for her muffled weeping. "Where are ya'll?"

"In North Carolina, Mom. Burlington, North Carolina."

"But I don't understand."

Vic explained that he and Hobart flew down to play golf, and he recounted the fateful takeoff, carrying the story through to when Hobart was loaded into the coroner's van.

413

"And you're all right? You weren't hurt?"

"I'm fine, Mom. Foss, the pilot, and I are fine. It wasn't even a crash. A scary sort of, I don't know. A non-takeoff."

"And you were down there to play golf for money, weren't you?" All vestiges of her drawl vanished, but she was still crying.

"Ma! Hobie's dead, for Christ's sake." Vic fought his own tears. "None of that matters. I don't know what to do. Who to call. Did he have any family?"

"No, none that I know of. He was a widower. His wife died years ago. He had one daughter, but she overdosed on drugs sometime back in the sixties or early seventies. When I met him, he was pretty much married to his tool rental business, but of course, he sold that."

"I loved that old guy, Mom," Vic sputtered, overwhelmed by the emotion he was now unable to keep on hold. "He was more of a father to me than ... anyone." He fought for control, but found himself beyond any ability to continue. "Just a minute," he croaked, laying the receiver on the nightstand. He blew his nose, wiped his eyes, and panted several deep breaths. "I'm better now," he breathed into the receiver.

"Oh, Allan. This whole thing is so tragic. I'm glad it wasn't more serious, that *you* weren't hurt." After a period of silence, she was the first to speak again. "So, what are you going to do now?"

Vic explained that he called in personal days, and was covered at work. While he jumped through whatever legal hoops would be necessary to get Hobart's body released and shipped back to Charleston, Foss would check out the plane. If it was airworthy, he and Foss would fly to Charleston as soon as arrangements were made for Hobart.

"Allan!" she screeched. "You don't mean to tell me you'd set foot on that little arra-plane *again*!" She'd resurrected her drawl.

"Why not, Mom? I mean, my God, I'm up in it almost every weekend. It's completely safe. Safer than a car. Foss is a master pilot. The thing with the geese was a fluke. The odds of anything happening again are astronomical."

"Odds," she echoed. "My, my. You really have become a gambler, Allan. I can't tell you how disappointed I am."

At that moment, another loss hit home. The realization was more damaging than the word "disappointed," his mother's equivalent of a .357 hollow point slug. Vic's voice iced over. "It isn't gambling, Mom. It's playing a game of skill for money. There's a difference between those two. But, it doesn't really matter anymore, because I think I can safely say those days are pretty much over."

Vic promised her he'd keep her up on what was happening, and after he hung up he walked back over to the window and sipped his drink. The conversation with his mother changed nothing. Alone. His world was so small, if a few of the players were removed, he was nearly the only one left. Alone. Alone and unbearably lonely.

It was no longer raining and the view was clear. The puddles in the wet parking lot reflected the lights of the surrounding buildings. Vic imagined the scene must have been very similar to the way the reflections looked from the window of a house on the Maumee River. He imagined himself standing at a window in a river house, watching the reflections on the water below. Standing by himself. Alone.

~ ※ ~

The coroner, after conferring with the emergency physicians who attended Hobart, and with Hobart's attorney when Merle West proffered the lawyer's name, ruled an autopsy would not be required. Hobart's age and physical condition were evidence enough as to why he was in cardiac arrest when the medics arrived at the scene of the aborted take-off. The attorney assured the examiner there would be no legal issues.

Vic connected with the lawyer over the phone, later that evening. "Can you get Hobie's body released to be sent back to Charleston?"

"I could, but you can do it yourself, Mr. Vickery. When Hobart came in to get the syndicate business squared away after he bought out Mr. Shymer and Mr. VanVorhis, he conferred you with power of attorney on his behalf." The lawyer chuckled quietly. "He was pretty forward thinking and matter of fact. He told me he spent more time with you than with anyone else. I guess he kind of figured something like this could happen, and he wanted you to be able to handle his affairs."

"So I can handle the funeral arrangements, too?"

"I think Hobart would have wanted that. Let me know if I can assist in any way."

~ * ~

As Vic reflected on Hobart Early, his most prominent quality was he was a man of simple tastes and simple pleasures. Although Hobart could easily have afforded rich complication, the kind many who have a lot of money indulge themselves with, Hobart delighted in things like a good plate of bacon and eggs, the seven-year old Buick he drove, or a comfortable pair of baggy, Dickie work pants. If he owned anything dressier than a bolo tie, Vic had never seen it. So, when he set about planning Hobart's funeral, simplicity was Vic's paramount goal.

Like Vic, Hobart wasn't a fan of organized religion, but according to Merle, Hobart was close friends with a pastor named Edward Thornwood. He came into Hobart's tool rental store years back, when there was only one location. Merle didn't remember what it was the pastor wanted to rent, but Hobart recently stocked it and wanted to familiarize himself with the tool so he could offer advice or precautions to future customers. He offered to help the pastor do the job and the two became fast friends. Over the years, they shared many rounds of golf, and even some dinners and drinks. Pastor Thornwood was the natural choice to officiate at Hobart's service. His simple little church sat atop an Appalachian foothill overlooking a holler with a mountain stream washing through it. The church was the perfect setting for the service because Vic had no idea how many mourners to expect. Rather than have a few folks spread thin, Vic favored the idea of a smaller church, and the pastor's whitewashed clapboard chapel comfortably seated only fifty. As it turned out, the extra twenty in attendance didn't mind standing behind the last row of pews.

Vic and Foss escorted Vic's mother to the front pew where they sat only feet from Hobart's coffin, in front of the pulpit. The lid was closed, in accordance with wishes Hobart expressed in a brief note his attorney gave Vic. Hobart wrote it years ago and it was originally addressed to his wife and daughter. But the "Dearest Clara and Autumn" had a line through it and Vic's name was penned in next to theirs, in Hobart's hand. "You know Hobart," the attorney said when Vic expressed his surprise. "I offered to have my secretary type up a new one for him to sign when he was in the office to assign you power of attorney, but he said, 'Why waste a good sheet of paper. This'un says it fine.'" The note went on to request no visitation or public viewing, and only a short funeral service for relatives and friends.

As the opening hymn concluded, Vic's mother leaned close. "Tissues in my purse," she whispered, while dabbing at her own tears. "I'll leave it open." Then she handed a tissue to Foss, who was seated on her other side, next to Merle.

The minister stepped into the pulpit as the music faded away. He broke into the gentle, peaceful smile all clergy seem to have mastered for such occasions. "What do you say about a man like Hobart Early?" he began, slowly shaking his head. "Some lives are too immense for the vocabulary we have to use."

The pastor started with the way he met Hobart, and since Vic already knew the story, his mind went its own way. He didn't resist, letting it wander amongst the many landmarks Hobart created in Vic's memory. He remembered little things. Hobart's big, homely grin, showcasing teeth with divergent ideas on alignment. The way he brayed, made worse by one of his few conceits, trying to rein it in. Hobart always asked Vic how he felt: if he was happy, hungry, or nervous. One of the qualities that set Hobart apart from most people was when he asked a question, he was in it for the answer. He cared. His attention was one hundred percent on the person he spoke with. When Vic was locked in conversation with Hobart, he felt as though he was the only other person in existence. Weak as Vic felt his efforts at Alexis had become, he did concentrate on emulating Hobart's level of engagement when Vic talked with his students.

Vic noticed his mother's sobbing, and that brought him out of his thoughts. He put his arm around her, and fished a tissue out of her purse for himself. He'd maintained dry eyes to that point, but the pastor sounded like he was nearing the end of his speech, and Vic wanted to be ready in case he caved.

"The last thing I'll tell you about Hobart is a story I think you'll all enjoy," the minister said.

"Hobe and I were playing up at Possum Run, a course near here we both favored. I missed an easy putt that would have won me the round, something I was rarely able to do. I've prayed long and hard for a good golf swing," he said, speaking with the back of his hand poised at the side of his mouth as though he offered privileged information. "But powerful as it is, prayer apparently has its limitations." He paused to let his listener's chuckle, which they did. "Anyway, I thoughtlessly took the Lord's name in vain when the ball lipped the cup. Hobart shrugged and said, 'Ed, once you think it, the sin's committed. You might as well go ahead and get it out of you.' Then he smiled and said, 'And don't worry none. This'll stay between you, me, and your God.'" Although Vic began to tear, the church filled with the murmur of soft laughter. The melody of *The Tennessee Waltz,* Hobart's favorite tune, began then. Vic never heard it played in a church before, and the organ's lilting vibrato added an element of emotion that left him weeping openly by its finish.

Pastor Thornwood rode in the limousine with Vic, his mother, Foss, and Merle. A tail of thirty or forty cars wagged behind them on the twisty road to the cemetery. Vic studied the minister, who faced them, but looked out at the sunlit countryside. Vic liked this pastor. He knew very little about him, but everything he knew made Vic believe, minister or not, the man was someone he'd easily call a friend. Besides, he was a friend of Hobart's, and that spoke volumes, as far as Vic was concerned. The pastor happened to glance and saw Vic looking at him. "Is there anything I can do or say, Allan?" the minister asked.

"Yes, sir. One of each." Pastor Thornwood raised his bushy eyebrows and it occurred to Vic the minister resembled Abraham Lincoln, but with silver-white hair, and without the beard.

"What you can say is to call me Vic. That's the name my friends use. And what you can do is play a round of golf with me at Possum Run, the next time I'm down this way to see Mom."

The minister chuckled. "Will you give me strokes, Vic? And, will you call me Ed?"

"I'll give you a stroke a hole," Vic said. "And I'll call you Ed, but not today. I need you to be Pastor Thornwood today. Is that all right?" The minister smiled. "And can I ask you a question?" The pastor nodded. "Do you believe that you, Hobie, and I will ever play a round of golf together?"

Vic's mother cut in, shaking her head in mock disgust. "He's not as religious as I'd like. He doesn't go to church."

The pastor reached to pat her hand. "I know of people who go to church every week, but aren't very spiritual. I don't know your son all that well, Mrs. Vickery, but he impresses me as the spiritual type." He looked at Vic. "As to your question, I'm not positive we'll play golf, but I believe we'll see Hobe again. And if there aren't golf courses, how could it be Heaven?" Everyone laughed, and when that passed, Pastor Thornwood asked, "And what about you, Vic? Do you think we'll all meet again?"

Vic winked. "If you asked me a year ago and I said yes, I'd have been fibbing. But I had a pretty life-altering experience not long ago, and now the answer is absolutely. I know we will."

The pastor smiled. "And if we can play golf with Hobe, will you give me strokes then, too?"

The limousine lurched to a stop. They were at the cemetery. Vic turned toward the minister. "If it's Heaven, Pastor, you won't need strokes from me."

The little cemetery where the short, graveside service took place was like something out of a Norman Rockwell painting. A white picket fence did its best to stay erect in the rocky soil, and trees with bare limbs and branches that appeared to be bowed sympathetically stood stark against the sunny, late afternoon sky. Regardless, the air was chilly, and Vic stood upwind of his mother, trying to shield her from the breeze. When Pastor Thornwood concluded his brief graveside remarks, four men lowered Hobart's coffin into the grave on silky-looking ropes. Then, another man stepped forward and tossed a shovel-full of dirt onto the coffin. Vic was caught by surprise. He'd seen that done in movies, but never witnessed it in person. One after the other, a number of the gathered stepped forward to contribute a shovel's-worth. It appeared to be voluntary. Vic made eye contact with his mother, pinched out a sad smile, then stepped carefully around the open grave. He sunk the spade into the mound of dirt, and tossed the soil in on the coffin. The dirt scattered across the pinewood's grain, small pebbles colliding like marbles. He burned that image, and the dull thud of earth against wood, into his mind, so he would never forget either of them.

Painful as it was to see Hobart buried, Vic was glad he was there to watch, and even to participate. Since the graveside service was cancelled because of the weather, Vic never saw The Old Man's open grave. He'd been buried in a steel coffin, which was enclosed in a cement vault, and Vic had fashioned a vague mental image he could pull up on his Halloween sojourns to the cemetery. Though he was certain he would make it back to this little burial ground, taking away a clear image of Hobart's plain wooden coffin snuggled into its blanket of orange-brown West Virginia soil comforted Vic in a way he wasn't certain he understood. As he and Foss guided his mother to the waiting car, Vic was thankful for the consolation.

~ * ~

Foss taxied the Comanche onto the tarmac at Hawk Air and shut down the engines. The silence the stilled engines created always caught Vic by surprise. He eased against the headrest and closed his eyes.

"Safe and sound, son." Foss chuckled.

"Aw, Foss. You know it isn't that. I'm wasted. Hey, you want some coffee before you head back?"

Foss checked his watch. "You buying?"

"Bet your ass."

The fueler walked toward them as they off-loaded Vic's luggage. "Tanks are good," Foss called to the kid in baggy coveralls. "I'm going in for a coffee. I'll have it out of here in fifteen minutes." The skinny boy waved and turned back toward the hanger.

The Hawk Air office was quiet. Vic saw no sign of Treese. The carafe on the burner was half full with coffee that Vic figured was hours old.

"Here you go, coffee-flavored pudding," Vic said, filling the pilot's cup.

Foss blew across its surface and sipped. "Could take the enamel off of your teeth."

"Hobie would have loved it. You couldn't make it too strong for him." The memory caused both of them to match sorrowful expressions.

"You did a great job of putting the funeral together," Foss said.

"You all helped. Turned out to be quite a deal, didn't it? I didn't know what to expect. I was afraid it might be you, me, Merle, and my mother, but old Hobe had quite a turnout."

"He didn't have any family to speak of, but he had plenty of friends. It says a lot about a businessman when even his competitors show up at his funeral." He sipped again. "It was nice to meet your mother. Hobie always spoke so highly of her."

Vic felt a stab of sadness. "Hobie was pretty well smitten, but Ma's kind of funny about men. After her divorce from The Old Man, she always kept them at a distance."

"Oh, I understand. After my Barbara died back in '77... " Foss shook his head. "I'm not lookin' for anything permanent. In fact, I guess you could say I've been kind of like a kid in a candy store ever since." His eyes twinkled.

"Christ, you sly old dog. No joke?"

Foss cocked an eyebrow. "What the hell do you think I do on those weekend layovers? I never smoked or drank, but women—now there's a fine weakness. You'd be amazed how many gals think a pilot is, oh, I don't know what you call it."

"Dashing?"

"Yeah. Maybe that's it. I mean, I can walk into a club, order tonic water, and most always find someone to dance with, have fun. Spend some time." He winked.

"Jesus, Foss. With all that stuff out there, the new immune disease and all, you better be careful."

The pilot throttled up his smile. "Vic, I'm pushing seventy. At this point, no matter what I die of, it'll be old age." He swallowed down his coffee and gripped Vic's shoulder. "Thanks for the joe, my friend. I have to get airborne."

"I'll walk out with you. I'm glad we had the chance to shoot the shit. Like with Hobe, I never got to know you as well as I'd have liked. We have lots of air-time together, but we never really talked about anything important." They were nearing the plane. "With him gone, well, this is it. And only *now* I find out you're a damned lady-killer."

"You'll be down Charleston-way to see your mother. Christ, give me a call. We'll have dinner."

"Dinner? *Bull*shit. We'll go to a club, order tonic waters, and I'll study your technique. Now that I'm young, single and free, I need to learn some of your moves."

"Then you can use 'em to land the little gal that runs this outfit. That'd be *my* first move," Foss said, taking Vic's hand. The handshake became a clumsy men's embrace. "You take care, boy."

Vic watched him climb into the plane. The starters made their strange whistling screech and, one after the other, the engines came to life amidst a fog of exhaust. Foss gave Vic an upright thumb and rolled out onto the taxiway.

In the waning minutes of Saturday's cold March sunlight, Vic elected to watch as Foss, half a mile down the runway, awaited clearance to take off. Minutes passed. Vic stuffed his hands in his pockets, determined to endure the chill for as long as he had to. At last, he heard the Comanche's engines rev. The plane hurtled down the runway and lifted off, directly across from where Vic stood. Foss tipped the wings as soon as he cleared the ground. Vic's wave ended in a swipe of his sleeve across his eyes.

~ * ~

On the drive to the apartment, a loneliness as strong as body-ache enveloped him. Angie and the Bittersweet house were gone. So was Roxanne. Hobart was dead and Foss was on his way back to Charleston. The camaraderie and excitement surrounding syndicate golf was gone as well. Kindling a relationship with Treese, as Foss mentioned, was an exciting possibility, but even that idea didn't do much to fill the hollow Vic felt in his soul. So much of what Vic became perished with Hobart and was buried in the rocky loam of a cemetery on a hillside above Charleston.

As he drove, he evaluated his situation. He still had his job. Even though he hadn't been much of a teacher lately, he knew he could resurrect the former Mr. Vickery. *At least teaching is an honorable way to make a living,* he thought. Playing the syndicates wasn't even honorable golf, a fact that chewed at his dying conscience like a flock of buzzards. And, between his winnings and the money he received from the sale of the Bittersweet house, he had over twenty thousand salted away; enough for a down payment on a house in a quiet Toledo neighborhood. He once dreamed of looking down upon such a place from the picture window of a river house, but no longer.

Finally, he still had his game. He couldn't wait to play real golf with his friends again, in games where he pulled for them to make good shots, even if it wound up costing him a beer in the clubhouse. And no more psyching out opponents, he vowed, wagging his head. Still, he found himself mourning the loss of his dreams. A river house and a fast boat. Thousands in syndicate money, won on courses all over the nation. He fell back into his regular routine—slithering like a lizard in the muck and mire of his misery. By the time he reached his apartment, he was very much at home in the primordial ooze. He smiled when he remembered Hobart's advice not to fight it.

Muldoon came running and leaped into Vic's arms when he opened the door. Vic always left plenty of extra food and water for just such an emergency, but Muldoon had been alone for eight days. Vic dropped onto the floor, petting and nuzzling him.

"I'm sorry, Mully. You don't have to worry, my playing days are over. Won't be leaving you anymore. Promise."

After petting and playing with Muldoon, Vic went through his mail, poured some Southern Comfort and set about unpacking. He came across a golf ball and rolled it in his fingers. "Raven's Roost," it said, below a medieval-looking coat of arms on which a large black bird was perched. Muldoon jumped onto the bed and sat next to the suitcase. Vic raised his glass. "'Quoth the raven, nevermore.'" He drank it down. "Written by Edgar Allan Poe, Mully, another guy who drank too much."

Vic put the glass on the dresser, tossed the ball in the air, and caught it. "Nevermore," he repeated, walking to the display rack on the living room wall. He picked up the marker and penned an inscription onto the ball.

Ray Prosser
3-7-82
LOST IT ALL

After blowing the ink dry, Vic placed the ball on the rack. There were seven balls: one from Cherry Hill where he'd beaten Blackstock, five from the syndicate matches, and the one Tom Bayer hit him with. Seven golf balls on a rack designed to hold two dozen. I better look for a smaller rack, he decided.

After a hot shower, he was sitting down with another drink when the phone rang. He had no idea who was calling.

"Hello, Allan. Wanted to see if you made it home safely."

"Yeah, Mom. No problems. I just finished unpacking." His tongue suddenly felt like it was thickening by the minute, and he concentrated hard so he wouldn't slur any words. "But, yeah, Mom. I'm good. You?"

"Yes. I believe I am. I've been thinking a lot about Hobart. He was such a wonderful man. Treated me like a queen. I have to say I didn't appreciate him as much as I should have. I really miss him." She paused. "But I also have to say I'm still angry about him getting you involved in gambling."

"Mom, for God's sake. I'm thirty-three years old. Don't blame Hobie for the things I chose to do. He never twisted my arm." He held his breath, hoping she didn't notice his slip.

"Are you drinking? If you are, hope you aren't going out anymore tonight." Her voice dropped into its reproving range. "Like your grandpa always said, alcohol is a liquid, but it isn't a solution."

"Maybe not," Vic said, looking at the rack of golf balls on the wall, "but I think I know where there's a liquid that might be."

~ * ~

It was getting on toward midnight. As Vic carefully guided his car along River Road, he slowed a bit to look at the river houses, their windows aglow with rich, warm yellow light. He was once so certain he would own one, but now he found himself feeling curiously detached from the idea. He couldn't even muster a lot of envy for those who did.

Next to a house north of Toledo Country Club, there was a stone road leading down a hill to a public boat launch. Vic turned onto it, his tires grumbling against the gravel all the way down the hill. He stopped, leaving the car nosed toward the river where there was a narrow strip of grass, between a parking area and the shoreline, and cut the raspy engine. He left his high beams on when he clambered out. His earlier liquor-flush had ebbed. When his capillaries lost their dilation, they forced his blood deeper into his limbs and the chill of the air hit him hard. He walked in front of the car, carrying a small bag of golf balls and his five iron.

Upending the bag, he dropped the seven golf balls on the grass. "Wish you could watch this, Hobe." Vic gazed into the moonless sky and chuckled. "And you, too, Bass. No more money games. No more gamesmanship. I guar-an-damn-tee it."

Using the head of his five iron, Vic guided one of the balls into position. He peered at it through the horizontal glare of the high beams. Bo McJunkins' name faced up. "I'm really damned sorry about what I did to you, boy," Vic whispered. "And I hope Reefer can forgive me." He set up and fired the ball out over the river. The headlights illuminated its proud splash.

Vic pulled Elwin's ball out of the cluster and giggled like a teenage prankster. "I should take my time hitting this shot, you blimpy-assed bastard, but I'm really not interested in any slow play tonight." Another swing launched Elwin's ball into the muddy waters.

Jonas Brown's ball was the next. "The only reason I beat you was because it was cold that day in Georgia, Jonas. Guess it's only fitting I'm freezing my ass off at this very minute." Vic hit the ball well.

As Jonas' ball made its barely audible sploosh, Vic pulled another into its place. "Sam Blackstock. I'm gonna blast this shot like a fucking dynamite charge, you son-of-a-bitch." He cackled. Taking a violent cut, Vic caught the ball sweet, sending it into the river with the others.

With three balls left, the next one he dragged over was Ray Prosser's. "Nah!" Vic said, knocking it away. "I played you last, so I'm saving you. Wingo, you crazed little shithead, you're next." The ball cleared the weeds at the river's edge and swept out across the choppy waters.

"Okay, Ray, now it's your turn. I couldn't beat you, but I sure as shit can sink you now." Vic caught the ball a little heavy and it rocketed up into the darkness, reappearing in the headlight beams before ripping the river's swirling surface.

Vic pulled the final ball into position, the one with Tom Bayer's name on it. This ball started him on his journey. This little Top Flite ball set him off on a tour through the southland to play money matches with Hobart and Foss, but the trek was about so much more than golf. True, when the ball slammed into his head, it dropped him into a coma where he met Bascolm and gained more skill at a game he loved than he ever dreamed he could possess. But after he emerged from the coma, he ran headlong into an affair with Roxanne, and out of his marriage to Angie.

Ultimately, Vic connected with Reefer and later journeyed to Mercywood, where he found Bascolm's vegetative body. Those two events kindled a belief that the boundaries of existence don't end where he once believed they did. Still, he couldn't help but consider how little good the last six months had done him, or how little good he was able to do with what he learned along the way. He managed to make a lot of money, but traded his feeling of self-worth in an attempt to get rich. Additionally, much of his original misery was rooted in the loneliness he felt when he was married to Angie. Now, many months and miles later, he stood alone on the bank of the Maumee River at midnight, still lonely. He wondered if hitting Tom Bayer's Top Flite into the river might drown his game along with the ball that set him off on his long magical journey. "At this point, how much could it matter?" he whispered.

As he set up to hit Tom Bayer's Top Flite into the Maumee, he heard the sound of tires on the gravel drive. He swiveled, and before its spotlight came on and bathed him in its radiant yellow candlepower, Vic saw a Toledo Police patrol car bumping down the hill. It groaned to a stop and the driver's door swung open.

The officer who emerged from the big Ford moved like a young man. He was a big guy with former lineman written all over him. Vic couldn't see much else with the wall of light blasting from the patrol car's spotlight, not to mention the beams of his own headlights.

"Evening, mister. What's going on here?" the policeman asked.

"Drowning my sorrows, officer." Vic turned back to set up for his shot.

"So you've been drinking?"

The officer's tone of voice hinted he was amused, but he was still merely a silhouette when Vic glanced at him to confirm his suspicion. "Oh, I had a few earlier, but I decided this was a better way to drown my sorrows." He pointed to Tom Bayer's ball. "This ball is the last one. You play any golf yourself?"

The patrolman shook his head. "I used to. I got a wife and a young boy. They take up most of my time."

Vic nodded his understanding. "This is what we call a 'difficult lie.' See the way the ball's trapped down in the grass? I've been getting a lot of these lately. But there's an old saying in golf. You only get the lie you give yourself." Vic used the head of his club to pull the ball up onto a hillock of matted turf. "I don't usually roll 'em like this, but there's no money on it tonight."

The policeman stepped toward Vic. "This is public access, so I guess it's okay if you hit golf balls here, but I need to check your license and registration before I go."

"No problem." Vic slid his wallet out of his pocket. "The address isn't correct on this, by the way." He handed the officer his license. "I used to live on Bittersweet, but now I'm up in Maumee. Haven't changed it because my birthday's in a couple months. Figured I'd do it then." He started for the car. "My registration's in the glove—"

"Wait a minute," the officer nearly shouted, peering at Vic through the strong contrast of the darkness and the light beams. Vic froze in place. "I thought you looked familiar, Mr. Vickery. Don't you remember me?" The policeman grasped Vic's hand. "Jim Casper." His smile was wall to wall. "Everybody called me Ghost. They still do." He dropped Vic's hand, lifted his patrolman's hat, and ran his palm across his brush-cut. "I had more hair back then, but no mustache."

"My God, I can't believe it. Jim Casper. You and, let me think, Morgan Loxley. Yeah, the two of you joined the Army."

428

"After we got kicked out of Alexis." The young cop lowered his head, but was unable to conceal a smirk. "Morg and I, we thought we were bad-asses. Mr. Vickery."

"Vic, Jim. You're out of school now, and that's what everybody calls me."

"Okay, Vic, as long as you call me Ghost." He almost palpably made the transition from former student to cop, as he spoke. Vic looked more closely and noticed he had the "cop eyes" Vic saw all too often on the off-duty officers patrolling the halls at Alexis. Eyes that saw too much in too few years. "Yeah, the Army straightened me and Morg around good. Hey, jump in my car. It's freezing out here."

The two of them climbed into the car. The passenger-side seat was cramped with radio equipment, and Vic bumped his knee on the shotgun which was clamped vertically to the dashboard, muzzle to the roof.

Jim Casper chuckled. "Sorry. Most always keep my passengers back there." He pointed through the steel mesh screen behind the seats with his thumb.

"Not a problem. And how's Morgan doing? Last time I saw him was right after you two finished boot camp. Four years ago?"

"More like six. We got booted out of Alexis in '76 and joined the Army later that year. But I had to recycle on my hell week because my appendix ruptured."

Vic grinned. "That's right. I remember now."

"Yep, Morg made it through and was starting his leave. He stopped at the hospital to see me before he left Fort Dix, and I told him, 'You get back to T-town, you stop around and tell Mr. Vickery you made it, and I'm going to."

Vic remembered how it touched him that two guys who were bully-tough in school cared enough to want him to know they changed their ways. He had to blink against excess moisture in his eyes, but found a convenient excuse. "Damn, after coming out of the cold, my damned nose is running." He wiped at his eyes with his sleeve.

The policeman turned the heat down. "In plain terms, we gave you a lot of shit, but less than we gave our other teachers. You were a good guy. I still remember the day you sat down and showed me how to draw a picture of my old Chevy."

"Your Nova. Man, that thing was a beast."

"Yeah. Wish I still had it." He paused. "So really, Vic. What's going on here?" He held up his finger, then picked up the handset for the radio. "Dispatch, this is unit two-five-six. Show me ten-seven at," looking at his watch, "twenty three-forty hours." He dropped the mic on his lap. "Break time. So, anyway, practicing golf in the middle of the night? What's the deal?"

Vic scuttled around in his mind, trying to decide what and how much to tell his former student. He began talking before he was completely certain where he was going with the story. "I started playing golf for money, here, about six months ago." Vic paused. "Big money."

"No shit? You talked about playing golf in class, but I never knew you were any good."

There was no way he was going to try to explain the whole coma experience in a few minutes, so he decided to leave that part alone. "I wasn't. Not until last fall. I ran across a great coach, and I worked really hard at it. Thing is, I was so caught up in golf and the money, I lost control of the things in my life that really mattered. Personal relationships. My career."

Jim Casper clicked his tongue. "Tell me about it. My wife and I are in counseling now. Cop life and marriage don't fit all that well."

"Things'll be okay? Did you marry a gal from Alexis?"

"Nope, Sonia went to Central Catholic. You wouldn't know her. But yeah, I think we're getting it together." He motioned toward the last remaining ball. "And so why are you hitting balls into the river? I don't get the connection."

"The balls I hit into the river were trophy balls; balls I bought to remember my victories." He gestured toward Tom Bayer's ball. "That's the one that started the whole thing."

"Purging," Ghost said. "That's what the counselor told me I have to do when I go off-shift. Get rid of the stuff that builds up on-duty before I get home. Maybe I should knock some street punks into the river." He laughed, his face tightly wrinkled with smile lines. "It'd be easier than purging emotions." He looked at his watch. "Ah, shit. I better get back in service. They like to keep us hopping." He shook Vic's hand. "Damn, great to see you. It's pretty rare I get to show off my cop skills to anyone I know."

"Yeah, well, I'm glad you didn't have to cuff me up for a DWI or something. Talk about embarrassing."

"You weren't driving your car. Most it could have been was physical control, and since you weren't even sitting in it ... " His grin faded, and he turned solemn. "Besides, I'd have given you a pass. Driven you close enough to your place that you could walk the rest of the way. You sure cut me enough breaks." He clapped Vic on the shoulder. "Keep your day job. You're good at it. Play golf on the side."

"And you go home and give your wife a big kiss," Vic said.

"That I'll do." the young policeman glanced at his watch. "In about six hours."

After their goodbyes, Vic slid out, closed the door and watched the policeman drive away. He leaned against his car, splitting his attention between the choppy waters of the river and the Top Flite lying on the matted grass bordering the parking lot. He remembered Cass Elliot believed the copper pipe that hit her in the head was magical. Was his Top Flite magical, too? The fact he was even contemplating the possibility made him wonder. *A thirty-three year old teacher standing by the river at midnight, with his magic ball,* Vic thought. Still, much of what occurred in the past six months was unexplainable, if not magical, and it was all set in motion by that ball. There was no rational accounting for what Vic experienced, without some form of other-worldliness factored in.

So, the question became not whether the ball held some mystical power, but whether or not Vic wanted to risk keeping it. Was he strong enough to turn down big money games in the future? What if Merle West called and said he wanted Vic to continue playing the syndicates? He doubted that would happen. Merle was never interested in syndicate golf. But if West did call, would Vic be able to limit himself to playing area amateur tournaments and beer-a-hole golf with his friends?

He recalled a man he'd taught with a few years back. Ted Bronner stopped smoking, but regardless, he was never without a cigarette. He even had one hanging from his rear view mirror, in a glass tube stenciled with the inscription, "Break in an Emergency." Vic once asked him why he always carried a pack of smokes, sometimes even walking around with an unlit cigarette in his lips. "Because you can't say you've beaten an addiction until you can dance with its temptation," was Bronner's answer, gesturing with the unlit smoke. Vic remembered how much he liked the way Bronner phrased his reply, and how much he admired the man's willpower.

Vic walked over, scooped the ball skyward with his five iron, and snatched it out of the cold March air. Then he got into the Mazda with his club and the ball, turned up the heat and drove home.

~ * ~

March seemed to pick up speed as it warmed into April, and Vic concentrated on getting his life back into a semblance of the order he was used to. He began looking at houses with a matronly real estate woman who proved to have a wit as sharp as her acumen in real estate. She called him anytime she saw something she thought might come close to the parameters he'd given her. So far, nothing had really clicked, but he looked forward to the afternoons he spent exploring bungalows in middleclass Toledo neighborhoods with her.

As far as women were concerned, Vic kept himself on hold. Still wounded by the revelation Angie set up housekeeping with Nathan and Roxanne chose to do the same with her husband, he decided to make certain he was at home with himself before he went looking for anyone else to try to get comfortable with. No more grabbing for another woman, simultaneous to leaving the last one. Or being left, in his case. Still, he thought of Treese often, and was determined to call her, but not until he was completely settled in his own personal life.

And of course, much of his personal life revolved around his work. Vic labored diligently at reclaiming his position as a solid teacher, and he enjoyed the effort. He couldn't tell if many of his students noticed the difference, but regardless, he did. Every so often, a student acknowledged Vic's new attitude and the smooth-running classes that resulted, but he learned to make certain his sense of worth as a teacher came from within, not from without.

He retrieved his easel and painting equipment from the storage locker. It was a scary moment when he first sat down in front of a clean, freshly-stretched canvas. He hadn't painted in weeks, and he worried he'd become rusty or, worst case, might have lost his moves completely. When he put them away, the brushes felt as familiar as pens or pencils in his hand. How would weeks of not holding one register? He used to joke with his students saying they shouldn't spend too much time staring at a pristine white canvas, or they might go snow blind. After too many minutes of doing that exact thing, Vic grabbed a stick of charcoal, and hit the surface with a smudge of black. That smudge eventually became a shadow under the eaves of a large Victorian building. Vic blocked in the pines around the structure before it occurred to him the building bore a strong resemblance to Mercywood. There were paintings he did because he wanted to see particular colors together, and paintings he did because he thought they would offer a challenge. When he realized this one came straight out of his subconscious, and represented a place that had a huge impact on his framework of beliefs, he was certain it would be one of his best, and couldn't wait to get home from school each day to work on it.

The teacher's golf league began in mid-April, and Vic discovered his game was as strong as ever. He found special pleasure in playing honest golf, and was amused when his friends cheated, as most hackers do. Guys kicked balls from behind trees, took illegal drops or "forgot" a stroke here and there. Vic would chuckle and shake his head, but he still won more beer than he wanted and was careful never to take liberties with the rules himself. He drew a first-year teacher as a partner, and by any standard, the guy was a lousy player. Vic enjoyed showing him the things Bascolm taught him, and the young man began to show promise.

One thing was certain, Vic no longer envied the PGA Tour players. He'd experienced the pressures they faced on a daily basis and knew a lush, green, rolling golf course made an excellent playground, but a horrible place of business. As much as Vic enjoyed being a legitimate player, it felt even better to play without pressure. If he hit a bad shot, or even had a bad round, he let it go. Golf was fun again.

An irony that wasn't lost on him was making golf his profession stole the fun from the game, but doing the same with teaching made it only more rewarding. One afternoon, after the final bell of the day rang, and his jubilant students evacuated to their personal lives, a girl named Sylvia Stoner came into his room. Sylvia wasn't in any of his classes spring semester, but she'd taken photography the preceding fall. Sylvia was a tall, heavy girl with a pretty face, who seemed to be involved in every activity she could find. Teens definitely show a cruel streak in regards to any deviation, physical or behavioral, from the standards set by the rock stars and actors high school kids adopt as their heroes. One way to avoid the nastiness is to become a diligent worker, a go-getter and a bubbly friend-to-all. Sylvia wisely chose that tack.

"Hey, Sylvy," Vic said. "Haven't seen you in a bit of a while. How's your semester going?"

"Oh, fine, Mr. Vickery, but I really miss photography." She approached his desk the way students did when they were going to ask to go to the restroom or request an extension on a deadline. After eleven years of teaching, it was easy for him to spot a student who was about to ask a favor.

"I miss having you in class, too." He pushed his chair away from his desk and folded his hands across his lap. "What can I do for you today?"

"I'm in charge of the prom this year, Mr. Vickery. I was hoping you'd help out with the decorations. You know, give us some ideas. Help us put it all together

"When is it?"

"Third weekend in May. I just got the job, and I wanted to give you as much advance notice as I could. Do you think you could help us design the decorations?"

Vic gave her a serious look, then brushed it away with a smile. "Yeah, I think I might be available. You have a committee?"

Her delivery was thick with enthusiasm. "Oh, yes. We have lots of kids to do the work. We only need to know what to do."

The thought crossed Vic's mind that Sylvia would put endless hours into the prom, and most likely would not get invited. He understood what she faced as the large girl in a world of guys looking for a local Bo Derek. "I'd be honored to help out," he said. "What's the theme this year?"

"Open Arms." Sylvia apparently felt comfortable enough to sit on the corner of a table in front of Vic's desk. "You know, from that Journey song."

"Very romantic. I saw that video this morning on MTV while I was getting ready for school. I think it's a great choice. Why don't you stop by after school tomorrow with your committee? We'll do a little brainstorming."

Sylvia beamed. "That's great, Mr. Vickery. Thank you so much." She turned and started for the door, but stopped and slapped her forehead Detective Colombo-style, dramatically indicating she'd forgotten something. "Oh, and would you like to be a chaperone? We need some of those, too."

"I could probably schedule that in. It would be a pleasure."

"Joanne Parker and I decided to go together."

Vic tried to mute his surprise. Joanne was a girl with an attractive face and figure, but her skin was masked with a terrible acne problem. The pebbly rash-like patches on her face were probably the reason she assumed she wouldn't be asked to prom by a boy.

"That's really neat," Vic said.

435

"Yeah. I think so, too. I'm sure we'll get razzed about being gay, but we know the truth, and that's all that matters. We decided the only way we'd get to our prom is if we went with each other, and we didn't want to miss it." She laughed. "Oh, and you'll never guess. We decided to rent tuxes. Heck of a lot cheaper than prom dresses, let me tell ya."

"That's very cool." He meant it. He recalled Treese mentioned she wasn't asked to her prom, and he was happy Sylvia and Joanne figured out a way to at least be there and enjoy the fruits of their labors. "The two of you will look terrific." He liked her style, he decided. A no-nonsense answer to a problem many wouldn't attempt to overcome. "So, bring the gang around tomorrow and we'll get started with the plans."

Sylvia waved and started for the door, but she stopped and turned again. "You watch MTV?"

Vic scoffed. "Probably too much. I kind of use it like radio when I'm at home."

Sylvia nodded, as if she decided that was okay. She waved and was on her way.

~ * ~

George Flanner, the woodshop teacher, stopped Vic in the parking lot.

"It's Duffy's birthday tomorrow," Flanner said. "I found a calendar with fat lady pin-up girls. I don't think one of them weighs under three hundred pounds. It's from, like, 1967, but he won't notice. He'll never take his eyes off the women."

"Good work," Vic said. "Want me to pick up a cake?"

"Nah, we don't want him to get the idea we like him *too* much. Maybe some donuts. I told some of the other guys, and they'll be stopping in his office tomorrow morning for coffee and the calendar presentation. A dozen donuts should be plenty."

Pixler's was the best bakery Vic knew of, but it was close to his former neighborhood. He'd purposely avoided the area around Bittersweet.

436

It was like favoring a bruise; it didn't hurt if it wasn't touched or thought about. But one of Pixler's selling points was they sealed the boxes in shrink-wrap. Donuts picked up the day before stayed fresh, which saved having to leave early to make a stop in the morning.

Once the donuts were stowed behind the seats, Vic decided to take Glendale the few blocks to River Road and turn south toward Maumee, where his apartment was. This route would take him past Bittersweet. *Dance with the devil,* he thought to himself as he turned onto River Road. This was more like a flirt with the devil, not a waltz. But it was a long time since he drove along the river, and he was interested to see if either of the river houses he'd hoped to own was still on the market. Now that he was out of the syndicate golf, there was no way he could afford a hundred-thousand dollar-plus home, but his idle curiosity begged to be fed. Besides, he wanted to test the effect driving past the street where he once lived with Angie, and began his affair with Roxanne, would have. Both women were long-gone, and he wanted to check to see if the wounds were healed

River Road made for a beautiful drive. Even in early spring, with many trees still appearing to be merely surrounded in wispy green smoke rather than full foliage, the tunnel-effect of the trees bridging the smooth asphalt roadway began. And sure enough, both of the houses Vic liked were still available. The larger of the two was an English Tudor manse, set far off the road with many old-growth oaks standing like scattered Corinthian columns. There was a banner across the realtor's sign proclaiming the price was reduced. "But probably not a hundred-grand," Vic said aloud as he drove by.

He passed the country club and rounded the gentle "S" curve leading to where Bittersweet cut off to the right, still a quarter of a mile distant. He girded himself for the drive-by when he noticed a couple strolling on the sidewalk. Strangely, he didn't realize who they were until he saw the dog tugging along on the leash the woman held. It was Mofus. Roxanne's other arm was wrapped around Tom's waist, and her head rested against his shoulder, tilted as though she was talking to him. Tom's arm crossed her back, his hand palming her hip.

Vic began to panic. Why had he come this way? The last thing he wanted was for her to see him. Even if he turned his head or ducked, she could still recognize the car. At least they're not walking toward me, he thought. Suddenly, as he was about to overtake them, a large Rottweiler charged out from a nearby house. Tom scooped Mofus into his arms, and both he and Roxanne turned to face the Rotty, which began to circle them, opposite the direction Vic was headed. As he passed them, their backs remained toward him, their full attention on the encroaching dog. In his rear view mirror, Vic could see the Rotty in retreat, and by the time they turned to continue their walk, Vic and his Mazda were safely distant.

Vic settled in his seat and began to sort his feelings. The major one was relief. He was delighted neither Roxanne nor Tom saw him because it would have implied something he now knew wasn't true. Until the moment he saw Roxanne and Tom, Vic couldn't have honestly answered the question, did he want her back? The Rottweiler succeeded in allowing Vic fly-on-the-wall status, and seeing Roxanne and Tom together, apparently very happy, added to Vic's feeling of relief by supplying that answer. Happiness is all Vic wished for her. Of course, he always assumed she would find her true happiness with him. She made the decision to recommit to her husband, and Vic wasn't sure she'd made the correct choice. Seeing the two of them together, looking like lovers, told him she probably did.

And how did that make him feel? For the entire span of their relationship, Vic was never certain whether he really loved Roxanne, or merely loved their lust. He wanted it to be love. But is that what it was? He wasn't sure he'd ever know, but he did know he didn't love her now. His ego had to endure a huge hit when she chose Tom over him. Vic always believed he was better for her, and frankly, a better man than Tom Bayer. When she chose to go back to her husband, Vic was bruised, but it was more mental than emotional. At least, that's how it seemed in retrospect. Which was exactly the way he felt when Angie told him she was going to Colorado with Nathan. Vic had long since fallen out of love with Angie, but it still hurt when she took up with Nathan, especially when Vic suspected some kind of relationship with her boss may have affected their marriage, back when he did still love her.

Vic was still plumbing the depths of his psyche when he pulled into his parking space at the apartment. He realized he felt much the same in regard to Angie's happiness as he did with Roxanne's. He'd always wanted Angie to be happy. If she was happy with Nathan, then Vic was at peace with that. Truly at peace. He shut off the engine, sat in the silence and realized he was smiling. Two pivotal relationships with two wonderful women were over, and neither had gone the way he wished. But, he realized both had ended well. The women were on courses that made them happy, and his involvements with both Angie and Roxanne helped him to become the person he was now. A better person. That made him happy, as well.

Vic walked up the sidewalk. As he neared the apartment building, the door opened and Olivia stepped out, an unlit cigarette in her hand.

"Hi, Vic," she said, quickly swinging her arm behind her back, like a child caught stealing a cookie.

"Hey, Liv." Vic tilted to the side to see what she held. "I thought you told me you were giving those up." He made certain his tone conveyed the joke.

"I'll tell you, you've become my conscience now. Every time I light one of these, the little voice in my head saying I shouldn't sounds like yours." She punctuated that with her laughter, which always sounded to Vic like bubbles rolling to the surface of some thick liquid. He enjoyed the sound.

"Don't worry, you'll kick it." He opened the door. "Life's a process," he said, before stepping inside.

~ * ~

Later that evening, while Vic graded sketchbooks, the phone rang. He glanced at his watch. It was 7:30. He had absolutely no idea who would be calling. "Yeah," came the guttural voice on the other end of the line, "is this the Allan Vickery who plays golf?"

"Golf? Yeah, I play golf. Who is this?"

"Then you're Vic, right?" the deep voice asked.

"That's what my friends call me. So who's this?" he asked again, a bit of impatience staining his reply.

"Vic, this is Mink Marroan. You played Bo McJunkins, my syndicate player, at Pine Lakes."

Vic careened into his memory. Mink. The big guy. Towered over Bo. The surly man with the bad temper and worse reputation, all of which he seemed to enjoy promoting. The guy who arranged a hit on the kid who broke into his car. Vic wondered how that all played out, but there was no way he was going to ask.

"Yes, sir, I remember. How have you been? How's Bo?"

"I'm good, but tell you the truth, Bo ain't. He got into a little, ah, altercation in a bar a week or so back. Bo thought he was fightin' one asshole, turned out that guy had a couple friends wanted to influence the outcome, if you get my drift."

Vic thought of the way The Old Man was murdered, in the bar in Redlands, California, all those years ago. *Times change, but people don't,* he thought. "Sorry to hear that." He really was.

"So was Bo. The three of them busted him up pretty good. He wound up with a broken arm, among other things." There was a pause. "Anyway, the reason I'm calling is I'm looking for another player."

"To fill in while Bo's laid up?" Vic asked.

"Partly. But, tell you the truth, after that match with you, Bo hasn't been playing worth a shit."

That, Vic *really* hated to hear. He wondered if there was anything he could or should do.

Maybe he could call Bo and tell him most of what he'd heard on the course that day was fiction. Vic decided that would probably only make the boy angry, not better. The damage was done. At this point, it would be like extracting bullets from a corpse.

"So I'm looking to see if you'd like to play for me, instead. I heard your syndicate kind of came apart, what with Hobart Early dying."

The mention of Hobart stabbed at Vic's heart. The image of his shovel-full of soil hitting the top of Hobart's coffin flickered in Vic's mind. "You heard?"

"Yeah, word gets around the syndicate circuit. I know you two were pretty good friends. Sorry to hear he's dead." Marroan's voice was flat and unemotional. "But I like your style. And your game. You got a good head on your shoulders. You worked Bo over good."

Vic wondered if Marroan had any inkling most of the story he used to topple Bo was invented.

"I think we could make a lot of money together, Vic. I'd be willin' to make you a sweet deal, because there's nobody else involved now. I'm the syndicate. It would be you and me. We could go halves after expenses. Half for me, half for you." He paused as though he expected Vic to respond, but when he didn't, Marroan kept talking. "Fifty-fifty, that has to be better than what Early gave you. You could make a heap of fucking cash playin' for me."

Vic couldn't make a sound. This came out of nowhere. It felt like he was spinning in a whirlpool, perhaps even sinking.

"Tell you what. I don't want you making a fast decision you'll regret later. I'll give you my number. Get back to me when you decide. Take all the time you need." Marroan's tone of voice indicating the phone call was coming to a close. "A heap of money, Vic. Think about it."

Vic scribbled the number down, and told Marroan he'd call him as soon as he made his decision.

"Thanks for thinking of me."

"Remember, Vic. We could get real fucking wealthy together," Marroan concluded, before saying goodbye.

Vic hung up and pulled out a Diet Coke. There was beer in the refrigerator, but he was cutting back. He walked into the living room and sat on the worn couch where Muldoon was asleep. The cat stirred and stretched as Vic relaxed.

"Ah shit, Dooner." Vic stoked the cat's silky coat and looked at the TV. "We have us a big-ass offer." The Steve Miller Band was in the middle of *Abracadabra*. Vic glanced at Tom Bayer's golf ball, where it sat on his desk. The way he played, Vic knew he had a lock on the old magic, whether it was due to the Top Flite or not. "Get back into the syndicates and knock down a hundred grand in a year or so." He looked at Muldoon. "Get you a nice place on the muddy Maumee. With lots of birdies for you to watch through big picture windows."

Vic spent a long time thinking about golf, about teaching and about his commitment to stop playing for money. Syndicate golf and its attendant rituals and ceremonies tickled pleasure centers in Vic's brain, and the resulting rush neared an addiction. The temptation to go back on the promise he made to himself was strong. There was a part of him that craved the intoxication of the money. The travel. That adrenalin rush when he walked onto the first tee, having no idea how good the other player would hit it that day. The excitement as the game unfolded. Studying the other player like quarry so he could analyze his strengths and discover his weaknesses. Once Vic spotted the other player's Achilles heel, and everybody has at least one, he savored the mental gymnastics he employed to capitalize on the other man's soft spot. It was like chess, or poker. It was fun, but it went way beyond mere pleasant diversion. He also thought about houses on the river, speedboats and about owning things a teacher's salary could never provide. Playing the syndicates for Marroan, Vic could have all that and more.

The syndicates had huge downsides, however. Vic knew them well. The very things that made the golf so exciting also sucked the life he cherished right out of him. It made him neglect his teaching career and his painting. It put personal relationships in peril. And it made him feel badly about himself because he did things in the heat of competition he regretted afterwards. Thinking back on his match with Bo, he had to admit he regretted his actions that day, even before he started in on the boy.

442

Premeditated mental assassination. In Vic's mind, that was not an overstatement. Sadly, he knew he was guilty. And now, after Marroan's call, he knew the effect it had on Bo.

Then, there was the loneliness. Vic thought back on his days of playing for Hobart's syndicate. Because he hid his winnings from Angie until after the divorce, he was never able to let his friends know what he was doing, and that cut him off from them. Sure, now that the divorce was final and Angie was in Colorado, he could tell them if he started with the syndicates again, but would he want to? Part of him would love to let them in on his exploits. They would admire and envy him for being able to use his skill to make big money, and that would certainly stroke his ego. But Vic also knew admiration and envy could breed bad feelings and drive wedges between friends, especially when money was involved. He had his hands as full as he wanted them, trying to soft-pedal the fact he was the best player his friends knew, let alone being the richest one. So, he probably wouldn't tell them if he accepted Marroan's offer. He also wouldn't be playing much golf with them if he was off playing the syndicates, either. And no explanation would be forthcoming. Another wedge.

If he went back to the syndicates, Vic would have to spend his weekends with Mink Marroan. That was a chilling thought. He remembered the night he had the go-round with the thug-brothers who tried to rob him outside the motel in Maryville, when VanVorhis filled in for Hobart on the trip. Vic experienced a life-and-death episode, and there was no one he could tell, or talk it over with. Marroan wasn't a man Vic could become friends with, but could he put up with the man for big money?

Finally, if Vic decided to play the syndicates, he'd be gone most weekends, which was prime time for dating. He missed having a woman to talk to. To share secrets and ideas with. And yes, he missed intimacy. Going back to the syndicates would put finding someone on hold. Was he ready to do that?

Vic stood up. "I think we're long overdue for me to make an intelligent choice," he said, walking to the phone. He searched several pieces of paper until he found the number he wanted, and dialed. The phone rang several times.

"Hello, Treese? This is Vic."

"Oh, Vic. It's so good to hear from you." Her voice was velvety smooth. "I've been a little worried. You must not be golfing anymore. I haven't seen you in weeks, but I really didn't feel comfortable about calling to see if you were okay. You haven't been sick, have you?"

"Not at all. I'm fine. And yes, I'm playing, but not doing the travel thing anymore. I play two or three times a week with my friends, after school and on the weekends. But golf was taking too much of the time I need for other things that are more important."

"That's neat. It sounds like you have your life right where you want it."

"I do, for the most part. But, you remember I told you I was seeing someone?" He paused, but Treese didn't respond, which worried him a little. "That relationship ended, so I thought I'd call you and see what your situation is."

"Oh, I've been dating a little, but I haven't been seeing anyone regularly." She paused. "You know, you still have to collect on that flying lesson I promised you."

"I'm really looking forward to doing that, but to tell you the truth, I called because there's a more pressing issue I need to deal with."

"There is?" Caution crept into her voice.

"Absolutely. Didn't you tell me you missed your senior prom?"

She laughed hard. "Actually, I didn't get *asked* to my prom. But a girlfriend and I went together. No way were we going to sit at home because some stupid boys wouldn't ask us," Her voice was loaded with resolve.

Vic thought of Sylvia. "Did you wear tuxes?"

"Tuxes?" She sounded puzzled. "No, we wore formals. Why?"

"I'll explain later." Vic chuckled. "The point is, Alexis's prom is in a few weeks, and I told the kids I'd be a chaperone. Now I'm looking for a date."

"I'd love to go."

"We've only been out once, though, so before you commit to something as important and life-altering as a high school prom, you might want to have a preliminary date. You know, to make sure I'm someone you would want to go with."

"Kind of a trial run?" She finished with a giggle.

"Sure. I mean, you don't take off until you taxi around a little, make sure the engine's making good power. Right? So maybe this Saturday, we could go on kind of a check-out date. See if you think I'm actual prom-date material."

"I'd love to go out Saturday night. You won't be nervous?"

"Nervous?"

"Like you said, I'll be checking you out."

"Oh, that's right. But don't worry, if you decide I'm not prom-worthy, I'll taxi quietly back to the hanger. No drama."

They talked for a few more minutes and agreed on a time. As soon as they said their goodbyes, Vic quickly dialed another number. Marroan's machine picked up.

"This is Mink. Leave a message," his recorded voice instructed.

"Yeah, Mink? This is Vic. Listen, I appreciate your offer, but after giving it some thought, I decided I'm going in a different direction. So thanks, but no thanks." Vic started to hang up, but stopped the receiver in mid-flight. "Oh, and tell Bo I hope he's out on the course hitting 'em good again soon. The kid's got all kinds of game. I'd stay with him, if I was you."

Vic hung up and followed a sudden urge to get out of the apartment and go outside. As he stood savoring the early spring evening, he was overwhelmed with a sense of belonging. He belonged to the community at Alexis High School. He didn't merely go there, put his time in, and come home. He was now part of what made the school function, both in and outside his classroom. He was in solidly with his friends, playing golf with them and hitting a bar or two after school on Fridays. Soon, he would find a house on a quiet street in Toledo and become part of a neighborhood. He would make a point of getting to know the people who lived around him, even the ones two doors down. That thought made him smile. He would be a better friend to the people who were important to him, and to Muldoon, as well. He would honor the memory of Bascolm by being a player his former mentor would be happy to share a fairway with. He would honor the memory of Hobart, and even of The Old Man, by being a man they would be proud of. In so doing, he would be a son his mother could take pride in, as well.

Lastly, and certainly not least, he would find a woman who was actually available for a relationship. Treese could be the one, or she may not be; but he wouldn't spend any more lonely hours hoping for happiness in the future. Instead, he would fashion happiness in the present, and enjoy it on into the future.

All this was a plan for life management, savvy as his course management. No more games of Take Me. No more kicking it out of the rough. From now on, if life gave him a difficult lie, he would play it straight and take the best shot he could. He smiled. Bascolm taught him to make the right decisions on the course. After months of missteps, he believed he finally made the right decision for his life.

A warm breeze rustled the fledgling leaves on a nearby tree, and he could smell the aroma of the grass Ames cut that afternoon. A bird sang nearby, and Vic thought of the poor robin he hit on his way to Heather Hills, that long ago day in September when his journey began. He looked around, but couldn't spot the bird to see if it was, indeed, a robin singing. Regardless, the nearly intoxicating sights, smells, and sounds of spring didn't seem to merely surround him. He felt like he'd subsumed them, as though he'd become part of this new season, while it became a part of him. Spring is the season of rebirth, and Vic was embarked on an exciting new life. He stood on the first tee, with a clean score card.

About the Author

Christopher T. Werkman lives on a few acres outside Haskins, Ohio with his partner, Karen Wolf, and a six-pack of cats. He completed a thirty year career as an art teacher in Toledo, Ohio. Following that, he served as an adjunct art education instructor at the University of Toledo for ten years. He still paints, and designed covers for several published novels and a short story collection, but his primary passion is for writing fiction. When he isn't writing, he plays too much golf in the summer, too much indoor tennis in the winter, and rides his Kawasaki Ninja whenever traction is adequate. His short stories have appeared in numerous literary journals and anthologies. *Difficult Lies* is his first novel.

That attitude does not fly w. me.

VISIT OUR WEBSITE
FOR THE FULL INVENTORY
OF QUALITY BOOKS:

http://www.roguephoenixpress.com

Rogue Phoenix Press

Representing Excellence in Publishing

Quality trade paperbacks and downloads
in multiple formats,
in genres ranging from historical to
contemporary romance, mystery and science fiction.
Visit the website then bookmark it.
We add new titles each month!